THE DARK OF YOU

Guardian Hostage Rescue Specialists

ELLIE MASTERS

JEM Publishing

~

Dedication

This book is dedicated to my one and only—my amazing and wonderful husband.

Without your care and support, my writing would not have made it this far.

You pushed me when I needed to be pushed.

You supported me when I felt discouraged.

You believed in me when I didn't believe in myself.

If it weren't for you, this book never would have come to life.

Also by Ellie Masters

The LIGHTER SIDE

Ellie Masters is the lighter side of the Jet & Ellie Masters writing duo! You will find Contemporary Romance, Military Romance, Romantic Suspense, Billionaire Romance, and Rock Star Romance in Ellie's Works.

YOU CAN FIND ELLIE'S BOOKS HERE:
ELLIEMASTERS.COM/BOOKS

Military Romance

Guardian Hostage Rescue Specialists

Rescuing Melissa

*(*Get a FREE copy of Rescuing Melissa

when you join Ellie's Newsletter*)*

Alpha Team

Rescuing Zoe

Rescuing Moira

Rescuing Eve

Rescuing Lily

Rescuing Jinx

Rescuing Maria

Bravo Team

Rescuing Angie

Rescuing Isabelle

Rescuing Carmen

Rescuing Rosalie

Rescuing Kaye

Cara's Protector

Rescuing Barbi

The Dark of You

Military Romance

Guardian Personal Protection Specialists

Sybil's Protector

Lyra's Protector

The One I Want Series

(Small Town, Military Heroes)

By Jet & Ellie Masters

EACH BOOK IN THIS SERIES CAN BE READ AS A STANDALONE AND IS ABOUT A DIFFERENT COUPLE WITH AN HEA.

Saving Abby

Saving Ariel

Saving Brie

Saving Cate

Saving Dani

Saving Jen

Rockstar Romance

The Angel Fire Rock Romance Series

EACH BOOK IN THIS SERIES CAN BE READ AS A STANDALONE AND IS ABOUT A DIFFERENT COUPLE WITH AN HEA. IT IS RECOMMENDED THEY ARE READ IN ORDER.

Ashes to New (prequel)

Heart's Insanity (book 1)

Heart's Desire (book 2)

Heart's Collide (book 3)

Hearts Divided (book 4)

Hearts Entwined (book5)

Forest's FALL (book 6)

Hearts The Last Beat (book7)

Contemporary Romance

Firestorm

(Kristy Bromberg's Everyday Heroes World)

Billionaire Romance

Billionaire Boys Club

Hawke

Richard

Brody

Romantic Suspense

Changing Roles Series:

THIS SERIES MUST BE READ IN ORDER.

WITH JET MASTERS

Book 1: Command Me

Book 2: Control Me

Book 3: Collar Me

Book 4: Embracing FATE

Book 5: Seizing FATE

Book 6: Accepting FATE

Romantic Suspense

EACH BOOK IS A STANDALONE NOVEL.

The Starling

~AND~

Science Fiction

Ellie Masters writing as L.A. Warren

Vendel Rising: a Science Fiction Serialized Novel

Vendel Rising: a Science Fiction Serialized Novel

To My Readers

This book is a work of fiction. It does not exist in the real world and should not be construed as reality. As in most romantic fiction, I've taken liberties. I've compressed the romance into a sliver of time. I've allowed these characters to develop strong bonds of trust over a matter of days.

This does not happen in real life where you, my amazing readers, live. Take more time in your romance and learn who you're giving a piece of your heart to. I urge you to move with caution. Always protect yourself.

ONE

Paul

～

Present Day

～

Sᴜʀᴇɴꜱ ᴛᴇᴀʀ ᴛʜʀᴏᴜɢʜ ᴛʜᴇ ᴀɪʀ ᴛʜᴇɪʀ ᴇᴀʀ-ᴘɪᴇʀᴄɪɴɢ ᴡᴀɪʟ ᴍᴀᴛᴄʜᴇꜱ the rapid beat of my heart. EMTs secure Forest's limp form onto a stretcher and hastily loaded him into an ambulance. His usual vitality and stoicism replaced by a chilling stillness that strikes a chord of terror deep within me.

The familiar comfort of Guardian HQ is instantly transformed into a chilling tableau of uncertainty and fear. As the ambulance takes off into the night, painting the surroundings in frantic streaks of blue and red, Sara and I can only watch, feeling helpless and scared.

"Come along." Sam's firm voice nudges us toward a car. "I'll drive you to the hospital." His actions instill a measure of control in the chaotic night.

We crawl into the vehicle, both in shock, and Sam chases the shrieking emergency vehicle through the desolate night. Sara and I hold hands and find solace in each other, our intertwined fingers echoing our shared fear for Forest. The road ahead is a blur, echoing the disarray of our hearts and our fear for the man we both desperately love.

The hospital greets us with a flurry of activity, a whirlwind of medical professionals rushing Forest away for urgent care. The words 'Emergency Department', 'Intensive Care', 'critical condition' hang heavy in the air. The updates are sparse, but he's still alive—a small beacon of hope amidst our growing fear.

Shaking, I pull out my phone from the pocket of my jeans, my fingers barely steady enough to dial my sister's number. It rings twice before a familiar voice answers.

"Hey, Paul. What's up?" Piper's perpetually perky and positive attitude is usually a comforting presence, but it seems too perky against the backdrop of the night's events.

"Hey, Piper." I try to steady my voice and fail. My nerves are raw, and exhaustion pulls at me.

"What's wrong? You sound…" Piper's voice is steady, comforting.

"It's Forest." I swallow hard, the lump in my throat making it difficult to speak. "He's been taken to the hospital. It's… It's bad."

"Oh, God…" There's a gasp on the other end of the line. "What happened?"

"We're not sure. It's all a blur. Sara and I are at the hospital. We're going to be here all night." My words tumble out in a rush, all my fears pouring into the phone line. "Can you…" Men aren't supposed to cry, but I swipe away an errant tear.

"Don't worry about Delia and Sebastian. I'll take care of them." A deep sigh comes from the other end. "Ah, Paul, I wish I could give you a hug. How is Sara holding up?"

"Weepy. Scared. We just don't know what's going on."

"Bent and I will take care of the twins." Piper doesn't hesitate. "We'll make it an adventure of tent camping in the living room, bingeing kid-friendly movies, and staying up way past their bedtimes. We'll make it fun. You focus on Forest. He needs you right now."

"I… Thank you, Piper." Relief washes over me.

"Forest is a fighter. He'll pull through." She tries to inject hope, but I'm not in a position to respond.

"I… I hope so."

"I'll let the crew know what's going on. If you need anything… A food run? Coffee run? Hug? Silence? I'll make it happen."

"Thank you. You're the best."

"Anytime. I love you, and it's going to be okay." She tries to bolster my hope, but I'm at a loss right now. I'm barely keeping myself together, putting on a strong face for Sara.

"Piper's got the twins." Hanging up, I pull Sara in for a hug and kiss her on the top of her head. Ours may not be a physical relationship, but we care for each other deeply.

"Oh, that's a relief." Sara shakes out her hands, trying to deal with her anxiety over Forest. Her arms thread around my waist as we stand together, supporting one another, staying strong for Forest.

We're not alone in this. We're surrounded by people who love Forest just as much as we do, and we'll get through this as a family.

I hope.

A little later on, we video chat with the twins, blowing kisses and giving great big air hugs. We keep the crew at *Insanity* updated with what little we know.

By dawn, we're camped out in Forest's hospital room. His steady breathing is a grim reminder of his fight for survival. Sara sleeps twisted in a reclining chair while I sit beside Forest's bed. I can't tear my eyes from his unconscious form. The impersonal hum and rhythmic beeps of the hospital monitors and equipment, while annoying, provide some sense of relief.

Forest's alive. He's still with us.

His chest rises and falls with the mechanical assistance of a ventilator, a cruel reminder of how fragile he has become. How close to death he might be.

Skye stands by the window, her worried gaze scanning the gloomy sky outside. Sara shifts in the seat, her sleep fitful at best. I clutch Forest's limp hand and close my eyes as exhaustion pulls at me.

With each passing hour, our confusion deepens. Despite Skye's medical expertise and calming presence, the lack of concrete information is maddening.

We hold onto her every word, but the reality is painfully clear: Forest's fate hangs in the balance, and all we can do is wait.

"Did they tell you anything?" My question is for Skye, who, as a physician, is helping Sara and me navigate the boggling medical landscape we're suddenly thrust inside. "Do we have any idea what's wrong or why he's so sick?"

Skye shakes her head; her usually stoic facade wavers. "They have to run tests. Figure things out. We have to wait and see."

She's not telling us the truth.

Or rather, she's not sharing her take on Forest's clinical condition. Skye's a formidable emergency and trauma physician, but she's also family. I can understand why she won't share her fears with us, as if voicing them out loud might make them manifest for real.

"Why is it taking so long? They took all that blood in the ER. Did X-rays. They poked and prodded…"

"It's not that simple. These things follow a certain order. Those results lead to the next round of tests."

"While we wait." I clench my teeth, tired of interminable waiting.

"While we wait. But for now, Forest's condition has stabilized." Skye tries to focus on the positive, but she's scared. I see it in the way she wrings her hands when she doesn't think I'm watching.

I run a hand through my hair, frustrated with what I perceive is either lack of ability from the docs, or them dragging their feet.

A flurry of memories with Forest flood my mind. His wedding to Sara. The day he begged me to be his Master. The joyous birth of our twin children. Seeing him now, vulnerable and broken, feels like my soul is being ripped in two.

"We'll get through this." Skye attempts to reassure me. "Forest will pull through."

Beside me, Sara stirs. "Did I fall asleep?" She rubs her eyes and stretches her arms over her head. "What time is it?"

"Early morning?" Honestly, I haven't looked at a clock in hours.

"Were you up all night?" Sara looks at me with concern.

"Yes."

"Paul, you shouldn't have let me sleep all night. You need rest too."

"I couldn't leave his side." I shrug but don't make a fuss when she climbs out of the chair and insists I take it. With a peck on the cheek, she grips my shoulders, providing a reassuring squeeze, then takes my hand, holding it in hers.

"Well, at least pretend to get some rest."

"I can't."

"Then don't, but close your eyes. I'll wake you if anything happens." With that, she kisses the back of my hand, then perches on the edge of the bed next to Forest.

She and I are the two halves that make Forest whole. She's the light to his darkness, while I'm the one who feeds Forest's deepest, darkest, and most depraved desires. In doing so, I help him navigate through his twisted and tortured mind. I help make things possible, like having a normal relationship with Sara and the twins.

"Remember when we found out about the twins?" Sara releases Forest's hand for a moment. "The way his face lit up? He was radiant, as though all his suffering suddenly disappeared."

I nod, a faint smile crossing my lips. Sara and I accomplished the impossible with a little help from Skye and her medical connections. Through the wonder of in-vitro fertilization, we implanted two embryos, siblings who share a piece of each of us.

Sara's pregnancy with our twins was riddled with challenges, and as for our children, Delia bears an uncanny resemblance to her father, adorned with a shock of white-blonde hair and eyes as clear as the sky; she's a charmer. Sebastian inherited my predilection for dark locks and an indomitable spirit. They both inherited Sara's strength, compassion, and patience.

We told Forest at Christmas a couple of years ago. It was a magical night at *Insanity*, the group home of the mega rock band, Angel Fire. Each member of the band lives there with their wives and children. The three of us live in a house adjacent to the massive estate. That Christmas, it was as if all the stars aligned because all the women, except for Spike's Angel, were pregnant at the same time, and they all kept it a secret until that night.

Sara and I were running late from the OB appointment, eager to share the good news with Forest. He was topping the tree when Sara and I finally made it. The women presented their stockings to the men, and each pulled out either a pink or blue knit bootie. Sara and I held up two: one pink and one blue.

"Do you remember the way his eyes bugged out of his head?" A smile pushes away my worry for a moment, reliving the joy of that moment.

"I can't believe we kept the whole thing a secret from him." Sara's fingers lightly grip my arm and squeeze gently.

Sara and I are neither romantically nor intimately involved with each other—there was that one kiss several years ago, but nothing further came of it. Now, we share Forest between us, knowing neither of us alone is what Forest needs. What we share is a unique bond and passion for the man we love.

And we're happy.

Sara's more than a dear friend to me. She's very much a part of the love I share with Forest.

"Do you remember the way the color drained from his face?" Skye turns away from the window. "I thought he was going to faint." Although meant to be light, her words fall flat in the room.

"Do you think he was sick back then? It's been over two years." My comment brings our short-lived happiness to an abrupt end.

My nose twitches with the smell of the hospital's disinfectant as one of the hospital staff cleans the floors outside Forest's room. The heart monitor's persistent beep is meant to reassure, but it's more of a relentless reminder of his precarious state.

Sara and I glance down at the man we love. His features, once vibrant, now appear pallid and are hardly recognizable amidst the invasive tubes and wires.

"I'm not going to do that and suggest you do the same." Skye's voice cuts through the oppressive lull in our conversation.

"What?" Her comment confuses me, as she didn't answer my question.

"Don't pick apart the past and second guess yourself. There's no way to know when the cancer began…"

"Cancer?" Sara's fingers tighten around my arm. "Is that what you think this is?"

Skye's been reluctant to share her thoughts. Now I understand why.

"I don't know what's wrong with Forest, and I didn't want to scare you if it turned out to be a simple virus. We don't know what's wrong, but it's in the differential."

"But you don't think it's a virus?" I point to Forest's frail form. "Viruses don't do this."

"Some do." Skye steps to the foot of the bed. "There are several that can. Ebstein Barr is one."

"But you think it's cancer?" I push her to commit, knowing I shouldn't, but needing to know. Sara and I exchange another worried glance.

"I just don't know." She remains hesitant to commit.

"And when will we know?" Sara pulls her hand from my arm to thread her fingers with Forest's hand.

"We should focus on what we know rather than speculate about what we don't know. All that matters is that he's stable for now." She looks down at her foster brother, a man with whom she survived some of the worst brutality a child could ever endure. The two of them created an indelible bond in the darkness of their abuse.

"If only I'd pushed him to see the doctor sooner. As his Dom…"

"As his Dom, you would never cross that line with him." Skye doesn't let me berate myself. "And as his Master, you would never violate his trust and use your position over him like that."

The dynamic Forest and I share is no secret. People understand the throuple thing, and they understand the BDSM thing between me and Forest. But none of them truly grasps it the way Skye and Sara do.

It's our unique bond.

And Skye's one hundred percent correct. I'd never violate Forest's trust, or the dynamic we share, by letting it intrude beyond the strict boundaries we've established. What we do is exceptionally private.

In public, we're lovers and best friends. Which puts me on the same footing as Sara. In private, we become something else entirely.

Like me, and Skye for that matter, we've all tried talking to Forest over the past year about his declining health. He chose not to listen. I can't help but wonder if I had crossed that line, and demanded as his Master that he go in for a checkup, if we could have avoided letting things get this bad.

"Well, I hope he wakes up soon." Sara barely holds her voice together. "When he does, the two of you are going to have to take a number, because I'm going to chew his ass off for not taking better care of himself." She sniffs and wipes at a stray tear. "Do you really think it could be cancer?"

"We just don't know." Skye shifts and returns to the window, where she places her palm on the glass. "And I'll be right behind you to light up his ass. Forest is a stubborn, obnoxious, infuriatingly stoic man who needs to be read the riot act."

A knock on the door halts our conversation. A nurse walks in, her eyes darting between us and Forest. "I just need to take his vitals and draw some labs."

Sara grips Forest's hand, staying by his side while the nurse does her job.

"His vitals are stable." The nurse gives us a brief report, but her words offer little comfort now that Skye revealed her fear about his diagnosis.

"What labs did they order?" Skye fixes her gaze on the bleak skyline outside while the nurse rattles off an alphabet soup of various labs. Skye nods, approving the plan, while I watch the entire exchange. I trust Skye's medical judgment, and I trust her with Forest's life.

But I wish we had answers.

Outside, the normally clear blue skies of California's coastline fill with gray storm clouds and rain. A gust of wind lashes at the glass, making Sara jump.

Once the nurse leaves, Sara's voice cracks with emotion as she tenderly cradles Forest's limp hand in hers. "What did all that mean?" Her eyes glisten with unshed tears, and I struggle to hold back my own as I see the pain etched across her face.

When Sara hurts, my heart aches. I brave a glance at Forest and can't help but feel a crushing weight of guilt settle over me. If only I'd been more forceful.

"They're working their way through the differential diagnosis. We should know something soon." Skye's tone shifts, turning gentle yet insistent. "Paul, you need to stop that."

"Stop what?" Can she read my mind?

"You can't blame yourself. We all tried talking to him. As much as I hate to say it, this is on Forest. He's the one who refused to listen to all of us. Don't shoulder guilt that's not yours to bear."

"I'll try, but it doesn't make it any easier." I clench my fists until my knuckles turn white.

"Maybe we should let him rest?" Skye once again tears her gaze away from the window to fix me with a solemn look. "There's not much more we can do."

"I'm not leaving." Nothing will pull me from Forest's side.

"Let me rephrase that. Why don't you and I get some rest? We'll take turns, making sure one of us is always here. That way, if he wakes up…"

"When he wakes up." I don't like the defeat in her gaze, or her choice of words. I'm not ready to let Forest go and I'm going to stand by his side fighting until the bitter end.

"When he wakes up, one of us will be here, but in order to be there for him, we need to take care of ourselves. Sara can stay for now. You and I will get out of here, clear our heads, and come back to take our shifts."

"I'm not leaving." How else can I make myself clear?

"Paul, you're of no use to him if you're exhausted and incoherent. When he wakes, Sara will call us." Skye turns her attention to Sara, who nods in agreement.

"Fine." I reluctantly agree, my voice barely audible. I push myself out of the chair, feeling as though I'm abandoning Forest, but who better to leave him with than Sara, the light to his darkness?

As Skye and I gather our things, Sara calls out, halting my retreat. "Paul, we'll get through this." Her eyes meet mine, filled with determination and love—a love that binds us together.

"You promise?" I can't help the way my voice wavers.

"Promise."

For a moment, I allow myself to believe her, to cling to the hope that somehow, we'll find a way to save Forest.

But I've never been more scared in my life.

The steady rhythm of Forest's breathing offers momentary calm.

"Come back to us, Forest," I whisper the words under my breath, a silent prayer for healing, while my heart breaks in two.

Forest is the foundation of our trio, teetering on the brink. Seeing him like this makes me wonder what a future without him might look like?

While complicated, our relationship has its own rhythm and unique balance. Forest, Sara, and I share intricately woven bonds of mutual respect, trust, and shared history. We don't fit into societal norms, but our triad works for us. In our world, love is fluid, respect paramount, and trust a necessary foundation.

Despite our different relationships with him, Sara and I find common ground in our shared worry for the man we both love.

What will happen to Sara if he dies?

What will happen to the twins?

Will Sara and I raise them together?

Or will we drift apart without Forest to hold us together?

I fear for our future.

The man has endured more than his fair share of life's adversities. His time in Snowden's captivity still haunts him, painting our happiness with streaks of pain. Yet, we've found a way to deal with it, an unconventional healing process through the complex dynamic of dominance and submission.

My thoughts can't help but drift back to the beginning of our unconventional relationship. It was born out of pain during a time when I was a different man than I am now. To a time when I served the vilest of men.

TWO

Paul

∼

Several Years Ago

∼

I PUSH OPEN THE DOOR TO THE DARK AND DINGY BAR. A GUST OF wind follows me in, swirling into the bar like a lost soul seeking solace.

Or maybe that's me?

The stale smell of cigarettes, sweat, and spilled alcohol greets me like an old friend. I scan the room, taking in the scarred wooden tables and booths that line the walls, their shadows flickering from the dim yellow lights.

The soft hum of whispered conversations and clinking glasses offers me a temporary reprieve from the torment of my thoughts. The dimly lit room is a sanctuary for those who seek refuge from the world, and if there's one thing I seek refuge from, it's the man I've become.

A flickering neon sign casts a ghostly glow on the stained walls, and the low hum of hushed conversations fills the air. Shadows cling tenaciously to every corner, hiding secrets and broken dreams.

As I make a beeline to the bar, my heavy boots make a soft sucking sound against the sticky floor. The weight of my past drags behind me, every step a conscious effort to keep moving. I glimpse my reflection in the cracked mirror behind the bar, and the reflection staring back at me is a stranger: hollow cheeks, dark circles, haunted eyes, and a stubbled jaw.

I barely recognize myself.

With a sigh, I pull out a worn barstool, its leather surface cracked and worn like me— fractured beyond repair.

The bartender, a scruffy older man who has surely seen his fair share of troubled souls, regards me with an air of understanding. He knows better than to engage in conversation with a man who radiates pain.

"Whiskey. Neat." My gravelly voice is raspy and raw.

The bartender pours amber liquid into a glass with practiced ease. The whiskey sloshes against the sides, creating tiny whirlpools that mirror the storm raging within me and outside this bar.

"Here you go." The bartender slides the glass across the counter. Our eyes meet briefly, and the bartender's gaze holds a mixture of pity and understanding—a silent exchange that speaks volumes.

I grip the glass tightly, my knuckles whitening under the pressure, and stare into the amber liquid, watching the distorted reflection of the bar's flickering lights within it.

I take a deep breath, inhaling the smoky scent of the whiskey as it mixes with the musty odor of the bar. The aroma is both comforting and suffocating, much like the memories that cling to me. Tension knots in the pit of my stomach, and I throw back the whiskey in one swift gulp.

The burn of the alcohol, as it slides down my throat, brings a fleeting moment of relief, the fiery sensation temporarily numbing the pain that's my constant companion. The warmth of the alcohol offers some solace from the icy grip of my past, but it doesn't last. It never does.

"Another," I grunt and push the empty glass across the counter.

The bartender obliges without a word, refilling the glass with practiced ease.

"Thanks." I take another sip and turn my gaze toward the flickering neon sign. It reflects my haunted eyes, a silent reminder of the torment I seek to escape—if only for a little while.

Questions swirl through my mind as I stare into the depths of my second drink,. Will I ever break free from the chains that anchor me to my past? Is redemption possible for a man bathed in darkness? I shake my head, trying to drown out the haunting whispers of doubt and despair that echo within me.

Just as I'm about to take another swig, the door to the bar bursts open. A gust of icy air blows in as a group of rowdy patrons stumble into the bar: five men and one pathetic whore; a woman who's been used, abused, and no longer fights against her oppression.

The men's laughter reverberates through the dimly lit space, grating on my nerves like nails on a chalkboard, shattering the fragile silence that envelopes my quiet corner of the world. I can't help but steal a glance at them, noting their raucous behavior as they jostle each other and shout over the din.

"Hey there, bartender. A round for me and my friends." The leader of the pack cups his hands over his mouth and shouts at the bartender. Although there's no need. It's a quiet crowd tonight. The burly man, with his unkempt beard and eyes that gleam with malice, reeks of trouble.

The bartender obliges, pouring drinks with a forced smile. I retreat further into myself, trying to tune out the men as I sip from my glass. But their voices grow louder, more insistent, worming their way into my thoughts despite my best efforts to block them out.

"Did you hear what happened last night?" One newcomer asks, his voice slurred and already thick with alcohol. Evidently, this isn't their first stop for the night. "Guy robbed this dude at gunpoint. Said he begged for his life. Pathetic, huh?"

I freeze, my heart hammering against my ribcage, as memories of my crimes claw their way through the cobwebs of my mind. Desperate cries for mercy. Fear in my victim's eyes. Power coursing through me as I stood over them and raged.

A cold shiver races down my spine, and I grip my glass, knuckles turning white. Fragments of memories I've long tried to bury claw their way back from the depths of my tortured mind.

"Man, that's nothing." Another man laughs, his words tumbling out like venom. "Remember that time we beat up that homeless guy? Just because we could?" The group erupts into laughter, each man trying to outdo the other with tales of violence and cruelty. "Dude just curled up and let us kick him. Didn't even try to get away. Pathetic."

I recall the faces of those I've hurt, the lives I've ruined, and shudder. Rivers of guilt and shame course through me, drowning me beneath a sea of regret. I squeeze my eyes shut, willing the images away, but they cling to me like a second skin, a scar that will never truly heal. That these men boast about such things? It pisses me off.

"Ah, those were the days," another patron chimes in, reminiscing. "We had power, money, everything we could ever want. Nobody could touch us."

"Power is for fools," I whisper under my breath, my throat constricting as bile rises in my stomach.

The rush of adrenaline, the exhilaration of control, the intoxicating allure of dominating others and forcing them to submit to my will. It's a drug that consumes me.

It turned me into a monster.

"Cheers to that!" The group raise their glasses in a toast.

My hand trembles, my glass quivering in my grasp. I can't take it anymore—their words are like daggers, stabbing into the raw wounds of my soul. I need to get out of here.

"Hey, buddy, you alright?" One of the rowdy patrons asks, his tone mocking, his eyes filled with disdain. "What's the matter? Can't handle a bit of fun?"

"Leave me alone." My hoarse voice is barely audible over the pounding in my ears.

"Aw, come on, we're just having some fun." The man sneers, reaching out to pat me on the back in a mockery of comfort. "Lighten up, will you?"

I can't shake the images in my mind, the echoes of past crimes reverberate through my skull. The surrounding air seems to thicken, suffocating me beneath the weight of my guilt and the cacophony of voices that taunt me, reminding me of who I once was—and who I can never escape.

The man laughs and turns back to his friends. The walls close in around me, trapping me in a prison of my making.

Amidst the raucous laughter and jeers of the rowdy patrons, the whore's eyes lock onto me. A cruel hand on her arm declares possession and ownership. Her pimp leans down and whispers in her ear. She takes a deep breath, plasters a sultry smile on her lips, and saunters over to me.

Her fingertips curl around the hem of her skirt. As she draws close, the scent of cheap perfume and stale cigarettes slams into me, battling for dominance with the bitter tang of alcohol that hangs heavy in the air.

"Hey there." A sultry purr, her voice grates on me. She leans against the bar, and I flinch at her invasion of my personal space. "I'm Silvie, and you look like you could use some company."

My heavy gaze fixes on the amber liquid swirling in my glass. The silence stretches between us as I take in her tattered dress and smudged makeup.

"I'm not interested."

"Come on, handsome." She tries again, coaxing me, her voice softer this time. She runs her fingers along my arm in a practiced, seductive gesture. "I can help you forget whatever's bothering you."

"Leave me alone."

"I don't bite… unless you want me to."

"I doubt that." A bitter laugh escapes my lips before I can stop it. "Move on to the next John, and leave me alone."

"My boss won't be happy if I don't make you feel good." Silvie's eyes flick toward her pimp, hovering nearby, watching our exchange like a hawk.

"Your boss can go to hell." I down the rest of my drink in one gulp.

"If I don't bring in some money tonight, my boss is going to be pissed." Her hand falls back to her side. For a moment, she drops the seductive façade.

The desperation in her voice strikes a chord within me, stirring up an unfamiliar protective instinct. I can't save myself from the darkness that haunts me, but perhaps I can spare this woman some measure of pain.

"Look, it's not going to happen." I meet her gaze for the first time. "I'm not interested in what you're offering."

She cocks her head and then her eyes light up in understanding. "You prefer men?" Silvie asks gently, having picked up on the subtle cues others might miss.

"Among other things," I reluctantly admit. My eyes shift away, haunted by my demons.

"Okay." Her voice shakes; her vulnerability a sharp stab to my useless heart. "Can we talk? If I go back without… I'll be in trouble."

"Fine." I relent, seeing the fear in her eyes and recognizing it as a reflection of my own demons. "What do you want to talk about?"

"Tell me about yourself." Silvie slides onto the barstool beside me.

"Darkness." I keep my voice low, as if confessing a terrible secret. "The kind that lives inside me, twisting and gnawing at my soul until I can't stand it anymore. The kind that makes me question whether there's any good left in me."

"Everybody has darkness in them." Silvie's reply is soft. Her hand briefly touches my arm in a gesture of comfort. "It's what we do with it, how we choose to overcome it, that defines who we are."

"I'll pay for your time, but don't touch me." I withdraw from her touch as if stung.

"Fair enough." Silvie sighs, a tentative smile curving her lips as she tucks a strand of dirty blonde hair behind her ear.

"Is that what you tell yourself? How we choose to overcome our darkness defines who we are?" Bitterness creeps into my voice. "Does that justify what you do? Selling your body for the likes of him?" I gesture toward her pimp.

"It's what keeps me going." Her admission hits me strangely. "Every day, I fight against the shadows and every night, I hope for a brighter tomorrow."

"Maybe we're not so different after all."

Something shifts within me as we sit there, sharing our pain amidst the cacophony of drunken revelry around us. A flicker of hope? Perhaps. It's hard to say. Or maybe it's simply the realization, that even in the darkest corners of the world, there are still those who understand the struggle against the demons within.

THREE

Paul

SILVIE LAUNCHES INTO A STORY ABOUT A CHILDHOOD ADVENTURE gone awry. Her words paint vivid images of laughter and innocence, a stark contrast to the darkness that shrouds her now.

She draws me into her tale, the warmth of her memories seeping into my own battered soul. The weight of my past crimes gradually recedes, replaced by the bittersweet ache of loss and a yearning for the simpler times she evokes. She reminds me, in some ways, of my younger sister, Piper. The little scrap of a girl I left behind when I took to the streets. I wonder what she's doing now?

Where did life take her?

For a moment, I allow myself to forget the shadows that haunt me—to believe redemption might still be within reach.

"Thank you." My voice cracks with an intensity of emotion threatening to spill over. "For sharing that with me."

"Everyone needs a break from their demons." Silvie's eyes fill with understanding. "Even if it's just for a little while. You don't have to let the darkness win, you know. There's always time to change, to be better."

I clench my jaw as the weight of her words bears down on me.

She makes me see her raw vulnerability as she shares her struggles. But redemption? That isn't something I can fathom.

Not for me.

She takes my hand in hers. This time, I don't pull away. Her touch is warm and soft, offering solace to my tormented soul.

"I appreciate your words, but you don't know what I've done or what I'm capable of. You don't carry the ghosts I do."

"Maybe not." Her eyes hold a deep well of sorrow that hints at her own share of pain. "But I've learned we need to forgive ourselves before we find redemption. I believe there's more to you than darkness."

My heart aches, touched by her unwavering conviction in the face of my hopelessness. I want to believe her, want to cling to that sliver of light she offers, but the shadows within me are too deeply rooted.

"Maybe you're right," I admit the possibility, my voice thick with emotion. "But I'm not sure I deserve that chance."

The raucous laughter of the group Silvie belongs to intensifies, fueled by alcohol and unchecked aggression.

Silvie's pimp stalks toward us; his face contorted with rage. He slams his glass onto the bar top and yanks Silvie away from me. The force of his grip makes her wince, and my heart clenches at the abuse. The man tries to loom over me—his eyes a storm of jealousy and rage—it's a mistake he'll regret.

"I didn't do anything wrong," Silvie pleads with her pimp.

"Then why are you wasting your time talking to this loser instead of fucking him?" The man sneers, turning his glare on me. "Trying to get some for free, huh?"

"Leave her alone." My words come out a low, throaty growl, and my anger builds. I rise from my seat and surprise the man when I tower over him by a foot. "We were just talking."

"Think you can have a heart-to-heart with my girl without payin' up?" He snarls at me, his breath reeking of cheap booze and stale cigarettes. "You got another thing coming, buddy."

"Think."

"Huh?" He looks at me without understanding.

"It's another think coming. Not thing." I correct the bastard, getting more irritated by the second.

"You lookin' for trouble?" The pimp's lips twist into a sneer. He's too far into his drink to realize he's outmatched when it comes to me.

"Leave him alone," Silvie interjects, her voice trembling but resolute. "He's not trying to get anything for free. He's going to pay. We were just talking."

I clench my fists, feeling the darkness within me stirring, urging me to lash out. I want nothing more than to wipe the smug sneer from this guy's face, but violence will only prove Silvie's words wrong—that I'm beyond redemption.

"Talking doesn't keep the lights on, sweetheart." The pimp's fingers dig into Silvie's arm. She winces in pain, but her eyes remain locked on me, pleading with me not to retaliate.

"Let her go." My hands ball into fists as every muscle in my body tenses, ready to strike. The darkness within me wakes, urging me to unleash my pent-up fury upon this man who dares to harm someone so undeserving.

"Or what?" The pimp sneers, tightening his grip on Silvie's arm until she cries out. "You gonna teach me a lesson?"

"Maybe I should," I reply, keeping my voice low and dangerous as I stare down at the man who stands between me and the fragile hope Silvie offered me. "She doesn't belong to you. She's more than a possession for you to control."

"Is that so?" Rick taunts me, stepping closer. Which only makes him crane his neck. At six-ten, I've easily got a foot in height over the man, and while lean, my muscles are whipcord strong. "You think I don't know what she's worth? She's damn good at what she does, and I'm not giving her up without a fight."

A feral growl builds in my throat as the pimp's venomous words lash out. The weight of every past sin and transgression presses down on me, fueling an inferno inside of me that will consume everything in its path.

As we face off, the weight of the pimp's words hangs heavy in the air. For the first time since I can remember, I stand up for someone other than myself. Normally, I'm the punisher and executioner.

But not tonight.

Maybe Silvie's right?

A small flicker of hope pushes against the darkness that threatens to consume me. And though I feel the familiar pull of violence tugging at my soul, I hold firm, determined to prove that I can still choose a different path.

"Get your hands off her." I spit on the floor, my voice laden with the anguish that's festering inside of me.

Silvie's eyes shimmer with unshed tears.

The pimp backhands Silvie across the face. The sound of flesh striking flesh echoes through the bar, followed by a gasp from the few remaining patrons as she falls to the sticky floor.

Rick's eyes blaze with fury, the veins in his neck bulging beneath his taut skin. He points an accusing finger at me. "You think you're so much better than me? You ain't no saint, pal."

"Never said I was a saint." My heart thunders in my chest, each beat echoing the anger coursing through me. My fingers twitch, itching to strike.

"Rick, please," Silvie pleads from the floor, her voice quivering with fear. "He did nothing wrong."

"Stay out of it, bitch." Rick, her pimp, snaps, not even sparing her a glance before turning back to me. "This is between me and him."

"Leave her alone."

My rage finally boils over. The last vestiges of my restraint shatter. With a guttural roar, I lunge at the pimp, fists flying like a storm-driven hail. Blow after blow rains down upon the man who dares to harm someone who showed me kindness, even if only for a moment.

We collide with the force of our pent-up aggression. Our bodies tangle, limbs flailing as we grapple with one another. The room dissolves into a blur of frenzied movement. The sharp tang of sweat and blood fills my nostrils as my fists connect with Rick's flesh, but with each strike, the darkness inside me grows stronger, more insistent.

Ravenous to inflict pain. To hurt another.

As much as I want to break free from the darkness that haunts me, a part of me is terrified of losing its familiar embrace.

"Enough!" The bartender's booming voice slices through our fight like a thunderclap. With surprising strength, he wrenches us apart, the force of his grip on my arms bruising and unyielding. "I won't have this in my bar."

My breath heaves in ragged gasps, the fire within me still burning hot and wild, but with nowhere left to direct it. The world around me blurs into a haze of pain and regret, each heartbeat threatening to rip me apart.

The bartender points at me. "You, get out of here. Now. Leave."

As I stumble toward the exit, the taste of blood in my mouth, I can't help but wonder if I have truly lost any chance of finding redemption? If it had ever truly been within my reach at all.

Silvie struggles to her feet, blood trickling down her cheek as she meets my gaze. Sadly, I can't save her. I turn away from her and she calls out, but the pain in my chest only grows sharper with each step I take.

"Goodbye, Silvie," I whisper the words, making them a silent promise that I'll carry the memory of our brief encounter forever.

The door slams shut behind me, casting me into the frigid night. The icy air cuts through my clothes, making me shiver violently, and the sickly sweet stench of blood and alcohol clings to my skin like a cloying perfume.

"Damn it." I drag a trembling hand through the disheveled mess of my hair.

Amidst the shadows and fog swirling through the empty streets, I spot a stray dog—thin and ragged, its fur matted with grime. Its eyes meet mine, seeming to see straight through to the darkness within me.

"Go away."

The dog tilts its head as if considering whether to approach.

"Leave me alone," I growl, turning away, and continue my aimless journey through the desolate night.

The dog seems to make up its mind and trots over to me. I look down at the shaggy beast and stretch out my hand, not caring if the dog bites me. It tentatively sniffs my hand and licks my fingers. Dropping to my knees, I rub the mangy mutt, then glance at a diner that appears to be open, although no one is inside.

"Stay here, pup." The dog whines as I trot across the street.

I return with a mixture of bacon, sausage, eggs, and biscuits. Kneeling down, I place the food on the pavement and sit back while the dog wolfs down the meal.

"I can't keep living like this."

It looks at me as if to say I'm wrong.

With one good deed done, I leave the dog and stumble down the deserted streets. My thoughts swirl like a storm, battering me with questions about my purpose, my morality, and whether redemption is possible for someone so thoroughly lost.

I walk for some time, wandering aimlessly, when coarse laughter stops me in my tracks. Laughter belonging to the cretins from the bar. I round the corner to find the men standing around a tiny figure curled in on itself on the pavement. The men relieve themselves, urinating on the body of the woman I met tonight.

"Silvie?" Horror creeps up my spine as I take in her mutilated body. Angry bruises and deep gashes mar her face. "God, no."

She tried to help me, to reach into the depths of my soul and pull me from the abyss. And now, she lies broken and lifeless on the dirty ground.

Rage surges through me like a wildfire, incinerating the shackles of restraint that held me back in the bar. My mind becomes singularly focused—the pimp will pay for what he did, for snuffing out a light that dared to pierce my darkness.

I growl through gritted teeth and stalk toward the men, driven by a savage thirst for blood. Darkness rises within me, an unstoppable rage ready to exact retribution for a woman I barely knew.

I tackle the pimp first.

"Silvie didn't deserve to die." I snarl as we grapple, our bodies slamming against a cold brick wall. The pimp fights back. His men join in.

But there's no stopping the fury that drives me.

I lay his men out on the street, one by one, barely breaking a sweat as they fall. When the pimp realizes he's alone, fear replaces his arrogance as my hands close around his throat.

"P-please…" His eyes widen as he gasps for air.

"Too late for that." With one final surge of strength, I silence the man forever.

The pimp's lifeless body crumples to the ground, and I stand over him, chest heaving. The fire of revenge extinguished as quickly as it ignited. A text comes through my phone. A summons from John Snowden, a man whose soul is blacker than mine.

Snowden: I've got a job for you. A man I need you to break.

A hollow emptiness settles within me, leaving me more lost than ever before. My dark urges flare to life. If there's one thing I'm good at, it's dispensing pain.

It's in breaking others.

And I need that right now. I need to embrace the monster I've become.

Me: On My Way.

I hit send and get ready to do what I do best.

"You don't have to let the darkness win, you know. There's always a chance to change, to be better." Silvie's words echo in my head, but it's not true.

My sole purpose is to make others suffer.

FOUR

Paul

———

~

Present Day

~

THE STARK WHITE WALLS OF THE HOSPITAL ROOM FEEL LIKE THEY'RE closing in. Overhead, fluorescent lights bore into my skull; their oppressive sterility makes it hard to breathe.

Forest sits on the edge of the bed. His hands folded neatly in his lap. The breathing tube and ventilator are gone, but the monitors remain. He's alert and looking more like himself, but still haggard and bone-weary.

I press my fingers to my temple and focus on what the doctor, an oncologist, is telling us. I try to block out his words, but there's no avoiding the truth.

"Non-Hodgkin lymphoma." Dr. Chen's words slice through the air like a scalpel. "I'm afraid it's quite advanced. Stage IV. It's treatable, but it's a long road to recovery."

It feels like a death knell.

But Forest?

He's so damn calm about it, as if he's made his peace with this nightmare. I want to grab him by the shoulders, shake him, and make him see that he needs to fight, not just placidly accept this news.

Meanwhile, Sara clutches my arm. Her nails dig into my skin, but I don't flinch. The pain's a balm to the horrifying diagnosis.

I want to rage at the universe, scream until my throat is raw, anything to wipe the detached look in Forest's eyes and erase Dr. Chen's words from existence.

"Paul." Sara's voice cracks, pulling me back into the room. Her eyes are red-rimmed, and she clutches at her sweater as if it's the only thing anchoring her to the earth. "Say something."

Forest's not with us. He retreats into himself, pulling away when we need him the most. I've seen him do this before—when tortured past what any human can stand by Snowden.

By me.

It's a coping mechanism he's honed well throughout his troubled life.

"I don't understand why you're so fucking calm about everything." I snap at Forest but regret it instantly.

Forest's composure barely cracks. "You need to accept this. Both of you." His voice is rough with suppressed emotion. "Skye, you as well."

"I won't accept it. We'll find the best doctors, the latest treatments. There has to be something…" My heart pounds, and my breath catches.

"Enough." The sharp command slices through my panic.

I fall silent. Forest never uses that tone with me. If he dared, I'd yank him down to our dungeon and light his ass on fire with my whip.

Can't do that here.

Wrong time.

Wrong place.

We're not in those roles out *here*.

Forest stands, pulling me into his arms. I cling to him, breathing in his scent. The familiarity threatens to undo me. He whispers in my ear. "None of us were meant to live forever. Let's make the most out of whatever time we have left."

Sara gasps beside me. I stretch out a hand and pull her to my side, including her in Forest's embrace.

"You're giving up?" My teeth grate together, annoyed and growing more pissed off by the second.

"Maybe that's how he's coping." Skye sits quietly from her perch on the windowsill. She gazes out at the gray sky as if searching for some hidden meaning amidst the clouds. "Bean? Is this your way of coping? Or are you just being an ass?" Like the rest of us, she's pissed at the way Forest reacts to the news.

It's almost as if he's relieved rather than drowning like the rest of us.

Poor Dr. Chen doesn't know what to make of the unusual family dynamics he stepped into. He sits at the foot of the bed, one foot on the floor, ready for a speedy exit.

"Forest," I try to keep the anger from my voice. It's not directed at him, but at the injustice of the situation. "You need to fight this. You can't give up."

"Who says I'm giving up?" His voice is soft, almost serene. It's infuriating. "Just because I accept what's happening doesn't mean I've given up, but there's only so much we can do." He turns his attention to Dr. Chen. "Right, Doc?"

Before Chen can respond, I grab Forest by the shoulders and give a hard shake, probably harder than I should with Dr. Chen watching.

"Your life is worth more than accepting what comes. We need to fight this. You need to fight it. You've fought so hard to get where you are now, and we've all fought alongside you. You can't let cancer win."

"What if I'm tired of fighting?" Forest looks me square in the eye as he drives a dagger into my heart. "You just said it yourself. I've fought so damn hard to get to where I am. Maybe I'm done fighting? It's my life. I get a say in how I want it to end. This doesn't seem such a bad way to go."

"How can you say that?" Sara's voice is barely a whisper, but it's enough to silence me for a moment. "I can understand you're tired of fighting, but this isn't about you. It's not about me, or Paul, or Skye for that matter. You have Delia and Sebastian to think about. Are they supposed to grow up without a father?"

"They have Papa Paul," Forest grumps at Sara's comment.

"They need both their fathers you insufferable brute." Sara's fingers curl into tiny, compact fists. "You need to be strong for them. Fight for them. If you won't fight for me, or fight for Paul, then you fight for your children."

"It looks like he's already given up on all of us." My words tumble out before I can stop them. "Like he's just waiting for the end to come. Fucking coward."

"Enough." Forest's tone is sharp and final. "I'm tired of *always* fighting something in my life. I never said I wouldn't explore treatment options or that I wouldn't consider them. All I said is, if this is what kills me, I'm okay with that."

His gaze meets mine, and the full force of his conviction slams into me. For the first time since we entered this hospital, I see a flicker of emotion in his eyes—determination, perhaps, or defiance? —maybe he simply needs control?

As much as I want to continue arguing, I have no right to impose my fears on to him.

"Fine," I relent, my jaw tight. "But don't think for one second that I'm going to let you face this alone. We're a team, remember?"

"Always." Even though his voice is steady, the faintest hint of gratitude shines in his eyes. Forest is tired. It's not until this moment, I realize how incredibly tired he is.

We stand there, a fragile web of pain, anger, and despair weaving around us while we each grapple with our demons, but we'll face whatever comes next together.

As a team.

Maybe that will be enough?

Sara's hand grips mine, her knuckles turning white, her anguish palpable. Forest may be acting like an ass, but Sara and I are in this together.

I glance at Forest, searching for any hint of fear or uncertainty in his steely gaze, but he remains impassive, like an island of calm amidst the storm of emotions threatening to consume us all.

"Tell me," Forest's voice is as steady as a rock as he turns to Dr. Chen, "What are my options?"

The oncologist hesitates for a moment, his expression solemn. "Stage IV lymphoma is treatable, but I must emphasize time is of the essence."

"Treatable?" I latch onto what hope I can. "How treatable? What are we looking at?" My words lodge in my throat as fear grabs me like a vice.

"Aggressive rounds of chemotherapy are often given as a first-line treatment for lymphoma at this stage." The doc doesn't hesitate. Likely, he's had this conversation hundreds of times with the various patients he's treated over the years.

"What does stage IV mean?" Sara's crystal-clear voice cuts through the panic raging within me.

I should've asked that question.

"The cancer has spread throughout Mr. Summers's body. Most often it spreads to the liver, bone marrow, and lungs. Stage III and stage IV are considered in a single category and they have the same treatment and prognosis. Stage III and IV lymphomas are common, still very treatable, and often curable, depending on the NHL subtype."

"NHL?" Sara continues to ask questions.

I'm too enraged by Forest's blind acceptance of his possible death to think rationally.

Skye clears her throat. "NHL is shorthand for Non-Hodgkin Lymphoma."

"Prognosis?" Finally, a word I understand, perhaps the most important word.

"The five-year survival for stage IV lymphoma ranges from 57% to 67% based on the particular subtype and response to treatment."

"What about immunotherapy and targeted therapy?" Skye shifts and leans against the window. "Will those be a part of his treatment plan?"

"Potentially, depending on the subtype and response to treatment. Radiation therapy, as well as BMT are also options."

"BMT?" I'm starting to think more clearly. "What's that?"

"Bone marrow transplant," Skye answers instead of Dr. Chen.

I'm glad we have Skye to help us navigate through the complex medical jargon.

"Bone marrow transplantation is considered an aggressive treatment for NHL." Dr. Chen shifts on the foot of the bed, settling into a more comfortable position. "It's generally used only for people with NHL whose disease is progressive or recurrent. For some NHL subtypes, such as mantle cell lymphoma and some T-cell lymphomas, we may recommend transplantation as part of the initial treatment plan to prevent or delay recurrence. Until we get the results of our subtyping, we won't know the best way to proceed."

"How long will that take? If Forest needs treatment, we need to start today." Hell, we need to have started this months ago when Forest first started looking haggard and pale. Once again, I curse myself for not insisting Forest seek medical attention sooner. Maybe then, it would've been stage I instead of stage IV?

"Our next step is to determine the subtype." Dr. Chen doesn't commit. "There are a few more tests we need to do."

"Such as?" Sara pipes up, her voice steadier than mine.

"Lymph node biopsy, a spinal tap. We've already sent blood for testing. Those results can take days to weeks."

"Weeks? We don't have weeks. He needs treatment now." I pride myself on self-control, but right now, I sound like a freakin' lunatic.

"Paul," Skye steps in, cutting off Dr. Chen's response. From the look he gives her, it's clear he's happy for the interference. "Typing of NHL is complex and the treatments for each individual subtype even more so. Not to mention new treatments and trials are ongoing. We don't want to jump to the wrong treatment."

"Dr. Summers is correct." Dr. Chen takes back control of the conversation. "We can do the lymph node biopsy today and the spinal tap. After that, as long as Mr. Summers feels up to it, there's no reason for him to remain in the hospital. We can discharge you and follow up in the clinic once we know what we're dealing with and how to proceed. In the meantime, I want to set you up with your clinical team. We offer a multidisciplinary support team, from dietitians, therapists, psychologists, and more, to form a cohesive plan of care."

"I can get out of here today?" Forest jumps on Dr. Chen's words.

"Maybe not today. We can get the biopsy done today, but we'll need to observe you overnight. In the meantime, I'll get our treatment team in here to introduce themselves. Tomorrow, as long as you're feeling up to it, you should be good to go."

"Any limitations?" Forest asks.

"As far as?" Dr. Chen's brows bunch.

"Activity." Forest gives him a look. "Like can I go walking, running, lift weights." Forest's gaze shifts to me. "Other more *strenuous* activities?"

Holy shit and no fucking way.

No way in hell are we heading downstairs for one of Forest's *therapy* sessions. The man's in no shape for my whip, or any of the many things we do down there to feed his masochistic needs.

No fucking way.

"There are no limitations to any activity. Your collapse was likely due to stress and dehydration. Our nutritionist will meet with you before you leave. The success of any treatment will be directly linked to your current state of health when we begin."

"Sounds great." Forest claps his hands together, making Sara jump at the sound. "Let's stick a needle in me and call it done. I'm ready to blow this joint, and blow something else." Once again, he looks to me.

Forest's sexual appetite matches mine. Which is to say, we're equally voracious. But in addition to sex, Forest requires constant attention to his darker cravings. When I don't feed him pain, those cravings bubble up to the surface, where they don't belong and can become dangerous to others.

Like Sara.

It's one of the side effects to the trauma he endured as a child. Most of Forest's sexual cravings are as dark, or darker, than what his abusers subjected him to as a child. He normalized what they did to him, and that's what I'm attempting to course-correct as his Master.

Forest entrusted himself to my care. He gave up all control over his sexual self to me. I'm the conduit through which he can share normal, healthy sex with the woman he loves.

I'm the one who keeps him from hurting her because of a triggering event.

The hunger in Forest's eyes right now? That's the darkness bubbling to the surface. But how the hell can I master him when all of this hangs over our heads?

What I know about Forest, and hate about him, is he will fulfill his needs. It will either happen with me, or without me. Part of our pact is a promise we swore to each other. He would never seek such things outside my control. In return, I would give him, not what he wants, but what he needs.

Fuck me.

He's going to need a significant session soon.

"Well, let's get started. I'm ready to get out of here." Forest tips his head to the ceiling and closes his eyes. I don't know if he's praying or running complex math in his head. One never knows with Forest.

"So, you *are* going to fight this?" Like me, Sara's a bit confused as to whether Forest is going to fight or give in.

FIVE

Paul

———

∽

Forest pulls Sara into his lap, folding his arms around her. She tips her head to lie against his chest. He turns his attention to me. Eyes solid. Voice firm.

"I'll fight until I can't." A shadow of a smile plays across his lips. "Until then, I plan to have fun and *enjoy* what time I have left."

He's like a broken record with the *"enjoy what's left"* shit. I'm going to have to talk to Skye once we're alone to find out how physical I can get with Forest.

"Forest," Sara whispers, tears streaming down her cheeks. "Please—don't be like that."

"Like, what?"

"Fatalistic."

"Not being fatalistic. Just practical."

"What you're doing is behaving like an ass to your wife. You have to fight this."

I agree with her. The way he's treating Sara pisses me the fuck off.

Forest may get his wish after all. If he continues to be flippant and cavalier about this diagnosis, I'm going to rip into his ass and make him suffer. The only problem with that is he'll soak up the pain like a reward.

"I will fight, but I don't want to lose sight of what truly matters." His tone softens; gentle, yet resolute.

Even after this diagnosis, he refuses to succumb to despair. He's either going to fight to his dying breath, or embrace it.

Knowing him, Forest's going to own this cancer in the same way he owns the abuse he endured.

He meets my gaze with an intensity that both warms and unsettles me. "Life is fragile and fleeting. I embrace my mortality, and in doing so, found a sense of peace."

"Peace?" Skye asks, her eyes wide with disbelief. "How can you be at peace with this?"

"Because it's liberating." Forest's normally deep voice is barely audible above the sterile hum of hospital machinery.

We exchange glances, each of us grappling with our own fear as we process Forest's words. This diagnosis has shaken us to our cores, yet here stands Forest, steady as ever, determined to make every remaining moment count.

Perhaps there is still hope—not just for Forest, but for all of us. We have an opportunity to grow, to learn, and to cherish the time we are given.

My gaze shifts to Sara. Everything will change for us if Forest dies. We're connected through Forest. Not with each other.

Forest's stoicism pisses me off more than it should.

"Should we get a second opinion?" My words are for Dr. Chen, but Forest reads the subtext.

I'm not happy with Forest, or his choices. I'm most definitely not a fan of the way he dismisses Sara's love. He's hurting her on purpose. Almost as if, in pushing her away, his death won't hurt her as much.

In that, Forest is dead wrong.

"If you desire a second opinion, we can definitely accommodate that." Dr. Chen clears his throat. "I only ask that we wait for all the tests to come in. Any second opinion will need that information."

"There's no need for a second opinion," Skye cuts in. "I have absolute faith in Dr. Chen and his colleagues. Just run the tests.

We'll be waiting to hear the results." She turns to Forest and shakes her head. "Bean, you're really being a selfish twat."

"Me? What have I done?" Forest acts like he's innocent.

Skye's only answer is a flick of her eyes over to Sara, who's drowning in tears.

"I'm just being realistic." Forest glares at his sister.

"Realistic?" The word comes out as a snarl, my chest tightening with each breath. "You're talking like you've already given up. Would it kill you to—I don't know—pretend you're not the only one hurting because of this news?"

"I'm the one dying from cancer."

Sara chokes on a sob. I pull her out of his arms, tugging her to me. Comforting her. Holding her. She may be Forest's wife, but she's my "other" other half.

"You're a fucking asshole." I'm going to shelter and protect Sara from the damage and fallout Forest's diagnosis rains down all around us.

"Paul, stop," Skye interjects, her voice trembling with emotion. "This isn't helping, and it's not what Forest needs right now."

"Don't you think I know that?" I take Sara's hand, threading our fingers together. When I bend down and inhale Sara's soft, floral fragrance, my eyes close as her essence infuses all my senses. She's everything Forest's not, soft to his strong, quiet to his loud, gentle to his abrasive exterior.

"I'm going to go home and see to Delia and Sebastian. Paul, can you stay with Forest?" She leans her cheek against my chest, seeking comfort in my arms.

"I'm coming with you." I sweep a strand of hair off her cheek and tuck it behind her ear. "You're in no condition to drive."

Besides, I need someone to talk to. Someone who shares the same pain as me.

"I'll stay." Skye pushes off from the window and comes to the foot of the bed. "Dr. Chen, we really appreciate you taking time out of your day to give us this news. What you do isn't easy, and I appreciate you."

"No problem." Dr. Chen stands then glances around the room. The confusion in his gaze as he glances between me, Sara, and

Forest is clear, but we get that all the time. "Are there any other questions?"

Our little throuple, our triad, makes sense only to the three of us.

"Not now." Skye ushers Dr. Chen to the door, then turns around with her fists propped on her hips. "Forest, I'm sorry you've got cancer. It totally sucks monkey balls, but we can do so much more than ever before. Do not give up on me now." She thrusts her pointer finger at him, punctuating her words. "Paul and Sara, I'll give you a minute alone." With those words, she stomps out of the room, leaving the three of us in an awkward silence.

"I don't know why the two of you have bugs crawling up your butts." Forest looks at the way Sara and I cling to each other. "I'm the one who has cancer."

If he had one wish in life, it would be for the three of us to be one. Not just two pairs united through Forest. He wishes Sara and I were intimate and that the three of us would express that intimacy together.

He wants a real three-way.

The only problem is I'm a Dom, a Master, and I'm gay.

"Did you really just ask if I had a bug up my butt?" Sara pulls out of my embrace.

"It's the truth. You act like you're the one they diagnosed." Forest's digging his own grave. If he doesn't stop with the flippant bullshit…

"You're a part of us," Sara says. "Which means this affects us all. Don't ever shut me out like that again. I've gone through too much with you to be treated like I don't matter. Yes, you have cancer. Yes, it sucks. Yes, I'm scared. I think we're all scared. But our strength is in how the three of us work together to push through and deal with whatever life throws at us. When I was pregnant with the twins, we all pulled together when things got bad, and we're going to do that again. We're going to do it because we love each other." She takes my hand in hers and grabs Forest's, placing our hands together in a stack, with Forest's hand in the middle.

"Sometimes strength isn't about fighting," Forest says softly, his gaze locked on mine, unwavering. "Sometimes it's about accepting what we can't change and making the most of what we have left."

"Please stop talking like that." Her voice cracks with the weight of her emotions.

"Like what?" He simply doesn't get it.

He and I are going to have a serious talk later.

"I can't lose you." Sara swipes at her cheek where an errant tear dared to fall. "Until the doctors know what kind of NHL you have, don't accept death because you're too scared to live."

"I'm sorry I hurt you, but I'm not afraid to face death." He turns to me and shifts his hand to grasp mine. His grip is firm and steady as his pale-blue eyes fill with tears. "You won't lose me. Not in the ways that truly matter. We need to face this without anger or denial."

"Forest…" My words come as barely more than a whisper, the pain in my chest making it difficult to breathe.

"Promise me." His eyes search mine for the acceptance I'm not sure I can give. "Promise me that we'll make the most of the time we have, however long that may be. When I say I've had enough though, respect my wishes. My life hasn't been the best life. I love you; I love Sara. I will always go to my knees and serve you as my Master, but, in this, I need your word."

I stare into his unwavering gaze, struggling to find the strength to support him. But stop fighting? How can I give him my word when I plan on fighting until the end?

"I don't know if I can do that."

"Please?"

"Fuck." I run my hand down my face, pulling on the skin. "Forest, you can't ask me to give up." We cement our unique ties in that moment.

"I don't want to give up. I plan on doing the chemo, or whatever else, but if things aren't helping, I don't want to go out like that. I don't want to die in a hospital. Please, promise you'll accept my decision when the time comes."

When? What the fuck? He's already resigned himself to this death.

"I'll try, but I can't give you my word."

"I suppose that'll be enough."

The three of us clasp hands, a symbol of our unity in the face of this devastating news. And yet, as I join my own hand with theirs, I can't help but feel a sense of unresolved tension beneath the surface, a storm threatening to tear us apart as we grapple with the implications of Forest's diagnosis.

"Now, come here." Forest stretches out his arm, not for me. We don't show affection in that way, but for Sara. "I'm sorry. You know how much you mean to me. I'll do whatever it takes to beat this, and I promise not to shut you out."

"You promise?" Sara asks.

"I do. Forever and always."

"Forever and always." She leans over and kisses him on the cheek. "But I do need to go."

"Delia and Sebastian can't wait another hour?" Forest asks.

"I hate to say this, because you can't leave, but this hospital room feels suffocating. I'm not like you. I need time to process my messy human emotions."

"I love your messy emotions." Forest kisses the top of her head.

"You barely understand people have emotions." She snuggles into his embrace.

"True, but I'm learning from you." He holds her for a beat longer than necessary. In that, I see the rawness of his fear.

Forest's terrified and putting on a strong face for us. Like Sara, I need out of this place; the beeping of machines is a constant reminder of Forest's mortality. He looks better after his collapse, but he's still a shadow of his former self.

Forest turns to me. He smiles—a sad and wistful smile that speaks to the pain he's endured throughout his lifetime.

"I've stared death in the face before. I've learned to embrace it as a part of living, but I'm not done fighting yet."

"Death isn't something to embrace." Anger and fear bubble up inside me once more, but I shove them to the side. "We're supposed to fight it, to cling to life with everything we have."

"True," Forest acknowledges, his expression turning somber. "But sometimes fighting only causes more suffering. Sometimes, accepting our fate can bring peace and liberation."

I frown, unable to grasp the concept of embracing mortality

when faced with such a cruel and unjust reality. "You really believe that?" My voice cracks under the weight of my emotions.

"It's how I survive." His eyes never leave mine. "I've experienced loss, pain, and betrayal, but found love, friendship, and purpose. It's more than most people." He reaches out, placing a hand on my arm, his touch warm and reassuring. "If my past has taught me anything, it's that life is fleeting, and our time on earth is precious. I refuse to spend whatever time I have left drowning in anger or despair. Or lying in a hospital bed. I want to come home. To you. To Sara. To the twins. I want to spend as much time as possible with you in the basement."

There he goes again, hinting about his needs.

"You make this harder than it needs to be." I grit my teeth, disliking everything about this conversation.

"How's that? We can't control everything in our lives. The only thing we control is how we react." He takes a deep breath, resolve etched into the lines of his face. "I choose to face this with grace."

Grace my ass.

His strength and acceptance in the face of such adversity are both humbling and inspiring, yet the thought of losing him still threatens to shatter me.

"I need you to promise me something." Forest's hand whips forward, grasping my upper arm. His grip is fragile and weak.

"What?"

"Promise you'll let go of your anger and fear. Promise me you'll focus on the time we have together." Forest's grip on my arm tightens ever so slightly. "I don't want anything to change between us, especially when we're alone."

Again, *another* reference to the basement.

I swallow hard, my throat thick with emotion. That's the closest Forest will come to telling me his darker cravings need my attention. It's the closest he'll come to begging.

"I don't know if I can."

"Try," he pleads, his eyes imploring me to find the strength within myself. "For me."

Unable to form the words as I seal the promise in my heart, all I can do is nod. Fortunately, Forest doesn't push and accepts the nod.

I glance at Sara, her eyes brimming with unshed tears, and reach for her. Our fingers intertwine in silent support.

I feel her pain, unable to do anything for the man I love. The man who taught me how to be strong, to embrace my darkness without losing myself to it.

But I won't be able to accept defeat. I'll fight for Forest to the bitter end.

Forest always says there's light in the darkness. I fear we'll fail to find the light as we navigate through this storm.

As Sara and I depart, a memory of holding the whip to Forest tumbles through my head. It was the first time I met his defiance head-on and found myself completely, and utterly, entranced by the one man who refused to break beneath my whip.

It was the moment I fell in love with him.

Paul

———

~

Several Years Ago

~

THE DOOR CREAKS OPEN AS I STEP INTO THE DIMLY LIT ROOM. MY eyes adjust to the flickering shadows cast by a single dangling light bulb.

The smell of Snowden's newest acquisition's sweat, fear, and blood hangs heavy in the air. I'm no stranger to the dark world of pain and punishment, but something about this particular assignment leaves me feeling dirty, like my soul is stained beyond redemption.

"Back again?" Forest's deep voice vibrates the air. "Needed a break?"

"Silence." I crack my whip, snapping the tip on his inner thigh, making him jump.

I'm the one with power here. I'm the punisher—the dispenser of pain—but an unsettling sensation clings to me, as persistent as the shadows overtaking the rough edges of the room.

Forest Summers, a once proud man, lifts his head at my entrance. His vibrant ice-blue eyes are shadowed and dull, but he rallies and jerks against the chains holding him against the wall. His unbridled rage is fucking intoxicating.

"Fuck." He hisses in pain, then closes his eyes and takes in a slow, deep breath. His voice changes, turns husky. Sexy. "Do it again." He glares at me, eyes full of fire and spite.

"Begging for my whip?" I close the distance between us and place the butt of my whip under his chin. This close, I feel him on a cellular level, and the sexual chemistry between us is ready to explode.

"Don't you know it." He shifts in his chains, pushing his chest out, bumping against me.

"Well, that's your first mistake." I reach down and grab his balls, squeezing tight.

Forest rises on his toes, hissing with pain as my fingers curl and twist his nuts.

This isn't our first meeting. Snowden assigned me to guard Sara when he takes Forest to be used and brutalized. I've watched the two of them together, envying their bond.

I want Forest.

I crave him on a visceral level.

"Stop playing with your toy." Snowden pulls me back to the reason I'm here. "You can fuck him later."

Snowden's not done playing with Forest. He's not at a point where he's willing to pass off his toy to me. As for Forest and me, we're still in the getting-to-know-you phase of our relationship.

While Forest grudgingly accepts my job as Sara's guard, the two of us dance around the sexual chemistry building between us. I've played guard duty for a while now, protecting Sara, watching Forest, but today is the first time he tasted my whip. I expected a response, but this blows me away.

We're fucking perfect for each other. Unfortunately, my father stands between us. My lip curls and I shrug off the possessive thoughts.

Forest's just another job.

Or, should be.

His battered body, taut with tension, is a magnificent canvas of reds, blues, the deepest purples, all spattered by the most horrific blacks.

Evidence of our previous go-around.

His eyes remain full of defiance, but something lurks beneath the surface—a flicker of challenge that makes my heart seize. Almost as if he dares me to break him. Dares me to show my true strength.

As if he wants it.

Needs it.

Craves it.

"You just going to stand there and hold my nuts? Or are you going to play with your whip?"

"Depends on which gets you hard first." His cock jerks as I shift my hand from his nuts and grip the base of his shaft.

Forest rocks back on his heels, rolls his lower lip between his lips and moans. The man fucking moans. And his flaccid cock surges to life.

"Does it matter?" His lids slowly open and we once again engage in a battle for dominance. "Shame he doesn't let you fuck me. The man gives me to his men, but you're the only one who hasn't fucked me. Why is that?"

I can't help but wonder what secrets hide behind his haunted eyes. I need to know this man. It's a visceral compulsion to crack him open and sift through his pain, savoring the agony he holds. The pain he bears for me.

"Perhaps I'm waiting for you to beg me to take you."

"That's a shame. Wanting me doesn't mean you get to have me. Not in the way you want."

"Fuck off." My fingers tighten around his turgid shaft.

"Love to, but I'm currently tied up."

I rear back and punch him in the gut. The man's got muscles for miles, but I'm stronger than he expects. He grunts as I drive my fist into his gut.

Like him, I'm painfully aroused. This dance between us stirs my deepest hunger.

Forest may be facing the desperation of a submissive struck by the potential of meeting his true match, but I'm caught in the same dilemma. This man is perfect for me.

Perhaps it's this that unnerves me?

In Forest, I see my other half. Only together will either of us be whole. He's the only man strong enough to accept the pain I must inflict. The only man capable of enduring the savage sadism within me. The only man who desperately begs for a Dominant worthy of his surrender.

"Paul…" Snowden's voice curls through the air like an unwelcome guest.

"What?"

"Get on with it." Snowden leans back, his cock already in his hand, stroking slowly as he watches me with Forest. He loves the spectacle of watching me torture another.

"With pleasure." I take a step back and shake out the whip.

"Do your worst." Forest softens his voice, low enough Snowden can't hear.

"Be careful what you ask for." This is our second go-around for the day. I spent the morning warming Forest up, getting in a workout with my whip.

"I'm not afraid of you. If this is your idea of foreplay, I'm afraid the main event will be a bore."

"Don't worry. I know exactly what you need." His defiance pisses me the fuck off. "But you're going to have to beg me to give it to you."

His body is now a tapestry of angry red welts and deep-purple bruising. There's not a patch of skin that didn't taste my whip. Except for his face. I won't mar that perfection.

"If I thought you deserved it, I'd consider that an invitation, but all I see is a man who's ruled by another. As long as you work for him, you don't deserve me."

When I whipped his cock, something that would break any normal man, Forest responded with a twitch. As if his cock woke up.

For me.

I lean in close, whispering into his ear. "You're wrong about that."

With eyes the palest blue and a chiseled face cut from stone, Forest is stunningly beautiful with his shock-white hair.

Forest outweighs me, but I'm whipcord strong. That alone might define the balance of power between us, but we are not equally matched.

I've spent my life learning how to dominate men like him.

Forest may be stronger than me physically, but he's nowhere near my match in a fight. I'll win every time if we're ever pitted against the other. I'll win because I know how to survive, and I know how to kill.

Forest has never traveled down that path. He's not a killer. His soul is pure. Not blackened like mine.

"You'll be exceptional when you submit for me. Unlike Snowden, however, you'll do it because it's something you want. Not because you're trying to protect—her."

His teeth gnash together, ready to spit vitriol and fire, but I don't give him the chance. Stepping back, I lay into him with my whip. If he wants to drown in pain, then I'm a firehose of pain, and I'm coming at him.

I hate that he isn't mine to master. I'm merely the tool of John Snowden, a man who spent decades scheming to get his hands on the boy who eluded his grasp so many years ago.

Only Forest is no longer a boy.

He's a force of nature.

And I want him.

As for why I'm the punisher and not Snowden, the passing years have not been kind to Snowden. Perhaps there was a time when he was stronger than Forest. Doing the math and knowing Snowden's predilection for young boys, it's not hard to put two and two together.

Forest would rip Snowden in half now. He's no longer the scared and helpless little boy cowed into submission by a monster of a man. Forest is grown now. An incredible specimen of male virility and strength, he makes my mouth water.

To master all that strength? To command the man Forest's become? I crave that more than I can describe.

Forest will be my downfall.

But he is not the only prisoner who occupies the room.

Sara huddles in the corner. She's the only thing keeping Forest from lashing out. The diminutive woman shivers with terror and hunkers in the corner of the room, as if that will make her disappear. She stares at Forest with wide, fearful eyes, silently pleading for mercy. My heart clenches at the sight.

Those two share a bond I will never touch. No matter how brutal, or how merciless, their bond will endure.

Forest's submission to Snowden comes at a price, a bargain the two men made. Forest submits to Snowden and, in return, Snowden promises Sara will not be hurt.

I guard Sara and ensure she's not hurt. Which means, I moved my quarters into theirs. While they're not intimately involved, it's clear they're madly in love with each other.

That love was Forest's downfall.

Unfortunately, there will be no mercy for Forest. Snowden wants Forest irrevocably broken. His will annihilated.

He needs Forest physically incapable of resisting before he takes the man into his bed. To do otherwise is a death sentence because Forest will kill Snowden if given the chance. But Snowden's smart. As long as Sara's safety is contingent on Forest's submission, Snowden can do anything to Forest.

Not once does Forest resist or beg for any of it to stop. He soaks up the pain because his love for the woman is greater than his need to survive. He endures rape by Snowden, and his men, to keep Sara safe. He'll sacrifice his life if it means Snowden never touches Sara.

Snowden thinks to dominate Forest, but he doesn't understand what he's creating. Forest will be the end of him, and if Snowden doesn't see that now, he will soon enough.

Until then, Forest is mine to do with as I please, and I very much desire to break him. To force his submission and make him mine.

Not Snowden's.

Mine.

Because I know this man was made to complete me. As for Sara? Something within me resists causing her any more pain than she's already suffered.

Not physical pain. Sara will endure no physical pain. Hers will be emotional, forced to watch the man she loves broken into a shadow of his former self.

As for the breaking, it's time.

Snowden settles into his chair. A massive, grotesque thing, it's his throne where he lords over Forest.

"Listen carefully, my boy, as I explain what I desire." Snowden preens from his throne like a cowardly lord. "Give me your body, your pain, and I will not harm Sara. She will be spared the attention of my men." A cruel smile curves his thin lips and a glint of sadistic pleasure flashes in his icy cold eyes.

"Isn't that what I'm doing?" Forest growls from his chains. "Submitting? Giving you my body to do with as you please?"

"No, my boy. You are enduring. Thinking to catch me when my guard's down. Regardless…" Snowden gives an imperial wave of his hand. "Watching you suffer brings me pleasure. Which means suffering for me should please you." He cackles like a lunatic, making the air bristle with malice.

This is more than breaking a man. It's personal between Snowden and Forest. Snowden turns to me, dispensing his commands like a jackal on a throne. His voice drips with malice.

"Forest is strong. Always was a defiant little boy. The goal is not just to hurt him, but to break him. Shatter his spirit until there's nothing left but an empty shell."

Snowden picks off a piece of lint from his shirt and flicks it to the floor. When his gaze shifts to Sara, she whimpers in fear. "Do we all understand our roles?"

My part in this is clear. Do as Snowden instructs, or risk not only my life, but Sara's as well.

Damn you, Forest, how did you get me to care about the woman who adores you when you pretend she means nothing to you?

"I gave you my word." Forest grits his teeth and struggles with his words. "I submit willingly. Whatever you want? Whatever price you need me to pay? I'll pay it. Just don't hurt the girl."

"Excellent." Snowden snaps his fingers, coldly, then forces Sara to her knees on the stone floor. A heavy iron chain wraps around her neck, a stark reminder her life is at the mercy of Snowden's pleasure.

"Please," Forest whispers, his voice strained and broken by pain. "Don't hurt Sara."

"Give me what I want." Snowden snarls and his eyes lock on Forest, like a predator eyeing its prey. "Give me your submission, your obedience, your suffering. Give me everything."

"Isn't this enough?" Forest's shoulders slump in defeat. "You've taken everything from me."

"And that's not even close to what you owe me." Snowden grins like a malevolent specter. "I want your spirit crushed beyond repair. I want you curled up in that cage, sniveling like the twelve-year-old boy I broke so many years ago."

Snowden turns his attention to Sara, yanking her from where she cowers by the chain around her neck. "And just for fun, this one will watch every moment until you break. She's going to watch you crawl to me and beg to be used, to suck my cock, to take me in your ass. She's going to watch you turn into my eager little fuck toy."

With that, he forces Sara to kneel on the cold stone floor where she can witness the horror about to unfold. Her gaze locks with Forest's, pleading and full of pain, but he isn't strong enough to hold her gaze. Forest knows what's about to happen. He knows Snowden's already won.

"Please, don't make her watch." Forest's voice comes out a broken whisper filled with pain and resignation. "I'll do whatever you want, just please let her go."

"But where would the fun be in that?" Snowden sneers. "Your little summer sky isn't here to help you, is she? She won't watch you crawl to me, but this one will."

As I prepare to carry out Snowden's orders, I look between Forest and Sara, at the love that shines between them. I'll never come close to touching what they share.

My heart hangs heavy with guilt, but there's no choice. Not for him and not for me. And so, with the heavy weight of their love pressing down on my shoulders, I dig into my dominance and unleash the sadist within. It'll be best to get this over quickly and crush Forest's spirit completely.

I'm a monster myself and not worthy of another's love.

But I can preserve their love as much as possible. There must be a way to save them both, even if it means walking the razor-thin line between loyalty and betrayal, right and wrong, desire and pain.

With a heavy heart, I steel myself for the task ahead, determined to find a way to protect Forest, and a woman I barely know, from the monster lurking in the shadows.

Protecting them from me.

I grab the whip, raise my hand, and bring it down on Forest with all the force I can muster.

And this is how we begin.

SEVEN

Paul

———

~

Present Day

~

THERE'S A CLINICAL STERILITY TO THE HOSPITAL THAT MAY BE comforting for most, a silent promise of the war being waged against disease, but for me, it's a cold reality check.

I walk behind Forest and Sara. She hugs his arm, leaning against him as he slowly makes his way to the front doors of the hospital.

"Can't shake it off, can you?" Skye's voice interrupts my worry.

"No." I run a hand through my hair. "This place looks like a place of healing, but when I think about what they're going to do? The poison they're going to pump in his veins… I wish I could spare him that."

"His condition…"

"I know. It won't get better without the chemo." The words feel like a punch in the gut. The cancer's spreading, doing its vile work, and this is the first step to stopping it.

Over the past few days, Forest's condition is no better. Not that I would expect him to improve. We haven't done anything yet. In the meantime, his cancer continues to eat away at him.

"Today, we start fighting back." Skye offers hope.

"Yes." A strange mix of dread and hope coil within me, settling uneasily in my chest.

Today we begin the fight for Forest's life.

This is the first of several chemotherapy sessions planned by his medical team.

"It's going to be tough, isn't it?" A knot of dread coils in my gut. Forest needs the chemo, but the chemo might kill him.

"There's a reason I went into emergency medicine and trauma. Most of our patients get well. Those who don't? Their suffering is usually short. I hated my oncology rotations." She wraps her arms around herself. "I hated getting to know my patients only to watch them…"

"Forest isn't going to be one of those. He'll make it."

"His odds are better than most. I'm thankful for that."

There's no doubt this is going to be a long and difficult road.

"How is he doing—otherwise?" Skye lowers her voice, keeping our conversation private. "Have you taken him for a—session?"

"I tried. He needs it, but he's not strong enough to handle what we normally do. I'm trying out different things. Reaching out to other Doms who've dealt with something similar."

"That's a shame. I see it in him, that feral hunger growing. No offense, I respect your relationship with my brother, but I wish he didn't need what you provide."

"None taken." As time passes, more and more of me wishes for the same.

The man we escort into the hospital barely resembles the vibrant and spirited Forest I know so well.

"Do you feel he's strong enough?" I've tried not to speak my fears out loud, but I value Skye's medical expertise.

What I really want to know is whether Forest can endure the poison infused into his veins? The toxic chemotherapy that will kill the good cells along with the bad. Leaving him vulnerable to the mildest viruses and bacteria?

"Chemotherapy is rough. I won't sugarcoat it. Beyond the side effects of the drugs, the nausea, vomiting, hair loss, brain fog, and fatigue, his immune system will be virtually nonexistent. Sepsis is my greatest fear."

"Why?"

"It can delay the chemotherapy regimen. In some cases, depending on what a patient's cell counts are doing, it can be fatal."

I take note of the way she switched from speaking about Forest to talking about patients. Is she aware of the switch?

Forest's stride falters as we near the Oncology department. The heavy doors loom like grim sentinels. Was that a stumble? A sign of weakness? Or does he falter because he's afraid?

"I wish it was me instead of him." My heart constricts painfully. If I could, I would bear this burden for him. Be the strength he needs.

"This is his fight. As much as we want to, we can't take his place." She looks at me with sympathy and understanding.

She's right. This is a battle Forest will face alone. The enemy is his very body that's turned against him.

"I know." I hang my head. "I just wish… I wish I could trade places with him." Non-Hodgkin lymphoma, the words still ring in my ears like a bad echo, refusing to fade.

Ahead of me, Forest stumbles again.

"You okay?" I rush to Forest.

He reaches for me, grasping my arm, a quiet plea for support that he tries to disguise with a warm smile. A mask, for Sara and Skye, so they won't worry, but I see the truth in his eyes, in the way his grip tightens. Fear, uncertainty, a whole gamut of emotions swirl in the pale-blue depths of his gaze.

"This doesn't seem real, does it?" His deep, rumbly voice is a shadow of its former self.

"None of this seems real." I exchange a look with Sara.

We're terrified of losing him.

Sara, with her fiery spirit and stubborn resilience marches beside Forest. Outwardly, she seems undeterred, matching Forest's strong facade with unwavering optimism. I'm the only pessimist in the crowd. Sara's all blue skies and smiles. I'm the black pits of despair.

Forest is ambivalent.

And Skye?

Skye looks worn, her usually vibrant eyes dull with inner turmoil. As an emergency and trauma physician, she's seen more life and death situations than any of us. But this, this is different. It's personal.

It's Forest.

"You ready?" Forest asks, his voice steady, as we get ready to enter the hospital.

"Not in the slightest, but the sooner we get this done…" My words trail off because I don't know what we're hoping for. I guess we're trying to kill the cancer and rid Forest's body of the malignant cells, before the chemotherapy kills him.

We're at war with an invisible enemy; a war that I'm terrified we might lose.

We check in and settle into Forest's room, one among many similar rooms occupied by cancer warriors waging their own battles against cancer. The walls echo with unspoken tales of grit and hope.

Forest heads directly to the bed, testing out the mattress and pinching the thin pillow with disdain. He says nothing as he sits and swings his long legs around. He sits there, looking like a patient instead of the powerful man I know, appearing ghostly pale and fading into the snow-white sheets.

I rock back on my heels, taking it all in. Flashbacks of seeing Forest whisked into the emergency room flood my mind. Him in the ICU hooked up to a ventilator until he was stable enough to breathe on his own.

Sara flits across the room, her movements disjointed, a physical manifestation of her anxiety. Her eyes, normally vibrant and full of life, hold an undercurrent of fear as she glances at Forest.

"Are you comfortable?" She moves to the head of the bed and takes one look at the flat excuse of a pillow. "I'll get Mitzy to bring your favorite pillow."

Forest places his hand on her arm. "No Mitzy. Not this time. I don't think I can handle her energy."

"Well, I'm sure we can get someone to bring it." She places her hands on her hips. "You barely fit on the bed."

Indeed, Forest's heels rest at the very end of the bed, pushing against the footboard. She fusses at him, getting him to pull back the covers and get comfortable. Each time her fingers brush against him, Forest relaxes, their connection is profound.

Skye, generally the most composed of us all, leans against the door frame, arms crossed defensively over her chest. Her eyes sweep the room and stumble each time they drift past Forest.

The door glides open with a soft whoosh and a nurse steps into the room, wheeling in a shiny cart that carries a set-up of transparent bags and tangled tubes. Her scrubs are starched, crisp, and her face carries a practiced calm.

"Hello, Mr. Summers." She greets Forest warmly, stepping closer. "I'm Janice, your chemo nurse today. We've got some saline solution to start with." She taps one of the clear bags with her gloved finger.

Forest acknowledges her with a tight nod, apprehension lining his eyes.

With professional ease, Janice unwraps a packaged needle, the metallic point glints in the harsh hospital lights. She continues talking, explaining each step.

"I'm going to clean your skin with alcohol first, then insert the IV."

The room fills with the sharp, clean smell of the alcohol swab as she rubs it on Forest's skin. The touch draws a visible shudder from Forest. When the needle punctures his skin, Forest's jaw clenches.

Considering the degree of pain I know he can tolerate, this surprises me.

"That's the tough part done." Janice keeps her voice steady and her eyes kind. She sticks an adhesive to secure the IV line, erasing the small dot of blood with a sterile pad.

"I'll let the saline run for a bit, then we'll be ready to start the chemotherapy." She hangs the bag of drugs on the stand with a gentle click, its liquid contents begin to snake down the tube, entering Forest's veins drop by slow drop. "Looks like we've got a crowd." Janice looks at Sara, Skye, and me with curiosity, but doesn't dig.

"I'm Skye." Skye moves forward to shake Janice's hand. "Forest's sister, and this is Sara and Paul." She doesn't say anything else, but Forest jumps in with a twinkle in his eye.

"Sara and Paul are with me."

"Nice to have friends with you. It's nice to mee—"

"They're not friends. Sara's my wife and Paul's my lover."

It's great seeing Forest have fun with the nurse. His humor's been virtually nonexistent leading up to *C-day*; his word not mine. Like D-day, C-day marks day one of chemo.

"Ah, well then you're doubly blessed." Janice's smile widens and she winks at me. Looks like Janice wins this round. "A wife and a lover? You're a lucky man. Now, the infusion takes a few hours."

She continues on, completely unfazed. "We'll hold you overnight for the first round. I'm sure Dr. Chen explained what to expect. The nausea is unfortunate, but we'll do our best to medicate through that and keep you hydrated. Barring nothing going wrong, you should be cut loose within a day or two."

"Fabulous." Forest slouches back in bed, but protects his arm with the IV from getting jostled out of place.

Janice glances at the IV bags and hits a button on one of the pumps. "And there you go. First round of chemo starting now."

The room plunges into a new rhythm, orchestrated by the quiet hum of the machinery. The palpable air of tension is broken only by the gentle beeping of the medical equipment, each an unsettling reminder of the battle we're just commencing.

Janice is a pro at this, leaving to give us space, returning to check on us. She brings a list of videos we can watch, and we all argue over what movie we want.

Forest's gaze meets mine, his eyes betraying a hint of fear, quickly replaced with stubborn resolve. I move closer, reaching out to squeeze his hand. His fingers wrap around mine, the warmth familiar and reassuring.

With the treatment started, I watch the liquid from the bag slowly making its way through the tubing, moving inch by inch until it disappears into his vein. The room fills with an eerie silence, save for the soft whir of the machines and the occasional words from Janice when she returns to check his vitals.

Skye takes the seat next to Forest, her hand resting lightly on his shoulder. It's her way of providing comfort, a touch that says, I'm here for you.

Sara, on the other hand, paces, her nervous energy a stark contrast to the calm exterior Forest is striving to maintain.

"Are you okay?" I move to stand beside his bed.

"Right as rain." His smile is strained, a flicker of discomfort in his eyes. He's not okay, far from it, but he's fighting, just like he's always done.

As the days wear on, the treatment takes its toll. The vibrant energy that Forest usually radiates is now replaced by a weariness that doesn't belong on him. And yet, he keeps that brave face, smiling at us through the fatigue, laughing at our attempts to lighten the mood.

But I see it, the pain that lingers in his eyes, the effort it takes to lift his hand, the ghost of a tremble in his fingers. It hurts seeing him like this.

And it's just the beginning.

I pray we have the strength to endure the battles that come after this.

Because it's only going to get worse.

EIGHT

Paul

⁓

THE AFTERMATH OF THE FIRST ROUND OF CHEMOTHERAPY IS A brutal wake-up call. Forest's vibrant energy dims beneath the onslaught of the toxic drugs.

His face, once animated with laughter, is now drained of color. His cheeks hollow. His body a gaunt skeleton.

The chemotherapy ravages his body, and I can't help but wonder if the cure is worse than the disease. It's a paradox, watching him deteriorate in the fight to get better.

Every time he gags and wretches, it hits me like a punch in the gut, shattering my semblance of self-control. Forest, stoic as ever, doesn't complain, even when he's up all night throwing up.

Either Sara, or I, are at his side in a flash, reaching out to hold his hair out of the way, offering silent support. Tonight, days after the first round of chemo, the intensity of his nausea spikes.

"It's okay, Forest," Sara whispers, her voice barely holding steady. Once he's done throwing up, she tries to get him to drink and keep him hydrated.

Meanwhile, I shoot off a text to Skye.

Minutes later, she strides in, carrying a basin filled with IV bags of saline and supplies. Meds to combat the relentless nausea. There's a benefit to having a doctor on speed dial.

She wears her professional mask, the one that's seen her through countless emergencies, as she threads an IV into one of Forest's veins and lets the saline run.

Beneath her stoic exterior, a flicker of concern flashes in her eyes. The basin she leaves strategically by Forest's side, a grim reminder of the side effects the doctors warned us about.

We've gotten to the point where we need two basins. One for Forest to vomit into and the other to take out and empty. It's an endless loop that keeps all three of us up all night.

Sara brings a cold cloth, placing it gingerly on Forest's forehead, her touch featherlight.

"Hang in there, Forest. You'll feel better once the IV runs in." Her voice barely rises above a whisper, as if the slightest noise might cause Forest more discomfort.

We're armed with the strongest weapon we have—our unwavering love for Forest—but if this is where we are after round one of chemotherapy, how are we going to make it through the rest?

As round two approaches, we orchestrate a surprise for Forest, hoping to buoy his spirits, but this evening, his hair started falling out, putting a damper on an already difficult day we must face tomorrow.

The night before the second round of chemotherapy, I find Forest staring into the distance, lost in thought. His eyes hold a hesitant fear that wasn't there before.

The relentless nausea from the first round of chemo stopped a few days ago, leaving him with a deceptive sense of being well.

"Are you okay?" I break the silence.

"Just trying to psych myself up for tomorrow." His response comes as a quiet rumble, a soft confession. "I don't want to be sick again." Despite the uncertainty in his voice, a steely determination underscores his words.

The next morning breaks cool and crisp, a stark contrast to the tension brewing within us. Forest's second round of chemotherapy is looming and, despite his best efforts, he struggles. As we prepare to leave for the hospital, he lags behind, his steps heavy, reluctant.

"You okay?" I exchange a worried look with Sara.

"Just dreading the sequel." He shrugs, and the corners of his mouth twitch in an attempt at a nonchalant smile, but his eyes betray him—they're wide and anxious.

"You're going to be okay." Sara, always the nurturing soul, moves to his side, offering a comforting touch on his arm. She searches his face, her own reflecting the worry etched in his. "We're getting better at knowing what to expect and will be ahead of the ball this time."

"Lost more hair on the pillow today." His frown deepens.

"Let's not forget the silver lining." Sara does her best, trying to lighten the mood. "I've been told I give a great head massage."

"Funny, Paul says I give great head too." Forest nudges Sara, teasing her.

"It's true; I trained you well," I jump right in, loving the banter. We've missed this.

At least he hasn't lost his humor, and it's true. Forest is exceptionally talented in that arena. I can't help but smirk when Sara catches my eye. She smiles, probably thinking the same things as me. Forest's humor is quirky.

We're open about our unusual sexual dynamics. That openness holds us together. There are no secrets. Sometimes, I like to watch Forest and Sara have sex, and they let me. Forest would prefer to have all three of us in bed. A three-way fuckfest. After the first few times I took Forest down to the basement, Sara came to watch, curious about our dynamic. She no longer does that, but she knows what we do.

"Ha ha," Sara fires back. "Funny, he says you never give him head."

"That's because he's too busy on his knees, giving me head," I fire right back. "Besides, he prefers my hand."

"You know…" Not to be left out, Forest joins in. "Sara could give me head, while I give you head?" Ever the optimist, he pushes for an open sexual dynamic between all three of us. "Or, even better, you could fuck me while I fuck Sara." For the first time since his diagnosis, Forest's eyes sparkle.

I glance at Sara, and we share a moment. The two of us simply aren't there yet, but maybe we can make it work for Forest's sake? If he doesn't make it through this, I'd hate to deny him one of his dying wishes.

When Sara and I find ourselves at a loss for words, Forest snorts, and we all chuckle. For a moment, the tension eases, replaced with a sense of family and togetherness.

"Someday, the two of you are going to figure it out." Forest shakes his head. "And I'll be the one on the sidelines, watching the two of you fuck each other." He grabs his wallet, then spins around. "Where are the twins? I wanted to see them before we left."

"They're still asleep," Sara says.

Just then, the sound of tiny feet padding against the floor pulls our attention to the doorway and away from our conversation. Our twins, Delia and Sebastian, have woken up, their sleepy faces peep around the doorframe.

"Daddy up!" Delia's face lights up at the sight of Forest. Sebastian mimics his sister's excited chant, tottering forward with a sleepy grin on his face.

"Up, Daddy." He stretches his tiny arms toward Forest.

Forest kneels down, opening his arms, and the twins rush into them. Their innocent laughter fills the room, a welcome distraction from the impending hospital visit.

"Morning, my little munchkins," Forest murmurs, pressing a kiss to each of their foreheads. "Daddy has to go to the doctor today."

"Why?" Delia asks, her brows furrowing adorably.

I step in and take Delia out of Forest's arms and carry her to the breakfast table, where I place her on my lap. Forest follows with Sebastian. Sara helps him get Sebastian seated at the table.

"You remember how Daddy hasn't been feeling well lately?" I wait for the twins to nod before continuing. "Well, the doctors are going to help Daddy feel better."

Sebastian looks at Forest with wide eyes. "Daddy, owie?"

"Just a little, buddy," Forest answers with a soft smile. "But Papa and Mama will be with me, and I'll be back home before you know it."

"Promise?" Delia asks, her small hand reaching up to touch

Forest's cheek. Her fingers curl around a few strands of Forest's hair and they fall out.

Sara's eyes widen and she quickly takes the fallen strands from Delia's tiny hands and gets to work putting breakfast on the table.

"I promise," Forest assures her, pressing a gentle kiss to her hand.

"We'll be home soon," Sara reassures them, pulling the twins into a group hug. "Till then, Aunty Piper will look after you."

"Cookies!" Sebastian squeals with excitement, his toddler language clear in his enthusiasm.

"Fort!" Delia giggles. "Piper make best forts."

It's a small victory, these moments.

Every smile counts.

We walk the twins the short distance from the house Forest built us adjacent to *Insanity*, the group home where the men of Angel Fire live with their growing families.

Piper's already waiting with Arwen, her little munchkin. Piper is a perpetual ball of energy. She's got more perk than anyone I know. She's also my sister, which makes Arwen my niece.

Unlike her mother's perky personality, however, Arwen peeks out from behind her mother. With thick black hair like her father, the stunning green eyes she inherited from her mother make her one of the most stunning kids I've ever seen. She's going to break so many hearts.

The warmth of Piper's smile does little to mask her worry, but she tries. She crouches down to the twins' level as they run into her arms.

"Ready to have some fun with Aunty Piper?" she asks them, her voice firm yet gentle. They nod, their eyes wide and curious.

Delia grabs Piper's hand, her small fingers curling around Piper's thumb. "We make fort?"

Piper chuckles, nodding. "Absolutely. A big, strong fort."

"And cookies!" Sebastian adds, his words slightly slurred, pointing toward the kitchen excitedly.

As Piper settles the twins with promises of forts and cookies, the front door opens and Skye appears, her husband, Ash, by her side.

Their two kids, Zach, who's a robust five-year-old, and their petite little girl, Sonnet, follow closely behind.

Even at their young age, Zach's easy confidence and Sonnet's sprightly charm mirror the charisma of their famous rock star father.

"We'll make the biggest batch of cookies you've ever seen," Piper promises, earning delighted giggles from the twins.

"Hey, munchkins," Skye calls out as she approaches, opening her arms wide. Delia and Sebastian toddle toward her, their faces lighting up at the sight of their aunt.

Skye swoops down to hug her niece and nephew, ruffling Sebastian's hair and giving Delia a gentle squeeze. "Are you going to behave for Aunty Piper?"

"Cookies!" Sebastian squeals again, his thoughts evidently on the promised sweet treats.

"Cookies?" Little Zachy suddenly gets interested.

At five, he's the eldest of all the kids, surrounded by a swarm of two-year-olds who are such *babies* in his eyes. He'll be the ringleader in the years to come, leading all the kids on great adventures they'll hide from their parents.

Our kids' lives will be rich and full of love—very unlike their parents.

"And forts!" Delia adds, not to be left out.

Skye chuckles, turning to include Zach and Sonnet in the group hug. "And what about you two? Ready to have some fun?"

Zach nods vigorously, his own excitement undimmed. "We can play superheroes!" He proposes, his grin wide.

Sonnet, ever the angel of the group, merely giggles and hides behind her big brother, peering out from behind his shoulder with wide, sparkling eyes.

As we say our goodbyes, I watch Piper and Ash usher the brood of kids inside after saying goodbyes. Skye will join the three of us, standing beside Forest as round two of chemo begins.

A pang of longing hits me.

This is what we're fighting for—family, laughter, love, and days filled with superheroes, cookies, and forts. With that thought, we leave the sounds of joy and love behind us, carrying it in our hearts as we head for the hospital.

As we leave, Piper stands with the twins, Zach, and little Arwen, waving goodbye, the sight both comforting and heart-wrenching. We wave back until they're out of sight, their innocent faces imprinted in our minds, a reason to fight, a reason to return.

Skye slips on her professional facade. Forest made it through the aftermath of round one with her IV bags and anti-nausea meds. It's time for round two.

With a collective sigh, we head to the hospital. Forest takes one last glance at *Insanity* as we leave the sanctuary of our home, heading out to do battle again, and sighs.

The ride is silent, each of us lost to our thoughts. As we draw closer to the hospital, Forest's grip tightens on the door handle, his knuckles paling under the strain. His other hand entwines with Sara's, their fingers locked in a silent promise of support and love.

When we park, Forest is the last out of the car. He steps out and takes a deep breath, preparing himself for another round of the toxic drugs.

Knowing round two would be difficult for him, Sara, Skye, and I orchestrated a little surprise. I pray it takes his mind off why he's here.

If only for a moment.

NINE

Paul

~

As soon as we step into the hospital, the smell of disinfectant overpowers everything. Forest walks between me and Sara, his steps slow, laden with the unsaid dread of what's to come.

"Poison time." He tries to joke, but it falls flat with the anxiety we all share.

After checking in, we're taken to a different treatment room. This one holds a chair instead of a bed. Janice, Forest's chemo nurse, ushers us in with a professional yet sympathetic smile.

"Nice to see you again, Mr. Summers." Her voice is a gentle breeze, lightening the mood. The corners of her eyes crinkle sympathetically because no one in their right mind would be happy to be here. "You ready for today?"

"No." His deep voice trembles.

"Well, let's see if we can't turn that frown upside down." Janice points to the treatment chair and maintains an upbeat attitude. Considering her line of work, I bet she gets tons of practice dealing with grumpy patients.

"No bed?" He glances skeptically around the room. Instead of a bed, there's a plush recliner clad in *pleather*—the fake leather that squeaks and makes all kinds of rude noises as a person shifts around.

"Nope. We'll keep you for a few hours after the infusion for monitoring, but there's no need to keep you overnight."

A wince flashes across Forest's face as he settles onto the cold *pleather*. I head out of his room to wrangle up extra chairs for Skye and Sara.

I'd rather pace.

Sara, ever the soothing presence, hovers close to Forest, her concern evident in her tightened features. She rests her hand lightly on Forest's shoulder.

Skye's in her own world, her fingers dancing over her tablet. Granted professional favors and access to Forest's medical record, she scans and re-scans the file with the intensity of a seasoned doctor. "The counts are looking better than last time." She speaks more to herself than anyone else, but it sounds promising.

Janice gets to work, and the room plunges into a tense silence, the only sound being the soft beep of the machines, a grim symphony of what's to come. She inserts an IV with the precision of a pro, but each second feels painfully drawn out. Forest's jaw tightens, but he remains silent, a picture of quiet resilience.

"I'll come back and check on you." Janice checks the pumps and seems satisfied. From here, we're basically on autopilot as the poison drips into his veins.

Once the chemotherapy starts its course, Forest leans back, his eyes fixed on the slowly dripping bag. He's silent. His jaw set in that stubborn way of his. Eyes tight, fending off the fear he doesn't want us to know about.

Except we do.

We're all scared.

Just as the silence begins to grow unbearable, a commotion in the corridor disrupts the bleak atmosphere. A beat later, the door swings open, revealing the wild energy of Angel Fire.

A rush of laughter and banter sweeps into the room. With hearts of gold, the band blows in like a storm, their infectious energy immediately lightening the mood and filling the air with chaos and cheer.

Ash, ever a force of nature, leads the pack. He strides in with an infectious grin filling his face, followed closely by Bash and Spike. Bent, Noodles, and Mitzy trail in, their laughter ringing through the room. "Thought we'd crash the party." Bent brandishes a deck of cards. "Wanna play?"

Forest visibly relaxes and a ghost of a smile tugs on his lips as his friends gather around him. The sterile hospital room transforms into a scene of camaraderie and laughter, lifting all of our moods.

"Cards? I'd think a rock band as big as Angel Fire would come with something more than a deck of playing cards. Like say, their instruments?" Forest tries to chastise the band, but they're not having it.

"You want us to serenade you?" Ash rubs at his neck, then looks to Skye. "Told you he'd want a song."

A hint of Forest's old spark flickers in his eyes. "At least you still know how to make an entrance." His voice is hoarse but filled with genuine gratitude.

"Never thought you'd be the one to hog all the attention," Ash teases, nudging Forest gently. "And here I thought it was Spike who liked the drama."

That earns him a smack from Spike, a swift retribution that has the rest of us chuckling. It's typical banter for them, a routine that feels reassuringly normal in our far-from-normal state.

"We doing the cards, or not?" Bent shuffles the cards; there's a hint of something I can't quite make out in his expression.

"Let's do it." Bash claps his hands. "I'm ready to get this party started."

As Bent shuffles the cards, he smirks. "Winner decides the loser's punishment. No backing out, agreed?"

The band members agree, their expressions oddly serene. They've got something up their sleeve, but what that might be eludes me.

"What are we playing?" I settle in beside Forest, eager for the distraction, even if only a lame game of cards.

"Spoons." Bent shuffles the cards and begins to explain.

"What the fuck is Spoons?" Forest grumbles, sounding more like his old self.

"It's a game," Mitzy responds in her snarky way. "Played with cards."

"I got that part." Forest shakes his head as if frustrated, but he's happy the band is here, and even Mitzy, his exuberant and highly talented technical genius.

Ash and Spike head out, begging for extra chairs from the nurses. They bring in a small table to play on. Once settled, everyone gathers around Forest. Bent grins and deals the cards. He looks around at the expectant faces and explains the rules.

"If you haven't played Spoons before, it's simple. I'll deal each of us four cards. The goal is to get four of a kind. I'll start by picking a card from the deck; I can either keep it or pass it to my left. We keep passing cards to the left, keeping or discarding until someone gets four of a kind."

"Sounds simple enough," Forest says, "but where do the spoons come in?"

Mitzy retrieves a handful of spoons from her bag, placing them in the center of the table, minus one. The simple utensils suddenly feel like coveted trophies.

Bent pauses, gesturing to the spoons in the center of the table. "Once you have four of a kind, you grab a spoon. After that, it's a free-for-all; everyone else tries to grab a spoon too. There's one less spoon than there are players, so one person will end up without one. That person loses the round."

"And what's the punishment for losing?" Bash drums the top of the table, his energy infectious and catching.

Bent's smirk broadens as he reveals his surprise. "You'll find out when you lose."

Laughter fills the room, the tension easing slightly, as everyone gets ready to play. The cards are dealt, the game begins, and for a little while, the hospital room feels just a bit more like home.

Forest's competitive spirit, despite his fatigue, shines through as he plays with the same determined grit he always does.

The first hand starts. Forest, despite his pale complexion and the IV tubing snaking from his hand, joins the frenzy. He picks up a card and discards another, the pace of the game quickening as each player tries to get four of a kind.

The energy in the room shifts, filling with adrenaline and anticipation. Forest's gaze flickers between his cards and the spoons, the corners of his mouth turning up into a smile. It's the most alive I've seen him since we walked into the hospital.

The cards blur in a whirlwind of motion, a symphony of color and noise. Spike picks up the card Bash discarded, and then it happens. Bent draws a card. He grins widely, a flash of triumph, as he reaches for a spoon. The room erupts in chaos, each player lunging for the spoons.

When the dust settles, Spike is left without a spoon. He swears, throwing his cards down in mock frustration. His attention flicks to Bent, who shakes with laughter.

Spike shoots him a faux glare. "Laugh it up, fuzzball. You'll get your turn."

Bent leans back, spoon in hand, looking entirely too pleased with himself. "Alright, Spike. You're up first." He produces an electric shaver.

The room fills with laughter as Bent flicks the switch, the buzz of the shaver filling the air. Spike rolls his eyes, but it's clear this is no surprise.

I planned the visit, but they planned this.

Are they…?

Forest's eyes go wide. His hand reaches out, gripping mine as the first lock of Spike's hair falls onto the sterile floor.

This is so much more than a game of cards. It's defiance in the face of adversity, a message loud and clear—they're in this together, and I can't help but smile. This is the family we've chosen, the family we fight for.

Spike winces as the buzzing fills the room, but he holds still as Bent deftly shaves his hair off. It's a shockingly tender moment, the band sharing looks of solidarity and support. Spike emerges bald, his scalp shiny under the fluorescent lights.

The card game resumes, the tension's back but accompanied with a sense of camaraderie. Noodles is the next to lose.

A slow smile spreads across his face as he pushes back his chair and makes his way to Bent and gets his hair shaved off. Ash loses next, then Bent; each one accepting their fate with grace, laughter filling the room as they all emerge newly shorn.

Bash, who already shaves his head regularly—a memorial to his twin brother who died from cancer as a kid—sits beneath the razor in solidarity. "Might as well clean it up." He shrugs, grinning at Forest.

When Mitzy loses, the room goes silent. She's known for her vibrant, rainbow-colored hair, her pixie cut glittering under the lights. She pauses, looking at the electric shaver, then at her friends. With a deep breath and a determined nod, she seats herself.

"Mitzy—no. Your hair," Forest protests, but Mitzy flashes a cheeky grin.

"It'll grow back." The room falls silent as she takes her place under the razor.

Her eyes gleam with love and support for Forest as the shaver buzzes to life. The vibrant strands of her hair fall to the floor, leaving Mitzy's head bare. The silence is broken by applause when Mitzy stands with her newly bald head held high, grinning wildly and bowing to the crowd.

When I step forward, eager to join their solidarity, Forest's voice cuts through the room, stopping me.

"No, Paul," Forest says, his voice choked. "Please, I need something of the old world with me." He points to Sara and Skye. "The same goes for the two of you."

Janice returns, more than a little star-struck by the band, now bald, and finishes up the last of the chemotherapy.

"Interesting group of friends you have, Mr. Summers," Janice flushes the IV line before removing the IV itself.

"They're the absolute best." His eyes mist with tears, but he sniffs and refuses to let them fall.

The room fills with nods of understanding and respect, each man, and Mitzy, taking a moment to share a look with Forest before they finally leave. The door closes softly behind them while we finish up with our instructions for this round of chemo.

Instructions such as how to deal with the unrelenting nausea and vomiting. I hate this. I hate every bit of this horrible disease.

The echo of the band's laughter lingers, and Forest leaves the hospital with a bounce in his step and a smile on his face.

When he's not looking, I give Skye a thumbs up for helping me arrange the visit. While Forest's attention is distracted by Sara, I shift back to Skye.

"Did you know they were going to do that?"

"I had no idea, but it's brilliant. Ash and Bash are talking about taking it on tour. Using their shaved heads to raise awareness and run a bone marrow donor drive."

"That's incredible."

"They never stop amazing me, but I don't think a tour is the right thing to do right now," she says.

"Why not? It sounds perfect."

"Forest's in no condition to run a tour, and if they have someone step in, I think it'll send the wrong message."

"Ah, I see what you mean."

It's a shame. The band could do so much to raise awareness, but I understand Skye's concerns. This is only round two out of many. Forest's health will decline before it gets better.

If it gets better.

TEN

Paul

———

∾

Days melt into weeks, and weeks into months. Forest's second round of chemo blurs into the third, then the fourth round. It's a monotonous cycle of hospital visits, intractable nausea, and watching the color drain from Forest's face until he's a shadow of his former self.

Yet, despite the physical toll, his spirit remains unbroken. He clings to hope like a lifeline, his quiet resilience shining through each day.

In the brief reprieve between treatments, we grab moments of normalcy. Forest's laughter rings through the house, albeit a bit weaker, his smile a touch fainter. But his eyes still hold that familiar spark, that stubborn refusal to back down.

After putting the twins down for bed, we huddle together in front of the TV with Forest comfortably nestled between Sara and myself. His head rests gently on my shoulder, his hand entwined with hers. We watch reruns of old sitcoms, the canned laughter ringing hollow against the somber atmosphere that clings to the room.

On a sunny afternoon, we decide to venture to the rocky beach beneath *Insanity*. The twins dart ahead of us, tiny figures in brightly colored swimsuits, their shared laughter mixing with the crashing waves and the cry of distant seagulls.

Sebastian and Delia, armed with buckets and nets, scamper amongst the pebbles, their small forms nimbly navigating the uneven terrain. Sebastian is fascinated by the tide pools, kneeling to inspect the marine life trapped within during each low tide. Each discovery—a snail, a small crab, a starfish—elicits squeals of delight from him.

Delia, on the other hand, seems more intrigued by the pebbles. She collects them by handfuls, her bucket soon filled with an array of colors and sizes. Occasionally, she holds up a particularly interesting one, her eyes sparkling with the simple joy of her find.

Forest walks slower, his steps measured and careful, conserving his energy. Despite the physical strain, he insists on making the trek himself. The sea, just like the laughter of his children, has a pull he can't resist. His determination is a sight to behold, and Sara and I share a glance, our silent communication filled with admiration and shared concern.

The twins poke at a tide pool when Forest finally settles down on a rocky outcrop, out of breath, but smiling.

"They're so much like you." His comment is for Sara. Delia takes after him while Sebastian looks like a miniature version of me. Each of the twins, however, carry Sara's gentle nature and determined inquisitiveness.

Delia points at a starfish, her white hair flaring in the sunlight like her father's used to. "Daddy, look! It's red with black bumps."

She looks expectantly at Forest, who breathes out slow. It's clear he wants to go to her, join the experience, but he's too weak to make the effort.

I jump in. "Wow, that's a pretty red starfish. Can you find an anemone?"

"Oh yes!" Given a task, Delia's on the hunt, her precocious mind already blooming with so much potential. In that, she's Forest's clone.

Sebastian tires of the tide pools and toddles over to Forest. His black curls bounce as he looks at Forest. "Daddy, why don't you have hair like me and Papa?" His innocent question hangs in the air, and for a moment, we're all silent.

We struggled at the beginning with what to do with the twins having two dads. Finally, they sorted it out for us. I became Papa Paul, which eventually became Papa, while Forest got stuck with Daddy. I love the little quirks of our unique family.

Forest smiles at Sebastian, a soft, tender smile. "Sometimes, people get sick, kiddo. And the medicine to help them get better makes their hair fall out."

"But it'll grow back, right?" Delia joins us, her pale-blue eyes wide and concerned.

"Yes, sweetheart, it will," Forest reassures her, his voice thick. He reaches out and tucks a loose strand of hair behind her ear.

"And the medicine will make you better?" Sebastian places his hand over Forest's bald scalp, feeling the smooth skin.

"That's what it's supposed to do." Forest tickles Sebastian, who dissolves in a fit of giggles.

Not to be left out of the fun, Delia wants to join in. Knowing that's too much for Forest, I grab her, lifting her high in the air until she screams and squeals with joy.

Sara's oddly quiet, deep in her thoughts, watching Forest and me play with the kids. There's a melancholy look in her eyes. I know exactly what she's thinking.

I wake up and go to bed with the same thought in my head.

How will I ever do this without Forest?

The rest of the day passes in a blur of laughter and exploration; the twins' innocent curiosity is a balm to the harsh reality of our lives. When the sun sets, it paints the sky with vivid hues of pink and orange. We pack to leave. Forest leans on me as we make our way back to the gondola that will take us up the steep cliffs. His weight's a reminder of the battle he's fighting.

And when I say weight, it's the lack of it that scares me.

I've carried him before, fought with him before, grappled with him, restrained him more times than I can count, and he's a shadow of his former self.

When we get to the top, Sara goes ahead with the twins, leaving Forest and me alone to watch the rest of the sunset.

"Tired?" I ask.

"Always." He leans heavily against me. With Sara and the twins gone, we slip into the roles we share in private. He leans against me, a more intimate touch. A submissive stance. "Are you upset with me?" His voice breaks as he slumps against me.

"Why would I be upset?"

"The basement? I can't be there for you." He claws at my shirt. "You know I crave our time together. I wish I could... I need..."

He refers to something that happened more than a week ago. Against my better judgment, Forest convinced me he was strong enough for one of our sessions. He wasn't. But it had been so long since we'd been together that I caved to his request.

What a disaster.

The first strike of the whip left a massive welt that bruised and swelled. In a panic, I called Skye. We never let others down in the basement. Sara's always welcome, but after the first few times she came down to watch, she now gives us the space and privacy to do, and become, what we are when we're together like that. We hide nothing of what we do from her. But no one else ever goes down there.

They wouldn't understand.

Skye knows what happens down there. I asked for her input on some of the design, but she's never seen the place in person.

She did that night.

And she saw the bleeding beneath the skin from the kiss of my whip. She called it a hematoma. After a quick trip to Guardian HRS's medical facilities, we were able to keep the incident out of Forest's official medical records. She pumped him full of blood products, platelets and clotting factors, to help his body stop the bleeding.

Afterward, she gave us an explicit rundown of what we could and couldn't do. How oral and anal sex were no longer options. How the chemotherapy drastically reduced Forest's body's ability to fight off infection, and how those two sexual acts were particularly dangerous for Forest.

Basically, everything's off the table. We can kiss and give hand jobs, but that's it. I can blow Forest if I want. It's no risk to me, but that's not something I normally do as Forest's Master.

Which means, we're reduced to handholding, hugs, kissing, and fucking each other's hands.

We're both frustrated.

All I can do is reassure Forest.

"We'll get back to all of that once you're well."

"Promise?"

"Damn straight. I love the way you moan when I fuck you."

"You love the way I moan when you whip me." He tries to laugh, but it's too forced.

"I definitely do." My cock twitches in response.

I can't help my cravings. They're just as strong as ever. I wrap my arm around his shoulders and tug him in close. Ever astute, Forest notices the tiny twitch of my dick.

"Want to head back down to the beach? You can put me on my knees in the gondola and make me give you a hand job?"

He's trying so hard; I do my best not to bring his spirits down. And while I shouldn't, from the look in Forest's eyes, he needs this tiny echo of what we are to each other.

"Fine." I release him and march back to the gondola. With a snap of my fingers, I point to the floor of the gondola. "Naked and on your knees."

While surprised by the *naked* command, Forest hustles over to the gondola, but he's too weak and out of breath to undress himself. I take over, pulling off his shirt. He kicks off his shoes, and I help him with his pants. Eyes alight with the spark of desire and need, Forest goes to his knees for me.

I let him free my cock and stroke it to life. But I need more stimulation than he's able to provide. This is perhaps the hardest part. Our dynamic thrives on pain and punishment, vigorous and brutal sex. Unapologetic power exchanged between two powerful men.

Fortunately, my mind has no problems bridging the gap. While Forest strokes me, I envision him in the basement and all the perverse things I want to do to him.

I come and Forest gets what he needs. His desire to serve is fulfilled. While down on the beach, I reward him the same. Like him, my touch is gentle. Unlike him, I do it to avoid unintentional injury and bruising to his cock.

We stay on the beach long after the sun goes down, enjoying a rare moment of intimacy while cementing the bond between us. And while we shouldn't, Forest begs to wrap his lips around my cock. I allow it, with a good bit of hesitation, but I'm only so strong. It takes every ounce of my willpower not to take over and fuck his mouth the way I enjoy.

Meanwhile, life continues.

There are bad days and worse days. Days when Forest can barely get out of bed. Days when Sara and I feel helpless, our hearts heavy with worry.

But we also have good days. Days when Forest's laughter fills the house. Days when the twins' antics bring a genuine smile to his face. Days when we feel like a normal family, if only for a little while.

But the truth remains—we're in a fight against time, and despite our best efforts we're losing the battle.

Forest's continued chemo sessions hit him hard. His once strong and vibrant body weakens, the disease and the treatment both take their toll. He loses weight. His skin grows pale. His hair is long gone, but the spark in his eyes, though dimmer, never fades.

With each session, the routine becomes more familiar—the cold touch of the IV, the harsh smell of antiseptic, the hollow echo of hushed voices. But familiarity doesn't make it any easier. It's a battle, each session another round in the ring with an opponent who never tires and is determined to win.

Sara and I do our best to keep Forest's spirits high, to keep the shadow of fear from clouding our days. We hold game nights with the band in Forest's hospital room. We watch movies, just the three of us, on a tiny portable screen, pretending for a few hours that we're back home in our living room, not in the sterile confines of a hospital.

With Forest and I unable to have sex, I move my control into the bedroom with Forest and Sara, where I take over, direct his interaction with Sara, and control his releases. I find my eye turning more and more to Sara, to the soft swell of her breasts, to the fullness of her lips as she gives Forest a blow job, to her gentle, feminine cries as her orgasm overtakes her. And oddly, she appears to get more turned on the more I command Forest and direct what they can and can't do.

Outside of the bedroom, however, the strain in Sara's smiles returns.

Skye, a physician who's used to saving lives, finds herself unable to wield her skills to save the life of her own brother. Her smiles become less frequent, her laughter a little more forced. The vibrant woman I've known is fading, much like Forest, replaced by a shadow haunted by fear and uncertainty. She knows before any of the rest of us when the chemo fails.

As for Forest, Sara, and I, we laugh, we cry, we bicker, and we make up. We act like normal people, but through it all, we support each other. Despite our struggles, the relationship between the three of us remains as strong as ever: united and unbroken.

And through it all, Forest fights.

He fights through the fatigue, the nausea, the pain.

He pushes through every session.

He endures every setback with the same stubborn determination that's always defined him.

But his strength fades. His determination deserts him.

We finally make it to the final round of chemotherapy, only to have our hopes destroyed. Our world in turmoil. Forest contracts a simple infection, and it nearly kills him.

ELEVEN

Paul

~

Forest has been in the ICU for weeks now, fighting an unrelenting battle against sepsis. The sterile, lifeless atmosphere of the hospital feels a world away from our colorful, vibrant home. Weeks pass like a time-lapse film, punctuated by handing the twins off to the family Forest built, visits to the hospital, long trips down the cold sterility of the hospital hallways, and finally, interminable hours spent beside Forest's hospital bed.

Each passing day is a struggle, but slowly, steadily, Forest recovers. He's moved back out of intensive care to the oncology floor, a sign of hope amidst the gray.

And the doctors give us great news.

Not only are they allowing a rare visit from the twins, but they're going to begin the final round of chemotherapy tomorrow.

The monotonous routine of quiet waiting is broken by the arrival of Delia and Sebastian. Their presence feels like the first warm day after a long, brutal winter—their laughter is a radiant beacon of hope that cuts through the pervasive gloom of the hospital.

"Daddy!" Delia bounces into the room, all white-blonde hair

and wide blue eyes. She's the spitting image of Forest. She squeals as she spots him, her voice echoing brightly off the hospital walls.

"Hey, princess." A gentle smile lights up Forest's face. His voice remains weak, barely more than a whisper, but laden with love.

"Daddy?" Sebastian, my doppelgänger with his wavy black hair and dark eyes, walks in after Delia. He's more solemn, carrying a weight that seems too heavy for his two years. He's reticent to approach the unfamiliar hospital bed, but eager to see his daddy. With a bit of encouragement from Forest, and sibling competition not to get left out of cuddles, he settles beside Forest, his tiny hand finding its way into Forest's larger one, offering silent support.

"Hey, champ." Forest reaches out and ruffles Sebastian's hair.

With the energy of a thousand suns, Delia explores the hospital room's weird machines with wide, curious eyes—identical to Forest's. She's a live-wire, her infectious laughter echoing through the clinical confines of the room, lending it a semblance of warmth and life.

Forest watches her every move, the corners of his eyes crinkling with a joy that has been too long absent.

We set up a small, sanitized play area in one corner of the room, taking every precaution to ensure Forest's safety from infection. As the twins immerse themselves in their games, Forest watches them, a faint, but genuine, smile playing on his lips. Despite the wires trailing from his arms and the lingering antiseptic smell in the air, for a while, we're not in a hospital room.

We're just a family, sharing a simple moment.

Forest insists on watching a movie with the twins. He holds them close, one on each side, their small bodies snuggled against him. We settle on a colorful animation about talking animals teaching life lessons. It's heartwarming, engaging, but as it progresses, the underlying theme—the circle of life—strikes an uncomfortable chord.

Forest's voice, although weakened, carries the same warmth as he explains the story to the twins, pointing out the characters, singing the songs, and joining their laughter.

"Daddy, what's circle life?" Delia's innocent question floats in the air as the film concludes.

Forest looks at her, his pale-blue eyes filled with love and sadness. "Well, princess," he starts, his voice soft, "the circle of life… It's kind of like seasons. You know how after winter comes spring, then summer, then fall, and then it's winter again? That's a circle, right?"

Delia and Sebastian nod, their eyes wide with curiosity.

"It's the same with all living things," Forest continues. "We're born, we grow, we live our lives, and then we…" He glances at Sara, tears welling in his eyes. He clears his throat and continues. "Well, we go to sleep. Then new life begins. That's the circle of life."

His explanation is simple, straightforward, and yet, it's everything. A lump forms in my throat as I watch our family nestled together in this hospital room. The twins are so young, there's no way they can understand that Forest is basically telling them about his death.

Watching him with the twins is a poignant reminder of what we're fighting for. These moments of normalcy, of love, of joy, they're our beacon of hope. They remind us that while the battle is hard, the reward—more moments like these—is worth the fight.

As the credits roll, and the twins cheer with joy, I can't help but excuse myself. I step out into the sterile hallway with my heart slamming inside my chest.

"Are you okay?" Sara joins me in the hall outside the room and slides her arm around me.

"He basically told them he's dying." I swallow my emotions and try to stand tall. Grown men don't cry, but Forest is gutting me with his acceptance of death.

"I think he needed to." Sara moves to stand in front of me and wraps her arms around my waist as she hugs me.

"Did he?" Without thinking about it, I wrap my arms around her shoulders and back, loving the feeling of holding her in my arms.

"He's preparing them. And us." Sara's voice is steady, but her tears wet my shirt. She doesn't try to hide her tears; there's no point. We're past pretenses now.

We stand there for a few minutes, silence enveloping us like a shroud. The beeping of machines and distant murmurs of hospital staff become background noise as we share a moment of quiet understanding.

Her hand slowly moves up my back, her fingers gently tracing invisible patterns over my shirt. It's a simple touch, but it sends waves of heat shooting through me. A touch I've come to crave more than I'd like to admit.

"Sara…" I tip my face to the ceiling and close my eyes. "I don't know if I can do this."

She cups my cheek and silences my half-formed words.

Her touch that leaves me breathless. There's a tenderness to it that resonates deep within me, stirring up feelings I don't understand. It's both surprising and confusing for a gay man.

But Sara?

She's different.

She makes me want things I've never wanted before.

When she rests her head against my chest, a rush of warmth floods my body. It's not emotional. It's physical.

My heartbeat quickens. My breath hitches. Her scent floods my senses. An electrifying sensation prickles at the back of my neck.

My body responds in a way it's never done before.

This isn't just a shared moment of fear and grief. It's a spark. A hint of something that could burn brightly, if given the chance. My reaction leaves me reeling.

Overwhelmed.

She's been my rock through all of this. My confidante. My friend. But now, the raw intensity of my feelings for her hums a different tune. It's more than friendship, more than shared concern for Forest.

It's an awakening.

Outside Forest's room, the hall is silent. We peek inside and catch the twins sleeping in Forest's arms.

It's been a long day, and their exhaustion finally caught up with them. My gaze travels back to Sara, who gazes at the twins with a soft smile on her face. My heart flutters at the sight, the affection in my gaze morphing into something more profound, more personal.

"Hey." I softly brush a loose strand of hair from her face. "You okay?"

"Yeah, I'm okay," She turns her attention back to me, her eyes searching mine. "They look so peaceful." Beneath her whisper, weariness and grief thread through her voice.

Reaching up, I cup her face, my thumb stroking her cheek. It's a comforting gesture I've done a hundred times before, but this time it feels different.

It'sintimate.

She leans into my touch, closing her eyes, making my heart pound wildly inside my chest. The pull between us is undeniable, magnetic. It's like gravity, drawing us closer, our breaths mingling.

Her eyes flicker open, meeting mine. There's an unspoken question in her gaze, one that mirrors my own uncertainty, my own disbelief at what's happening between us.

We draw together, the space between us shrinking until there's nothing but the whisper of shared breaths. The warmth of her lips, so close to mine, gives birth to a whirlwind of emotions.

Just as I'm about to close the gap, and taste the sweetness of her lips, reality hits me like a bucket of ice water.

I'm gay.

I've always been gay.

What am I doing?

Before my mind can fully spiral, I shift slightly, aiming my mouth upwards. Instead of a passionate kiss, I place a tender kiss on her forehead. It's a gesture of affection that leaves a lingering sense of something unfinished.

I pull back, meeting her gaze again. Her confusion is mirrored in my own eyes, but there's also understanding.

And acceptance.

We don't speak, don't address the unspoken question hanging in the air. Instead, we settle back into our roles, nursing our thoughts, knowing that when the time is right, we'll have to face this thing growing between us.

The silence stretches between us as we share the moment. We're on new ground here, neither of us brave enough to give a voice to whatever this thing might be.

Together, we turn back toward the room, back to Forest, the

man who binds us as one. The intensity of the moment lingers. It's a shift, a turning point.

And I wouldn't have it any other way.

In the midst of everything, this thing with Sara feels right. I find myself clinging to it, to her, because if there's one thing I need, it's a beacon in the storm.

Sara is my light.

We stand there, supporting each other, slowly coming to terms with the reality of Forest's condition and the emotional upheaval stirring between us. It's an intimacy born out of shared pain, shared love, and the growing realization we're falling in love.

A sense of calm washes over me. I squeeze her hand, grateful for the comfort she offers, but not ready to explore these new feelings.

Finding strength in Sara brings back memories of when Forest confused me, intrigued me, and woke the fierce hunger to dominate him within me.

Those were troubled times, but I wouldn't change a thing.

TWELVE

Paul

———

~

Several Years Ago

~

Nᴏᴛ ᴏɴᴄᴇ, ɪɴ ᴀʟʟ ᴍʏ ʏᴇᴀʀs ɪɴ ᴛʜɪs ʙʀᴜᴛᴀʟ ʙᴜsɪɴᴇss, ʜᴀᴠᴇ I hesitated. Yet, Forest's ice-blue eyes and defiant glare stays my hand.

The room closes in around me, turning the flickering shadows into phantoms dancing on the walls, mocking whatever this struggle within me might be.

My conscience screams to alter what I do—inflict pain in a way that will satisfy us both—but the coldness in Snowden's eyes, and the eagerness in his breath, remind me of the job I've been commanded to perform.

Still, I hesitate, my whip raised above Forest's battered body. There's a battle being waged in this room. It's not between Forest and Snowden but rather between me and my unwilling victim.

I thought Forest would break easily. I'm very good at my job. Despite the bruises and welts that mar his skin from our initial encounter, he remains stoic and unyielding.

Defiant.

Fierce.

And glorious.

He endures and will do whatever Snowden demands because of the woman hunkering on the cold stone floor with tears streaming down her face. What he will never do—and what is beyond my capacity to force—is submit to the man who controls his fate.

"Please," Sara whimpers from her place on the floor. "Stop this."

"Never." Snowden shifts his bulk, eyes gleaming, mouth salivating, his cock stirring in anticipation of the violence to come.

I drown out her anguished cries and center myself, preparing for the session that will bring Forest to his knees.

Forest looks at me. Our gazes tangle and weave together, fighting for dominance as he challenges me to do my worst—while begging me to drown him in pain.

To take him through and past the point of suffering into a place where he can embrace the darkness within himself.

He straightens his slumped form, digging deep into hidden reservoirs of strength, to stand proudly in front of me.

Christ, the man is stunning.

I lift a cruel whip from the table beside me. Made of elephant leather, its long strands bite deep and deliver stunning blows without drawing blood.

Instead of fear in Forest's eyes, something else lingers.

Rage.

Challenge.

Anticipation?

Eagerness?

Need?

Can it be?

It's almost as if he welcomes what's to come?

No man survives a session with the elephant-leather whip. He should know this, but it's as if Forest craves the pain and humiliation that's about to be inflicted upon him. That acceptance stirs a visceral reaction within me because I'm a sadist who craves dispensing pain. My cock stirs in response, standing up at the call of this man's need.

Fuck if Forest isn't the perfect man for me.

My grip tightens on the whip. With a vicious flick of my wrist, I send the tail cracking through the air. It slams into Forest's flesh with a punishing thud.

Forest gasps with the impact. He staggers beneath the blow, his breaths coming in ragged gasps as he processes the pain. I give him no respite, feeding his inner masochist more pain than it can handle.

My whip snaps through the air, again and again, until Forest trembles, his body overloaded with pain.

Sweat pours down my face. I rip off my shirt and toss it to the floor. Then I approach Forest, grab the hair at his nape, and yank his head back. My bare chest presses against his sweaty back and a bolt of lightning shoots through me.

"You will not survive much more. Submit to Snowden, and I will spare you more pain."

"Never." Pain grinds through Forest's voice. "I will never submit to him."

"Snowden will see you dead."

"No. He'll keep me on the cusp of death. Bastard needs me alive to fuck me." Through all the pain raging through this man's body, he's still able to defy Snowden. God, I love that about him.

I love the way he soaks up my pain.

"I see the darkness in you. The way you crave the pain. Devour it and absorb it. I'm here to tell you, that will be the end of you. I know what you are."

"And what is that?"

"I want you to admit it. Tell me."

"Never." His shoulders lift and rise with his breath.

"Do you fear me?" I lean in close, breathing into his ear, then nip at the tender outer shell.

"No." He trembles as my teeth bite down.

"You should."

"And why is that?" He grinds out the words.

"Because you submit to Snowden out of fear."

"I don't submit to him. I do as he asks to keep Sara safe. It's different. And I don't fear you."

"You're right. There's no fear in you when it comes to me. There's something else."

"There's nothing."

"Desire." I lick along the shell of his ear, loving the way his body trembles.

"No." Barely a whisper, but Forest hangs his head as the truth sweeps through him.

"You'll submit to me because you know what we can become, and you yearn for something like that."

"As long as you work for Snowden, that will never happen. You're his lapdog and nothing more. I won't serve a man who serves another."

Blood rushes to my cock. He has yet to say it, but Forest gives away much with his words. He wants to serve me. Or rather, he wants me to prove to him I'm dominant enough to earn his submission.

Christ, each word he says dances around a powerful truth. Despite my best intentions, my body responds to this man and the potential he presents.

"The world is a complicated place." In the blink of an eye, I reach around and grasp Forest's cock, making him jump at the invasion. My grip tightens until I get what I want. "You won't submit because you crave the pain. You get off on it."

"Pain always gets me off." Forest tries to suppress a moan as my fingers tighten around his cock.

"You fight me. Force me to give you what you need by topping from the bottom. Which I allow for now. When you're ready to get out of your own way, you'll discover an essential truth."

"What truth would that be?"

"You're hard for me, not Snowden."

"As long as you work for him, I'll never…" His cock pulses in my hand, growing more engorged by the second as desire stirs within him. His admission steals my breath. "I won't yield to you."

I dig my nails into his shaft, inflicting pain until Forest lifts onto his toes in a desperate need to escape the pain, but when he tips his head back against my shoulder, both of our bodies vibrate at the same frequency.

He's right about one thing. Pain might make him hard, but that's not what he craves. Snowden doesn't understand how to feed the needs of a submissive masochist. All he knows is how to inflict pain and destroy others.

But I know. I know how to feed the darkness within Forest.

If I didn't work for Snowden, is it possible Forest might do the same for me? Can he feed the darkness within me?

I no longer see him as a captive to be tormented but as a kindred spirit. He's a sadist's wet dream.

My wet dream.

A true masochist strong enough to endure the most feral pain I can dispense. He won't yield to Snowden, but he'll yield to me.

I know this as a fundamental truth. We're evenly matched and perfect for each other. I decide to give Forest a small taste of what we'll become.

"This is what you crave." I shift my hand from his cock, moving it around to his balls, cupping the heavy sack in my hands. Slowly, I squeeze until Forest's entire body shakes in pain. He gulps air as I dig my fingers into his balls, squeezing the tender jewels contained within.

His eyes shut, and he rolls his lower lip in, biting it with his teeth to forestall the orgasm threatening to crash through him.

"You crave a dominant. A man strong enough to carry you through the darkness infesting your mind. A man who knows the kind of pain you need to feel normal, and you need a *Master* willing to give it to you."

"Fuck you." His toes curl, and his breaths deepen as I inflict pain. On the verge of losing control of his release, he pants and gulps as the truth washes through him.

"Your cock wakes in my hand, eager to give me what I want. Or, do you deny what's happening now?"

One thing people don't understand is none of this is about pain and pleasure. Dominance is a mental game. Right now, Forest and I are locked in a battle; one I'll eventually win.

"It's just a body." He speaks the phrase like a longtime prayer.

Maybe something he used in the past to endure the defilement of his body by men like Snowden, and Snowden himself?

"You should never have let me discover this secret about you. I will use it to break you." I lean in close and whisper. "I plan on fucking you, dominating you… And one day, you'll beg me to be your Master."

"Fuck me. Dominate me. Do your worst." His words come as a silent plea; the desires of a true submissive willing to travel the darkest paths with the one who will carry them through and beyond. "If you wish to Master me, you're going about it all wrong."

"Stop with the infernal whispering." Snowden's brash voice breaks the connection Forest and I gingerly build. Just like that, the power crackling between us disappears.

"Forgive me, Forest," I whisper into his ear, knowing Forest can't forgive what comes next. "Snowden demands this."

I take a deep breath and step back, giving myself room to work my whip. With a cracking in the air, I bring the whip down with all the force I can muster. All Snowden cares about is dispensing as much pain as possible until Forest breaks and begs for release. He's not interested in the intricate bond between a dominant and his charge.

Heavy leather strikes flesh with a thud, filling the room with Forest's pained grunts. Bruises blossom across his back, spreading like crimson flowers that deepen to purple and black. But Forest never cries out or begs for mercy. Instead, he clenches his jaw. His muscles absorb the pain. His knuckles turn white as he grips the chains binding him.

"Again!" Snowden commands me to continue, his voice cold as ice.

I hesitate, my hand shaking as I raise the whip. The weight of Sara's fearful gaze drills a hole between my shoulder blades. Her silent plea for mercy cuts straight to my core, but I ignore it. If I don't give Snowden what he wants, he won't hesitate to end her life.

Forest's resilience is awe-inspiring, but as the torturous session wears on, his strength falters.

"Stop," Forest gasps at last, his voice barely audible over the sound of his ragged breathing. "Please stop."

"Have you had enough?" Snowden asks, stepping into the sliver of light that illuminates the room. "Are you ready to submit to me?"

"Does it look like I'm resisting?" Forest rasps through gritted teeth, a mixture of blood and saliva dripping from his split lip. "You want me to kneel and serve you. That's the bargain we struck. As long as you keep your side, I'm yours." Forest hangs his head in abject surrender.

"Leave us." With a snap of his fingers, Snowden dismisses me. I wish I could spare Forest the degradation to come, but that is not within my power. What I can do is protect Sara from witnessing the vile things Snowden does to the man she loves.

I rush Sara out of the room before Snowden puts Forests on his knees.

THIRTEEN

Paul

∾

Present Day

∾

IN FOREST'S FIGHT AGAINST THE CANCER RAVAGING HIS BODY, I'M not sure where I stand. The hospital room feels colder each day, a chilling reminder of the battle we wage. Forest lies frail and faded on the sterile bed, a stark contrast to the vibrant man he once was. I feel like I'm living a nightmare, and no matter how hard I try, I can't wake up.

The days become a blur of hospital visits, whispered conversations with doctors who give only bad news, and restless nights filled with worry and fear of a future without Forest.

Sara, Skye, and I take turns staying with Forest, but I often find myself lingering. I sit by his side, our hands entwined, trying to lend him my strength through the mere touch of our skin.

There's a certain helplessness in watching the man you love fade before your eyes. But I swallow down my despair, push back my tears, and steel myself to be strong. Forest needs me.

Sara needs me.

Skye needs me too.

I can't afford to fall apart, not now.

The thought of losing Forest haunts me. We're not at the end. Not yet. There's still a chance, however slim, things can turn around.

And so, I cling to hope. Even on the hardest days, when Forest's smile is but a faint flicker, when Sara's eyes are teary, and when Skye's guilt is almost too palpable to bear, I hold onto hope.

I wear my strength like a shield, protecting not just me but the people I love from the harsh reality that Forest's light is fading. It's a heavy burden, but one I carry willingly. I don't know if it's enough, but for Forest, for us, I'll continue to fight.

Tonight is a treat because we're not in the hospital. I enjoy nights like these, rare moments when Forest isn't hooked to machines.

We're home. The kids are in bed. Sara's asleep, catching up on much-needed rest. I sit with Forest outside, where we gaze out from the steep cliffs of *Insanity* toward the horizon, enjoying the breeze coming off the ocean.

His hand is limp yet warm in mine. Despite the translucent skin stretched taut over knobby knuckles, there's a strength that lingers, a will that stubbornly refuses to be extinguished.

Forest has always been the life of any gathering, his infectious laughter enough to brighten the gloomiest days. Cancer has whittled him down to a skeletal shell of his former self until he's not much more than a living ghost.

In a moment of clarity, his pale-blue eyes slowly open, and he weakly smiles at me. Though it's faint, it's filled with warmth that spreads from him to me.

"I had a dream." His voice was barely audible.

"You did?"

"Yes." His voice is almost too quiet, too weak, to be heard.

"A good dream or a bad dream?" My brows furrow with curiosity, but also concern. I squeeze his hand, offering comfort, connection, and support.

He tries to be brave, but beneath his mask of courage, the man I love is scared and uncertain.

He takes another deep breath before speaking. "I want you to know that no matter what happens, I will never stop loving you, nor regret the life we've shared together."

I dislike his fatalistic talk, but I'm here to support him, not rage at him. Instead of responding in anger, I turn the conversation back to his dreams.

"Do I dare ask what you were dreaming about?"

"You." His wan smile is an attempt at levity, but it falters and dies in the space between us.

"Me?"

My heart clenches at his attempt to joke, to keep things light despite the direness of the situation. It's so very like him, refusing to let his condition dampen his spirit.

"It was the day we met. Do you remember?"

"I do."

Snowden assigned me to guard Sara when he took Forest for his use. When I arrived at their quarters, Forest and Sara were in the shower.

"I thought you were fucking Sara in the shower."

"We weren't fucking." He jabs me in the shoulder with his bony finger. "You fucked me first, if you remember."

"True, but you kissed her first."

"You and I didn't do much kissing back then."

"True. So, it's a bad memory?" I swallow against the sudden lump in my throat. Our beginning is filled with violence and pain.

"Bad and good."

"Well, what I remember is we fought over keeping the doors open. You kicked my ass and tied me up." The memory brings a smile to my face. "Not the way I usually begin things with my subs."

"You saw past my bravado to who I really was." His voice trails off, and for a moment, I think he's fallen asleep, but then his deep rumble fills the air. "You were—*magnificent*."

"Magnificent?" A laugh escapes me as I cock my head in disbelief. "If anyone was magnificent, it was you."

"Me?"

"The way you raced out of the shower when Sara screamed after seeing me on the couch. You were like a protective warrior, every muscle engaged and visible beneath your skin, your magnificence only rivaled by your impressive cock."

"I thought Snowden was messing with me when you showed up."

Both Forest and Sara were Snowden's hostages. As part of his bargain with Snowden, Sara was not to be harmed. In return, Forest agreed he would do whatever Snowden asked.

In addition to torturing Forest for Snowden, I was assigned to protect Sara against Snowden's men.

"I'll never forget it. You were buck naked, challenging me, demanding to know who I was. The way the water dripped down your body… I couldn't miss your magnificent cock."

"We need a new word other than *magnificent*. You were never intimidated by me. Most people are."

"We're nearly the same height. Not many men intimidate me." I smirk and meet his gaze with a playful glint in my eyes. "It's why we fit."

This is what we used to be—playfulness giving way to dominance, submission, and countless moments of agonizing pleasure.

"Here's a new word for you." I pause and nudge his shoulder. "You were *glorious*."

"Glorious?"

"You do strike an image. Viking king? Norse god of thunder? Glorious cock." My cock twitches thinking about Forest.

"Those are very alpha-dominant words."

"You strike fear into the hearts of those who don't know you. You're very Alpha dominant."

"Except you. You never feared me." His lips twitch into a smile as he takes in my words. "You always treated me with respect in front of others. I appreciate that, and you've always been able to give me what I need when we're alone. You take me deep into my darkness and don't judge the things I need—or the things you make me do. You take me to places where I don't have to be strong, or tough, or a Viking King. I can just be your…"

He always has trouble saying the word. It goes against the grain of who he feels he needs to be around others. I'm the only person in the world who's ever seen Forest laid bare.

"There's no yang without yin. No Dom without the sub. No Master without the slave. You've never judged me for the things I need either. It goes both ways."

"You tell me that all the time."

"What we do alone, and explore alone, is no one's business." I miss our sessions in the basement I built for Forest.

I miss the raw and feral nature of what we become. How we feed off each other's desires, as depraved as they may be. Perhaps someday, he'll be strong enough to return to our basement where we can embrace our natures without judgment?

"Did you know?" Forest's curiosity gets the better of him.

"Did I know, what?" I raise an eyebrow, feigning innocence.

"When you first saw me, did you know what I was?" He leans closer, his voice dropping.

"That you were bi?" I chuckle softly.

"Thought that was obvious, but I meant… Did you know I needed…" Forest's expression turns serious.

"I saw the darkness in you from the beginning, if that's what you're asking." I finish his thought, knowing how difficult it is for him to accept that part of himself.

"I always wondered when you figured it out." A flicker of realization crosses his features when he sees the answer he seeks reflected in my gaze. "For a guy my size, people often assume I'm the Dom. You never thought that."

"From the moment our eyes locked, despite your strength and confidence, I knew." I trace a finger along his jawline, my voice laced with confidence. "I've always known."

"How?" Forest's voice trembles.

"It was in your eyes." I lean even closer, my lips almost brushing against his ear. "You begging for release from your pain."

Forest shifts uncomfortably, his arousal responding to the memory.

"There was something in your eyes, a spark. A desperate need. I just knew you craved more than physical domination. What

Snowden tried to force was never going to happen, but I knew someone would bring you to your knees. The person fortunate enough to capture your submission would have to embrace your strength and satisfy your desire for pain. I decided then, and there, that person would be me."

"You knew all of that?" Forest's eyes widen, a mix of surprise and intrigue. "At first sight?"

"You ignited a desperate hunger I couldn't articulate. Do you remember how the air crackled? How your body responded to me?" I nod, a smoldering intensity in my gaze.

"I was hard because of Sara." Forest's voice turns husky with desire. "We'd just exited the shower, so I was..."

"You were *aroused* by her, but not hard. You hadn't accepted your attraction to her. That came later." A smirk plays on my lips. "Your response to the challenge I presented made you hard for me, and that's when I knew."

"But I knocked you out." Forest leans closer, his voice filled with a mixture of curiosity and desire. "I demolished you in our fight."

"You did, but when we fought?" I chuckle softly, rubbing the back of my neck. "It was..."

"Magnificent? Glorious?" Forest smiles with the memory.

"It was *intoxicating*. I wanted nothing more than to explore the depths of our connection. No matter who won or lost that fight." Once again, I nudge him with my shoulder. Shifting gears, my curiosity gets the better of me. "When did you know?"

"Know, what?" Forest meets my gaze, his eyes burning with intensity.

"That I would betray Snowden for you?" I hold his gaze, my voice filled with conviction.

"When you couldn't tear your eyes away from my cock."

"I'm being serious. When did you know?"

"I'm not lying. Poor Sara had that flimsy towel wrapped around her, and all you did was stare at me." A hint of vulnerability flickers in his eyes. "But it was the way you did it. The glint in your eye told me things would only flow one way between us, and that's why I got hard. From the first time we met to all the times Snowden made you..." His voice trails off.

"You were the only man I couldn't break. Your strength made Snowden so angry."

"I didn't think of it as a torture session. I focused on you. Pretended you were my Dom. Then I pictured you as my Master, forcing me to submit. I took Snowden out of the equation and let my fantasies go wild."

"Is that how…"

"God, yes." His voice turns throaty and aroused. "I fantasized about you. About how you'd force me to take your whip, endure your pain, do all the depraved things I wanted you to do to me. It's why I never broke. At least not for Snowden. I did whatever it took to keep Sara safe, every depravity Snowden visited on me, I accepted willingly, as long as he didn't hurt her. But I would never submit to him. Not in the way he wanted. He controlled me, but he never had my respect. He never ignited my desire. You turned me into a raging inferno." Forest's gaze locks with mine, desire and uncertainty mingling in his eyes. "I always wondered if that's why you challenged me about the doors. Why did you insist the doors had to remain open?"

"I wanted to see what you would do." I huff a low laugh, my voice filled with a mix of amusement and desire. "I wanted to see what it would take to Master you."

"And?"

"Like you said, you knocked me out, tied me up, and left me on the floor while you and Sara went to bed with the door closed. Fuck, I woke to the hardest erection I've ever had. Then I freed myself, took the doors off their hinges, and waited to see how you'd respond."

"I don't think I ever felt what I felt that night."

"And what's that?"

"For the most part, up and until that night, men did things to me. I never got to choose."

"You were sexually active with other men before I came into the picture. Didn't you choose them?"

"I spent most of my twenties drunk, on drugs, and sexually promiscuous with men. It was something I needed, my way of coping with my trauma. It was never something I wanted. Not the way I wanted it with you. I dabbled in BDSM, tried both sides of the whip, but for the first time in my life, after meeting you, I desperately wanted someone to master me for real. I wanted you."

"And it all worked out in the end."

If not for his cancer, this is exactly the kind of shit that would make me drag Forest down to the basement for a really deep session.

"I tossed and turned all night last night." Forest's sudden shift from past to present takes me by surprise.

"Why?"

"It's been too long. I need you to take me downstairs. Force me to…" Forest shifts uncomfortably. "You know… Make me do those things in the way only you do."

"Forest, we can't. You know what Skye said. The risk of infection…"

"I'm better now. Stronger. I need this. You need it too. It's who we are. Cancer or not, I'm still yours." His words send a shiver down my spine. He looks so vulnerable—his eyes begging for something he's in no condition to endure.

I take a deep breath and exhale slowly, trying to decide what to do. He begs for something he shouldn't.

His thin frame quivers as if his body is already anticipating the pleasure and pain that lies ahead. If I take Forest in the way he needs, it could be too much for him.

He's been through so much—his body already ravaged by the chemotherapy—but I can't deny the intensity of my desire.

"We do this one time." I take his hands in mine and look into his eyes. "We go slow. You tell me if I need to stop. This is about being safe and not pushing beyond your limits."

He responds with a fervent nod, understanding this is the only way it will happen. His body shudders against mine, the heat of his skin burning me like flames.

It's been far too long.

The electricity between us is palpable. We stand there in silence for what feels like an eternity before I take his hand.

"Come." Neither of us can deny our need. We can't escape our nature.

The next few hours are filled with a sharp mix of pain, pleasure, and aggressive sex. It's not the intensity either of us craves, but it's enough to deepen our bond.

I move slowly, but deliberately, taking time between each activity to check in on how Forest is feeling. I put him on his knees and stand tall over him, forcing him to serve me. I bring out a light flogger, forcing him to accept my pain. The night is full of whispers and caresses that leave us both wanting more, but I remain aware of the risks involved in taking things any further.

With certain adjustments, I give Forest what he craves most, from sharp pain to light bondage. The intensity between us is palpable as we explore the limits of our pleasure and pain together. I bind his hands above his head and take my time exploring his body with my hands and tongue, teasing him toward orgasm, then firmly denying his release. He moans as I stroke him, eliciting a gasp when I bite down on his nipples.

When he's ready, I spin him around, use lots of lube, and drive into him slowly, before building up to harder thrusts that leave us both panting.

Our bodies move together until my second orgasm rushes through me in a wave of intense pleasure. I collapse over him, my cock spent and my heart full. Then, I reach around, taking his cock in my hand, and finally allow pleasure to course through his body. Our breathing returns to normal as we savor the connection between us.

It may have been risky, but it's worth it—this one night is something neither of us will ever forget.

"Thank you." Forest leans against my chest as I hold him. His once towering form feels *less* in my arms.

He tries to brush away a tear rolling down his cheek without me seeing it. Not wanting to ruin the moment, I let him believe I didn't, and realize this may well be the last time we're ever together in this way.

Cancer is a brutal disease, but chemotherapy is worse.

And Forest desperately tries to keep his hopes up.

His resilience is awe-inspiring, making our resolve to fight alongside him even stronger. Sara and I stand right beside him, supporting him as only we can.

Forest—the heart of our trio—isn't just fighting for himself. He's fighting for us and the family we built together.

A week later, however, we rush Forest to the hospital when he collapses in front of the twins.

On our arrival, the news is not what we expect.

FOURTEEN

Paul

⸺

THE MOOD IN THE HOSPITAL ROOM IS BLEAK. FOREST LIES motionless, his weakened body connected to various machines and IV lines. The aseptic hospital air hangs in the room, mingling with the tension vibrating between Sara, Skye, and myself.

Dr. Chen enters the room, his expression grave; we instinctively brace ourselves for what's to come. He clears his throat and takes a moment to gather his thoughts. His voice carries a mixture of compassion and professional detachment as he addresses us.

"I'm afraid I have some difficult news to share with you."

Skye nods, her face a mixture of concern and understanding.

Dr. Chen meets Skye's gaze, appreciating her medical knowledge and her ability to comprehend the complexities of the situation. He takes a deep breath and delivers the news with utmost care.

"Mr. Summers's latest round of chemotherapy has not yielded the desired results. The lymphoma has shown signs of spreading to his bone marrow."

Sara's hand tightens around Forest's. "But what does that mean for his treatment? Is there something else we can do?"

Dr. Chen adjusts his glasses and continues, his voice gentle as he delivers the bad news. "Given the spread to his bone marrow, an autologous bone marrow transplant is no longer a viable option. However, we could consider an allogeneic bone marrow transplant."

"What does that mean?" I shift unsteadily on my feet.

"An autologous bone marrow transplant," Skye explains, "is where you take bone marrow from the patient and use the patient's own healthy bone marrow for the transplant. Since Forest's cancer has spread to his bone marrow, it's no longer an option because any bone marrow we take will have cancer cells in it. All we'd accomplish would be to give him back the cancerous cells."

Well, shit.

"What's an allogeneic transplant? You said that's an option?" Sara sniffs and wipes at her tears.

"An allogeneic bone marrow transplant involves receiving bone marrow from a genetically matched donor. Typically, this would be a related donor, such as a sibling," Dr. Chen answers Sara's question with hesitation.

"Is it hard? To find a donor?" Sara lifts Forest's hand and places his palm against her cheek. Her voice trembles with a mixture of desperation and determination. "Forest is an orphan. He doesn't have any siblings."

Dr. Chen's gaze softens as he looks at Forest, acknowledging the strength and resilience within him. "We'll explore all possible options, including the possibility of finding an unrelated donor."

Forest stirs, his eyes fluttering open. He grips Sara's hand tightly, finding solace in her presence amidst the uncertainty that looms ahead.

"What's going on?" He looks around the room, his gaze landing on Skye, the one person on this earth he trusts the most. "Why am I here?"

The bond Sara and I share with Forest is tight, but it's nothing compared to the bond between Forest and Skye. Their bond is unbreakable.

Dr. Chen takes a step closer to Forest's bedside, his voice filled with empathy. He explains what he told us.

"I know this isn't where we wanted to be," Chen keeps his focus on Forest, his patient, but his words are for all of us. "We'll do everything we can to find a donor."

Forest's eyes close as he absorbs the information. "What are the chances of finding a match? Is it even possible?"

Dr. Chen considers the question, then picks his words carefully. "The likelihood of finding a match among unrelated donors varies depending on multiple factors, including ethnicity and genetic compatibility. It may take time, but we have seen successful transplants even in challenging cases."

Sara's grip on Forest's hand tightens, her voice filled with determination. "We'll do whatever it takes, won't we, Forest? We won't give up."

Forest's gaze shifts from Dr. Chen to Sara, his expression turning somber. "I need to be honest with all of you."

"About what?" Sara's brows furrow, concern etching her features.

His grip on her hand weakens slightly, his voice strained. "I'm tired. Tired of fighting. Tired of enduring the pain and uncertainty. The thought of going through a bone marrow transplant, the endless search for a donor, and the grueling process ahead… It's too much."

Skye's eyes well up with tears as Forest struggles with his emotions. "Maybe this isn't the best time to make life-defining decisions? You need rest. Let's deal with this infection. We'll talk about the bone marrow transplant later, when you're feeling better."

"Better? I feel like shit, and it's not going to get better."

Dr. Chen maintains a compassionate demeanor, fully aware of the weight of Forest's words. "Mr. Summers, I know how challenging this has been for you. The treatments, the setbacks, it's been a difficult road, but I agree with your sister. This kind of decision needs time."

Forest's voice fills with resignation. "I don't want to go through that again. I don't want to spend the last bits of my life puking from chemotherapy while waiting for a donor that never comes."

Sara's voice trembles. "Forest, we've come so far, fought so hard together."

Forest reaches out and gently wipes away Sara's tears with his thumb, his touch filled with tenderness. "This isn't about giving up. It's about choosing how I want to spend the time I have left."

The room falls into a heavy silence as Forest's words hang in the air, and we grapple with the weight of what he said.

Sara's tears flow freely, her voice choked with grief. "I agree with Skye. This isn't the time for these kinds of decisions. You need rest."

"It's not like I haven't thought about it." Forest closes his eyes. "My decision's made."

Throughout the entire conversation, Forest doesn't look me in the eye once. He knows what he'll see, and he's afraid of my reaction.

"We're not done, Forest. We'll find a donor." What the fuck is Forest thinking? Can't he see he's hurting Sara?

Forest's gaze meets mine, filled with both love and sorrow. "This is my journey, my body, my pain. I don't want to spend what time I have left confined to a hospital bed."

Skye's gentle voice fills the room. "I hear you, Bean. I really do, and while I understand your right to decide, I urge you to reconsider. We can explore palliative care options, focus on ensuring you're comfortable, while still keeping the possibility of a transplant open. It doesn't have to be an all-or-nothing decision. And you're not making that choice today."

The soft glimmer of the bedside lamp catches the exhaustion in Forest's eyes. He's fought hard, much harder than anyone I've ever known. He manages a weak smile, reaching out to hold both Sara's and my hand.

"I'm tired." The words are barely audible, but they echo loud and clear, ringing with the weight of his admission.

"We know." Sara leans in to press a gentle kiss to Forest's forehead. "But we're not giving up, not yet. You need rest, and we'll talk about this tomorrow."

With that, Dr. Chen leaves us alone. Skye and Forest talk about what it would mean to move forward with the bone marrow transplant while Sara and I hold onto each other, clinging to the promise of another day, another battle, another chance to save Forest.

FIFTEEN

Paul

———

A week later, Forest recovers from the infection, which nearly killed him, and is cleared for discharge home. We brought him home last night and woke to a bit of weather outside as a storm blows in off the Pacific Ocean. It's a melancholy day, and the steady rain patters against the window, a mournful soundtrack playing in opposition to the tension crackling in our dimly lit living room.

Forest sits hunched over on the couch, his eyes distant and hollow. The shadows cast by the flickering flames of the fireplace accentuate the gaunt lines of his face, making him appear more fragile than ever before.

"Forest, you have to consider the transplant." My voice is barely audible above the driving rain.

He doesn't look at me; his gaze remains fixed on the fire as it dances and sways in a hypnotic ballet. It's as if he's losing himself to the flames, retreating further into his own self-reflection.

"Leave it alone, Paul." Where my voice is intentionally soft, his is hoarse and weak.

The words cut through me like a knife, slicing away at the bond we share. But I can't let him give up. The thought of losing him forever is unbearable.

"This isn't something you can wish away." My desperation

mounts the more he withdraws. I clench my fists, trying to contain the boiling anger that surges within me. "We need to fight."

"What don't you get? It's my life, and I'm done." Forest snaps, finally turning to face me. Pain, betrayal, and defiance fill his eyes to overflowing. "It's my decision."

I stare at him, heart pounding, mind racing. "How can you be so stubborn? You're isolating yourself from everyone who cares about you, pushing us away when you need us the most. I love you." My voice cracks with emotion. "And I can't stand by and watch you give up on yourself."

"You love me?" Forest scoffs bitterly, his eyes brimming with tears. "You love *dominating* me. You love when I go to my knees for you. If you really loved me, you'd respect my wishes. Instead, you're trying to control me and take away the only thing I have left: my choice."

"Forest…"

"Enough." He stands suddenly, swaying unsteadily on his feet, his body weakened by the relentless assault of the cancer. "The first round of chemo was hard enough. The infections were worse. If I do the bone marrow transplant, that chemo is far worse. Not to mention the radiation. I don't want to go through that. It was hell. I don't want to spend the time I have left in and out of hospitals fighting a battle I can't win."

He stumbles toward the door, leaving me feeling helpless and broken. He's spiraling, and I don't know how to stop his fall.

As the door slams shut behind him, I'm left alone in the dark room, the rain outside echoing the storm raging within me. The wind howls like a wounded animal as it whips through the branches of the trees outside, and I want to go out there and howl with my pain.

The weight of Forest's words, the depth of his pain, threatens to crush me, but I refuse to let go of the hope. He can still beat this.

I stand next to the fireplace, but its warmth barely touches me. I've always been there to guide Forest, to help him navigate the murky waters of his past and teach him how to trust again.

He's right. I fiercely guard our connection because it's unique to us. I love when he goes to his knees, when he displays his vulnerability and bares his most private self with me. We're yin and yang in that respect—two halves of an imperfect coin.

But now, faced with this insidious disease eating away at him, I find myself powerless, unable to make him see reason, or take the treatment that could save his life.

It's like watching him drown, refusing the very life raft that could pull him from the depths.

"Will you please come to bed?" Forest's soft voice startles me out of my reverie.

He stands in the doorway, his once-strong body gaunt and frail, barely able to support his weight.

"Not until we talk about this."

"There's nothing more to say." His jaw tightens, bracing for an argument. "I've made my choice."

"I refuse to watch you throw your life away."

"Who are you to decide what's best for me?" Anger flashes in his eyes. It seems all we do is argue these days. "Just because we have our arrangement doesn't give you the right to dictate my choices when it comes to my own body."

He's right, and that's what makes this an impossible conversation. Our dynamic is built on trust and consent, and I swore never to overstep those boundaries, but the thought of losing him terrifies me. My role comes with a responsibility to protect him, even from himself.

"The survival rate is sixty to ninety percent. How can you ignore those odds?"

"It's fifty-seven to eighty-six percent." Of course, Forest corrects me. "Which means a forty-three percent chance I go through all that hell and wind up dead anyway. I'll spend the last few months puking my guts out, in and out of the hospital, becoming more of a skeleton than I already am. I don't want the kids to see me like that. I don't want their last memories of me to be—that. And I don't want to stand here, arguing, when I'm tired and just want to go to bed."

"But what if those aren't their last memories? They're toddlers. They're not going to remember any of this, but they will grow up without a father."

"They'll have you."

"And you think I'm father material?"

"You're great with kids."

"I'm good with *our* kids, but my track record isn't promising. Or did you forget what my father did to you?"

"That's a low blow." His pale eyes cloud with remembered pain.

I meant that one to hit below the belt, and I'm not sorry. I'll do whatever it takes to convince him to see reason.

"Snowden groomed me to be his right hand. To torture his victims. That's what I have to offer Delia and Sebastian."

"You're different than your father. You killed him."

"With my bare hands. You want a murderer raising your kids?"

"*Our* kids and you did it to spare me…"

"I know why I did it, but you think a murderer is the best role model for the kids? Or do you think having their daddy, a man who's saved so many lives, is the kind of role model that should groom their young minds?"

"Doesn't matter what I think. I won't be here. And you're wrong. Snowden's death was justified. If you're going to argue, pick something that makes sense."

"I killed him to spare you having that taint on your soul, but I also killed him because of what he made me. I never want our children to know that about me."

"Then don't tell them."

"I won't lie."

"This is a waste of time. Life's not guaranteed for any of us. We never know when we're going to die."

"We've been over that."

"And it's worth repeating. Something awful can happen to any of us at any time. Tomorrow isn't guaranteed for anyone."

"But…"

"Paul…" He takes small, unsteady steps toward me. When he closes in, he breaches my personal space to rest his forehead on my shoulder.

I wrap my arms around Forest, holding him tight while his muffled voice reaches my ears and breaks.

"You don't know what it's like, feeling your body betray you, knowing that every day brings you closer to the end. I want to live life on my terms, not tethered to machines and trapped in a hospital room."

"Then let me help you. Let me guide you through this nightmare." My voice trembles, raw with desperation. "Let me be your Master here, outside the basement, where you need me most."

"No." Forest pulls back, and I let him take the space he needs.

"Why not?"

"We agreed." His voice rises in anger. "Don't cross that line."

"I don't remember ever agreeing to that. Maybe it's time we renegotiate because it looks like you need me to step up."

"Do that and you'll lose me forever."

His words cut deep, leaving me reeling from the impact, but the fear of losing him overwhelms any reason or logic. I'll do anything to save him, even if it means crossing that line.

"Forest, please," I whisper, my voice choked with tears. "Don't make me choose between honoring our agreement and saving your life. I can't bear either outcome."

"Then don't." Deep lines etch his face with pain. "Just… Just let me go. Let me face this my own way. Respect my boundaries."

With that, he turns away, leaving me standing in the dimly lit room, my heart heavy with the knowledge our bond may never be the same again.

The silence that follows suffocates me. I take a deep breath, burdened with the choice I must make.

"Wait," I call out, my voice barely more than a whisper. "Come back."

Forest slowly turns around. He takes a hesitant step toward me.

"Let's go downstairs. I know what you need." My voice shifts an octave, assuming my role as his Master.

For half a beat, I think he'll say no, but then he pivots toward the stairs leading to our special space.

SIXTEEN

Paul

~

"Remove my clothes," I issue the command, and immediately, it's as if a weight lifts from Forest's shoulders. He takes in one haggard breath, then stands taller.

He complies, slowly unbuttoning my shirt and sliding it off my shoulders.

"Touch me." The cool air caresses my skin.

He places his hands on my chest, then runs them down my arms, tracing the contours of my muscles.

The sensation is electric, sending a current of energy through me that ignites a fire deep in my core. My breathing turns shallow as Forest explores with his hands, slowly mapping out every inch until I tremble with desire.

My cock hardens in Forest's hands, and the heat radiating from his palm warms me from the inside out, chasing away my fear.

"Tell me what you need." I take control effortlessly, but then Forest gave me power over him years ago.

"I need what you did to me at Snowden's." Raw and raspy, desire slurs his words.

I knock his hand off my cock, then point to the floor in front of me. "Strip."

Forest strips off his clothes and kneels without me having to ask, shaking with anticipation.

With the chemo and the changes to his body, anal penetration isn't possible, although I ache to take him like that again. It's the one true way to physically dominate him.

Anything with the possibility of resulting in another life-threatening infection is off the table. We're not able to be brutally physical, which is what Forest asked for when he mentioned Snowden.

His eyes turn heavy with desire, his body quivering as he awaits my commands. I take in the sight of him, my heart soaring at the trust he places in me. Then there's a dizzying fall.

If I do what I must, I could lose him forever.

I need this last session as much as him.

My hands shake as I touch Forest's face, tracing a line from his forehead to his chin. The heat radiating from his body sets me on fire.

"Touch me," I whisper into the darkness.

He wraps his hands around my waist and pulls me to him. Our bodies lie flush against each other's, locked in an embrace so intimate it's too much to bear. Our hearts beat as one. Our breaths mingle in a symphony of blissful silence before I take his hand in mine. I guide him to the bed, then kneel by the edge. His cock comes into view, and I do something I rarely ever do when we're like this.

I take him in my mouth.

Forest squirms beneath me, the sensation of my mouth driving him insane.

We spend the rest of the night downstairs.

I wake early the next morning to find Forest sleeping peacefully beside me. My heart breaks with the fear of losing him because I've made a decision.

I'm taking control outside the basement, without his consent. It goes against everything we've built together.

Forest can beat his cancer. I feel it in my bones. He's too strong to let something like that hold him back.

If I can find a donor, there's no way Forest will say no. He'll do it for Sara and the kids, if not for me. I don't want our children growing up without their dad.

But first, I need a donor. Which means I need a way to find one without him finding out. Fortunately, Spike is an expert at the process. He's been a bone marrow donor three times. Time to have a talk with Spike.

For a moment, I consider involving Sara in my decision but decide against it. Forest is going to need her in the days ahead, especially if he throws me out on my ass.

Again, if it means Forest lives, I'm willing to do whatever it takes. It's a betrayal of Forest's trust and might very well be the end of our dynamic.

I can't imagine a life without Forest in it, but I'll risk everything if it means he gets to live. Watch our children grow up. Grow old with Sara by his side.

I'll risk it all, for him. Always, for him.

The shower door opens, interrupting my thoughts.

"May I…" He gestures with his hand.

"On your knees." One thing I've learned is to never break our dynamic while we're in the basement.

I no longer demand he refer to me as Master when we're alone. That moniker was critical in the beginning. I never forced Forest to be my slave. He's the one who stepped across that line. This is something he chose.

"I wish we could stay down here forever." He bows his head in submission as he kneels before me. "I wish I could give you want you need."

"Sara needs time with you too." We came downstairs to be alone and disappear into our private world.

Down here, there are no calls to interrupt our flow. No distractions to pull Forest out of the headspace he desperately needs to keep the rest of his life in balance. No children begging for attention. With the doctors' appointments and chemo, we haven't had a chance to be alone in the way we need to be.

Forest responds to the flow of power between us by reverently leaning forward and placing the lightest kiss to the tip of my cock.

I ache for more. I ache to hold a strap in my hand and whip his back as he gags on my cock. I ache to tie him down and take him in the ass. I ache to string him up and force him to stand on the tips of his toes while I flay his skin and watch him writhe in pain. I ache for the moment when his pain and torment turn into visceral, unstoppable pleasure as Forest breaks for me and finally allows himself to feel my love.

"Touch it."

The moment his hand is on my cock, waves of pleasure course through my body. I'm going to enjoy this. His lips tease my cock. The lightest of butterfly kisses. The firm rasp of his tongue makes my hips buck, needing more stimulation.

I imagine gripping the back of his head, fingers buried in his hair, as I force him to take more. But, I can't do that. His hair is gone.

Cancer sucks.

I focus instead on the way his hands feel. I will myself to relax, to let myself enjoy the sensation.

When his lips wrap around my cock, I gasp. "Forest, we can't…"

He leans back and stares at the water spiraling down the drain, then he looks up at me. "Cancer's taken so much from me. Last night, you pleasured me. Today, let me pleasure you. I need this." His gaze shifts to my cock. "I need it to feel normal."

Eyes open, he pleads with me. I shouldn't allow this, but a feral monster stirs within Forest. He needs me to tame the beast and put the monster back in its cage.

Over the years, I've taught Forest how to enjoy sex with and without the pain. Occasionally, Sara allows me into her bed with Forest. Not as an active participant, but rather as Forest's Master, controlling him as he learns how to make love to a woman.

When I was horny teenager experimenting with sex, Forest was brutalized during sex, forced to endure what happened to him, or he was forced to have sex while brutalizing his partner. In almost every case, that partner was none other than Skye. For years after they rescued themselves from that living hell, Forest couldn't stomach touching Skye out of fear over what would happen next.

His relationship with sex is more than complicated. It's a twisted tangle of dark, and dangerous, cravings.

Most nights, the three of us sleep in one bed, with Forest in the center, as he's supposed to be. Then there are nights like last night when Forest and I need to be alone and fully embrace our dynamic. And there are days when Forest and Sara take off for romantic getaways.

People don't understand our dynamic, but it works for us.

And it works for Forest.

Slowly, he's healing his childhood trauma and learning how to manage his sadomasochism. Right now, what Forest needs is for me to give him exactly what he wants.

"Open." I force him to take me. Like always, he resists at first. Forest eternally fights against my dominance, needing me to assert myself again and again.

But this is the way.

I force him to take me, and the moment his lips wrap around my cock, I moan. His mouth is so warm. So hot. His lips pull at me, and his tongue flicks along my shaft, desperate to please me. I can't stop myself from pulling his head down, forcing him to take me deeper.

"*Fuuuuck!*" I cry out as he swallows my cock, and his lips hug my shaft.

He's not just kneeling for me. His eyes are closed as his head bobs up and down, working me. I palm the back of his head, pulling him toward me. He uses his tongue to lick along my shaft, and I'm about to lose it. I'm about to come.

Everything about Forest drives me crazy. His submission. His love for me. His love for Sara. His loyalty. His devotion to us both.

I'm about to lose it, but if I take him quickly, maybe we can ignore the doctors' warnings. I'll be as gentle as possible.

I pull him off my cock and step back. "Turn around. Kiss the ground."

He complies without hesitating, breathing heavily. He always breathes heavily when he submits to me.

Always excited. Always eager.

I want to be inside him.

Forest craves pain; he needs to feel the sting, the bite, the ache, the burn. But we have to be careful.

I reach around and grab his balls. Maybe this will be enough for him. My fingers curl and squeeze the heavy sack until he pants from the pain. He pushes back against me, begging to be used. My cock drags against his ass cheek, and while I know we shouldn't, I can't help but fuck him one last time.

Love him, one last time.

SEVENTEEN

Paul

~

THE DIM GLOW OF *INSANITY'S* BAR LAMPS CASTS A SPECTRAL HUE across the bar. I nurse a glass of whiskey. The ice clinks against the glass, a hollow echo in the silence. I take a sip and the whiskey burns a path of fire down my throat.

Three days have passed since Forest and I spent the night in the basement. Three days that he spent with Sara and the twins, *'making memories.'*

That phrase echoes mockingly in my mind and stirs my anger.

I hate it. I hate everything about this disease.

Sara, like me, is at a loss about how to combat Forest's decision to let nature dictate his fate.

But I have an idea.

Spike, the lead guitarist of Angel Fire, strides into the bar just as I swallow another mouthful of whiskey. I perch on a barstool, watching the monotonous dance of rain against the panoramic window. It's one of those gray, dreary days that matches my mood perfectly—overcast and brooding.

"Thought I'd have to drink alone." Spike flashes a wry grin as he saunters toward me. His facial piercings glint in the dim glow of the lamps, bringing an otherworldly look to his face. "Looks like I have company."

"What's your poison?" I gesture to the vacant stool beside me, a clean whiskey glass waiting for him on top of the bar. "Didn't know if you were a whiskey guy."

Spike chuckles, sliding onto the stool. He picks up the glass, cradling it thoughtfully in his palm. "I never met a liquor I didn't like. Just depends on the day."

"Does today call for whiskey?" I pour him a generous portion.

The amber liquid shines as the light hits the liquid. "It does. It's been one of those days, you know? What did you want to talk about?"

A dry chuckle escapes me. I clink my glass against his before taking a slow sip. The conversation we're about to have hangs heavy between us, an unspoken elephant in the room.

"I didn't realize my attempts to get you alone were that obvious."

Spike's a smart guy.

I catch him in a side glance, contemplating how to broach the subject that's been weighing on my mind for the past few days.

"I've seen you lurking, you know." Spike's voice cuts through the silence, his grin teasing, but his eyes are serious.

"Lurking, huh?" I smirk, playing along. "Well, wouldn't want you to think I was stalking you."

Spike raises an eyebrow, a hint of amusement playing in his eyes. "Is that what you've been doing?" He sips the whiskey, waiting for my response.

I glance at him, a ghost of a smile on my lips. "Maybe. You've got an interesting history."

"History?" His laughter rings out, filling the bar. "Do I need to worry about my past catching up with me?"

"Depends." I set my glass down and turn to face him squarely. "What are your feelings on bone marrow drives?"

"Well, that's not what I was expecting…" Spike's grin fades, replaced by a frown. His eyes are thoughtful, a touch of confusion swirling in their depths. "Are you asking because of…?"

I watch him for a moment before taking another swig of

whiskey. Spike's always been good-hearted, a lifesaver, literally. I can only hope he'll understand why I've been so persistent, so *stalkerish*.

"Let's say hypothetically, someone close to us may benefit from a donor."

"Someone close to us? Okay." His fingers drum rhythmically against his glass. He understands the gravity of the situation without needing it to be spelled out. "I can see why you'd think of me. I'm in. What do you need help with, exactly?"

A wave of relief washes over me. It's a small victory, but one in the right direction for Forest, even if he's blissfully unaware of my machinations.

Before the silence stretches out uncomfortably, Spike's grin returns, lightening the somber mood. "By the way, you make a pretty terrible stalker. Might need to work on your skills."

"Yeah, well," I offer a half-hearted smirk, "I figured I'd use my terrible stalking skills for something good. I want to set up a bone marrow drive for Forest."

"Forest won't like that." Spike raises an eyebrow, his glass pausing mid-air. "We were gonna do that."

"I'm aware," I respond, a bitter taste rising in my throat.

"Ash said Forest wouldn't be able to act as band manager and might send the wrong vibe, but we're totally up for it."

Before I can continue the conversation, the rush of approaching footsteps catches my attention. Skye walks into the bar. Her expression grim. Eyes sparkling with unshed tears.

Forest's decision is taking a toll on all of us, but Skye has been his rock for as long as I've known them. Seeing her this upset worries me.

"What won't Forest like?" Skye's voice cuts through the silence. Her eyes are focused on me, a question etched in their depths.

For a moment, I consider not telling her, shielding her from my scheme, but Skye is just as much a part of this as the rest of us. She deserves to know. So, I take a deep breath and meet her gaze.

"I'm planning to set up a bone marrow drive. For Forest."

She blinks, surprised. A moment later, understanding flickers in her eyes, followed by a hint of rebellion. "He won't like that." She echoes Spike's earlier statement. "Told Ash in no uncertain terms what he'd d0 to Ash's balls if he tried something like that."

I nod, the bitterness in my throat deepening. "I know."

The silence that follows is a sobering reminder of the fight we have ahead.

Spike finally breaks the silence. "You know, when I did it, I just signed up with the national registry to be a donor, but I've heard of drives organized for specific people too. You might need to work with a local hospital or clinic for something like that."

"Forest won't want it. You know that." Skye sits on the barstool next to me. "He'll see it as us not respecting his decision."

"I know." I meet her gaze. "But if there's a chance… Don't we owe it to him to try? Regardless of what he wants?"

"He's going to resent you." Her shoulders droop. "But if we can do it without him knowing, and if we find a donor, I wonder if he'll reconsider?"

"That's what I'm hoping."

It's all I think about anymore.

Skye's expression softens at my words. She understands. We're all in the same painful boat, desperately trying to navigate these rough waters. But she nods slowly, giving me a small, sad smile.

"I guess we're doing this." She rubs her palms on her jeans and bites her lower lip in distress.

With Skye in agreement and Spike offering his experience, I feel like I've got a fighting chance to set this plan into motion. If anyone can save Forest, it's the family he's chosen in *Insanity*, our home.

No matter what Forest wants, we'll fight for him, every step of the way.

That's what families do.

"I'm worried, though." Skye blows out a breath.

"Why?"

"He'll see it as abusing your power." Once again, Skye offers a word of caution. "He won't forgive you."

"Perhaps. Forcing him to accept treatment feels like a breach of trust, but I can't sit by while he dies. I accept whatever fallout happens. He's too important to lose."

My voice trails off, swallowed by the heavy silence in the bar.

Skye looks at me with understanding. She knows what it's like to love Forest, to want to protect him at all costs.

"I think…" Her voice is slow and thoughtful, "We can do it through health immunizations. Call in all of Guardian HRS and do a little bone marrow drive on the side. He wouldn't have to know. But *you* should know the likelihood of finding a donor is exceptionally small."

"Doesn't matter. It's something." For the first time, there's a glimmer of hope.

The bar door swings open and in strides Mitzy, gadget in hand. Her psychedelic hair has grown back after she shaved it in solidarity with Forest. She fiddles with the device in her hand.

She takes a stool at the end of the bar. "I've got a better idea."

"Were you eavesdropping on us?" I turn to Mitzy, not nearly as surprised as I should be.

"I've been watching your horrible stalking skills, wondering why you'd want to talk to Spike. Considering Forest needs a bone marrow transplant, and Spike's got experience as a donor, I put two and two together. It wasn't that hard. And immunizations, while a good idea, aren't going to fool Forest." Mitzy's a straight shooter, but she does like to make an entrance.

"Remember how Alec's tracker was compromised when Artemus Gonzales captured him?"

"I remember."

Alec, along with Barbi, one of the roommates Bravo team seems to have gone *ga-ga* over, was kidnapped by Artemus Gonzales, a now-defunct human trafficker. During Alec's captivity, both of his embedded trackers were removed.

Trackers Mitzy's team uses to locate Guardians anywhere in the world, precisely for situations like that. It's a great system, thought to be foolproof until Alec's trackers were removed.

I raise an eyebrow at her, silently prompting her to continue.

"Well, we've been working on a new method to embed the trackers more securely. We're going to need everyone to get new ones implanted, and the sooner the better. We could use that as a cover for the drive."

Her suggestion is simple, straightforward, and genius. I feel a glimmer of hope as the pieces start falling into place.

"That could work." My mind spins with ideas. "You're a genius."

She shrugs, her smirk broadening. "Just doing my job."

"I like it." Skye nods. "It's a reason to pull people in, rather urgently. Involves the medical staff, so we can kill two birds with one stone. Best of all, we can do it all right under Forest's nose."

With Mitzy's solution, our plan feels more solid, more feasible. I finally feel like we have a chance. All we have to do now is set it in motion and hope it's enough to save Forest's life.

As our plan takes shape, Skye offers a word of caution. "Paul, you're crossing a line with this. Forest is going to be pissed at me and Mitzy, maybe Spike as well, but it's going to be different for you. You're violating the trust and boundaries you both agreed on. Overstepping your role. Are you prepared for the rift it's going to create between the two of you?"

"I'm aware of the consequences. I just can't sit back and watch him give up. He's been fighting all his life. I refuse to let him stop fighting now. If this means…"

My throat closes up with emotion, and I struggle to clear my throat. "If he kicks me to the curb, ends our relationship, then that's a price I'm willing to pay."

"You sure about that?" More than anyone else, Skye understands the dynamic between me and Forest. She may be the only one who approves, but then she understands the darkness in Forest.

"Is there really any other choice?" My frustration boils over. "If I don't do this, he could die. Trust can be rebuilt—but not if he's gone."

Mitzy interjects, her tone thoughtful. "Forest is a stubborn man. Always has been. If he thinks we're disrespecting his wishes, he'll react. Badly."

"How can you smile when you say that?" Sometimes, I can't figure out the energetic young woman with a brain nearly the size of Forest's.

She grins, her eyes twinkling with resolve. "Because that's the

Forest we know and love. The one who fights. Who doesn't back down. That's the man we need to bring back."

"Can't disagree with that." Skye nods, a determined look in her eyes. "When will the new trackers be ready?"

"Already ready. We can start now."

Skye takes a deep breath and stares at me for a long moment before finally nodding. "We start tomorrow."

I pull her into a hug, squeezing her gently. A sense of unity passes between us, solidifying our resolve.

We'll save Forest. Whatever the cost.

EIGHTEEN

Paul

⁓

OVER THE COURSE OF THE NEXT TWO WEEKS, MITZY AND SKYE throw themselves into the enormous task of replacing all the trackers and establishing a bone marrow registry. Both of them are whirlwinds of energy and determination, their shared focus on Forest creating a powerful bond between them.

As their plans take shape, I meet them over at Medical, where they've assembled Alpha Team: Max, Knox, Axel, Griff, Liam, Wolfe, as well as Jinx and Lily, to get the new trackers implanted.

I hover on the fringes, watching their progress with a mixture of guilt and admiration. I hate that we have to deceive Forest, but it's the only way. Every new development, every swab collected, and tracker replaced only amplifies the drumbeat of urgency reverberating in my chest.

One afternoon, Forest wanders in. He stops eyes narrowing at the sight of the team gathered together.

"What's going on?" The muscles in his jaw tick as he takes in the assembled team.

Mitzy, engrossed in her task of updating Knox's tracker, looks up at Forest. She has become a master of subterfuge over these weeks, her face revealing nothing of the grand scheme beneath the surface.

Without missing a beat, she answers with a calm that belies the deception we're all participating in. "Tracker updates."

"Tracker updates?" Forest's voice rumbles.

"We can't afford a repeat of what happened with Alec. Everyone needs an upgrade."

Forest's expression eases at the plausible explanation, but his sharp gaze scrutinizes her every move. Eventually, he nods, seeming to buy into the lie.

Skye skillfully collects buccal swabs for the bone marrow registry as the team members get their new trackers embedded.

Each sterile swab brushes against each team member's cheek, collecting precious cells. It's a masterful performance, the real intention behind each swab hidden under Forest's unsuspecting gaze.

With each collected sample, we move a step closer to saving Forest's life, and he remains oblivious to it all.

"Hey, Forest." Mitzy's lips tug into a playful smirk. "Since you lost all your hair, you should ask Lily to donate some hers if you want a wig."

Laughter ripples through the room.

Forest throws a mock glare at Mitzy before his gaze lands on Lily. His brow furrows for a moment, but it's fleeting.

Knox quickly redirects attention, flexing his hand and grinning at Mitzy. "Are you sure this new tracker won't pop if I flex too much?"

"Positive." Mitzy rolls her eyes, tossing a piece of sterile gauze at him.

As the laughter dies down, the room returns to its usual rhythm of good-natured banter and camaraderie. A faint smile creeps over my face. We need more moments like this. Moments that remind us why we're fighting so hard.

"Hey, Paul," Forest's voice breaks through my thoughts. He looks at me, an eyebrow raised in question. "Are you next?"

"Um…" I stammer, but Mitzy saves my ass.

"You want to get in line behind him? We've gotta update your trackers too."

Hadn't intended on getting one of the new trackers, but I have to have some reason for being here. I kick off the wall I've been leaning against and stroll over to Mitzy.

She preps a new tracker, her movements steady and sure. There's no hesitation in her eyes as she takes my arm, her touch professional and detached.

Forest watches, his gaze flicking back and forth between us. He doesn't say anything, but there's a tightness around his eyes. He's suspicious but not enough to say anything.

Forest follows me, rolling up his sleeve. Mitzy inserts one of the new trackers like a pro.

For now, our secret is safe. But I can't shake the feeling we're walking on a knife's edge. One slip and everything could come tumbling down.

"Want to grab lunch?" Forest pulls me aside.

"Sure." We file outside and I take a deep breath, ready to continue the charade, but Forest pulls me up short.

His eyes meet mine. "What's really going on?"

"They're taking precautions. That's all."

For a moment, Forest looks like he wants to argue. But then, his gaze drops to the ground. He's either not sure something's going on or too tired to deal with it.

For now, Forest chooses to let the lie stand.

NINETEEN

Paul

~

Piercing blue, the sky mocks my turbulent state of mind. The sun bakes the land, the heat relentless, much like the turmoil in my head. It's been a couple of weeks since we set up the bone marrow drive for Forest, and the days are a blur of anxious waiting and false cheer.

Meanwhile, the cancer spreads.

A buzz from my phone jolts me from my internal tumult. It's a text from Skye.

Skye: *We need to talk. Meet us at the office.*

Us?

A chill pricks at my skin despite the oppressive heat. The air feels too thick, too heavy all of a sudden. The urgency in her message feels like a stranglehold around my throat. With one last glance at the deceptively serene sky, I climb into my car and speed toward Guardian HRS.

There's only one thing she would urgently want to discuss, and either outcome leaves me in ruins. No match found, and Forest is on borrowed time. A match found, and I must face the reckoning of what I've done in direct violation of Forest's wishes.

Either way, I stand to lose him.

When I wander into Skye's office, an uneasy silence hangs heavy in the air. She and Mitzy huddle around a small, glowing screen, their faces etched uncharacteristically by confusion.

The knot in my stomach tightens.

They're so focused on whatever's on that screen that they don't register my entrance.

Something's wrong.

Clearing my throat, I try to sound casual, but my voice betrays a tremor. "What's up?"

Skye and Mitzy glance up, a mixture of surprise and something deeper reflected in their eyes. They exchange a long look before turning to me. There's something raw and apprehensive in their gaze that knots my stomach. A moment of stillness follows before Skye breaks the silence.

Her voice is steady, clinical, and detached. "We've been going through the preliminary results from the drive. There's—something you need to see."

Mitzy's high-pitched voice squeaks more than usual. "Usually, it takes months, even years to find a match, even with a national registry. But we…" She trails off, and Skye takes over again.

"We got lucky." Skye's voice is thick, constricted. "Or rather, Forest did."

"Lucky?" My mouth is dry, and my heart pounds against my ribcage. "How?"

Skye's gaze locks with mine, her normally vibrant eyes mute with worry. She turns the screen toward me, pointing at a name that makes my heart stutter.

"Lily?" The name falls from my lips in a stunned whisper. "Sh-she's a match?"

I glance between the two women, wondering why they aren't excited by this. "This is amazing news. Why are the two of you freaked out about it?"

"Not just a match." Skye's voice is barely audible. "A sibling match."

"Sibling?" I glance at the screen, and my heart stops. There, in clinical, black-and-white is Lily's name. "Forest doesn't have any living family members."

"Evidently, he does." Skye points to the screen.

"Lily?" My voice barely rises above a whisper. "How?"

"Genetics don't lie." Skye leans back and pinches the bridge of her nose.

A series of images race through my mind: Lily's white-blonde hair, her pale eyes, the subtle resemblance to Forest I've always shrugged off as a coincidence.

The room spins, the implications of this revelation monumental. Lily—a sibling match for Forest.

"How is this possible?" I look to Skye. She knows everything about Forest.

"I don't know." She shakes her head as silence descends between us again.

Time freezes. My mind struggles to digest the enormity of this revelation. Lily? Forest's sister? A match?

"She can save his life." My voice sounds distant as I struggle to process the news.

Everything just got a lot more complicated.

A sliver of hope sweeps through me. We have the power to save Forest's life, yet it comes wrapped in layers of lies, littered with betrayal.

As reality sinks in, an overwhelming sense of dread swirls in my gut. We have the means to save Forest, but at what cost?

It's time to come clean.

"We need to tell him." Skye's voice cuts through my spiraling thoughts, grounded and resolute. It jerks me back to the present and the grim reality we have to face.

"This was my idea." My mind races. "I'll tell him."

"Your idea, but we set it up." Mitzy runs her fingers through her psychedelic hair, making it shimmer in the light. "Besides, I wouldn't want to face Forest alone. We should stage an intervention."

"Intervention?"

"You know, gather all his loved ones around him? Present him with the news…" She gives me a look, like I'm an idiot. "What's he going to say? '*I'm not going to do it?*'" She shakes her head. "He can't *not* move forward with the transplant."

"Does Lily know?" I ask.

Mitzy shakes her head. "We wanted you in the loop first. We didn't want to do anything until the three of us discussed it. This isn't something we want circulating until we've spoken to Forest."

I feel a pang of sympathy for Lily. She's on the precipice of being thrust into a whirlpool of deception and lies, all while potentially being the key to Forest's survival.

My web of secrets is about to unravel, and all I can do is brace for the storm.

"So, who do we tell first?" Mitzy asks. "Lily, Forest's savior? Or Forest, the reluctant beneficiary?"

The decision feels like a tightrope, each step threatening to tip us into a pit of recriminations.

"Maybe we should tell Lily first," Skye suggests, her voice tight with apprehension. "The shock of a long-lost sister might help when we break the news to Forest."

Doubt swirls within me as I consider what to do next.

"Sara," I blurt out her name. "She should know first."

"Can she keep it a secret until we talk to Forest?" Skye's gaze sharpens, her face a mask of clinical detachment, but her eyes betray her worry.

"Sara deserves the truth."

They all do.

An uneasy compromise forms in my mind. I reach for my phone.

"Let's get them both here." I send them both a text.

Waiting for them to arrive is nerve-racking.

When Sara finally walks into the office, her smile fades at the grim expressions on our faces.

"What's wrong?"

"Have a seat." I gesture to one of the chairs.

"What's going on? Is it about Forest?" Her expression shifts to fear and worry.

"I really think you should sit for this."

"Okay?" She takes a seat, concern etching her features as she glances between me, Mitzy, and Skye.

I debate telling Sara while waiting for Lily to arrive, but Lily walks in shortly after. Her wide, innocent eyes scan the room in confusion. "What's going on?" The confusion in her voice mirrors Sara's.

I glance at Skye and Mitzy, who give me small, encouraging nods. When I begin, my voice cracks with emotion. "There's something I have to tell you…" I choke up, but Skye rushes in to fill the gap.

As she explains everything, the look of shock on their faces mirrors mine when Skye and Mitzy called me in. The silence that follows is deafening.

"A match?" Sara's first reaction is a sigh of relief. Her eyes shine with unshed tears, but then her relief transitions into surprise, then concern. "Why wasn't I told about this?"

The weight of her question hangs in the air, tension stretching between us.

"We didn't want to get your hopes up," Mitzy says gently. "It was a long shot."

"I organized it in secret." I look at Sara, my throat tight. I have to be brutally honest with her.

"Forest doesn't want it." Sara twists her fingers in her lap, conflicted and hurt.

Mitzy attempts to take some of the blame off my shoulders. "Forest didn't want any of us to get tested, but how could we not?"

"And you didn't tell me." Sara ignores Mitzy and stares directly at me. It's not a question but an accusation, her eyes icy. "Why didn't you tell me?"

"I couldn't." I've lied long enough. "I'm sorry."

"Because you knew I wouldn't keep something like that from Forest?"

"Yes." I flinch at her words, the guilt cutting deep.

"You had no right to keep this from me. Or from Forest." Sara's voice is firm, carrying a reprimand that has Mitzy flinching.

"I know." Guilt hangs heavy in my voice. "I was desperate to find a solution."

Her gaze holds mine for a long, uncomfortable moment before she sighs heavily, the fight leaving her. "I don't agree with what you did. You violated Forest's trust. Our trust." She pauses, her voice trembling as she continues, "But I also can't ignore the fact that we have a match. We have a chance to save him."

Her gaze softens, but her disappointment is clear. Yet, when she speaks next, her voice carries a hint of understanding. "I get why you did it. But it doesn't make it right."

"I don't understand?" Lily appears to have recovered from the initial shock. "How can this be?"

"Ash would say fate intervened." Skye runs her fingers through her hair. We wanted to let you know first, make sure you want to be a donor. Forest is going to fight this. He's been very clear about enough being enough."

"Well, that's just silly." Lily grabs her hair and pulls it over her shoulder. "I heard he decided to stop treatment, but he's just being obstinate. Aren't the odds in his favor?" She absently plaits a braid.

"They are," Skye says.

"Then, why doesn't he want to fight?" Lily releases the half-formed braid and shakes her head. "I don't understand."

"He's tired," Sara provides an answer. "He says his entire life has been one battle after the next, and he just wants to stop."

"But how can he?" Lily glances around the room. "He's got you and Paul, and little Delia and Sebastian. He's got Skye? All of Guardian HRS depends on him. And now…" Her eyes widen. "I can't believe we're related. So what if his entire life's been a battle? Look at all the good he's doing? What he's created is remarkable. Sister…" Lily's brows bunch, clearly still taking it in.

"It's a shock to us all, but…" Skye crosses the room and pulls Lily into a hug. "I couldn't be happier." Tears stream down her face. "He might bitch about the bone marrow drive, but he can't bitch about finding you."

When Skye pulls away from Lily, she props her hands on her waist. "We all agree Forest is giving up too soon. He's not going to take this lightly. He's going to be pissed we went behind his back. Hopefully, this softens the blow."

"What do we do next?" Sara's voice is barely a whisper. Though still reeling from the deception, she can't help but revel in what we found.

This is more than a lifeline—it's a tremendous gift.

The room falls into silence, each of us lost in our thoughts, the atmosphere thick with mixed emotions. We are on the precipice of a chance we had hardly dared to dream of.

We have a match.

We have a chance.

Despite the lies, the overwhelming feeling is one of cautious optimism.

Next comes the difficult part.

"We tell Forest—together." The words trip on their way out of my mouth, too small for the enormity of the task ahead, too simple for the complexity of the emotions involved.

I dread the moment Forest looks into my eyes.

I see the scene clearly in my mind and feel the icy fury in his eyes, the hurt and betrayal etched on his face.

The simple truth is this: telling Forest, regardless of whether this saves his life, will destroy our trust. That, more than anything, terrifies me, but I knew that going in.

I did it for Forest.

For his future.

The five of us plan for the impending intervention and head back to *Insanity* to tell Forest he's going to live.

TWENTY

Paul

~

A DEEP SIGH ESCAPES MY LIPS. FOREST DESERVES TO KNOW, BUT HOW do I drop a bombshell like this? To tell a man that one of his employees is his sister? That his team, his family, conspired behind his back to find a way to save his life? That I, his Master, violated the very tenets of our relationship? That gnawing dread in my gut grows heavier with each passing moment.

We decide to break the news together, as a team.

As a family.

Sara doesn't want to wait.

That night, we gather in the joint living space at *Insanity*, each one of us shouldering a heavy burden.

We debate inviting the whole Angel Fire crew, but Skye wants to keep it as intimate as possible.

Ash and Spike are the only other members present. Bash, Bent, and Noodles took the kids and women down to the beach below the cliffs of *Insanity* for an impromptu barbecue and S'mores-fest.

The tension in the room is palpable, a silent, ticking time bomb ready to detonate at the slightest provocation.

At first, I suggested Sara bring Forest to the meeting, but there's no way she wouldn't tell him on the way. Therefore, Skye and Mitzy arrange to ride home with Forest from HQ.

Forest walks into the spacious living room, a look of curiosity etched on his face, his eyes sharp and probing. He can tell something is off—we've never been great at hiding things from him. He takes a seat, his gaze flitting between us all, a mixture of impatience and trepidation coloring his features.

"Well, get on with it." He gestures with his hands, telling us to lay it on him.

The moment is here. There's no turning back.

"There's something I need to tell you." My voice is barely a whisper, heavy with guilt.

"Go on." His eyes narrow, suspicion creeping into his gaze.

"I organized a bone marrow drive." My voice falters, the confession as bitter as poison on my tongue.

His gaze turns arctic cold.

"Everyone at Guardian HRS signed up as potential bone marrow donors. For you." Mitzy's high-pitched voice wavers and cracks, her intent clear—to share the burden of blame.

Forest's face goes white, his jaw clenching as his eyes swirl with fury. The revelation hits him like a physical blow. The color drains from his face as his gaze hardens, darkened by an anger that is both palpable and terrifying.

"You did what?" He practically snarls with anger.

"Forest, we're trying to save your life," Skye interjects, her voice wavering.

His gaze turns icy, a piercing glacial glare that silences my attempt to justify what I did.

"You had no right." His booming voice echoes painfully through the tense silence of the room as he rages against me. Forest may be a shell of the man he once was, but his voice still carries his strength.

All I care about is will he fight? Or has he already resigned himself to his fate?

"Stop." I modulate the tone of my voice, using vocal registers Forest responds to when we're alone, when I dominate him, but Forest doesn't cave.

"How dare you?" Forest seethes, his fists trembling at his sides. "How dare you use that tone with me. Here? Of all places? You went behind my back? You had no right. You *have* no right."

"We did it for you," Skye jumps in, seeing how the conversation spirals out of control.

"By lying? Manipulating me?" He shouts, and I flinch at the raw pain in his voice. "Is that how little you think of me?"

"Forest, please…" Mitzy begins, attempting to intervene, but Forest whirls on her.

"Stay out of this, Mitzy. All of you. This is between him and me." He roars, his fury turning on everyone in the room, but it's me who bears the brunt of his wrath. "How could you?" He runs his hand over his bare scalp. He looks at his hand, and it's like watching a mountain crumble.

"How could I not?"

"You had no right." He repeats what he said, his voice barely above a whisper but filled with an intensity that makes me flinch. "No right."

"Forest," I begin, my voice low and strained, "I never wanted to betray you, but I couldn't stand by and do nothing. Not when we have a fighting chance of beating this."

"You overstepped, and you know it." He glares at me with fury-filled eyes. "You had no right to make that decision for me."

"I disagree." My heart pounds against my ribs. "I have a responsibility to protect you."

"Responsibility? Protect me?" Forest scoffs, running a shaky hand over his bare scalp. "You think this is protection? This is control, Paul. It's the worst kind of control, and the fact you can't see it?" He shakes his head and falls silent.

The depth of his anger is no surprise, but his disappointment is a sucker punch to my gut.

In the silence that follows, Forest's condemnation stretches and the atmosphere in the room becomes unbearable. I watch his anger brew behind those pale, yet stormy eyes—a tempest fueled by anger, pain, and betrayal.

Did I push too far?

My greatest fear might just come true—Forest may never be

able to forgive me, and in my desperate attempt to save his life, I may have lost him forever.

"And what about you?" Forest turns on Sara. "Were you a part of this? Keeping secrets behind my back?"

"I didn't know." Sara's soft and gentle voice isn't enough to take the edges off Forest's anger.

"And yet you're here, with them, giving me this news."

"I only just found out. I didn't hide anything from you."

"Maybe, but he did." Forest turns his anger back at me. "How could you?" He stammers and can't finish his words.

"Forest," Sara says softly, reaching out to touch his arm. "I know you didn't want this, but what will you do if a match is found? Will you consider fighting? For the sake of our children? Can you at least consider it? Or would you rather leave me and Paul to raise them alone?"

Her words hang heavy in the air, and I watch as Forest's anger slowly crumbles, replaced by an unbearable sadness. The room feels suffocated by the weight of our collective guilt, our desperate attempts to save a man who may not want to be saved.

There's an uneasy silence, the air thick with emotions we can't put into words.

Then, out of the blue, Ash speaks. "Aren't you curious, Forest?"

"Curious about what?"

"Who you matched to?" His melodious voice is calm, but firm, grounding us all in the face of the storm that's just taken place.

"There's a match?" Forest glares back, a burning anger mingled with an unwilling curiosity in his eyes. He doesn't answer, but the silence he gives is enough of an answer.

"Don't you see the rarity of this situation? It's a miracle. The chance of finding a match from a bone marrow drive with a few thousand people is infinitesimal. Yet they found a match. And not just any match."

"What does that mean? A match is a match." Forest hangs his head and massages his temples.

Ash pauses for a moment, allowing his words to sink in before he drops the next bombshell. "It's a sibling match."

The room goes deathly quiet at the revelation, the magnitude of the situation not lost on anyone. Forest's face drains of all color as the implication of Ash's words sink in. He looks shell-shocked as if he's been hit by a freight train and is still reeling from the impact.

"I have no siblings."

"Forest…" Skye steps forward and places a hand on his arm. "You do."

"Who?"

"Me." Lily clears her throat. "It's me."

Poor Lily looks so uncomfortable. She's a part of the Guardians but not a part of anything here at *Insanity*. The outsider stepping in, her life's been flipped on its head.

"This is fate, Forest." Ash's voice is heavy with conviction. "It's fate screaming at you, giving you not just one, but three signs. The match, and Lily. It's telling you what to do. It's telling you to live."

Forest takes a long, agonizing moment to process Ash's words; his gaze bounces from one face to another, gauging reactions. Then, as if reaching an arduous conclusion, he nods slowly, his voice hushed when he finally speaks.

"That's only two signs. What's the third?" Forest swallows thickly.

"Today, you found a sister. Not too long ago, Skye found a brother in Chase. Don't you see? Do you know what the universe is trying to tell you?"

"I don't know what the fuck the universe is telling me, other than it wants me to die."

"Forest!" Sara gasps, then chokes back a strangled cry.

"You and Skye found family in each other. Then she found me, and the band joined your family. You created the Guardians, and they became your family. Sara is the first foster kid you rescued, and now she's your wife. You found Paul and the three of you added Delia and Sebastian to your family. Skye found Chase, a miracle in its own right, and now the universe gifts you with the sister you never knew you had. A sister who may just save your life. It's a sign, and if I were you, I'd take a long, hard look at what the universe is trying to tell you."

"And what would that be?"

"It's not your time to die. You still have things left to do."

Ash doesn't pull his punches. As the youngest child and black sheep of a large family, with a father who is a pastor, his relationship with religion is complicated. But if there's one thing Ash believes in, it's fate.

"My little beanpole who's grown so large…" Skye cranes her neck to look at the towering giant Forest became. "You know my thoughts on religion, but this feels as if a higher power is trying to send a message. Please, if not for me, if not for Sara, or for Paul, or for the twins, do it for all the lives we've yet to save. For all the kids trapped like we once were. Do it for them."

Forest hangs his head, and his shoulders slump. He turns his back to us and moves over to stand in front of the floor-to-ceiling windows that look out across the water.

Sara takes a step toward him, but I catch Lily moving out of the corner of my eye. I grab Sara's arm and hold her back, gesturing toward Lily. "Hold up."

Lily closes the distance to stand beside Forest. She says nothing at first, staring out the window like him, but then she reaches out, her fingers seeking his hand. When they touch, their fingers intertwine. The rest of us stand in silence, waiting for— something?

Lily turns toward Forest. Says something none of us can hear. Then she twists to stare back out across the ocean. Silence descends for several minutes, the time passing like molasses.

"What's he doing?" I keep my voice below a whisper and turn toward Skye.

"Thinking? Brooding?" She shrugs. "With Forest, it's hard to know."

Forest and Lily exchange more words. The rest of us wait. Then, he executes an abrupt about-face and returns with a grim expression on his face. He looks at everyone in the room: Sara, Skye, Mitzy, Ash, and Spike.

He looks at everyone, but me.

"I'll do it," he concedes, but each word is laden with reluctant acquiescence.

A flicker of hope ignites in the room, quivering and fragile, yet present. We lean forward, collectively holding our breaths.

"But on one condition." Forest finally turns to me. "Paul leaves." His voice is firm. Cold. Resolute.

The world drops out from beneath me.

The room descends into shocked silence, punctuated only by the sharp intake of breaths.

"Forest…" I manage to whisper, my voice barely audible over the deafening silence. "You don't mean that."

"You heard me." Forest's gaze locks onto me, blazing with a combination of pain, anger, and firm resolution. "I'll do the transplant. But you leave. I don't want you around anymore."

"Forest, you can't do that," Sara jumps in, her eyes wide and terrified. "The kids…"

Forest's weighty gaze shifts to Sara. "He can see them, but I never want to see him again."

The reality of his demand hits like a punch to the gut, knocking the breath out of me. Before I can utter another word, Sara intervenes, her voice a potent mix of shock and anger.

"You can't be serious. We're a family. Paul is Sebastian's father. You're Delia's dad. You can't cut him out of our lives."

"I have no intention of cutting him out of your life. I'm cutting him out of mine. I won't do the transplant if he stays." Forest turns to her, his features softening slightly, but his decision is unyielding.

"But, Forest…" Sara pleads, tears glistening in her eyes.

Forest raises a hand, silencing her. "I don't want there to be any misunderstanding or confusion. In front of all of you…" He keeps his voice low, but steady, "I rescind my consent and release Paul from his role as my Master."

The room plunges into stunned silence at his proclamation. It feels like a physical blow, ripping through the very fabric of our connection. The air grows heavy, burdened with a sense of loss and looming dread, and it feels like the end of everything we've built together.

The end of us.

Forest's gaze locks onto mine, his stormy eyes reflecting a world of hurt, betrayal, and pain.

"You ruined it." His voice is barely above a whisper, yet it resonates louder than any shout could. The words hang in the room like a spectral echo, intensifying the silence around us. "You ruined us."

"I did it to save you."

The weight of his words descends upon me like a shroud, blanketing the room with a cold, hollow emptiness that gnaws at my heart.

"You want me to fight? Well, I'll fight. I'll fight for Sara. I'll fight for the twins. I'll fight for Skye and Mitzy and all the rest. But what I won't do is fight with you by my side. I asked for one thing. For you to respect my wishes. You're no better than your father."

"Forest!" Sara cries out. "That's cold." She turns to me. "He doesn't mean it. Forest, tell Paul you didn't mean that."

"I never want to see him again. Not when I can't trust him," Forest continues, his voice straining under the weight of his raw emotions. His words rip into me, each syllable a blade slashing at the bond we share.

Shared.

It's all gone now.

Not that I should be surprised. This was always a risk, and how often did I say I'd pay the price willingly if it saved his life?

Well, it's time to pay.

Once filled with warmth and shared secrets, his gaze now holds cold rejection that stings more than any physical wound.

"I'll never kneel for you again." Each word echoes the death knell of our relationship. Our bond as Master and slave severed. Our friendship erased. Our love lost. "And I want you gone."

My heart shatters in my chest, a painful echo to his words. This is my greatest fear, losing Forest, losing us. And now, it's no longer an abstract fear.

It's a terrifying reality.

"I made the right decision, and I'd do it again in a heartbeat." Despite the pain of his words, I hold firm. "The love I have for you, our children, Sara, and our family, forced my hand."

"You took my choice and ripped away my control. Made it so I have no choice. Snowden did that, and now you did it too. I can't believe…" He runs his hand over his bare scalp. "I didn't want to have to live through that again. It was horrible."

"Forest…" I stand and keep my voice barely above a whisper in the silent room. "I would do it again. Even knowing this outcome, I would still do it again. Because you'll live."

The hurt and anger in his gaze stings, but there is no end to the lengths I'll go to save him.

With one last look, I turn and walk away, each step echoing in the silent room. The door closes behind me, a physical barrier that mirrors the one Forest erected between us.

I'm cut off from the man I love.

But if this is the price to pay for Forest's life, then I willingly pay it. I'll endure the loneliness, the isolation, the heartache without him. I'll bear this burden for the man I love.

For our family.

For his future.

And for that, I'm willing to endure anything.

Even losing him.

Because the battle for Forest's life has only just begun.

TWENTY-ONE

Paul

———

~

Rain spatters against the windowpane in a cadence that
matches the drumming of my heartbeat. The chilly beat fills the
empty apartment with its somber song.

The coldness of the room sinks into my skin, a stark reminder of
the warmth I left behind. The happy squeals of the twins. Forest's
booming laughter. Sara's lyrical voice.

I hate how unfamiliar these quarters feel; my refuge ever since
Forest dismissed me from his life. I moved out of the home we share
and into the staff dormitories located on the grounds of *Insanity*. I'm
close enough to still see the kids, yet far enough away to respect
Forest's decision to '*never see me again.*'

His absence is a raw, open wound, bleeding and infecting every
corner of this unfamiliar place I now call home.

My chest tightens as I stare into the darkness outside—an abyss
swallowing all comfort and light. It's a mirror image of the
bleakness of my soul. But I welcome it because it's less daunting
than the shifting shadows in the room that draw sharp parallels to
the murkiness of my thoughts.

With just me inhabiting the space, the silence is deafening, interrupted only by the relentless ticking of the clock and the pitter-patter of rain on the windows.

A soft, familiar knock echoes behind me. Without needing an invitation, the door swings open, a boundary respected by familiarity rather than intrusion. The gentle pad of Sara's footsteps echoes in the room, each step resonating with the depth of our shared history, an intimacy as intricate as it is untouched by physicality.

"Paul?" Sara's voice washes over me like a gentle breeze, carrying a soothing warmth that chips away at the icy loneliness infesting my heart. "You're brooding again. Wallowing."

"Just replaying past mistakes." My words come out harsher than I intend, bitterness soaking into each syllable and echoing with the emptiness gnawing at me.

The air subtly shifts as she moves closer. Her gaze on me, sharp and knowing. Sara has a gift. She's always been able to peel away the layers to see the raw emotional turmoil underneath the brave facade I present to the world. She gives a knowing look, like she can see right through me.

"Who cares if I'm wallowing in my misery? God knows, I've tried to become a better man for Forest. A better Master. But I fucked that up. I can wallow if I want."

"Wallow away." Her expression softens as she closes the distance between us. She touches my arm and a spark of electricity zaps us both. "You shocked me."

"Actually, I think you shocked me." I try to laugh it off, but more than static electricity flew through me. I'm viscerally aware of her presence.

"Do you want to talk about your wallowing?" She grips my arm, lending support.

"I'd do it again. I'd do it in a heartbeat to save him."

Her fingers tighten around my arm, her silence a testament to our shared sorrow. "I know you would, and eventually, he'll come around. Just give him time." The warmth in her voice and the sincerity in her eyes comfort me. Our shared love for Forest makes our bond unique.

"How is he?"

"Horrible. Brooding like you. Angry at you. Wallowing in his misery—like you. He's scared and lost. He misses his Master who keeps the darkness at bay. He misses his best friend. He misses the other half of his heart." She hugs my arm, and I'm surprised how that slight contact makes my heart pound. "He's grumpy. He'll never admit it, but he misses you. He misses his better half."

"You're his better half."

"Well, I'm sweet, soft, and tender, but Forest also needs strong, hard, and fierce. He needs someone who will call him out on his shit. He needs the push and pull only you provide."

"I can't get him out of my mind. I keep going back to when we first met. He compared me to my father." The sting of those words still reverberates within me. "I didn't deserve that. Do you think I treated him like Snowden treated him?"

"Ah, the dark and bleak times. I see we're firmly wallowing in the past." Sara lived that darkness. She was there at the very beginning of Forest and me. "Why now?"

"What do you mean?"

"Why are you thinking about Snowden now?"

"Because Forest said I was just like him." Didn't she hear him? She was in the same room when Forest banished me.

"I will never accept that horrible man was your father." Her nose wrinkles in disgust. "And you're nothing like him. Forest was just lashing out, looking to hurt you the only way he could."

"I wasn't really thinking about my father, but you know what's ironic?"

"No, tell me." Sara snuggles up to me.

We're close, but not intimate, yet this feels—intimate. I'm not sure what to make of it, except while I miss Forest, I miss Sara too. Like him, she's a part of who I am.

"The irony of this entire situation, and it's a bitter reminder, is despite my wish to protect Forest, I was once the person who caused him the most pain."

"Snowden caused that pain. You were merely his instrument."

"A loyal son who beat and brutalized so many."

"A son he kept in the fighting rings until he started losing money on you. He brainwashed you from such an early age. Made you think he was your savior when he was something far worse." She props her chin on the tip of my shoulder. "What he did to you was just as bad as what he did to Forest."

"You know…" I lead Sara to the couch and sit. She snuggles up to me as I lean back and pull her into my arms.

"Do I know, what?" She places her hand over my chest, feeling my heartbeat, providing comfort as a dear friend.

"The first time I saw Forest, he took my breath away."

"He does have that effect on people." She breathes out a swoony sigh. "He rescued me from an abusive foster home, and I loved him from that moment on. He took my breath away as well. My first crush. My first love. And the most infuriating man for taking so damn long to figure out he loved me too."

"Why did it take the two of you so long?"

"Because he was gay, silly." She slaps my chest and wiggles beside me. The soft swell of her breast brushes against the side of my chest. Something *shifts* within me: a sudden catch in my breath, a dropped beat of my heart?

"He's always been bi." I nudge her playfully.

"But I didn't know that. He only ever dated men. Actually…" She laughs softly. "He once told me he never dated men. He fucked them. He never showed any interest in me. Little did I know the thought of sex with me terrified him."

"He only knew brutal sex before you came into the picture. I can see why he was worried about hurting you. Especially after what he was forced to do to Skye."

"You know, not to waste too much breath talking about your father, but Snowden brought us together. Forest gave Snowden what he wanted to protect me. It was a knee-jerk reaction, but during our time there, Forest finally realized he didn't do it out of duty, but out of love, and we were more than work colleagues. I hate Snowden, but without him, we wouldn't be where we are today. Isn't that a horrible way to look at it?"

"A lot changed during that time. I felt something for him the moment I laid eyes on him." I struggle to find the right words. "Even though he wasn't mine—I knew someday Forest would belong to me. I didn't know how. But I knew."

She moves closer, her hand still on my chest, but moving down the hard planes of muscle to rest on my abs. "Forest has a way of—of getting under your skin."

"And those eyes… God, Sara, his eyes were filled with so much pain but shined with this indomitable spirit. I was thunderstruck."

"Yeah, he's something else."

"Forest saw the real me, not as his captor, but as a fellow captive in the twisted game my father orchestrated." Even though we're past all of that, guilt still gnaws at my conscience.

Sara says nothing, her silence urging me to continue.

"I remember the tone of his voice when he accepted his fate. How he protected you. The way he knelt to my father, but his eyes remained defiant. His strength… It stirred something within me. It was the beginning of my downfall—and the beginning of my redemption."

"You've come a long way from who you were."

"Forest made me want to be more than I was. And for the first time in my life, I dared to hope that might be possible. With Forest, it felt like I could change."

Sara's embrace tightens, her silent support anchoring me in this storm of my own creation.

"Do you think he'll ever forgive me?"

"He needs time." She places her hand over mine. "He loves you; we both do. But right now, he's hurt, and he needs space to heal."

I nod, understanding her words even if they feel like a punch to the gut. "I miss him, every second of every day."

In this, Sara and I are one. Our minds and hearts are tied to the same man, the man we both love, the man who is the very core of our existence.

The silence stretches between us, both lost in our own thoughts about Forest. I glance at Sara, her eyes mist with tears. She's beautiful in her vulnerability, reminding me so much of him.

There's a push and pull between us, a shared pain and a shared love that draws us together in this moment. When I look at her, really look at her, there's a faint stirring, a recognition of something deeper in our shared history.

She meets my gaze, her eyes reflecting the same turmoil. Placing her hand over mine, she leans against me. The heat of her hand seeps into my skin, her fingers gently tracing circles over the back of my hand. It's a small gesture, but it sends sparks dancing along the nerves of my hand.

My heart pounds, its beat echoing loudly in the silence. The distance between us seems to shrink, the warmth of her body drawing me closer.

The air shifts, the tension pulling taut.

"Sara," I whisper, my voice catching in my throat, thick with emotion and something else—an unfamiliar longing. Her name feels new on my lips, intimate in a way it's never been before. A whisper shared between the hush of our heartbeats.

She meets my gaze, her eyes wide and expectant, mirroring my own uncertainty. There's a magnetic pull tugging at me. A spark of something crackling in the air between us. I lean in, slowly, giving her a chance to pull away, but she doesn't.

TWENTY-TWO

Paul

~

The distance between us melts away.

Her breath hitches. She closes her eyes. I lean in, and the whole world seems to hold its breath with us.

Is this really happening?

Her warmth radiates outward, burning my skin. Her soft exhales ghost over my lips, carrying the sweet scent of her to flood my senses and stir my desire. I close the distance between us, my lips brushing hers in a soft, hesitant kiss. The moment our lips meet, it's like touching a live wire, a current that sparks and hums with eagerness and desire.

It's nothing like the fierce, dominating kisses I share with Forest, but it's just as intoxicating. It's gentle and exploratory, a kiss that speaks of shared pain and shared love. Her lips are soft, softer than anything I've ever known, and sweet against mine, a contrast to the roughness of men that I'm used to.

And I like it.

It's different, new, something that's ours. My heart skips a beat, then roars into life with fierce intensity and raw desire building within me.

She leans into the kiss, her hand squeezing mine, a featherlight touch that sends ripples of warmth cascading down my spine.

It's not the explosive, rough passion I've experienced with Forest. This is a slow burn, a simmering heat that builds and builds, until I feel it in the very marrow of my bones. Her hand squeezes mine, an anchor in the swirling sea of new sensations. The taste of her lips, the feel of her breath mingling with mine, the gentle press of her body against mine—it's all so incredibly intoxicating.

Soft.

Gentle.

Feminine.

I pull back, reluctantly breaking the sweet contact. My breath comes in ragged gasps as if that simple kiss stole the air from my lungs.

Her eyes flutter open, wide and surprised, reflecting my own shock. She's beautiful, her cheeks flushed and lips slightly swollen from our kiss. And suddenly, I realize how deeply entangled we've become in this intricate web of shared love and pain.

Our eyes meet in the silent aftermath of the kiss, confusion and surprise mirrored in our gazes. The moment feels suspended, our breaths held captive as our hearts race in tandem. We've trespassed a boundary that was always there, invisible but inviolable.

I pull away slowly.

"I-I…" Words fail me. My mind races to comprehend the seismic shift our relationship has just experienced. We're no longer united only through Forest. This kiss reshaped everything.

Just when I think I've gathered my thoughts, Sara gently cups my face, her thumb tracing the line of my jaw in a touch that feels electric. Her gaze is intense, burning into mine with an emotion I can't decipher.

"Paul…" she begins, but then she leans in again, her lips brushing against mine. A spark ignites, consuming my thoughts in a wild inferno.

Like a dam bursting, I surge forward, my hand cupping the back of her neck, pulling her closer.

Suddenly, I kiss her back with a fervor that shocks me. The quiet intensity from before morphs into a wildfire raging through my body, a firestorm of want, need, and desire for more. My fingers thread through her hair, pulling her closer. The feel of her against my body, the taste of her on my lips, it's all too intoxicating.

Our bodies move in sync, lips and tongues exploring, as if guided by an unseen force. I flip her around, laying her down on the couch, and lean over her as our lips fuse with the kiss.

Our second kiss isn't soft or hesitant. It's a declaration, wild and untamed. It's everything the first wasn't—hot and needy, the languid pace replaced by desperation. Our bodies press closer, a frisson of passion and desire. A surge of energy, primal and fierce, rushes through me, unlike anything I've ever experienced.

My lips move against hers with a fervor that shocks me. I taste the surprise in her gasp, feel it in the stiffening of her body, but then she melts against me, kissing me back with a passion that matches my own.

Her fingers thread through my hair, tugging gently, and the sensation sends sparks shooting down my spine. My fingers thread through her hair, gripping tight, pulling her even closer. I explore her mouth with my tongue, a dance of passion and desire, her taste intoxicating me.

My other hand skates down her side, feeling the soft curve of her waist, the flare of her hip, before it comes to rest on her thigh. Then my fingers move up, slipping beneath her shirt to explore the soft swell of her breasts.

She gasps into my mouth, a soft, breathy sound that sends a jolt of heat straight to my core. Emboldened, I hitch her leg up over my hip, pulling her flush against me. The heat of her pussy stirs my cock and I grow long and hard for her.

Our bodies align perfectly, a puzzle piece fitting into place, and the feel of her pressed so intimately against me…

It's overwhelming.

The room fills with the sounds of our ragged breaths and quiet moans, a symphony of desire as we kiss and explore.

Sara's fingers clutch at my shirt, tugging me closer, and I drown in a sea of sensations. Together, we rip off my shirt and I'm right back in there, kissing her again. Every brush of her lips, every caress of her hands is a spark that feeds the wildfire within me. The tension coils tighter and tighter, the edge dangerously close.

While my hands cup her breasts and my fingers tease her nipples, Sara begins her own exploration. She runs her hands down my back, fingers gliding across my shoulders, feeling around my waist where she tugs at my pants. Her hands brush against my erection, then her fingers slide beneath the waistband of my pants to touch me there.

It's a whirlpool of heat and desire, pulling us deeper. I can't recall ever feeling so consumed by anyone or anything like this. It's an intoxicating mix of fear and excitement. This is unknown territory, and we're reckless in our rush to explore everything.

My hand moves from her thigh to the heat of her core. Then, like her, my hand slips beneath her waistband. Her soft sighs fan the flames of my desire.

My hips jerk as her fingers curl around my cock. The sensations consume me, igniting nerves I didn't even know existed. I'm hard for her.

Hard for a woman.

Is this happening?

It's a whirlpool of heat and desire, pulling me in deeper and deeper. This is spiraling out of control. It's too much. Too fast. Too unexpected, and then reality rushes back, tossing a bucket of cold water on our desire.

What are we doing?

Forest—our connection, our love for him is tangled in this moment, making it both exhilarating and confusing.

"Sara," I gasp, pulling away. My breath comes out ragged and raw. "We… We can't."

The reality of what we're doing, the line we're crossing… It's all too much. The taste of her is still on my lips, the warmth of her body still presses against me. But this isn't right. Not without Forest.

"Why not?" she asks, her voice breathy, her lips glistening from our kisses.

"Forest…" I trail off, the reality of what we were doing hitting me like a punch to the gut. Forest. Our shared link. The man we both love.

"It's not fair to him," I manage to say, my voice barely more than a whisper. "We can't do this without him knowing. It… It wouldn't be right."

We sit in silence, trying to digest the reality of our actions. What we've done can't be undone. And yet, even amidst the turmoil, I can't find it within myself to regret the kisses we shared.

The implications of our actions heat the air.

Things between us will never be the same.

There's no turning back. Whatever happens next, we can't ignore the truth any longer. We're more entwined than we ever knew, and like Forest, I'm not gay. I'm definitely bisexual and I want to have sex with Sara.

I stand firmly on the line with one foot firmly planted on each side. My entire life, I thought I only liked men, but my body's desperate to take Sara and claim her as mine.

A bubble of panic begins to swell within me, a dread that I may have just crossed a line that can't be uncrossed. "Sara…"

"It's okay." She places a finger against my lips, silencing me. "I don't regret it."

"I don't want to drive an ever-bigger wedge between me and Forest. I don't want him thinking I'm doing anything behind his back."

The rain continues to drive against the windows, a stark contrast to the heated silence within the room. It's a strange moment of stolen time, but it's also a moment of understanding, of shared emotions that run deeper than any physical intimacy.

That kiss was an inevitable collision of shared love and longing, a quiet realization that we're more than just a throuple, two couples united through Forest. We're bound by something uniquely our own.

We're a triad. Three people deeply in love.

It's uncharted territory for both of us, and we should tread carefully, considering not just ourselves, but also Forest. The man we both love, the man who brought us together, the man whose absence forced us to confront feelings we've always dismissed as platonic.

"Where do we go from here?" Sara asks, her voice barely above a whisper.

"I don't know," I confess, meeting her gaze with an intensity that matches hers. "But Forest needs to know."

The reality of what we've done begins to seep in, washing over me like the aftermath of a storm. There's fear, of course, fear of what this could mean for us.

For Forest.

But there's also something else—a sense of relief, of rightness, that I can't quite put into words.

"We'll figure it out together. After all, isn't that what family does?" She squeezes my hand in silent agreement. Then she laughs.

"What's so funny?"

"The one thing Forest's always wanted is for the three of us to have sex. Maybe that will tempt him into forgiving you."

"I doubt it will be that easy."

She rolls her eyes, then fixes me with a serious look. "How does something like that work?"

"Something like, what?"

"Well, the three of us, together?"

"Sleeping?" I can't help but tease her.

"Having sex?" She rolls her eyes and playfully shoves me.

"Hmm, I can think of several ways, depending on how adventurous you want to get."

"Um, when you say adventurous, are you talking about—downstairs?" She gulps, barely getting the words out. "Because I don't think…"

I can't help but laugh. "I was thinking about anal sex, not dominance and submission."

"Oh, good." She holds up a hand and dips her head, showing her unease. "I don't think I'm ready for that yet. Although, I can definitely see why Forest lets you dominate him."

"You can?"

"You're pretty fierce. Very yummy; Alpha strong. Honestly, I don't get the whole pain thing, but the getting tied up bit?" She nibbles on her lower lip and can't meet my eye.

"You like getting tied up?"

"Never tried it."

"Being dominated? Told what to do?"

"Never tried it."

Holy mother of… I shake my head, dispelling that thought. Sara and I are a long way from any of that. Her mention of Forest makes me picture him on his knees. My cock weeps for him, but Forest's not speaking to me.

The basement will have to wait.

"Are you secretly submissive?" A tingling sensation rushes through me.

"Don't know. Never dated a dominant man before, let alone have sex with one." She shrugs, but there's a grin on her face and a sparkle in her eyes. "Forest seems to enjoy it."

"Thinking about you tied up in my bed is making my cock stand at full mast." Fuck, I'm hard and aching for her.

"Then we should hurry up and tell Forest."

"He's not speaking to me. You tell him."

"I don't want to hide this from him," she shakes her head. "It's not right, but I also don't want to tell him without you."

We take a breather, talking about Forest, about the past, about redemption, and I realize although my heart aches for Forest, it finds comfort in the shared understanding I have with Sara.

We're drawn together by the man we both love, but as we sit together, it's clear we're also bound by a new love—one blooming between us, slowly but surely, in the most unexpected of places.

She's as much a part of me as Forest, and it took losing Forest to see what's been right in front of my face all along. She's here, supporting me, holding me together when I feel like falling apart.

We continue to talk, our conversation meandering from the past, to the present, and into an uncertain future. I don't know what will happen next, but I feel a glimmer of hope for the first time since Forest kicked me out.

And I love how Sara cares enough about me to keep checking in on me. If there is a path back to Forest, she will build that bridge.

Eventually, Sara leaves, needing to get back to Forest and the kids. Unfortunately, that leaves me with nothing but my thoughts.

And who do I think about?

Dream about?
Forest fills my dreams.
And for the first time, Sara's in there as well.

TWENTY-THREE

Paul

~

THE FOLLOWING NIGHT FINDS ME AT THE EDGE OF THE CLIFF looking out over the ocean. My mind dares to traverse the twisted maze of past memories, settling on a poignant encounter with Forest —a haunting memory that revisits like a ghost reluctant to pass on to the other side, but a disturbance in the air, my eyes flutter open, snapping me out of my nightmares.

"Ash thought it was you out here. Do you want company?" Skye smiles as she approaches. Her eyes cloud with concern, mirroring the torment inside me. "Were you dreaming about him again?" My dreams are private, but the fact they torment me is public knowledge.

"I can't stop thinking about him."

"Bad dreams? Or good ones?" She slips beside me, letting her legs dangle from the observation deck.

After Forest kicked me out of our home, I should've moved into *Insanity* grounds. It would lessen the constant torture when I see Forest in the distance, but Delia and Sebastian are as much mine as his. He can't keep me from seeing them.

I run my fingers through my hair and rub the sleep from my eyes. "It's late. What are you doing here?"

"I was in the kitchen with Ash for a midnight snack when Sara came through, eyes puffy and fighting tears."

"She was crying?" The urge to go to her overwhelms me.

"Does it surprise you? Why are men so thick-headed?" She rolls her eyes, then draws her legs to her chest, propping her chin on her knees. A light breeze blows wisps of her hair in her face.

"What's that supposed to mean?"

"Do you really not know?"

"Know, what?"

"This whole thing is hard on Sara. Sometimes you and Forest are so freakin' blind. She loves you."

"I love her too."

"Okay, let me put it another way. Sara is *in love* with you."

I return a blank stare. How does Skye know? One hundred percent, I'm certain Sara would say nothing about what happened to anyone.

"Geez, men are hopeless. Sara's been cursed in life that the men she loves are idiots."

"I'm sharing my life with Sara." An intense ache pulses within me. I want to stop pretending there's nothing going on between me and Sara.

"You share Forest with Sara while being blind to how things have changed between you and her. Think about it."

"Our dynamic is challenging for most people to understand."

"I'm not most people, and instead of going to bed like I should, I decided to come here to knock some sense into your head. Sara loves you. She misses you. And she's terrified of losing you over this thing with Forest. Yes, you're a throuple. And yes, Forest kicked you out. But that doesn't mean Sara wants you gone. The poor thing is trying to raise two kids, deal with a husband who's the most obstinate man on the planet, manage his illness, and *oh by the way...* she's terrified of losing you. She doesn't just share Forest with you. Sara honestly loves you, and like any woman, she craves emotional and physical intimacy with both of the men she loves."

"I know." I shouldn't say anything, but I can't deny my love for Sara.

"I've seen the way she looks at you. The way the two of you hold each other." Skye pauses. "Wait. You know what?"

"That she loves me."

"I love Forest like a brother and I can definitely say we never look at each other the way you and Sara look at each other. Have the two of your ever…"

"No!" I jump at Skye's comment. "I'm gay."

I don't want it getting out that my feelings for Sara have changed, or that hers for me have changed. The first person who needs to know is the one man who's not speaking to me.

Not Skye.

"Yeah, that's what Forest said and look where he is now? A man with a Master and a wife, both of whom he loves unconditionally."

"I'm not his Master anymore." The words land like a bare-knuckle blow to the stomach, leaving me breathless as if all the air has been punched out of me.

Skye's presence comforts me, a reminder of our shared experiences. She's silent for a moment, her gaze fixed on me. I can almost see the gears in her head grinding together.

"You'll always be Forest's Master."

"I think that boat sank. With me on it."

"Sank?"

I think it's supposed to be 'that boat sailed,' but I was on the boat with Forest, Sara too, and now it's nothing but wreckage and flotsam. I royally fucked my life and the ones I love.

"Tell me about your dreams." The sudden shift in conversation takes me by surprise.

I need to tread lightly. This conversation could open up old wounds, but if anyone can understand me, it's Skye. She's been through the same hell, victim to the same man—Snowden.

"My dreams?"

"You never answered my question."

"What question was that?"

"Are they good dreams, or bad dreams, about Forest?"

"Everything about him." I find myself chuckling humorlessly. "The good. The bad. The ugly."

"Tell me."

"You really don't want to hear…"

"I love everything about Forest. Which means I love you like a brother. Sara like a sister. And even Forest when I want to throttle him. Honestly, it looks like you need to talk, and I'm really good at listening. Not to mention, I've lived his pain. Who better than me to talk to?"

I cock my head, debating whether to talk to Skye. How much to open up to her. In the end, losing Forest is a raw, bleeding wound, and I'm not coping well.

"I was dreaming about one of the first times I saw him holding onto his pride like a shield."

"Sounds like Forest. Was that the first time you saw him?"

"No." A coarse laugh escapes me. "The first time was something else entirely."

"Tell me." She leans back, getting settled.

"I'll start with my dreams." I lean back and gaze at the stars.

"A good place to start, but I'm really curious about the day you met."

"All I can say is he stole my breath the first time I saw him, but seeing him chained and bruised, yet still proud and fiercely defiant? Now that pulled at something within me." I pause, recollecting my dream and everything it encompasses. "Are you sure you want to hear this? It's not pretty?"

"I lived *not pretty* with Forest. Nothing you can say will shock me, and like I said, I'm probably the only one, besides you and Sara, who knows what Forest can endure. And what he likes. There are no secrets."

"I can't get him out of my mind. His image… His spirit… It haunts me. God, he was so defiant. Battered, chained… Yet so proud. He intrigued me. My father wanted me to break Forest, to force him into submission, but all I saw was a man refusing to break, even under the most monstrous pressure. How much do you know about the time he spent with Snowden?"

"The CliffsNotes' version." She shrugs. "Forest never shared with me. He had you and Sara. The three of you lived it, but I know bits and pieces."

I meet her understanding gaze. "Snowden wanted me to be the cause of Forest's pain. He wasn't strong enough to force Forest's submission. His obsession with Forest was… It was sickening. Snowden watched my every move, relishing the pain I inflicted. He saw in me a reflection of his own youth, a time when he was strong enough to exploit a defenseless boy caught in the horrors of the foster system."

"Yeah, those are difficult memories." She rubs her arms.

"Sorry, I didn't mean to…"

"No, it's okay. I want to hear how you fell in love with my brother." Her voice trembles when she responds, her eyes filling with unshed tears. "We were both Snowden's victims. But Forest… Forest was different. Even as a kid, he was—resilient."

"I wouldn't call it falling in love. At least not at first. Snowden's obsession with Forest was a palpable force. He wanted to break Forest. He saw it as a victory—his revenge on Forest. The more Forest suffered, the stronger he became, the more I saw how pain fueled his reason to keep fighting."

"Forest's always been a fighter." Her voice fills with a sad kind of pride. "No one could break him, not even Snowden."

"As you know, the cost of Sara's safety was Forest's submission to my father's vile desires—a price Forest willingly paid. Forest didn't hesitate. He dropped to his knees and bowed his head. He did everything and anything to save Sara." I swallow past the lump in my throat, my voice hoarse with emotion. "It was horrific."

"I remember." She was there the day Forest fell to Snowden's power.

"My father made me the harbinger of Forest's pain. I was supposed to shatter him, and a part of me—the darkest part of me wanted to do it—but the more I saw into Forest's mind, the more I hurt him, the stronger he became."

Skye doesn't respond for a moment. When she finally speaks, her voice is steady. "Forest has always been a survivor. He turns pain into power."

"He sure as shit does. Although stripped bare and vulnerable, he displayed a tenacity that baffled me. His fiery spirit ignited a spark of empathy within me. He held onto his fierce resolve—an unspoken promise that he wouldn't be broken, not by me, not by my father, not by anyone.

"I can see him doing that."

"I found his courage disconcerting." A smile tugs at the corners of my mouth. "I became obsessed with him, not as my victim, but as an equal. I saw myself in him, in his resilience. He wasn't *just* a captive. He… He became my reason."

"He became your salvation."

"Yes." I pause, collecting my thoughts. "His resilience stirred something within me. I admired him, feared him—and wanted him. God, did I want him. His endurance in the face of despair… It was inspiring. Every brutal command from my father, every lash, brought me closer to losing my humanity, to morphing into my father's image. Yet, in the midst of despair, Forest remained resolute, a beacon of survival and endurance. He was the light in my darkness, illuminating a path toward redemption. That was the start of my transformation into the man Forest needed, the man I yearned to be."

She watches me intently, absorbing my confession. "He brought out the best in you. When you saved him, he saved you."

"I don't know about that, but I do know this: I'm not the monster my father wanted me to be. And I owe that to Forest."

A silence descends upon us, both lost in our thoughts. After a while, Skye breaks the silence. "Forest is a testament to survival. He reminds us of the strength we possess. That what we endured doesn't define us."

Another memory claws at me. Like the rest, it refuses to be diminished by time.

A room faintly lit by the harsh glow of a bare bulb, the air tainted with the stench of fear and pain, a constant testament to Snowden's depravity. In the heart of that grim tableau stood Forest.

Chained to the wall, he didn't strain against the restraints. He couldn't. Any resistance put Sara in jeopardy. Yet, he still radiated a quiet strength.

A billionaire locked in a war against my father's empire of

human trafficking, he embodied everything my father despised. It justified the pain I inflicted on Forest, viewing him as my enemy.

Yet, as I faced him, his calm unsettled me. His icy gaze seemed to cut through me, forcing me to face a truth I had been avoiding. His ice-blue eyes radiated an intensity that stoked an attraction I couldn't ignore.

"You know," I shift to a more comfortable position, "in the beginning, Forest was just another challenge, nothing more. But as time went on, the initial resentment I harbored for him evolved."

"How so?"

"Instead of seeing him as another victim for my sadistic pleasure, I paid attention to his unique response to pain. How it strengthened him. How his eyes ignited with something raw and intoxicating. The more he fed on my pain, the more I supplied."

"He was trained to only experience pleasure through pain," Skye says. "But I think his darker cravings were always there. Pain and pleasure are intricately bound together within Forest's basic makeup. Much like how sadism is such an integral part of who you are. You both crave the pleasure only pain can bring."

"It took me a long time to understand that. Each step toward Forest felt like a betrayal to my father, but I was too engrossed in the enigma that was Forest, and my growing attraction to him, to care. Forest didn't just endure the pain; he harnessed it, thriving under its influence."

"That sounds like a turning point."

"That epiphany shifted our dynamics." It's hard to explain how Forest turned everything I thought I knew about myself on its head. "Our sessions evolved over time. With each lash, each moan, each heated exchange, an unspoken connection formed. We shared an intimate dance of pain and pleasure, dominance and submission. Depravity, degradation, and more."

"Forest was no longer your captive."

"He became my reason to live. Approaching him sent shivers down my spine. My job was to break him, to force his submission to Snowden, but his gaze—the way he begged for my pain—it gave me pause. And the way he responded to my touch…"

I lean back, and smile. I couldn't have this conversation with anyone but Skye. With her, these glimpses into my relationship with Forest, the dark way they evolved, doesn't feel wrong.

"And his eyes… Those ice-blue eyes held an intensity that delved all the way down to the black pit that was my soul." My heart hurts being separated from Forest. "There was something magnetic about him. Even in his broken state, he radiated a quiet strength that drew me in. I couldn't help but admire him. At the time, I didn't understand how deeply Forest craved pain, or how he needed it to keep the darkness within him at bay."

That understanding came much later, and in part, has to do with Skye—in what he was forced to do to her when they were in foster care.

"But you do keep that darkness at bay. His relationship with Sara is a healthy one because of you. It's full of love and tenderness. You allowed that growth within him. He's come an incredibly long way, in a large part because of you."

It wasn't until after Forest and Sara's rescue that Forest and I became Master and slave, sadist and masochist, engaged in a dark dance where the rhythm was set by my whip and the beat punctuated by his stifled moans.

He transformed the basement beneath our home into a space where pain and pleasure melded; a gruesome dance floor where we pirouetted in this perverse ballet.

It was there where he knelt before me for the first time, asking to bind his will to mine. Begging me to master him. His eyes glinted with so much defiance, yet simmered with the fiercest need to be used and degraded. He always challenged me, pushing me to go further, to delve deeper into his masochism. Begging me to feed his inner demons.

"Forest and I are two sides of the same twisted coin."

"I couldn't agree with you more. It's why I know things are not finished between the two of you. The three of you, actually. I challenge you to explore the feelings you have for Sara. Open a door."

"Open a door?"

"She's your path back to Forest."

"Forest made his wishes clear."

Our darkness mirrors each other, our pain resonates on the same frequency. We're a pair of paradoxes—two men bound by our mutual need for pain, and linked by a bond that's far more profound than I ever expected to find in this life.

In the end, I never broke Forest.

No man can break the towering giant. Even cancer hasn't broken his will.

Forest opened his soul to me. He invited me in. He swore an oath to be mine for a lifetime.

He became my reason to live.

As Skye looks at me, her gaze softens with understanding. I'm glad I finally had this chance to sit down with her and confide in her. The things I've done to Forest, both during his time with Snowden and after, have always made me uncomfortable when I'm around her—as if she judges me and doesn't approve of the odd relationship Forest chose with me and with Sara.

This wall of silence has stood between us for too long.

"Skye…" My voice chokes with the weight of the unspoken. "Thank you for sitting here, listening to me. I feel like I've needed to do this from the beginning and clear the air."

"Clear the air?"

"The things I did to your brother were horrific. The things we do together are questionable."

"I know Forest, and I've never judged you. I know what happened between the two of you. I know what the two of you do when you're alone. Forest came to me when he wanted to ask for your collar, needing you to be his Master. I understand what drives Forest. I don't judge him, and I've never judged you. As far as talking, I'm always here if you need me."

"Thank you. That means the world to me." I take in a deep breath. "You know I would do anything for him."

"I know."

"But I broke his trust. I shouldn't have used my position to circumvent his wishes." The words tumble out, the relief of sharing the burden almost unbearable.

She nods slowly. "You did it to save him. Forest may be angry, but he knows why you did what you did. Don't forget, Mitzy and I were right there with you, and don't forget what you gave him."

"Gave him?"

"You gave him the sister he never knew he had. That's a tremendous gift. In this, I'm of the same mind as Ash. A greater power is at work here."

"I would do anything for Forest."

"I would too. He inspires loyalty."

"There's something else. I don't think it ever made it into the after-action report, but when the Guardians came to rescue Forest, he tried to strangle Snowden. I couldn't let him do that—have that stain on his soul. So, I… I killed Snowden for him." The ghost of my past actions looms large. "I killed my father to save the man I love."

Skye reaches out, her hand closing over mine. Her eyes reflect a strength I've always admired. "I understand that need to protect Forest at all costs. You're not alone in killing someone to save him. We both share that sin."

"What…?" I stammer, my heart pounding in my chest.

TWENTY-FOUR

Paul

~

THE SILENCE BETWEEN SKYE AND ME THICKENS, PUNCTUATED ONLY by the booming of the heavy surf below the cliffs. The soft glow from the moon paints her face in stark relief. Her eyes glisten with unshed tears.

My own confession hangs in the air like a specter, a truth that binds us in an unexpected way.

She grips my hand, as if anchoring herself, but then her grip slackens and she withdraws, using it instead to wring her fingers nervously in her lap.

"I'm going to tell you something. Something I've never told anyone." She glances at me, the vulnerability in her gaze chilling. "It's about Clark Preston, our foster father. He brought Snowden into our lives and Snowden was not kind to either of us."

My heart pounds, a drumbeat that quickens with her every word as a sense of foreboding overcomes me. This secret of Skye's feels heavy. Ominous. Her voice is soft, as delicate as porcelain, yet a steeliness underscores her resolve.

"Forest and I were seventeen. Forest was months from aging out of the foster system. I was weeks behind him. Snowden was closing in. He knew he would lose us if he didn't do something."

Her eyes get lost in the past. "He had his sights set on us, on Forest. He wanted me as his slave, but he wanted Forest for his death rings. You know about those?"

"That I do."

A shudder courses through me at the mention of the death rings. I know them well. I survived them, tossed into unimaginable violence when I was just a kid. Forest in such a scenario is a thought too terrifying to entertain.

RANCID SWEAT, GREASY FOOD, AND THE STENCH OF STALE BEER CLING heavily to the humid air. I wrinkle my nose, my empty stomach roiling with nerves as I'm shoved into the dingy warehouse. Harsh overhead lights illuminate a makeshift fighting pit circled by shouting, leering men. The throbbing, pulsing mob presses close, their eyes feverish and lips wet with depraved excitement as crumpled bills and coins exchange hands for wagers.

A meaty hand clamps down on my bony shoulder, steering me toward the pit where another boy stands hunched and trembling. He can't be more than ten, maybe eleven, the same as me. Grimy tear tracks mark his hollow cheeks.

My pulse hammers as the shouting intensifies, the crushing grip propelling me closer. Blood roars in my ears, nearly drowning out the surrounding din. The men leer with feverish, depraved excitement, pressing so close I can smell their sour breath. "Fight, you worthless runts!"

The man holding me gives a rough shove between my shoulder blades. I stumble into the pit, chest heaving with panic, my heart slamming against my ribs. The other boy won't look at me, thin arms wrapped tightly around his frail body as it trembles uncontrollably.

"I said fight!" A beer bottle shatters on the concrete near our feet.

I cry out as shards of glass slice into the soles of my bare feet, searing pain radiating up my legs. The other boy howls as a shard pierces his heel. Rivulets of blood mix with the grime on the floor, the slick wetness causing us to slip. We thrash wildly trying to stay on our feet.

Behind the smeared dirt and lingering baby fat, his eyes swim with the same paralyzing fear gripping my insides. He meets my gaze, eyes round with shock and animal panic. Then his face hardens with desperate resolve. Before I can react, his small fist plows into my gut.

I double over, wheezing as bitter bile surges up my throat. No choice now but to fight back. I tackle him onto the unforgiving concrete, glass digging into our knees and elbows. He struggles wildly as my fists pummel his face.

Revulsion wells up inside at having to hurt this innocent boy. But failure means punishment, means death at the hands of the monsters who've taken us.

With a feral cry fueled by blind panic, I launch myself at the boy. He yelps, dodging my wild swing. My fist just grazes his jaw in a clumsy blow. I don't really know how to fight.

The men roar approval, stomping and hollering, oblivious to our pain. I feel his nose crunch wetly under my knuckles, but he doesn't stop fighting back. We thrash and punch, united in desperation, our feet bleeding, the floor slick.

Our young lives are mere entertainment, worth less than their wad of cash collected after only one of us limps out alive.

I strike again, but the boy scampers back. Silent tears stream down his grimy cheeks, but he makes no move to hit me back. He's already given up hope. But I can't. Not if I want to survive this hell.

I rush him in a panic, slamming us both to the hard concrete floor. He doesn't resist as my small fists pummel his face over and over, his life traded for mine. The brutality sickens me, but I can't stop.

I have to win.

At last, his blows weaken until his head lolls limply aside, eyes empty and staring. I roll off him, gasping raggedly before dragging myself upright on rubbery legs. The men's cheers ring in my ears, but all I hear is the roaring silence of his shattered life bleeding out on the pit floor.

My knuckles throb, and my soul shrivels. I stand hunched, awaiting judgment for my violent victory from the monsters who've forced me to become one of their own. The metallic stench of fresh blood now mixes with the other foul odors clinging to the humid air.

I clench my stinging fists and stare numbly ahead. Something in me dies along with that boy in the dirt. But another part hardens, already adapting to survive this vicious world I've been plunged into.

Over the next few months, I'm pitted against boy after boy, and my skills only sharpen. I become a machine of precise, unfeeling violence. Survival demands it and hones me into a devastating weapon.

A sure bet.

I no longer hesitate when the metal door screeches open, and they drag me to the next fight. This is what I must do to see another sunrise.

At first, I avoid their frightened eyes, granting them that small mercy. But soon, I can't afford even that shred of humanity. Meeting their gazes forces me to acknowledge the terror and despair of innocent souls condemned to death for sport.

I learn to stare through them, their faces blurring into a series of faceless opponents. My blows turn mechanical and cold, lethally efficient. Motions necessary for survival, devoid of feeling or meaning. I try to dispatch them quickly and efficiently, staring just over their shoulders or at the dirt turning crimson beneath our feet. I kill and kill and feel nothing.

I'm just a means to an end.

The rabid cries of the men batter my ears as I enter the bloodstained ring. The crowd roars and stomps, a cacophony that reverberates through the concrete floor and up through the soles of my bare feet. I'm a crowd favorite, no longer a scrawny boy but a lean and deadly force of nature. Shouts of "Red Devil" follow my movements, both taunts and twisted endearments. I am their champion, death walking in a boy's hollow frame.

No boy leaves my ring alive anymore.

My cell remains solitary now between fights. Friendship engenders weakness, so I keep my distance. Speaking is unnecessary; communication wastes breath between the brutality. I simply eat, sleep, and eliminate the next nameless victim.

A shell forms around me, my humanity buried deep beneath the monster they created. I'm numb to the horrors committed by hands I no longer recognize as my own.

One less nightmare to haunt me as long as the beast they forged keeps fighting. He will never stop, and I'm grateful for the numbness.

But beneath the hollow brutality, anger simmers. Dark fury at the monsters who forged me into this merciless creature. Outwardly I am ice, but flames rage inside, building in intensity. One day, the inferno will ignite, and they will burn. But not yet.

For now, this shell keeps me alive. So I embrace the emptiness, knowing my chance for retribution will come. And on that day, the devil they created will rain hellfire down upon them all without mercy. Only then will I be free.

After one more effortless victory, the door screeches open, but no one grabs me. The boss man stands back, gesturing sharply for me to exit. His eyes shine with newfound fear. He sees the monster he helped create.

I'm marched upstairs to a smokey office. Behind a heavy oak desk sits a man who can only be the BOSS himself. His smile is cruel when he motions me forward. "The prodigy returns. Quite a winning streak you're on, Red."

I stare numbly ahead, face blank. John Snowden's reputation paints him as a sadist without equal. I must be careful.

Snowden taps his fingers on the desk. "Almost too impressive. Men are grumbling about the lost bets." He smirks. "Seems you're too good at your work."

I stay silent, sensing danger in engaging this viper.

"But so much talent shouldn't go to waste." He leans back, regarding me thoughtfully. "How would you like to work for me directly? I could use someone with your killer instincts. And you need a new way to be...useful."

Every fiber of me wants to refuse, but Snowden's stare makes it clear this offer is not optional. I bow my head in acquiescence.

Snowden grins, satisfied at this proof of his absolute power. But beneath my hollow exterior, the flames of rage burn hotter. One day I will be the death of him, I vow it silently.

For now, I am his creature. But once I'm strong enough, the devil they created will finally turn against them all. My hour will come.

Snowden studies me, his smile shrinking into a contemplative line. "Never thought a scrawny runt like you would be the last one standing. I figured you wouldn't make it past the first week."

My fists clench involuntarily. Something sinister lurks beneath his falsely congenial tone.

"Especially after I slit your sister's throat." He snaps his fingers. "Piper, wasn't it?"

Rage ignites in my core, momentarily cracking my hollow facade. He murdered my sister? My hands tremble with the urge to wrap around his neck and squeeze.

Snowden's eyes glint, relishing my reaction. He misses none of this. "Yes, let the hate flow through you. Can't deny my blood in your veins, boy."

I go perfectly still, unsure I heard him correctly over the roaring in my ears.

He bares his teeth in a mocking grin. "Surprised?"

My knees nearly buckle. Son? This vile demon spawned me?

"And your whore mother, she squealed real sweet when I gutted her." Snowden drags his fingernail across his neck, his smile growing. "Should've known my seed would be a survivor. But I had to see if you had the stomach for it first. You'll do well in the family business. Welcome home, son."

I sway, gutted by these revelations. The monster who forged me into a killer, and murdered my sister, is my father. He slaughtered my family? Bitter bile rises in my throat.

Snowden may have created me, but he does not own me. I swear my sister's death will be avenged.

For now, I bow my head, the obedient son. But when my moment comes, there will be no mercy.

He should've killed me when he had the chance.

~

I stare out at the inky blackness where the sky and the ocean become one. Wind whips up the steep cliff, ruffling my hair as Skye continues her horrifying story.

"I-I couldn't let that happen. I couldn't let Snowden take Forest. At the time, even though Forest was seventeen, he was still spindly and weak. He was my Beanpole for a reason. He didn't grow into what he is now until his mid-twenties. He would have died in those fights." Skye swallows, her throat bobbing with the effort. The next words she speaks are almost too quiet, a murmur lost in the hush of the room. "So I killed Clark Preston."

Her confession rings in my ears, a harsh, dissonant echo. Skye, the woman who had suffered so much, a woman who dedicates her life to saving others, took a life to save Forest?

What a terrible, twisted sacrifice.

"It was our only way out. His death freed us from that life. I had a choice. I chose Forest, and we chose to stick together. To be a family." Her voice steadies, the raw edges of her confession smoothing over with a veneer of determination.

"How does no one know this?"

"Nobody knows. Nobody but you. Ash knows some of it, but not the worst part. The official record of what happened is Clark Preston tried to rape me and I fought back in self-defense. But I planned the whole thing. It's a secret we swore to take to the grave." Her eyes brim with unshed tears. The room hums with the weight of her admission, her act of protection now a tangible entity between us.

"Why tell me this?"

"Because I believe you love Forest as much, or more than I do, and that you would never do anything to hurt him. It's why I helped with the bone marrow drive. It's why I'm sharing this with you now."

In that moment, I understand the depth of Skye's bond with Forest. She, like me, would do anything to protect him. The lines that once demarcated our lives blur and intersect. We're united in our sins and our desperate love for the same man.

"The road ahead is going to be tough. Tougher than what he's been through so far. Tough enough that he chose not to face it for good reason. It's easier to embrace death instead of the chemo and radiation he faces. He's going to need you now, more than ever."

In the oppressive silence, our shared confession resonates, a testament to our shared love for Forest. Two souls marred by their pasts, intertwined by horrific experiences and a love that knows no bounds.

"Forest is hurting right now. He feels betrayed. But he's strong, stronger than anyone gives him credit for, and he'll find a way to forgive you." Skye's eyes bore into mine, pooling with compassion. Her hands wrap around mine, the warmth seeping into my cold, clammy skin. "He'll find his way back to you."

She offers me hope. A slender thread, fraying at the edges, but there, nonetheless.

"I don't know if he can forgive me." I manage to choke out, the lump in my throat threatening to cut off my voice. "He said he never wants to see me again."

I let the words hang, raw and filled with pain. The man I love more than anything, the man I would kill and die for, wants nothing to do with me.

But Skye shakes her head, her gaze steady, her grip on my hands firm. "Forest says a lot of things when he's upset or hurt, but he doesn't mean half of it. You know that. You know him. In you and Sara, the kids, and now Lily, he has a chance at what he lost as a child. He has the chance to have a real family and a somewhat normal life."

Her words are meant to be comforting, but they feel like tiny barbs digging into my already wounded heart. Because I know Forest. I know his strength, his resilience, his fierce spirit. Forest isn't a man who forgives easily.

We lapse into silence, Skye seemingly lost in her thoughts. The only sound is the crashing waves far beneath our feet and the rustle of the wind blowing off the ocean toward land.

"Forest's anger is like a storm. He rages and screams, and

sometimes, he destroys. But storms pass. They always do." Her voice hangs heavy with a wisdom born from years of shared hardships and battles fought.

I look at her, trying to find some assurance in her words, some promise that the storm that is Forest will pass and he will let me back in.

"Give him time." Her gaze remains soft but unwavering. "I can't promise he'll forgive you. That's something only Forest can decide. But I know he loves you. Despite everything, that's something I know; just… Just—give him time. He's going to need you in the days and weeks to come."

There is an undercurrent of truth in Skye's words, a sliver of hope amidst the overwhelming despair. I nod slowly, absorbing her words, taking them in as the lifeline they are.

I'll give Forest as much time as he needs.

Because I love him.

Skye's grip on my hand loosens, but she doesn't let go, her presence a comforting reminder that I am not alone in this. We sit in silence, united in our shared hope for the man we both love. The man we both killed for, and would again. A twisted bond, born from the darkest corners of our souls, but a bond nonetheless. The bond of love, of sacrifice, of a willingness to traverse the darkest depths for the one we care about.

And so, I'll wait. For Forest. For forgiveness. For a chance to mend the bond I destroyed. Even when it hurts. Especially when it hurts.

My hands tighten around Skye's, a desperate plea seeping through the silent contact. "But what if…" The words catch in my throat. "What if we run out of time?"

Her eyes meet mine, understanding flashing in their depths.

I swallow past the lump in my throat. "What if I never get to apologize? What if I don't get to tell him how sorry I am? How much I…" My voice breaks, the words trailing off into the suffocating silence. The fear, so long repressed, now grips my heart in a vice-like clench.

What if we never get a chance to reconcile?

What if Forest—dies?

Skye doesn't answer immediately. Instead, she gives my hands a gentle squeeze, her touch a balm to the roiling storm within me.

"You can't control the *what ifs*. You can only control the *right nows*. And right now, you need to hold onto hope."

The word hope hangs in the air, a tiny glimmer of light in the dark abyss of my fears.

Hope.

A word so small, yet carrying so much weight. A word that is both my lifeline and the bane of my existence.

"Forest is a fighter. You of all people know that. He won't go down without a fight. And you… You need to fight too. Fight for him. Fight with him. Fight against your fears and insecurities. Fight for Sara. But most importantly, believe in his love for you."

Her words are a rallying call, a battle cry against the dark forces threatening to overwhelm me. I nod, drawing in a shaky breath, allowing her unwavering faith in Forest to seep into me, to bolster my own crumbling defenses.

In the deafening silence that follows, her words resonate and stir a renewed sense of determination within me. I will fight.

For Forest.

For Sara.

For them both.

Because the possibility of a world without him, a world where we never get a chance to reconcile and mend the wounds inflicted by my betrayal, is a possibility too painful to contemplate.

It's not just the fear of losing Forest that terrifies me. It's the regret. The regret of things left unsaid, of apologies never given, of love not expressed.

Forest deserves better, and I intend to fight for him.

TWENTY-FIVE

Paul

~

Trapped in the sterile confinement of the staff dormitories flanking the grandeur of *Insanity*, dawn seeps through the cracks in the shutters, casting a hazy, unwelcome light on the stark reality of my day.

From the second-story window, my gaze trails the sprawling estate of *Insanity*, toward a heart-breaking scene.

The shared warmth of our home, our love, our connection is reduced to a distant echo. My spirit roils, still trembling from the aftershocks of Forest's rejection, our once loving ties torn apart by the very act meant to save him.

He chooses to live without me, and God willing, he lives a very long life.

Just past the manicured gardens, over the pristine drive, and beyond the grand main house, there's a steady stream of activity at the home Forest built for our unique family. His absence is my constant shadow.

I catch sight of Forest and pull out the binoculars. I purchased them specifically to spy on my former lover. His hunched figure makes its way to a waiting car, Sara a constant presence by his side.

The harsh morning light casts the drawn features of his face into stark relief, highlighting the cruel reality of his illness.

It's as if the cancer steals more than just his health. It erodes the essence of the man I know and love.

Forest, my inscrutable, unyielding, relentlessly passionate Forest, bears a striking resemblance to a rag doll, worn and frayed at the edges. The sight twists something inside me, a well of emotions surging upwards—regret, anger, an overwhelming fear, but most of all, an indescribable sense of helplessness and loss.

Every fiber in my being screams for me to rush out there, to take his hand and tell him I'm sorry.

But reality isn't that kind.

It's been weeks, going on months, and the impenetrable wall of his resentment, and the tangible barricade of my guilt, keep me chained to the sidelines where all I can do is watch the battle he wages for his life.

A part of me recoils at the sight of the once proud Forest Summers shuffling to the waiting car, wanting to ignore the undeniable proof of his decline, but I force myself to watch, to confront the uncomfortable reality of our situation. This is the man I betrayed, the man I'd do anything to protect, now wrestling with a demon far greater than any of our past enemies.

And there's Lily.

They've grown close. She's over there nearly every day. Forest's long-lost sibling stepping in to fill the void I left in his life. I watch as she exits the main house, her shock-white hair a beacon in the morning light, a ray of hope in this bleak existence where I now find myself on the outside looking in.

She's become his literal lifeline, his bone marrow donor, and his newfound family. They're reconnecting, building new foundations of a life without me in it. A part of me yearns to join them, to be a part of what they share, but the boundaries set by Forest are clear and nonnegotiable.

I'm not welcome in his world.

With a rumble, the car moves off, carrying Forest away for yet another round of chemotherapy in preparation to receive his gift of life from Lily. The harsh grating sound snaps me out of my reverie, grounding me back into my own reality.

I'm just the estranged lover, watching from afar as Forest battles for his life.

As the vehicle disappears into the distance, my grip tightens on the worn fabric of my shirt, right above my heart. This is my reality now—a spectator to his pain, an outsider to his fight.

A notification chimes on my phone, pulling me roughly from my thoughts.

My thumb hovers over the screen, a new message blinking in bold. It's a message from someone I never thought I'd hear from again. A specter from a past life, a time before Forest, before I escaped the dark and twisted world my father, John Snowden, forced me into.

A time of heinous acts committed in the name of the monstrous man who plucked me—a survivor of the death rings—from one hell and dropped me into another.

At least, until the day I met Forest, and my life changed forever.

The sight of Josh Davenport's name is not welcome. The mere sight of his name sends a ripple of unease slithering down my spine; a chilling echo of a life I thought was securely locked away. My pulse quickens with a mixture of apprehension and an old, familiar dread. Josh reaching out can only spell trouble, yet, a part of me can't help but be drawn to his call.

Joshua Davenport.

It's a name that reverberates with the echoes of my haunted past. Josh took down Zane Clarkson's death rings several years ago; a man who worked for my father before Josh relieved Clarkson of the burden of his life.

When Josh shut down that operation, he faked his own death— technically, it had to do with a life-debt owed to a crime boss in Asia. That debt was paid in full by Josh, and other than minor facial reconstruction, he reclaimed his life.

Josh is another tortured soul, a mirror image of my past. Forced by his sadistic father to brutalize women, then condemned to watch as their lives were extinguished. His past is as grim as mine.

Like me, he found redemption and forgiveness.

The floodgates of my memory open, unleashing a grim slideshow of young boys forced into a battle for survival while wealthy men made bets on who would live and who would die. I killed without regret, and I survived to fight again. My brutal past is best left in the past, but somehow it keeps resurfacing.

Kill or be killed.

Bound by a shared past tainted with the malevolent scheming of our fathers, Josh and I are kindred spirits.

Not friends.

Not adversaries.

We're survivors.

And we each play villains in our past.

His message is succinct yet ominously potent, a request to meet. A plea to join him in the fight against a nightmarish underworld that preys on innocent lives, turning them into grotesque spectacles of violence.

Death rings.

I endured and survived them as a child—victorious, but forever changed. Death rings that almost ensnared a young Forest, once upon a time.

The thought of Forest, condemned to the living hell I survived, sends a fresh wave of dread washing over me, but it also brings something else into sharp focus.

Skye's confession.

Her raw, chilling admission about the lengths she went to protect Forest from this very horror. She killed the foster father who abused both her and Forest. Clark Preston died by Skye's hands, a premeditated act committed to keep, a then young and vulnerable, Forest out of those rings.

I swallow hard, my gaze gravitating toward the vacant space where the car had once been, a stark reminder of the monumental struggle that lies ahead for Forest.

My thumb swipes over the message; requesting more information.

A coded message screams urgency. This missive from Josh is not a light in the darkness. It's a storm brewing on the horizon. A plea for help to resurrect the ghosts of our past, a chilling memory of battles fought and victories won at the cost of our innocence.

Our shared past is a labyrinth of pain and tainted victories, a cruel ballet performed under the cold, watchful eyes of our malevolent fathers.

It portends not rescue, but a reckoning with the ghosts of our past. His cryptic words conceal an urgent plea, a call to arms, to revisit the horrors we once escaped.

His words are carefully chosen, concealing a desperate request. Every letter a carefully constructed code pulsing in the deep wound that is our shared past. A veiled reference to the death rings, a brutal arena where the outcome is measured in life or death, where only the strongest, or the most cunning, emerge alive.

My memories of that time are monsters lurking in the depths of my mind, their eyes glinting ominously as Josh's message draws them out.

I thought I left those specters in the past when I killed my father. Yet here they are, rearing their ugly heads, snapping their mangled jaws, ready to snap and swallow me back into the abyss.

I sit on the edge of my bed, the depressingly bare walls of the dormitory seeming to press in on me as I hold my head in my hands and rock back and forth. The metallic tang of fear mingles with the bitter taste of past regrets, the specter of what I did to survive and who I became.

Among these dark recollections, a ray of hope flickers—Guardian HRS—Forest's creation. A name that signifies a fight against the darkness that once consumed Josh and me. But now, ostracized and isolated, I find myself grappling with the stark reality—I'm alone in this. Stripped of my authority, distanced from the organization I once served, I have to face this single-handedly.

I clutch the message tightly. A spark of resolve takes root. My own past may be tainted with blood and regret, but here lies a chance to protect others from enduring the same horrors. Despite the discomfort of these resurfacing memories, a strange sense of satisfaction overcomes me.

Josh didn't seek out just anyone for this mission; he came to me.

His coded plea hints at a trust that persists despite our tainted past—a faith in my abilities to face the horrors we once endured. The prospect of seeing someone so intimately tied to my past is daunting, yet necessary.

I owe it to the boys still trapped in those rings.

I owe it to myself.

I owe it to Forest, to show him the man I've become because of him. That I'm still worthy of his love.

With a newfound determination, I decipher the rest of Josh's message, focusing on the location of our rendezvous and draw back sharply when I see who else will be there.

Kate Summers—no relation to Forest and Skye—was instrumental in Josh's journey. She hunted him and nearly lost her life by his hands. She saw the darkness in him, exposed it, but then gave him an opportunity to redeem himself.

Their lives are a testament to resilience, redemption, and forgiveness. Three things I sorely lack. Facing them will be no easy task, but the daunting challenge holds the promise of a deeper understanding, a possible path to my own salvation.

If Forest's forsaken me, maybe this is my chance to find purpose again. To fight the darkness I once knew and rescue others from the abyss I narrowly escaped. I feel like he'll respect that.

I can just hear the maniacal cackles of my father, laughing because of my fall from grace. Loving that the man who turned me against my father has cast me out.

Fuck him.

Like me, Josh is a tortured soul, a man forced by his own father to commit heinous crimes, trapped in a horrifying cycle of abuse and murder.

I may not be a Guardian, or a Protector, but I am a fighter. I survived my own brutal hell, and I'm ready to face it again to save others. If I can't be with Forest, I'd rather be out doing something good other than peeking through a pair of binoculars as he heads off to his chemotherapy.

With resolve coursing through me, I dress quickly, choosing nondescript clothing for our meeting. I take one last look at the unadorned space that's been my home for the past couple of months, the walls bearing silent witness to my despair.

Tonight, my past converges with my present, and the urgency of Josh's plea propels me into action. After confirming our meeting place—an old, greasy burger joint just down the road—I leave the austere confinement of the dormitory and head out.

But not before a long look at myself in front of the mirror.

The bright fluorescent lights deepen the shadows of my face while illuminating the ghostly pallor of my skin. Stripped of my authority, abandoned by Forest, I'm a shadow of the man I once was, but there, in the depths of my eyes, I see a spark—the will to fight.

All I need is a purpose, and if that's not to be Forest's Master, maybe I can help Josh end the nightmare he discovered.

A cool breeze rustles through the sprawling estate as I slip outside. Clouds cover the sky, turning the world shades of washed-out gray and steely blue, a somber palette that mirrors the tumult within my heart. The whisper of the light wind envelops me, broken only by the distant booming of waves crashing against the secluded shoreline, a haunting symphony of nature's defiance in the face of coming storms. I grab a car and navigate my way toward my meeting with a ghost from my past.

TWENTY-SIX

Paul

~

"Manny's Place" is a living, breathing relic from the past. Its neon sign flickers in the late afternoon, a beacon for lost souls seeking solace in greasy comfort food. The potent mix of grilled burgers, stale beer, and decades of embedded cigarette smoke assaults my senses the moment I step through the doors.

It's a portal to another time.

A place of comfort, serving good food and good memories.

I'm not there for either of those things.

I scan the room, and there, seated in a dimly lit corner, I see him.

Joshua Davenport.

His features are nearly identical to the man sitting across from him, but time has etched a story of suffering and hardened survival on Josh's face, setting him apart from his twin brother, Jake. Seeing Josh again hits me like a sucker punch—a physical reminder of our similar pasts and shared pain.

In addition to Jake, Josh is joined by the indomitable Kate Summers, now Kate Davenport, wife to Josh's twin. The echoes of the formidable Mistress of Pain flicker in her eyes. Her past may have been stained with scandal, but the fierce determination that drove her to bring Josh to justice, and later redemption, remains today and is just as powerful as ever.

Josh locks eyes with me and a flicker of mutual understanding passes between us. We're survivors. We've walked through the flames and emerged, forever scarred but still standing. As I approach their table, anticipation surges within me.

The time has come to confront my past to ensure that no other child is thrown into the ruthless death rings. In this, I'm victim, villain, and predator.

As a victim, I fought to survive in those rings. Took more lives than I care to count. Truthfully, I never cared to count how many lives I took. Then, under the tutelage of my father, I turned from victim into predator. I found young boys. Groomed them to fight. Then, I set them loose on each other; barbaric entertainment for our auspicious clientele. I became the villain when my father set me to breaking Forest.

Josh, Jake, and Kate look up at me as I reach the table, an odd family bound together by a shared purpose. Their faces, etched with the weight of their past and the fear of the task that lies ahead, offer a grim reflection of my own thoughts. I square my shoulders, forcing a steely determination into my gaze.

When I reach the table, Josh stands.

"Josh," I acknowledge, keeping my voice low. Even after all these years, the guilt in his eyes is unmistakable. Like me, he'll carry it for the rest of his life.

"Paul." His voice is heavy with a myriad of unspoken apologies and gratitude.

Remaining seated, Kate and Jake glance up at me, acknowledging my presence with a nod. Kate's eyes are keen and alert. Her time as the Mistress of Pain leaves a mark of discerning vigilance in her gaze. Jake is a quiet but powerful dominant by her side, his supportive silence speaking volumes.

"It's starting again." Josh wastes no time on pleasantries. The gravity of his words hangs in the chilly recycled air. "They're organizing in Mexico."

My fists clench at my sides; old, almost forgotten, rage threatens to consume me. Me, leading the charge against the very horror that robbed me of a normal childhood feels like coming full circle, a chance to finally exorcise the ghosts that haunt me.

I've been given a chance to strike back at the rot that caused so much pain in my past. Is it condemnable that I find solace in this old, familiar hurt, rather than confront the raw, gnawing guilt of the wounds I inflicted on Forest?

Looking at the trio before me, their faces grim yet hopeful, I nod. The decision is surprisingly easy, an undeniable calling.

"What do you need?"

Kate nods toward a folder on the table. "There are connections with some influential figures. They're hidden and protected. I could use Mitzy's talents on this."

There was once a time when Guardian HRS's formidable technical leader was none other than the lowly assistant to Kate Summers, Private Detective. Mitzy was the key to bringing Josh to justice, and the key to saving Kate's life.

Grasping the folder, I rake my gaze over its damning contents. Images, stark and brutal, intermingle with clinical dossiers and bank statements. It's a grim testament to the monstrous underbelly of humanity, a machine tirelessly grinding away at life itself.

"I can get this to Mitzy, but you should know I'm not with Guardian HRS anymore. That's Forest's organization, and I've been ostracized." The familiar tang of bitterness hits me at the mention of Forest's name.

"What happened?" Josh invites me to sit, and I slide into the booth.

Like me, Josh is a Master. Jake as well. Kate's a former Mistress. We're fierce dominants, genetically wired to dominate and control others, as we also aim to protect them. The three of us share this trait. As does Kate, the once Mistress of Pain who set aside her whip to serve the man who stole her heart.

"I shattered his trust. Violated the terms of our arrangement." There's no reason to explain beyond that. They grasp the magnitude of my transgression against Forest—a sin seen as monstrous, even unforgivable, within the confines of our society.

Kate's eyes widen. As a former Mistress, she recognizes the enormity of such a sin. Jake stirs beside her; a powerful dominant and well known in the south for his club, *Stripes*. To him, my words are heretical.

Kate recovers, but her eyes narrow. "And you think that makes you useless?"

"I've been expelled. He wants nothing to do with me. If you're looking for help from the Guardians, you should've contacted Mitzy instead of me."

"Kate wanted to, but I insisted on speaking with you first." Josh wrangles back control of the conversation, which I appreciate.

Admitting my violation of Forest's trust is not how I want to spend my evening. Using my knuckles, I rub my breastbone, trying to soothe the ache Forest's absence leaves in my heart.

"We need you." Jake's voice resonates with quiet conviction. "You know how these rings operate, and maybe this is a fight you need to fight." His skill as a Master is evident in his choice of words.

He's right.

Absolutely right.

I let out a long sigh, grappling with memories of a painful parting and the shadows of a horrifying past. After a few moments of heavy silence, I come to a decision. My voice thick with resolve, I speak the words that will take me from Forest.

"I'm in."

Their relief is palpable as they share a look amongst themselves. And then, Kate adds, "If we can't have Guardian HRS—we still have Xavier."

"You can have Guardian HRS if you need them. You just can't have them and me. Forest will never allow it."

We order food, but I barely touch my meal. Our meeting ends soon after, leaving me alone with a folder full of nightmares and a daunting task ahead of me. As I square my shoulders something within me stirs.

Jake was right.

My past might be filled with ghosts, but I'm ready to face them. It's easier than living without Forest.

A sense of purpose.

It feels as if this is what I need. A rush I haven't felt in a long time flows through me. The ghosts of my past are still there, but I have the power to fight them. I need something to do. Something to help me forget Forest.

Let the fight begin.

TWENTY-SEVEN

Paul

———

～

Inside the colossal estate of *Insanity*, away from the world's prying eyes, Josh, Jake, and Kate join Mitzy and myself in the communal living room. It's a peculiar picture we paint—five grown adults huddled in quiet discussion, surrounded by a whirlwind of chaotic play and toddler antics.

My twins, Delia and Sebastian, immerse themselves in the realm of make-believe. Their youthful glee provides a stark contrast to our somber discussion, their laughter echoing around the room like musical notes composed by innocence itself. Suddenly, a high-pitched squeal slices through the laughter.

"Kai!" Mitzy calls out, as her rambunctious toddler pinches Delia, leaving my daughter blinking back tears. "Sorry, Paul."

"And there's Kai right on cue, disrupting a peaceful afternoon." I give Mitzy a look, saying I forgive Kai. He's not trying to hurt Delia. Like any boy, he simply wants her attention.

Mitzy's little tornado of a toddler, a relentless dynamo of childhood energy and destruction, ventures too close to his mother. Quick as lightning, she hooks Kai by the waist and hoists him into her lap where he squirms.

Right on cue, Sebastian comes to his sister's rescue, slapping Kai on the leg. Kai squirms out of Mitzy's lap, escaping time-out, and is on the rampage. The room turns into a whirlwind of chaos as Mitzy and I try to parent our wayward toddlers.

Kai's fast and evades his mother's half-hearted attempts to recapture him. He navigates the room with a captivating mix of clumsy determination and joyful abandon, leaving behind a wake of upended toys and a toppled, once carefully tended, potted plant.

A knock on the door reveals Noodles, Angel Fire's keyboardist and father of the hellion in our midst. So unlike his son, Noodles is renowned for his Zen-like demeanor, a soothing undercurrent of tranquility that echoes through his music and permeates his existence.

There's a contemplative quality about him, a sense of serenity that seems to hum gently under his skin, grounding him in a state of perpetual calm. It's as though he moves to a slower, more deliberate rhythm, a personal metronome set to the pace of mindful tranquility.

"Heard a ruckus. A squeal. And a crash? Need help?" While offering to help, Noodles doesn't venture into the room. He quietly scans the chaos created by his son with smug pride.

"If you don't mind, but aren't you guys recording today?" Mitzy, isn't the least bit frazzled by Kai's antics.

"Just finished. Was going surfing, but I can take Kai if you want."

"As long as surfing doesn't mean hanging out with Old Joe." Mitzy refers to Noodles's pet shark, a great white known for patrolling this expanse of coastline.

He and Mitzy are a conflagration of polar opposites, with Mitzy's OCD and hyperactive brain balancing out Noodles and his perpetual calm. Kai is the result of that union. Of the same age as my twins, his vibrant embodiment of unrestrained energy and exuberance, mirrors his father's passionate spirit, albeit in a more tempestuous form.

Where Noodles serenades the world with the gentle keystrokes of his keyboard, Kai conducts a symphony of joyful chaos, dictating the tempo with his bounding steps and gleeful laughter. Yet, there's a shared rhythm that bridges the divide between father and son, a harmonious synchronization beneath their outward differences.

Despite the discordant melody of Kai's energetic display and Noodles's serene demeanor, there's an undeniable unity to their beat, a rhythm that speaks of a deep-seated bond forged in love, laughter, and music.

"Come on, Kai, let's get your swimsuit on. You want to surf with your papa?"

"Yes, Papa!" Kai's laughter is a pure, unadulterated sound that fills the room, providing a heartening soundtrack to our otherwise somber conference. It rings through the space, a spontaneous composition of childish delight, offsetting the serious tone of adult deliberation.

"Thanks." Mitzy balances a laptop on one knee and continues speaking as if the whole exchange never happened.

Despite their antics, Delia and Sebastian are sad to see Kai go. Their smiles droop and Delia sniffs back fake alligator tears. It's all an act. She's a master at manipulating the men in her life. Growing up in *Insanity*, she has more uncles than she knows what to do with and knows exactly what it takes to manipulate each one into doing what she wants.

"Come on." Noodles glances over at me, silently asking permission to take the twins. After I nod, he opens his arms for the twins. "Papa Paul won't mind if you join us."

"Yay!" My kids run to Noodles, completely forgetting I exist in their excitement to spend time on the beach with their uncle Noodles.

Meanwhile, Mitzy continues speaking. "Guardian HRS has a lot of resources. We've got people, equipment, connections… You name it."

"But we need Paul." Josh shakes his head. "Y'all do great work, but Paul and I need to infiltrate their organization before sending in the calvary. We share the pasts that will open doors."

No need to elaborate on what that means. It's the one thing Josh and I share. We were both monsters in our former lives.

"And I don't want to overstep with Forest." A true dominant, Josh is protective of my former partner and judgmental of the sin I committed against Forest.

A shared look passes between Josh, Jake, and Kate.

I miss Forest. Once the compass that guided my decisions, his absence is a gaping hole in my life. I feel him like the pain of a phantom limb, an ache that will never go away.

"I can handle the tech work. Check out the backgrounds of the names on your list. We don't need the Guardians yet, but we will once you and Paul finish your initial survey," Mitzy states, breaking my train of thought. "I suppose, if you need help sooner, we also have Xavier and his team in the wings."

I glance at Josh, seeing him echo my surprise. "Are you sure he'd want to get involved?"

Mitzy gives a half-shrug, her eyes on Kai as he races back into the room to collect his favorite toy truck to take down to the beach. "He doesn't like death rings any more than you do. We've worked together before. He'll do it again."

"Then I'll get him on board," Kate jumps in, agreeing to bring in Xavier. "But I agree with Josh. This is a two-man mission. Sending Josh and Paul is complicated enough. Let's hold Xavier's men in reserve. When we need the Guardians, we'll…" A determined look is etched across Kate's face, but she pauses when a new person enters the room.

Skye steps inside. Her startled gaze sweeps across the room, landing on the upturned plant, our group, and the whirlwind of toddlers racing down the hall.

"Mitzy—what's happening?" Skye looks at each person in turn, trying to place how, where, and when she might have come across them in the past.

"Skye, meet Joshua Davenport. His brother, Jake, and Kate, his wife. Josh worked a case in Manilla, taking down a death ring run by Zane Carson, one of Snowden's associates."

"I see." Skye's gaze shifts to me, her confusion morphing into realization. "And you're here for Paul?"

"Correct." Mitzy nods.

Skye crosses her arms, her gaze narrowing as she processes the information. She knows who Xavier is, how crucial he was in Forest's rescue when he and Sara were kidnapped. A silent understanding passes between us all, hardening our resolve.

"Paul told them we couldn't use Guardian resources on account of Forest," Mitzy explains, "but I can provide tech support."

"You're going to need every resource you can muster." Skye meets each of their gazes in turn. "We can't do this half-assed. Not when it comes to dealing with Snowden's legacy." Skye's words are a solemn declaration, her tone hard with unwavering conviction. She sweeps her gaze over all of us, her eyes glinting with a determination that belies the gentle curve of her lips. Her gaze lingers on me, a silent conversation passing between us.

Kate's attention shifts between Skye and me, a hint of curiosity in her eyes. Josh and Jake remain silent, each lost in their own thoughts. The room is steeped in a momentary silence, heavy with the shared understanding of the risks we're willing to take to destroy the remaining vestiges of Snowden's operation.

"Skye's right," I break the silence, my voice echoing in the stillness. "We need all the help we can get." I shift my gaze to Skye, her eyes holding a depth of understanding that goes beyond our shared history. We're connected by secrets, by the knowledge of what she did to protect Forest, what I had to endure, and the crimes of my past.

The weight of our silent vows and our shared commitment to eradicating such horrors solidifies our resolve. Despite my estrangement from Forest, she's not willing to let that get in the way of doing what's right.

I admire that about her.

Noodles returns, grinning like a Cheshire cat. The twins and Kai barrel into the room, each sporting bright swimsuits and carrying an array of colorful swim toys. Delia, ever the charmer, convinces Noodles to hoist her onto his shoulders. She giggles gleefully, her small fingers playing with the fine wisps of Noodles hair as it grows out. Sebastian and Kai race ahead, their laughter echoing through the room to blend with the distant murmur of the sea.

Their youthful joy provides a stark contrast to the somber reality we discuss. As Noodles takes his leave, with the children in tow, their laughter fades into the distance. We return to the conversation at hand.

Skye leans back, crossing her arms. Her voice, when she finally speaks, is a quiet yet firm admission,

"I was waiting for this day." She meets our curious glances, her eyes holding a haunting resignation. "The world is a hell, and no matter how many times you put down evil, it always manages to find the light and take root."

Her words hang heavily in the room. A shared understanding, a universal truth, one that we all acknowledge. It's the very reason we're here.

She turns to Mitzy, a new determination in her eyes. "Do we know if these new death rings are a resurrection of the ones Snowden operated, or is it a new player in town?" Skye's question lingers, drawing us back to the purpose of this gathering.

"Don't know." Mitzy's reply is concise and to the point.

"What's the plan?" Skye asks.

The energy in the room shifts as we finally address the looming question.

Josh and I exchange a glance. We both know what we have to do.

"Paul and I will gather intel, get to know their operation from the inside." His gaze meets each of ours in turn. "It's the most effective way." His words hang in the air, a silent challenge daring any dissent.

My heart pounds with the echo of old fights, the specter of death rings rearing its ugly head once more.

"It's the fastest, most direct way to tear these operations apart from the roots," I jump in, knowing this is the only way. "I've been in the rings, fought in them, ran them. I know how they operate. We can offer a—partnership. Something guaranteed to get us an *in* to whoever's orchestrating the fights."

"Paul…" Skye's voice cracks. "Do you really want to resurrect that part of your past?"

"It's better than sitting in the dormers pining for Forest." I hate the way my words sound and regret them immediately. "I'm sorry. I didn't mean to be flippant about…"

"It's okay." Soft and soothing, Skye blows out a breath. "We're all hurting."

After weeks of watching Forest continue battling for his life, without me by his side, I'm once again filled with a sense of purpose. I have something to do.

It's a dangerous path, haunted by the ghosts of my past, but for the sake of the future and innocent children like Delia, Sebastian, and Kai, it's a path I'm willing to take.

"Forest may be an ass," Skye explains for the benefit of our guests, "but he's not the be-all and end-all of Guardian HRS. I have a say in where we focus our efforts." Her words, though biting, carry an unmistakable weight. "Whatever resources you need, we have them, and they're yours." There's a quiet strength in Skye's stance, a silent pledge in her words.

Despite the uncertainty, the danger that lurks in the shadows of our path, her declaration ignites a flame of hope.

"Thank you, Skye," Mitzy speaks softly, gratitude softening her usually sharp features that she won't have to operate behind Skye's back.

With Skye's assurance of resources, Mitzy's promise of technical support, and the unyielding determination etched in all our hearts, it feels like we've entered the fight.

Josh and I, our histories entwined in ways no one else can fully grasp, share a glance. We've danced with death before. I did it in the death rings. He did it in prison. It is a dance we know too well, its rhythm etched into the marrow of our bones. He speaks, his voice heavy with the weight of the past and the gravity of our task.

"It's settled then." Josh's gaze flicks to each person in turn. "Infiltration. An offer of a partnership. That's our best bet. We resurrect our pasts, get inside, understand their operations."

I swallow down the knot in my throat. Memories surge, filled with blood-soaked sand, the metallic taste of fear, and the hollow victories I claimed in the death rings.

But I'm not that scared boy anymore.

Mitzy's gaze fills with a silent plea. She's seen the aftermath of our kind of childhood, the scars we wear beneath our skin. It's a world she's terrified to expose her child to, and I share her fear as a father.

Mitzy nods, determination creeping into her features. "We'll prep the tech, ensure we've got a solid line of communication at all times. And if we could get Xavier…"

Jake's calm demeanor is marred by a tightness around his eyes. He's a silent pillar of support, his contribution often soft-spoken, but with a weight that tips the balance. "His team will be an invaluable asset, and he's already agreed to help."

I meet Josh's gaze again. His eyes, a mirror to my own apprehensions and resolve, speak volumes. We're going back to the nightmare that molded us. It's a gamble, a throw of the dice in a deadly game. But the payoff… It's worth the risk.

"Then it's settled," I say, a newfound purpose steeling my voice. "When do we move?"

The past is a nightmare I can't forget, but I can correct those wrongs in the present. While I can't negate what was done to me, I can protect the innocence, that was stolen from me, from being taken from another child.

But if I do this, it takes me further from Forest. If something goes wrong, I may never have a chance to reconcile with the man I love.

Skye invites the others to stay for dinner and they make their way into the communal kitchen. As the room empties, I'm left alone with my thoughts.

Images of Forest, pale and fighting for his life, flash through my mind, followed swiftly by the echoing laughter of Delia, Sebastian, and Kai. I'm doing this for them and for all the children who have yet to lose their innocence to this monstrous operation.

But the reality is inescapable. If things go sideways, I may never see Forest again. The chance to reconcile will be lost.

I leave the room to join the others, and pause, resting my hand against the wall.

Forest.

The kids.

The operation.

It all converges into a painful knot in my chest.

I can't shake the feeling of an unseen clock ticking away, each tick a step closer to an uncertain fate.

TWENTY-EIGHT

Paul

~

THE DAYS THAT FOLLOW ARE A BLUR OF MOTION AND EMOTION, A whirlwind of preparations I'm keenly aware lead me further away from Forest. As much as it tortures me, I steel myself against the pull of my heart, focusing instead on the imminent mission.

Mitzy proves to be a tech genius, her nimble fingers working wonders with gadgets that seem straight out of a sci-fi movie. She shows me and Josh bumblebee drones. The small machines whir to life and flit around the room, demonstrating how they look exactly like the real thing.

"See how they can attach to a person without their knowledge?" One of her drones lands on the back of Josh's collar. "They're designed to map and relay data back to us. All you have to do is get one of them on whoever you want followed." She explains how they'll function as our eyes in places we can't physically be, assisting in navigating unknown spaces.

"You're not afraid of needles, are you?" She preps a tracker for Josh.

"It's not the needle that scares me," Josh says, "but the idea of being monitored."

His words dredge up old memories of a life under constant surveillance, of feeling like a pawn in a deadly game, but Mitzy's voice is a steady anchor, bringing me back to the reality that this is our choice, our fight.

"Trust me. These trackers are passive. I don't monitor them and only activate them if anything goes wrong. We have your back." Her voice is firm, resolute.

With every passing day, the tension in the compound grows, the knowledge of our mission hanging like a shroud around us. The twins and Kai seem to sense a change; their laughter is a bit quieter, their smiles hesitant and unsure. It tears at my heart, this change in them, the innocent casualties of our war.

As the days roll on, I find myself dreading one thing. I need to speak to Forest. Sara updates me on his health, but it's been weeks since I've seen him.

Months.

I long to be there, holding his hand through his battle against cancer, but I can't. I'm preparing for a different battle, and I don't even know if he's aware I will be gone.

I finally find an opportunity. With everyone else busy preparing, I slip away to visit him.

When I reach the hospital, I sign in at the front desk, nodding to the receptionist, a woman who recognizes me after countless visits before Forest gave me the *old heave-ho!* I take the elevator up to the cancer ward and swallow hard, fighting back the surge of emotions that threaten to overwhelm me.

Forest's room is at the end of the hall. I hesitate before the door. Taking a deep breath, I push open the door and step into the room. Forest looks pale against the stark white hospital sheets. His gaze flicks toward the door, and the ghost of a frown forms on his face when he sees me.

"What part of *I never want to see you* again do you not understand?" His voice is cold, devoid of emotion. "Did I stutter? Was it not clear?"

"Come on, Forest, you can't…"

"The only reason I agreed to the bone marrow transplant was if you left for good. Yet here you are, once again breaking my trust."

The words hit like a punch in the gut. I swallow, searching for my voice, aware that I need to tread carefully.

"I know." It's a struggle to force the words out. "I need to talk to you. Just in case…"

"Just in case, what?" His eyes narrow with suspicion.

"Just in case…" I trail off, words failing me. How do I tell him I might not return? That this conversation could very well be the last one we ever have?

"Joshua Davenport contacted me. He found something."

Forest pauses at the name. His attention sharpens, but he doesn't ask the obvious question. It's up to me to fill in the gap.

"A death ring," I blurt it out, the words tasting bitter on my tongue. "In Mexico. He asked me to help him take it down."

Forest recoils, his eyes betraying a fleeting moment of panic before the stoic mask returns. "And?" he asks, his voice clipped.

"I said yes." The words are out before I can second-guess them, my resolve cementing with each syllable. "We're leaving soon."

A bitter laugh escapes Forest. "So, you came to say goodbye?" The words are laced with sarcasm, but there's an undercurrent of something else, a mixture of hurt and resignation.

"Not goodbye." My voice is a mere whisper. "I wanted to apologize and tell you how sorry I am."

Forest's gaze meets mine, and for a moment, we're lost in the unspoken words that hang heavy between us. His anger, my regret, our shared loss—it's all there in his ice-blue eyes.

"You never cease to amaze me." His voice carries an undercurrent of bitterness. "You think after breaking my trust, you can just waltz in here and have a heartfelt talk? You think it makes things better? That I'll forgive you because you may not make it back? What a fucked-up apology that would be. You're not doing it because you're sorry. You're doing it so you can leave and not feel guilty about what you did to me. What you took from me."

He doesn't need to elaborate on what I took. I took his ability to 'devolve' into what he is with me. I shattered his trust. Forest can't help his sexual cravings. They were imprinted on him when he was a prepubescent boy of twelve. Forged by pain and brutality, it's an essential piece of who he is.

That's what I took from him.

It's something he can't share with anyone else. A headspace he may never be able to embrace again. He can with me. He can because I was once one of the people who brutalized him. I know what it takes to get him where he needs to go. It's not something he can ask someone else to do.

What I do to him—for him—is brutal escapism. It makes no sense to anyone but us.

His words sting with truth, but I can't change the past. I can't undo my mistakes.

"I hurt you, and I'm sorry it changed us, but I can't leave without trying to fix us."

"You can't fix what you broke." For a moment, something softens in Forest's eyes. It's a flicker, a glimmer of the man I once knew beneath the sharp angles of bitterness and anger that he's become. The moment is fleeting, and his gaze hardens once again, turning cold and distant.

"You didn't just break my trust. It's more than that." His words slice through the silence. "You undermined the very foundation of our relationship. You destroyed everything we had."

His words are a visceral punch to the gut, raw and potent. I take his anger. I don't look away. I can't. Because as much as his words hurt, they're true.

"I'm sorry." The words feel hollow and inadequate, but I don't know what else to say.

"Sorry doesn't change anything," Forest snaps. "Things will never be the same."

"I'll make things right. I owe you that."

Forest scoffs, a bitter, cynical sound. "And how do you plan on doing that?"

I hesitate, knowing my next words will either bridge the gap between us or widen it further.

"Your needs aren't going away." I keep my voice steady. "What happens in the basement… You need that. You need me."

"You're wrong." His eyes flash with anger. "I don't need you. Not anymore." There's the slightest tremor in his voice. He tries to deny it, but I know the truth.

"You need me as much as I need you. I'm not going anywhere."

"I said no."

"I know what you said, and I refute it."

"You no longer have my consent. You no longer have the right."

Here is where I either break us forever or forge the path to our future.

"You're wrong." I keep my voice firm. "I have every right. I will always be your Master. You can't break that bond. We'll address punishment later. As for today, I came because I needed to see you in case I don't make it back."

"Fine, you see me. Now, leave me."

"Not until we talk this out."

He doesn't respond, his gaze steely; he's listening, even if he doesn't want to admit it.

"When I return…" I clear my throat. "I'm going to fix what I broke between us. I owe you that much. And as for what you need, I don't need your permission to give you that. I didn't the first time, and I don't need it when I return." My voice sounds firmer as I continue. This is our truth, and it's about time I remember it. "The next time you see me, you'll remember *why* you knelt for me that first time, because as much as you need me, I need you more."

Forest's eyes meet mine then, and there's a raw vulnerability in his gaze that nearly breaks my heart. But he's quick to mask it, to retreat behind his walls once more.

"You're not my Master anymore." His words are heavy and final.

"Is that what you think?" I acknowledge his hurt, but that's it. "You can say that all you want, but it doesn't change who you are to me. Or what I am to you."

His jaw clenches. A battle rages within him, and I don't back down. I can't. Not when there's so much at stake.

"I'm going to prove we belong together, but if this is the last time we speak, I want you to know."

"Know, what?"

"You belong to me."

This isn't the end. Not for us.

Not now.

Not ever.

In the lingering silence, something changes in Forest. The cold, indifferent mask he wears shifts ever so slightly. It's the barest acknowledgment of the truth I've spoken, a quiet concession that hides beneath his lingering resentment.

"But what if I can't forgive you?" He finally accepts what I have to say. It's a confession, raw and painful. It costs him much to admit it. "What if… What if I can't forget how you broke us?"

"I don't expect you to forgive me," I say gently. "But I don't need your forgiveness. When I return, and you're still alive, it means I was right. That I did the right thing *as your Master* in looking out for your best interests. I'll never regret saving your life. And just so we're clear, when you stepped into the slave circle and went to your knees, you promised to be mine *forever*. I warned you what kneeling for me meant. There would be no escape clause. That it was forever. You still went to your knees willingly. I was wrong to allow you to think you could withdraw consent. Consent isn't a part of what we are. It never was. You're mine, and we are what we are."

His fingers curl in the sheets of the hospital bed. The war between his anger and the undeniable truth is a battle I know all too well, one I've been fighting myself since the day I became his Master.

It's going to take time, and maybe leaving on this mission will give him the space he needs to forgive me.

I am his Master. Always will be. But I want to be his friend and his lover. I want to explore my feelings for Sara—see where those might go—and I want to do that with Forest. I want to give him the one thing he desires most in life: a true triad instead of this throuple we share.

"You hurt me." Forest glances away.

"I know. I'm going to give you space, but when I come back, we're going to settle this." I linger for a moment, my heart aching with the desire to turn back, but I resist. Forest needs space.

As I step out into the cool night air, a chilling realization washes over me. I'd rather die on this mission than live without Forest. If there's even the slightest chance, I owe it to Forest—and myself—to fight for us.

TWENTY-NINE

Paul

~

Departure day is nearly upon us, and Mitzy's lab thrums with activity as we scramble to wrap up last-minute preparations. The air is heavy, a palpable mix of technical wizardry and anticipation.

Josh and I are seated across from Mitzy. We're honed in on the different devices strewn about the table. The lingering taste of bitter black coffee taints my tongue as Mitzy begins her explanation.

Held gently in her hands are a pair of drones, each no larger than a bumblebee. She guides us through the process of deploying them, her fingers deftly handling the tiny machines. The soft, metallic hum of their wings is indistinguishable from a real bumblebee.

"These drones," Mitzy begins, her voice steady and practiced, "are not just simple surveillance tools. They can land on a person without detection, follow them wherever they go, even map out structures from the inside. They transmit high-definition video and clear audio. Essentially, they are your eyes and ears on the inside. Or rather, my eyes and ears."

"Really? Bumblebee drones?" Josh expresses his skepticism. "That seems a little—far-fetched."

Mitzy smirks, clearly expecting such a comment. "Oh, you want proof?" She taps a few commands into her computer and suddenly, a screen lights up on the wall. It shows the three of us, sitting in the lab, from a bird's-eye view. The footage is crystal clear, the audio perfectly matching our conversation.

She points to the screen. "That's us, right now. This feed is coming from a drone perched just inside that vent." She points to an air-conditioning vent overhead.

I crane my neck, squinting at the ceiling, and sure enough, a tiny drone, almost indistinguishable from an ordinary bumblebee, pops out from the vent. Its wings buzz softly as it hovers in place and the screen changes as the drone's vantage point shifts.

"Now do you believe me?" Mitzy chuckles, her eyes sparkling with a mix of pride and satisfaction.

I can't help but laugh, shaking my head in disbelief. "That's impressive."

"Now, about the trackers," Mitzy continues, her voice steady amidst the whirl of preparation. "They're implanted and passive. They don't emit a signal unless activated. These new ones are completely undetectable, so no worries about them being discovered.

"Now, if you need extraction," She reveals another piece of equipment, slightly larger and designed to curve along the jawline. "It's a piece of biotech that, when lodged in the tissue just under the skin, sends out an urgent SOS. It's surgically implanted, so Skye's team will take care of that once we're done here."

"And how does that work?" Josh rubs at his arm, checking for bleeding underneath a two-by-two piece of gauze.

"The activation is simple." Mitzy pulls out a dummy model. "Just apply pressure here, and it will send a signal."

The reality of the mission I'm about to undertake weighs heavily on me. Josh and I exchange a look, our faces hardened as we steel ourselves for what's to come.

A week later, we arrive at the airport and check into the first-class lounge while waiting for our flight to Mexico City to board. The memory of our departure from Guardian HQ plays like a movie in my mind. The last looks, the tight hugs, the promises left unsaid. Kate and Jake's farewell on the tarmac is etched into my memory. Kate, her hand lingering in Josh's, her eyes glistening. Jake, his hug full of silent promises and unspoken words.

In contrast, my farewell with Forest was cold, and distant. A stark reminder of the chasm that's grown between us. The chill of his dismissal still lingers, a bitter sting of broken trust.

But amidst these goodbyes, there's one that stands out, one that I keep coming back to.

Sara.

Her farewell was something else altogether. It was tender and raw, yet filled with the spark growing between us. I didn't ask her to see me off. It didn't occur to me that she would want to say goodbye.

But Sara came.

She came, her gaze holding me captive, her hands gentle on my arms.

There is a softness to her, a vulnerability that she usually hides behind her tough exterior, but in that moment, as she stood on her toes to meet me, she was open. Honest. Real.

Her lips, as she brushed them against mine in the tenderest of kisses, were soft, softer than I remembered, and when they met mine, a bolt of electricity shot through me. It was a kiss full of promise, of unexplored territories and shared experiences yet to come. It was her way of saying she'll wait, that she understands, and that she's there for me.

As she pulled away, her hand brushed against my cheek, a silent promise lingering in her touch. "Come back to us," she whispered the words, her voice filled with an emotion that caused a lump in my throat.

Come back to us.

To her and Forest.

Sara is my greatest ally in the fight to bring Forest back to me.

Her words echo in my mind even now as I sit in the plane, the drone of the engine swallowing my sighs. Her goodbye is a soothing balm to the sting of Forest's cold dismissal. I steal a glance at Josh, who appears lost in his thoughts, his focus trained on the notebook in his lap. He glances at me when he notices me looking.

"The buyer angle, it's solid." Josh's attention never leaves the notebook in his lap. "But we need to be careful, subtle… They're not idiots. They'll smell a rat if we push too hard."

My fingers absentmindedly trace the buttery, smooth leather of the seat. This high-risk mission demands our full attention, yet a part of me is still in that sterile hospital room with Forest, reliving Forest's bitter words and hurtful glances.

"We can't afford distractions." Josh's voice pulls me back to the present, sharp and commanding.

"Excuse me?" I'm a little taken aback by his tone of voice.

Josh's hard gaze softens a fraction, a rare show of empathy from the usually stoic man. "Look, whatever happened with Forest… you need to shelve it. At least for now. I need you focused."

His words hit home. They need to. For now, my personal turmoil needs to take a back seat. We're on the brink of infiltrating one of the most dangerous black markets in existence. I need to be focused, determined, prepared. For now, my hope for a future with Forest needs to be locked in the deepest corner of my mind.

"I've got my shit locked down." I meet Josh's gaze, my jaw set in a determined line.

"You sure about that?"

"Definitely, and as for the job, a subtle entrance isn't going to cut it. We gotta make a splash, you know?"

"What are you thinking?"

"Once we land, we make some noise." I raise an eyebrow at him, waiting to see if he gets it. "Expensive restaurants. VIP clubs. Beautiful women."

"What about men?" Josh gives me a look.

"Those too." Although the thought of having to play my part sickens me. There are only two people I'm interested in sexually: Forest and Sara. "I'm gay, and whoever's watching us should know that. And besides, it might look more legit if I have a mix of both. Whatever it takes to bring these rings down."

Josh claps a hand on my shoulder, a silent nod confirming our shared determination. The plane slices through the air, the world outside forgotten as we step deeper into our assumed identities.

Tension coils and uncoils in the space between us, the undercurrent of danger a constant reminder of what's at stake.

The thought of flirting with anyone, male or female, leaves a sour taste in my mouth when the only man I truly want is lying in a hospital bed, fighting for his life, back home.

When Josh and I exit the airport in Mexico City, all around us is a hurricane of color and noise. The clatter of suitcases on tile, hurried goodbyes in a thousand different accents, the piercing whine of the PA system—it's an assault on the senses, but I'm not here for any of that. I'm here to do a job, to play a part, to pretend that I'm something I'm not. I spot the tail almost instantly, just as expected. A pair of men, nondescript and completely forgettable in the way only professional watchers can be, follow us.

Taking a deep breath, I force a grin onto my face.

The game is on.

We traverse the city in a taxi, the dense urban landscape unfurling around us in a chaotic blend of the modern and ancient. High-rise buildings compete with historical landmarks for space in the sky, and the air is filled with a cacophony of blaring horns and vendors shouting their wares, the smell of spicy street food and exhaust fumes mix in the air to create a scent that's uniquely Mexico City.

Arriving at our hotel, we make a flamboyant display of our wealth, our clothes and demeanor painting a vivid picture of two rich playboys here for a good time. We request the penthouse suite, and without batting an eye, arrange for a bevy of male and female escorts to be sent to our room.

Our first night in the city, we hit the club scene. The pulse of the music is a living thing, seeping into my bones and making my heart pound in time with the beat.

The escorts are pros, masters at their craft. They touch, they dance, they flatter. But every touch, every whispered sweet nothing, is a punch to the gut.

I want Forest, not these strangers.

But I have to play the part. I smile, I laugh, I dance, and all the while the ache for Forest is a constant burn in my chest. What I don't do is touch them back. Instead, I force them to have sex in front of me, orchestrating lewd acts while I watch with disdain.

It asserts my predilection for controlling others. Showing how little I value the opinions of others.

Days pass like an eternity. Each morning dawns with a feeling of anticipation, of danger just on the horizon. We keep to our routine, knowing it's the best way to remain inconspicuous. Nights filled with lavish parties and loud clubs. Days navigating the bustling city under the watchful eyes of our tail. Late at night, way past midnight, we drop in on organized street fights, the dirtier the better.

With each passing day, my disgust grows.

Then, finally, there's the break we've been waiting for. An invitation slipped into my hand by our escort for the night, her scarlet lips curled into a knowing smirk. "We've been expecting you, Señor Montenegro." Her Spanish accent wraps around the false surname I've adopted for this mission.

I try not to react, keeping my expression schooled into a casual smirk. "I've been looking forward to something more adventurous," I reply smoothly, trying to emulate the nonchalance of a wealthy thrill-seeker.

She passes me a sleek black envelope, her manicured nails brushing my fingers. "The instructions are all in there. But one thing to remember, Señor Montenegro," she adds, her dark eyes gleaming under the dim club lights. "There are rules. No weapons. No interference."

"No problem," I assure her, my fingers curling around the envelope. "Anything else I should know?"

She leans in closer, the heavy scent of her perfume momentarily overwhelming. "Should you need anything—booze, women, men?" she says with a sly wink. "Don't hesitate to ask."

The offer, though part of this elaborate masquerade, sends a wave of revulsion coursing through me. A revulsion I expertly hide behind a nonchalant grin. "I'll keep that in mind, but I prefer not to mix business and pleasure."

We need to sell ourselves as potential investors, rather than wealthy thrill-seekers eager for a piece of this brutal world. Every handshake, every fake smile, every insincere word is a calculated move in this dangerous game. As for the fights, we place token bets and appear as bored as humanly possible.

"Business? We were not aware of such an interest?" She cocks her head, being flirtatious and failing.

"Tell your boss we come with a proposition. Something he will find quite interesting. If we're satisfied the matches are as advertised, we may discuss it further with him."

"Of course." She's smart enough not to ask too many questions and I'm certain my message will be delivered to the appropriate recipient.

With the delivery of the invitation, the final phase of our plan is set into motion. We've got our foot in the door. Now it's time to kick it wide open.

"Until then, we look forward to the fights." My voice oozing false enthusiasm. I've mastered this persona. It sickens me, but it's necessary.

Her laughter echoes through the air, a rich sound that's both alluring and sinister. "That's what we like to hear, Señor Montenegro." She steps back, but not before giving my cheek a playful pat. The touch is fleeting, but I feel a phantom burn long after she's withdrawn. "A car will arrive for you tomorrow night. The driver will take you to the venue and bring you back to your hotel. Anything you desire—it will be provided."

"Thank you. That's very gracious."

"Until then…" As the woman saunters off, leaving behind a trail of seductive perfume and lingering anticipation, I can't help but glance at Josh. He's been remarkably stoic throughout this exchange, his eyes a steady anchor amidst the storm of our charade.

"So, this is it," Josh murmurs, moving to stand next to me. His voice, barely audible over the thumping club music, carries a heavy note of finality.

"Yes." The envelope clutched in my hand draws my eye. It feels heavier than it should, a potent symbol of the danger we're about to walk into.

We spend the rest of the night, and the following day, in a tense silence, each lost in our thoughts. The wait until the next evening is excruciating.

As dusk sets, it's time to put on our masks once more. We dress in our sharpest suits, the expensive material a stark contrast to the grim determination etched on our faces. There's no need for words as we wait for our ride, the heavy silence speaking volumes.

The car arrives on time, a sleek black limousine that screams over the top opulence and wealth. As we slide into the plush leather seats, I can't help but feel like we're crossing a threshold, leaving our familiar world behind.

The city blurs by as we drive, the vibrant heart of Mexico City slowly giving way to the grungy outskirts. As we draw closer to the venue, the buildings become more dilapidated, abandoned factories standing like silent sentinels. The further we go, the more pronounced the industrial feel becomes. An unsettling air of desolation, forgotten lives, and broken dreams lingers in the air.

The car pulls up in front of a warehouse. Its hulking form looms menacingly under the harsh glare of twin floodlights illuminating a parking area. Graffiti-covered walls, broken windows patched up with wooden planks, and a rusting iron door that screams danger complete the look. It's the perfect setting for the underground death rings.

An overwhelming stench of decay, mixed with old oil, hits us as we step out, the harsh cacophony of the bustling city replaced by an eerie silence, broken only by the distant sound of a crowd going wild.

Time to step into the belly of the beast and embrace the crimes of my past.

THIRTY

Paul

~

The dimly lit warehouse reeks of sweat and blood. Tension and anticipation clots the air. Josh and I stand shoulder to shoulder in the crowd, our eyes locked on the makeshift ring where two young boys will battle for their lives.

The crowd roars with anticipation, hungry for violence as two boys are led into the ring. There's a lanky teen with a feral intensity in his eyes that chills me to the bone. His spindly, scrawny frame is covered in scars from past battles, each one telling a story of survival in this hellish world.

He's a survivor, a killer who knows how to play this sick game.

Facing him is a lean, terrified boy, no older than twelve, who's clearly out of his depth. His pleading cries echo through the warehouse, sending shivers down my spine. No one cares about his desperate pleas. His fate was sealed the moment he was forced into this nightmare.

"Please, help me." The boy screams, tears streaming down his face. My heart clenches at his desperation, but there's nothing I can do. We have to play our part, blend into the crowd, and gather information if we're going to bring this brutal operation down.

As I watch the terrified boy, a fire ignites within me. He's untrained, weak, and terrified. His pleading cries for help go unanswered, drowned out by the bloodthirsty spectators. I want to intervene, save him from his fate, but we have to choose our moment with care.

Unfortunately, it won't be in time to save the poor boy. I resign myself to witnessing his fate.

"Begin!" A disembodied voice cries out the command, and a desperate battle commences.

The terrified boy tries to shield himself, but the lean champion strikes with precision, landing blow after brutal blow. The fight is every bit as gruesome as I feared. The lanky teen launches himself at the terrified boy, his fists flying mercilessly. The boy tries to dodge and defend, but it's clear he's untrained and outmatched. Blood sprays across the floor, and the terror in the boy's eyes intensifies as he realizes there's no escape. It's almost too much to bear when the crowd roars its approval.

The fight rages on, each brutal punch and kick etching itself into my memory. The brutal scene triggers memories of my own dark past. The smell of blood and sweat, the echoing screams of pain, and the taste of fear—it all comes flooding back. With each blow that lands on the boy's fragile frame, my determination to end these fights grows stronger.

My heart aches as the terrified boy crumples to the floor, defeated by his merciless opponent. The lanky teen stands victorious over the boy, his eyes cold and empty. His heart not yet hardened enough for murder.

"Finish him." The order comes from somewhere in the shadows, but the teen backs away, shaking his head and pleading into the shadowed depths of the crowd. Despite his brutality, it's clear this is the part of the fight the teen hates.

"Finish him now, or join him." The dark voice forces an impossible choice on the teen.

With resignation, the teen kneels beside the battered boy who struggles to breathe, but still has life in him. The teen leans down, whispers into the boy's ear, then quickly snaps the kid's neck. Next, he vomits on the ground.

The crowd goes wild, screaming and shouting as bets are won and lost. The teen rises to his feet, shoulders hunched, spirit crushed, soul defeated. He's escorted out of the ring, leaving the battered, broken body of the young boy behind. The crowd disperses, the thrill of violence sated for now. Josh and I exchange grim glances, knowing we have our work cut out for us.

The image of the terrified boy's bruised and lifeless body haunts me as I lean against a cold metal wall, trying to gather strength for what lies ahead. Memories of my own past flood back, unbidden, refusing to be ignored. My hands tremble with rage, fists clenched so tight that my knuckles turn white.

In my mind's eye, I see myself at the same age as the terrified boy, thrown into my first match and forced to fight a stronger, more experienced opponent. The memory is visceral—the acrid scent of sweat and blood; the feeling of bone crunching beneath my fists, the sickening terror knowing that one of us wouldn't leave that ring alive. By some miracle, I emerged victorious, but every subsequent fight was just as brutal, just as raw.

My hands turned bloody while my soul turned black as death. Like the victor of this fight, at first, that final kill was difficult. Later on, I felt nothing.

I push away from the wall with renewed determination. It's then that I notice the figure approaching us from across the dimly lit room: a man past his prime, with short-cropped hair that's starting to gray. He studies me with cold, calculating eyes. His stocky build exudes an air of authority as he moves through the crowd, sizing up potential clients.

Our invitation came from him.

"*Ah, mis amigos!*" Carlos Mendoza's oily smile gleams in the low light. "I trust you enjoyed the show?"

"Quite an adrenaline rush," Josh replies smoothly, the perfect picture of nonchalance.

"Indeed." I try to keep my voice steady despite my seething rage. This man profits from the suffering of children and deserves death. It's a struggle to keep my disgust in check. "We're always looking for something new. I hear you're the man to see if someone wants to get more involved in these—events?"

"Depends on what you mean by *involved*." Mendoza studies us with a predatory gaze. "You looking to place bets or step into the ring?"

"Actually…" I do my best to conceal my true intentions, "I have experience organizing fights. High-stakes, high-reward kind of stuff. We'd like to explore options, perhaps offer our services, to help make your operation even more profitable."

Mendoza's eyes narrow as he assesses our proposition. We both know how dangerous it is to get close to someone like Mendoza, but we also know it's our best chance to bring down the whole operation from the inside.

"An interesting proposition, but I don't kiss on the first date." Mendoza cackles at his joke. His tone cautious but intrigued. "And I don't know you. Not to mention, I don't need American help. You understand."

"Of course," I reply, trying to maintain my composure. "Trust must be earned."

"Indeed." Mendoza cocks his head, then shifts his weight to leave.

Before he does, I reel him back in. "Perhaps we can discuss what we offer in a less public place? Something more intimate. Quieter?" I can't help but feel nauseous at the request, but it's necessary to continue our charade.

"Of course," Mendoza agrees, his eyes narrowing with suspicion before he continues. "I do admire persistence. I'll arrange a private viewing for you both. I'll send a car to pick you up. Say seven o'clock, tomorrow?"

"Sounds perfect, but before we go…" I glance at Josh, knowing he's going to hate this, but there really is no other way. "I'd like to see the boys you've got lined up for the fights tomorrow night. Perhaps we can start with an investment in a young fighter?"

"One of my boys?"

"Yes. I'd like to train him to become a champion."

"American's are crazy," Mendoza replies, a predatory grin spreading across his face. "It will cost you."

"Money is no object."

"I've never had someone pick a boy to train."

"I like control when it comes to my bets. Much more willing to put money on a boy when he has at least a fighting chance of winning. That fight…" I gesture toward the empty ring. "It wasn't a fair fight, and not worth my time, or my money. Get a man *invested* in the outcome of a fight, and you'll be surprised how much he'll wager in return." I cock my head, trying to see if Mendoza is as smart as I believe.

"And is this how you will *help* me?"

"It is only one of several things. Do we have a deal?"

"If you want a boy, and are willing to pay, then yes. But it's still too soon for a *first kiss*."

"Understood. I appreciate your caution. We'll take things slow. Start with holding hands, and you giving me a boy."

"Give? Do I look like a man who hands out gifts to strangers?"

"Consider it a business investment." I'm not afraid to push. A man like Mendoza expects it and I aim to give him everything he expects and more.

"We are not in business." He stands firm, but from the shifting of his feet, it's a test of my resolve.

"Not yet, but we will be. Give me a boy to train and let's see what I can do with him."

"Do with him? Or to him?" Mendoza arches his brow, confirming what I already know. He had people watching us last night.

"Does it matter what I do to the boy?"

Mendoza bursts into laughter, tipping his head back, letting loose with a deep belly laugh. When he composes himself, the cold, calculating businessman returns. "Well, I'm game. Ten-thousand American dollars and you can pick out any boy. I think you'll find plenty of potential here."

"One hundred." I low-ball his offer, knowing the lives of these boys mean little to him. The only thing he stands to lose is in the profits of his bets.

"Now, that is an insult." He covers his chest, as if physically wounded.

"It's a boy. An untrained child. A hundred is more than enough."

"One-thousand." His eyes narrow as we barter over the life of a child. "A steal considering the boy will be sucking your dick for free."

"One hundred, or I take my customers and walk."

"Customers?"

"I did mention this was a business proposition."

"But you didn't mention customers."

"Because, we've yet to have our *first kiss*. Isn't that what you called it? Look, I'm no fool. Money is no option, but my time is valuable. Give me a boy, and we can discuss how I can triple your profits in three months, and triple them again within a year's time. Dick around with me, haggling over what should be a gift, and I walk. I have something you want, although you don't know it yet. You're only one operation I'm considering. Simply put, you need me, but I don't need you."

THIRTY-ONE

Paul

＊

Mendoza takes a step back to reassess both me and Josh. His oily gaze takes us in, weighing, measuring, judging.

"You are brave speaking to me like that." He spits on the ground, barely missing the leather of my shoes.

I don't flinch.

"I wonder if you have any idea who I am? Because, if you did, you would never dare speak to me like that."

"I know everything about you." I play my role well as an arrogant businessman. Josh, as my security, says nothing, but he makes his presence known. "Carlos Mendoza, the man who stands atop the pyramid of Mexico City's organized crime. You didn't get here overnight. Born to wealthy industrialist parents, Hector and Luisa Mendoza, you've always had a taste for power, but not for school or business. Your father owns a network of textile factories across the country, and your mother is the heiress of a powerful real estate mogul. Their riches could have offered you a life of comfort and luxury, but they disowned you when you chose the path less traveled, one littered with danger and thrills. You cut your teeth on the streets of Mexico City, navigating its darker corners with an uncanny ease. Your rise through the ranks was as swift as it was brutal. One by one, your rivals fell to your ruthlessness. You may not have a head for traditional business, but you're an expert at strategy and cold-blooded execution."

"How do you…?" His voice grows silent as I continue.

"You married Sofia Aguilar, a union more strategic than sentimental. Sofia, daughter of a high-ranking government official, brought connections and influence, extending your reach and increasing your power. You have three children, eldest son Hector, named after your father, a daughter, Rosa, and your youngest, a son, Eduardo. However, your eye wanders, and you claim many mistresses, most notably Lucinda who fathered at least two known illegitimate children, a daughter, Lucia, who you dearly love, and a son, Carlos Jr., who you're grooming to one day take over your empire."

Every detail of his life, his climb to the top of the criminal underworld, his family ties, his illicit relationships, all meticulously studied and stored in my memory. And now, as I face the man himself, every bit of information is a weapon, ready to be unleashed.

Carlos Mendoza remains silent for a long moment, his cold, calculating eyes studying mine. I meet his gaze steadily, refusing to be the one to break the silence.

"You have done your homework, Señor Montenegro." A shrewd man, he keeps his voice steady, giving no hint of his inner thoughts. "It's true, many of these facts are not hidden. But I wonder, how did you learn about Lucia, about Carlos Jr.? It seems you know more than just public records." He crosses his arms over his chest. "And you, a businessman from the States, a man of power and influence. Owner of Montenegro Tech, a leading company in the world of technology and digital innovation. One of the richest people in the world, although your name would never grace Forbes Top 100 Wealthiest Men. Quite an impressive resume you have. And yet, you are here, in my world, wanting to do business with me."

He leans forward, violating my personal space to see how I'll react. "Señor Montenegro, I'm intrigued by your proposition, but I need more than just your word to trust you." There's a challenge in his eyes, a silent dare. He's throwing down the gauntlet, and now it's my move.

His challenge hangs in the air between us, a tangible tension that electrifies the atmosphere. I lean back, studying him as he studies me, the relentless hum of the crowd a steady backdrop to our negotiation.

"Here's my word," I begin, my tone casual yet firm. "I have contacts, wealthy men with deep pockets and deeper desires for thrills of a darker variety. Men who would gladly pay to have a say in the game. Men who would invest not just money, but also resources to train their own champions."

I let my words sink in, watching as Mendoza's eyes gleam with the promise of potential profit. "They will choose their champions from your stock," I continue, my gaze never wavering from his. "Kids they select. Kids they train. People pay for the chance to play god. Give them the opportunity, and they'll pay whatever you ask." I lean in close. "And they're arrogant enough to bet millions on the boys they trained."

Mendoza shifts back, retreating from his intrusion into my personal space, a thoughtful look crosses his face. I can see the cogs turning in his head, calculating the profits, weighing the risks. He's silent for a long moment, his gaze unfathomable.

"Your proposition intrigues me, Señor Montenegro. If I give you a boy, I need assurance that you're not just going to disappear."

"When I say I'll do something, I do it. I'm offering you an opportunity. A chance to not just increase your profits, but to transform the game. If you're not interested, there are plenty of others who would jump at this chance."

His cold eyes meet mine, and for a moment, a spark of interest flashes in them. But I also see something else, something darker. A predator recognizing another predator, perhaps. The game is far from over, and the stakes have never been higher.

"Well played, Señor Montenegro. Let me show you what I have." With a nonchalant wave of his hand, Mendoza signals for us to follow him away from the chaos of the fight ring. The harsh fluorescent lights of the warehouse dim as we leave the frenzied spectacle behind, stepping into the underbelly of this sinister operation.

The sounds of the roaring crowd and the bone-crushing blows recede, replaced by the chilling echo of our footsteps on the concrete floor. As we journey deeper into the warehouse, I pick up a faint, but distinct odor—a blend of mustiness and the sharp scent of fear.

We're led through a series of industrial hallways, the stark brutality of the place reflected in the corroded metal walls and cold, cement floors. The air is cooler here, with a certain stillness that sends chills down my spine.

Our path is lit by intermittent lights overhead, casting long, looming shadows that dance eerily against the walls. It's as if we've crossed into another world entirely—one where humanity and compassion no longer exist.

Eventually, we reach a series of metal doors, each leading to a grim-looking cell. They're rudimentary and minimalistic, with nothing more than a rickety cot for comfort. Each cell contains a young fighter, their eyes hollow and haunted, bodies battered and bruised. It's clear the boys housed in these cells are valued for one thing only: their ability to fight. Not to mention, these are temporary cells.

Does he really intend to fight a dozen boys all in one night?

As we walk, my heart pounds in my chest, and I try to keep my breathing steady. We're surrounded by ruthless criminals who would kill us without hesitation if they knew our true intentions.

"An impressive collection." The words leave a bitter taste in my mouth. The children stare at me; their hope turns into disappointment as I barely glance at them and move on. I'm not the savior they're praying for, but just another monster to exploit them. The guilt weighs heavily on me, but I remind myself, this is all part of the act.

Mendoza stops at the end of the corridor. His hand comes to rest on the bars of the last cell. Inside is a young boy. His body is lean and fit, but his eyes tell a different story. They're filled with a grim determination, a will to survive that's as heartbreaking as it is admirable.

He looks just like I did when I was that age.

"Meet Alejandro," Mendoza's voice echoes off the cold, stone walls. "One of our most promising fighters."

"Very nice." I look at the boy, my heart sinking. He doesn't cower or avert his gaze. Instead, he meets my eyes, a silent challenge.

Mendoza's gaze narrows at my audacity, a dark glint in his eyes. For a moment, I fear I may have pushed him too far, but then, he lets out a grating laugh that sends chills down my spine.

"Bravo." His laughter echoes off the walls. He turns to a guard standing nearby. "Bring me the keys."

The man disappears down the corridor, only to return moments later with a set of rusted keys in his hand.

Mendoza takes them and walks over to Alejandro's cell. There's a resounding click as the lock gives way, and the door swings open. He steps inside, the young fighter watching with wary eyes. Mendoza reaches for the chains around Alejandro's hands and, one by one, unlocks them. The metal falls away, clattering against the stone floor.

As he walks out of the cell, Alejandro's steps are unsteady, cautious, as if he doesn't trust this newfound freedom. He shouldn't. The boy is far from free. Mendoza claps a hand on his shoulder, guiding him toward me.

"Consider Alejandro a—*gift*," Mendoza says, the words curling off his lips with a sly smirk. "Good for fighting and for fucking."

The boy flinches at that comment. His shoulders slump, and his chin drops in defeat.

A knot forms in my stomach as I look at the boy. He's just a kid, younger than Forest would've been if subjected to the death matches. Older than I was when I survived the ring and killed for the first time.

"Come, if you want to live." I extend my hand, and he takes it, his grip firm, his eyes filled with a silent plea, but there's no hope in his eyes.

It died like mine did after I won my first fight and killed for the first time. I was him once.

On the ride back to the hotel, Josh and I are silent, each lost in our thoughts. There's a sense of urgency now, a ticking time bomb that's Alejandro. I've seen the beast, and it's as horrifying as I'd imagined. I will bring this vile operation to its knees.

For Alejandro.

For Forest.

For all the others whose names I might never know.

The mission has become personal now. It's no longer just about bringing the rings down, it's about saving these kids, giving them a chance at a life they've been robbed of. As the city lights pass in a blur, I make a silent vow to end this, no matter what it costs.

Mexico City, being what it is, nobody makes a fuss when Josh and I manhandle the terrified boy through the lobby and take him up to our room. To my surprise, the boy doesn't attempt to escape.

As soon as we step into the penthouse, I turn to Alejandro, a grimace pulling at my lips. "You need a shower, kid. You smell like shit, piss, and fear." I gesture to the en-suite bathroom. He flinches at the blunt statement but doesn't argue, just nods and shuffles away.

Josh watches him go, then turns to me. "Don't get attached."

"That's not going to happen. This isn't about attachment. This is about doing what's right." I shoot him a cool look, my heart pounding with a mix of adrenaline and exhaustion.

Josh doesn't respond, but the concern in his eyes tells me he's not entirely convinced.

The water runs in the bathroom and I move to one of the sofas, sinking down into the plush cushions. The penthouse suddenly feels grotesque; the glitzy décor of bloated wealth stands in stark contrast to the squalor we left behind.

As I listen to Alejandro's quiet movements in the bathroom, a thought strikes me. This is the first time in a long time the boy must have felt the comfort of warm water, the simple luxury of cleanliness. The disparity of our lives is so profound it feels like a physical weight on my chest.

Turning my gaze to the cityscape beyond the window, my determination solidifies. We'll bring this nightmare to an end. No more kids will be trapped in this deadly game. As I watch the lights of Mexico City twinkle in the distance, this mission has become more than just a job.

It's become a calling.

The metallic taste of blood still lingers in my mouth from the arena. The screams of the crowd echo in my ears, a haunting reminder of that terrified boy's final moments.

Moments that may very well be Alejandro's last, if I don't teach him how to survive.

I suddenly know what drives Forest. I thought I knew, but I didn't understand the depths of Forest's passion to save others from the fate he endured. With my thoughts turning to Forest, wondering how he's holding up, whether they've started the bone marrow transplant, I ache to call him on the phone.

To hear his voice.

To know he's okay.

My greatest fear is I'll never see him again.

THIRTY-TWO

Paul

As the first rays of dawn stream into the penthouse, my eyes flick open. I find myself already wide awake, the urgency of our mission a stark reminder that there's no time to waste. Lying on the sofa, I turn my gaze toward Alejandro. He's asleep on the other sofa across the room, his body curled in on itself as if to ward off the nightmares that undoubtedly haunt his dreams.

I push off the sofa and move toward the kitchen. The penthouse is quiet, the distant hum of Mexico City slowly coming alive despite the soundproofed windows. Not long after starting the coffee maker, the aroma of coffee percolates through the air. Its familiar scent is a comfort in the chaos that has become my life.

I glance over my shoulder, watching Alejandro's peaceful form. There's a certain innocence about him when he sleeps, one that's painfully juxtaposed against the hardened survivor he has to be when he's awake. It stirs a protective instinct in me that I didn't know I had, fueling my determination to save this boy from the death rings.

When the coffee is ready, I pour a cup and take a sip, the bitterness a bracing welcome to the day. The silence of the morning washes over me as I plan the day ahead. We start Alejandro's training, which means we need to gain his trust. Not really sure how that's going to happen.

By the time Alejandro stirs, room service delivers a simple breakfast: slices of fresh fruit, granola, and yogurt. His bleary eyes blink open, squinting against the morning light spilling into the penthouse. He sits up slowly, his movements cautious and deliberate. I wonder how long it's been since he's woken up without the immediate threat of violence.

"Breakfast," I announce, gesturing to the food. Alejandro's gaze flicks to the spread, his brow furrowing before he pushes off the couch and shuffles over. He says nothing as he takes a seat, his weary gaze flicking between me and the food. The boy is hungry but not trusting enough to eat.

Josh emerges from his room, his hair disheveled from sleep. He grunts a good morning and goes straight for the coffee, his movements a mirror of my own earlier this morning. We exchange a glance over Alejandro's head, a silent acknowledgment of the gravity of the task ahead.

As Alejandro tentatively begins to eat, I study his sunken eyes that are alert and watchful. A profound weariness stoops his shoulders, as if he's already accepted his fate: that this life will be short and brutal for him.

That strikes a chord in me. This kid has seen too much. He's suffered too much. But he's still willing to fight. I can work with that.

"Eat." I kick his plate under his nose and wait. When he's done, I have him clear the dishes before bringing him into the living area.

Time to get down to business.

"We're going to teach you how to fight." I face him and his gaze locks onto mine.

"Why?" His back straightens as if bracing himself for a blow.

"Don't you want to survive?"

His eyes widen, but he doesn't argue or protest. Instead, he nods, his jaw setting in a grim line of determination. That's a start. And in this deadly game, every small victory counts.

In the penthouse, with the sprawling cityscape of Mexico City as our backdrop, our makeshift training camp begins. The task is daunting, the stakes higher than ever, but as we start, I'm buoyed by one singular thought: we're not training Alejandro to fight. We're training him to live.

The days roll into a kind of rhythm, the penthouse transforming into a sanctuary of sweat, grunts, and grim determination. Josh and I take turns training Alejandro, utilizing our respective strengths and skills. I teach him the art of subterfuge and strategy, using one's mind as a weapon, which is as potent as a fist or a kick. Josh brings his expertise as a former prison inmate, teaching Alejandro to play dirty. How to immobilize an opponent quickly and efficiently.

Our training sessions are intense, a grueling mix of physical exertion and mental gymnastics. Alejandro is a quick learner, absorbing our teachings like a sponge. Yet, his haunted eyes serve as a constant reminder of why we're doing this. The threat hanging over him is not a hypothetical one.

It's real, and it's lethal.

When not training, Alejandro stares out the window. I don't ask what he's thinking, but something's on the boy's mind. I'm here to teach him how to fight and give him the best chance at survival. I'm not here to pry into his past. Josh warned me not to get attached, but I wonder about the boy.

Every so often, I find my thoughts drifting to Forest. His determination, his unwavering resolve, it's all become a beacon of sorts for me. What would Forest do in my place? The answer is clear as day. He'd fight. He'd fight with everything he's got. He'd make sure Alejandro survives. That's exactly what I'm going to do.

As another day of training comes to an end, Alejandro drops onto the couch, exhausted and gasping for breath. His skinny body is starting to toughen up. He's steadier on his feet. His awareness sharpens. His moves become more deliberate. More calculated.

He's far from ready, but there's progress.

Just when things settle into a rhythm, a sharply dressed man in a suit knocks on the door of the penthouse. Are we compromised?

"Señor Montenegro?" The man extends a hand. "My name is Emilio. I work for Señor Mendoza. He sends his regards."

I keep my face neutral, my grip firm as I shake his hand. "What brings you here?"

Emilio glances at Alejandro, who watches the exchange with wide eyes. "Señor Mendoza is curious about the progress of his—*investment*. He wishes to see a demonstration."

This is dangerous. I glance at Josh who tenses. If Alejandro doesn't perform to their expectations if he reveals too much of what we've taught him…

"I'm afraid I'm not ready to provide a demonstration. We're still working on his conditioning and building his strength."

Emilio's gaze flicks to Alejandro again, a cold assessment that has the boy stiffening. "Señor Mendoza expects results. You have one week."

"I'll see what we can do."

After Emilio leaves, I turn to Josh, anxiety gnawing at my gut. "We need to accelerate his training."

"Agreed." Josh nods, his jaw clenched. "Let's get back to it then."

We return to the grueling routine, the urgency even more palpable now. Each day brings us closer to the inevitable, a moment of truth that could very well spell the end for Alejandro and our mission.

We train.

We strategize.

We plan.

Above all, we hope.

Because Alejandro faces insurmountable odds.

One morning, Alejandro's gaze lingers on the television as a soccer match plays out. The players dart back and forth across the green field, the announcer's rapid-fire Spanish filling the penthouse with a semblance of normalcy.

"You enjoy football?"

"I used to play." Alejandro's voice is soft, his eyes distant. "Before…"

Josh raises an eyebrow from across the room, but doesn't comment. His words about not becoming attached run through my head. I wish I could save Alejandro from his fate, but my hands are tied. Instead, I teach him to fight and hopefully survive.

But survive what?

To fight again? To kill again?

When I was in Alejandro's shoes, I lived week by week, fight by fight. Weeks turned to months. Then months turned to years. When I turned seventeen, Snowden removed me from the ring.

I was too good and people stopped betting against me. I once thought Snowden saved me from the ring, but he was really only looking out for his business. My victories cost him because no one bet against me.

The next day, I surprise Alejandro. After an intense morning of training, I call for a break. We sit down in front of the large TV screen, game controllers in hand, a soccer match awaiting us in the virtual world.

Alejandro lights up. He may not be on a real field, but the joy of the game remains the same. He laughs. He cheers. He groans when his team loses a point. For a moment, he's not a fighter. He's just a kid enjoying a game.

As the days roll on, our routine becomes more structured. Josh takes on the task of building Alejandro's physical strength and endurance, pushing him to his limits and then some. I focus on honing his tactical thinking and survival instincts, running him through countless scenarios and strategies, making sure he's prepared for every possible outcome.

Our training sessions are intense and demanding. Alejandro is a quick study, absorbing our teachings like a sponge. One evening, after a particularly grueling session, I stroll over to where Alejandro sits by the window, gazing out at the city lights.

"It's a stunning view, don't you think?"

His gaze remains on the city lights. When he finally responds, his voice is barely above a whisper. "Can I survive this?"

His question hangs heavy in the silence. We both know what he's asking—not just if he can survive the upcoming fight, but if he can survive this world that's forced him into a cage.

I don't sugarcoat my response. "I don't know."

The following day, we push harder in our training. Each punch, each move, each strategy is not just about fighting—it's about survival.

As we continue to train him, he surprises me with his progress.

The boy is a quick study. He's a far cry from the terrified boy we first brought into the penthouse.

During a quiet moment after dinner, Alejandro stands with his back to the window, his gaze unwavering as he confronts me. "You're not just training me to fight. You're teaching me how to win."

"I have a lot riding on your victory." I lean back in my chair, studying him carefully.

"When Señor Mendoza gave me to you, I thought…" He shuffles on his feet. "You haven't…"

"I fuck men, not boys. My interest in you begins and ends with how well you fight."

"If I survive."

"When you survive, it means you fought well." No reason to sugarcoat it.

"But I must kill." The muscles of his jaw clench.

"I don't make the rules."

I wish I could tell him the truth, but Alejandro is young, impressionable, and incapable of keeping a secret. My intention toward him is completely self-serving, and perhaps I should be judged for my actions. I justify what I do to Alejandro believing the end justifies the means.

But that's a load of crap.

I'm using the boy.

"Why are you working so hard?"

"I have a reason to live." He swallows hard, his fists clenching at his sides.

"And what's that?" My curiosity is piqued.

Alejandro takes a deep breath before he utters words that send a jolt through me. "When Mendoza took me, he took my sister too. I don't know what he's done with her, but I know what men like him do to girls."

His plea hits me like a physical blow, knocking the breath out of me. The desperation and fear that lurks beneath his bravado twist my guts. I can't make any promises; the road ahead is too uncertain, but I find myself nodding.

"You can't save her fighting in the ring."

"But if I win…"

"You have years ahead of you." I wish I could explain—share what happened to me—but Alejandro is too young to understand.

His nod is barely perceptible, but it's there. He knows his fate.

His words, however, add another layer of complexity to our mission, but in the end, it's all the more reason to fight, to win, and to bring down the man who causes so much suffering. For Alejandro. For his sister. For all the kids who've been ensnared in this vile operation.

The mission has indeed become a calling. Unfortunately, the week is almost over. We leave tonight, and Alejandro will either take what he's learned and survive, or he will perish.

THIRTY-THREE

Paul

Once again, I wake to a new day. Morning light pours into the penthouse, painting the high-end décor with streaks of vivid golden hues. The opulent surroundings stand in stark contrast to the pulsating grit and bustle of Mexico City awakening outside.

The day of Alejandro's demonstration is upon us. We've trained him relentlessly, but will it be enough?

Today, he will live, or he will die.

I take a moment for myself, needing to hear Forest's voice. I clutch my phone, tracing the smooth edges as I dial Forest's number. Will he pick up?

The call goes to voicemail.

"Forest, it's me." My gaze shifts to Alejandro, his young form moving through a practice routine with Josh. Grim determination fills the young boy's face.

"I—I need to hear you. Know you're okay." He should be getting his bone marrow transplant any day.

The deafening silence that follows Forest's message is a slap in the face, a void filled with the impersonal tone of an automated voicemail message. Swallowing the lump in my throat, I disconnect the call. Forest's absence is a festering wound growing inside of me.

Sure, it was Josh who brought me on this mission, but Forest's rejection is why I came. The pain is harsh, a constant reminder of how I violated his trust. How I ruined us. With a sigh, I put my phone away and focus on what matters.

Across the room, Alejandro shadowboxes with a fierce determination that makes me momentarily proud. It's been two weeks. Two weeks of grueling training, and the boy's shown remarkable progress.

But will it be enough?

Alejandro's life is on the line.

I call out to Alejandro, my voice deliberately calm. "Time to wrap up and rest for tonight."

Alejandro pauses, meeting my gaze with a steady one of his own. We've had him for two weeks, yet the boy staring back at me has aged years.

He gives a single nod before completing his practice routine, each move precise and calculated.

I can't shake the gnawing worry clawing at my insides. Despite our best efforts, despite the countless hours spent training him, I can't shake the fear it might not be enough.

But there's no backing out now.

My phone vibrates and the screen lights up with Sara's name. With a quick glance at Alejandro, I step away, pressing the device to my ear.

"Thanks for calling." After trying to get a hold of Forest earlier, I called Sara. She didn't answer me either. At first, I thought maybe she'd forsaken me as well, but she texted back that she was busy. Forest was back in the hospital. "How bad is it?"

Sara sighs on the other end, the sound heavy with concern. "It's… It's rough. Another infection. The doctors say that once he recovers from this, we can move forward with the transplant."

A lump forms in my throat, the words bitter as they hang in the air. I press my hand to my forehead, my mind spinning with concern for Forest.

"How are you holding up?"

"I'm—I'm okay." Her voice trembles ever so slightly. "Just taking one day at a time." Her strength is a silent testament to her love for Forest.

"And the twins? How are they?"

"They're strong. Like their fathers." The compliment stings, a bitter reminder of the physical distance separating me from the ones I love. "They really don't know what's going on."

We fall silent, but there's something else I need to address.

"Sara…" I hesitate before I plunge ahead. "About us…"

"Do you regret kissing me?" She falls silent.

"I only regret not kissing you sooner." I take in a deep breath, steeling myself for what I'm about to confess. My heart races as I push forward, compelled by a force stronger than fear. "You've awakened something I've never felt before. Something I want to explore, but without Forest, and his blessing…"

"Paul…"

"No, let me get this out." My throat tightens. "If I don't make it back…" It's a risk, a real possibility given the danger we're about to face. "I need you to know that I love you. Not as a part of our throuple, but in the way a man falls in love with a woman. I'd like to explore it further—if we get the chance, but I don't want to do anything without Forest's consent." I hold my breath as I wait for Sara's response.

I brace myself for rejection, for anger, for confusion, but when she speaks, her voice is barely audible over the line.

"I love you too. I've been trying to figure out how it's going to work. Like do we… Do the three of us… Or…" Flustered, she can't continue.

"Sara," I cut in, my voice calm despite the whirlwind of emotions inside me. "We'll figure out the mechanics of a threesome later. I just… I needed you to know I want that with you. I want all of it with you. Not just sex. I want it with Forest. I want it with both of you. He's been hoping for a threesome forever, but I figure, sometimes, it'll be just the two of us."

Her silence stretches, but it's not as suffocating as before. It's heavy, but there's an undercurrent of understanding. I don't know how it will all work out, but we've always been unconventional.

"I want that too." Then she giggles. "And it will totally blow Forest's mind if the three of us…" She pauses. "Never in my life would I have ever thought I'd be involved in a threesome. I need to do some research."

"Love, you don't need to research anything. I know exactly what to do."

"Does that mean you'd be my Dom as well?"

"I wouldn't be against it, but some people simply aren't wired for that kind of relationship. I don't think it's a good fit for you. At least not yet. I'll top you instead."

"Top? What's that mean?"

"Makes me the one who does stuff to you, and you're the one who has stuff done to you by me. Like I said, don't worry about it." A weight lifts off my chest. It's out there now; Sara knows my feelings and the depth of my affection for her.

"We'll talk when I get back," I promise, the words tasting like a vow. "Stay strong, love. For Forest, for the twins."

"For you. I will." She promises to do so, her voice strengthening with resolve. We say our goodbyes, each returning to our respective battles. As I end the call, a sense of purpose propels me.

For Sara. For Forest. For the twins. And Alejandro. I've got battles to fight, and I intend to win them all.

My gaze flickers to Alejandro. This boy whose life now hangs in the balance means more to me than he should. Josh warned me not to get attached, but I'm attached and emotionally invested in Alejandro's success.

I pocket my phone, hardening my features into a mask of determination. The upcoming fight will be a test of our training techniques, a harsh reality Alejandro must face.

"Remember what we taught you." Josh places his hand on Alejandro's shoulder as he leads the boy out of the room. "Stay alive."

Alejandro doesn't respond; just gives us a curt nod.

We travel back to the warehouse, the journey passing in tense silence. The warehouse is just as I remember it, teeming with dangerous men. It's an arena of savagery, a place where childhood innocence comes to die. And we're walking Alejandro right back into it. The guilt gnaws at me, but there's a grim purpose behind our actions. A mission we cannot afford to fail.

Mendoza's men have done a good job hyping up the return of their little 'champion.' Betting is rife, money exchanging hands with unseemly eagerness.

As Alejandro steps into the ring, I steel myself for the battle ahead. I take one final look at the kid we've come to care for before turning to find the monster that started it all.

The opponent Alejandro is up against is a good foot taller and much bulkier than him. Alejandro looks like a small and utterly outmatched rabbit cornered by a wolf. The crowd, always hungry for blood, roars its anticipation, the cacophony deafening.

The sight of Alejandro in the center of the blood-stained ring makes my stomach churn, but we lit a fire in Alejandro. He isn't giving up. He's aware of his size disadvantage, but there's a fire burning in him that's undeniable.

The larger fighter lunges first, a powerful fist rocketing toward Alejandro. Alejandro's response is swift. His body coils and snaps like a tightly wound spring. He sidesteps the blow, the teachings from our training sessions echoing in the movement. He answers with a punch of his own, quick and calculated, straight to the gut of his adversary.

The fight is intense, brutal. Every punch Alejandro throws, every dodge, every kick, is a fight for survival. He's agile, quick, using his size to his advantage, ducking beneath the older boy's wild swings and getting in his own jabs where he can. A wave of roars and cheers breaks from the crowd, an audible reflection of the adrenaline surging through Alejandro's veins.

He becomes a tempest in the center of the ring, a flurry of punches, dodges, and kicks that blur into a deadly dance. He's nimble, sliding beneath the larger boy's telegraphed swings with a grace that belies the lethal intent of his moves. Each blow he lands —a jab to the ribs, a hook to the exposed flank—is a declaration of his tenacity.

With each punishing blow landed on Alejandro, a vise tightens around my gut, but every successful retaliation inflates my chest, pride threatening to burst forth. This fight lacks any semblance of elegance; it's a manifestation of raw survival instincts, a brutal ballet of clashing fists and gritted teeth.

Alejandro maneuvers, pirouettes, his body flexing and bending around the larger boy's strikes, absorbing, redirecting, and countering each attack. His lithe frame bears evidence of punishing blows with a deepening palette of bruises, his skin smeared with grit and sweat, yet he never stops. The boy is a study in grit and resolve. He's bruised. He's bloodied, but he holds his own. That's the difference between winning and losing.

The fight drags on. Then, as if in slow motion, Alejandro sweeps his foot low, catching his opponent off balance. Seizing the moment, Alejandro rushes forward, connecting a punch square to the opponent's jaw.

There's an audible crunch, a gasp from the crowd, and then his opponent falls. Alejandro stands victorious over the unconscious fighter; a boy learning how to kill.

A deafening roar fills the air, a mixture of boos and cheers. Alejandro stands in the center of the ring, panting heavily.

He won.

Against all odds, he survived.

But the look in his eyes tells me he feels anything but victorious. His survival comes at a heavy price.

"Finish him." Again, that cold voice calls out. A voice that belongs to none other than Mendoza himself.

Horror ripples through Alejandro's face, but he lets it pass and steels himself for what must be done. He takes a knee. Places his hands on the older boy's face. Like the fight we saw the other night, Alejandro leans down and whispers something drowned out by all the noise. With a quick snap of the boy's neck, Alejandro leans back, tears streaming down his cheeks.

A man enters the ring, grabs Alejandro's arm, and whisks Alejandro away. I turn my gaze to the bloody spectacle and rage boils inside of me.

The taste of victory is bitter on my tongue, tainted by the blood spilled on the ground. We trained him to survive, but it's a gruesome fate that requires him to kill.

I drag my gaze away from Alejandro's retreating figure to meet Josh's stern gaze. Our mission isn't about saving one boy, it's about dismantling this operation. It's about ending this cycle of violence.

Just then, a burly guard approaches, his large frame casts a long shadow. "Señor Mendoza wants to see you."

This is it, the next step in our mission. It's time to bring Mendoza down from within, to crumble his empire piece by piece. The weight of our responsibility settles heavily on my shoulders as we follow the guard, leaving behind the noise and bloodlust of the crowd.

The guard escorts us to the back offices of the warehouse, an opulent oasis in the midst of chaos. Mendoza sits behind a large mahogany desk, his eyes cold and calculating.

"Please, take a seat." He gestures to the plush chairs across from him. "Your boy fought well tonight." Mendoza's voice is devoid of any warmth or sincerity.

"You doubted us?" I force a polite smile.

"I don't know you. Now that we're getting better acquainted, things are different." Carlos Mendoza leans back, draping his arms over the plush arms of his leather chair. The gold on his fingers glints in the room's dim light. "You mentioned a business proposition."

"Oh, I've got a proposition that'll have you grinning like a fool." I let a chuckle slip, just a light, easy one. My fingers tap a rhythmic tattoo on the armrest of my chair.

The barest hint of interest flickers across his guarded features. His fingers drum on the armrest, a silent invitation for me to continue.

Clearing my throat, I fold my hands together in my lap. "You've got a stable full of prime prospects here. Boys itching for a chance to prove themselves in the ring. Now, imagine my buyers getting to choose their champion."

"And what do I charge for this? A thousand? Ten-thousand?"

"No. You give the boys away for free."

"Free?" His sharp eyes bore into mine, skeptical, but intrigued.

I flash a knowing smile. "Exactly. For free. Like you did for me. Handpicked for their potential.

"And where is the profit in that?" He leans forward, a glint of curiosity, and greed, shining in his eyes. The earlier skepticism seems to recede as he realizes there's more to this deal.

I continue, driving home the crux of my proposition. "My buyers aren't training the boys for their health. They're running them in the rings, same as you. But, they're betting big, and they're betting often. They'll want to bet in your ring because that's where the best fights are. That's where the money is. It's where the spectacle is. Your reputation benefits, and more importantly, so does your bottom line."

His eyes narrow at that, but he doesn't look angry. If anything, he looks thoughtful, like he's mentally calculating potential gains.

"The betting profits you'd rake in would dwarf what you'd make selling the boys. Now, imagine what happens when the rivalries start? My clients competing against each other? Training their champions to win? Their bets will escalate. The crowd will shift their bets from the boys to the men who trained them. It's a feeding frenzy, and all you have to do is prime the pump." I lean back and fold my arms. "Everyone wins. You get richer. My buyers get fighters. And the spectators get a show they won't forget."

There's a heavy silence as he digests my words. His eyes are sharp, considering, as they bore into mine. His fingers tap a rhythmic beat on the armrest, the only sound in the room as he contemplates the business before him. He looks thoughtful, like he's mentally calculating potential gains.

We tread on dangerous ground, a single misstep could blow our cover. But I hold his gaze, projecting an air of confidence.

"Help it grow?" he asks, a smirk playing on his lips. "And what do you get out of it?"

"Money, power." I shrug, falling into the role of a cold, calculating businessman. "The same things we all want."

Mendoza's eyes glitter with intrigue. He leans back in his chair, considering my proposition. The silence stretches as he weighs his options.

Finally, he leans forward, a devilish grin on his face. "Very well," he says. "Let's talk business."

Our plan is set in motion, a dangerous dance with a deadly partner, but we're ready to face whatever comes our way. For Alejandro, for his sister, and for every other victim of Mendoza's vile operation.

THIRTY-FOUR

Paul

~

SEVERAL DAYS LATER, WE FIND OURSELVES INVITED TO MENDOZA'S estate. We bring with us a potential client as a proof of concept for Mendoza. To do this, we're joined by Xavier, a man who straddles the line between what is, and is not, illegal. Xavier's connections run deep, and he's exactly the kind of client we want Mendoza to think we bring.

A gracious host, our invitation comes with car service. After an hour's drive outside the city limits, we find ourselves pulling up to an impressive retreat.

The heat bears down on the three of us as we exit the black limousine. Our tailored shirts stick to our backs, the oppressive humidity a tangible reminder of the environment we've inserted ourselves into.

Xavier steps out behind us, his eyes hidden behind dark sunglasses. The heat doesn't seem to affect him. He's calm, cool, and collected. The man is a mystery, his conncction to our cause only deepening the enigma.

"Quite a place, isn't it?" I venture, my voice steady despite the unease swirling in my gut.

"Unmistakable charm, I'll give him that." A wry smile pulls at the corner of Xavier's mouth. He takes off his sunglasses, revealing a gaze that, while calm, holds a sharpened edge.

Josh chuckles, his humor touched with a bitterness that speaks volumes about his feelings toward Mendoza and his operation. "Carlos Mendoza is known for his flair. He peddles a decadent fantasy that hides the brutal reality of his business."

"As we discussed, Mendoza isn't selling seats to watch the fights. He's offering you a chance to play god." I hesitate, glancing at the driver before continuing in a lower tone of voice. "You'll be able to pick a boy, train him, guide him. You'll be the puppet master pulling the strings."

Xavier nods, a grim understanding in his eyes. "The stakes are higher, the game more personal. I'm intrigued." His voice is neutral, his comment a well-rehearsed line in our shared narrative.

We march toward the grand estate, the tension humming like a live wire between us. Our objective is clear: infiltrate, gather intelligence, and bring down Mendoza's operation; no matter the cost.

We're greeted by Mendoza's guards, their imposing figures casting long shadows in the early evening light. They stand like specters, cold professionalism etched into every line of their bodies, their eyes sharp and calculating beneath the brims of their caps. Silent threats resonate from their very stance, a warning of the power they represent.

One by one, they pat us down. Their touch methodical, impersonal, and utterly invasive as they search for concealed weapons. The rough fabric of their gloves grazes my sides and I suppress a shudder. The silent assertion of power is an unspoken insult, a veiled challenge.

Beside me, Josh endures the same treatment. His body is rigid, his face an impassive mask, but there's a hard glint in his eyes, a spark of rebellion. He says nothing, accepting the indignity with a forced calm.

Their gaze finally settles on Xavier, their scrutiny lingering as if expecting to find a hidden threat. Xavier meets their gaze head-on, a slow, confident smile spreading across his lips.

"This is how you greet your guests?" Xavier's voice breaks the charged silence, his tone light, but carrying a subtle edge. "I'm not used to such a—hands-on welcome."

"Standard procedure." One of the guards, a burly man with a scar bisecting his face, responds with a noncommittal grunt.

Xavier's smile doesn't waver, a display of self-assured defiance that even the Cheshire Cat would envy. "Well, your standards need to be improved." Somehow, he manages to keep his tone breezy despite the undercurrent of tension.

As the gates open to welcome us into Mendoza's estate, we share a silent pause. The game has truly begun.

Inside the gates, Mendoza's estate is a testament of extravagant wealth. The splendor is a chilling contrast to the brutal blood sport Mendoza peddles. I glance at Josh, our eyes briefly meeting, and I can sense the shared unease. We exchange a few hushed words, attempting to maintain our charade amidst the opulence that conceals the horrors lurking beneath the surface.

As we follow Mendoza's guards through the grand halls, the sickening reality of Mendoza's operation becomes even more apparent. Young females, mere girls really, drift aimlessly through the corridors, their fragile bodies clad in revealing attire that leaves little to the imagination. They move with an unsettling grace, their vacant eyes scanning the passing guests, searching for an opportunity to offer comfort and companionship.

Their presence is a haunting reminder of the depths of depravity to which Mendoza and his operation stoop. The broken smiles they wear, masks of forced happiness, can't conceal the pain and anguish etched into their fragile beings.

Some bear bruises and marks of violence, silent testimony to the abuse they endure. Others carry themselves with vacant eyes, their spirits broken and hope extinguished. It's a chilling sight that wrenches my heart and stokes the fires of determination within me.

A girl approaches, her steps measured, her voice laced with seduction, and her eyes shimmering with submission. "Sir, I am a gift from Señor Mendoza. Please allow me to attend to your needs."

I'm taken aback by the girl's submissive demeanor and the implication of Mendoza's offering. I hesitate for a moment, my discomfort evident, and clear my throat, trying to find the right words.

"Thank you, but I'm here on business and respectfully decline."

Another girl approaches Josh, her countenance demure and her voice barely audible. She holds herself with an air of innocence, her eyes downcast. "Sir," she whispers gently, her voice filled with vulnerability. "Señor Mendoza has bestowed upon me the honor of serving you. Please allow me to provide you with comfort and pleasure."

Josh is as startled by the girl's submissive offer as me. He struggles to find his words, glancing at her with a mix of sympathy and concern.

"Thank you, but no."

A third girl approaches Xavier, her eyes cast down and her voice trembling. She radiates an aura of vulnerability, her presence submissive and unassuming. "Sir," she breathes delicately, her voice filled with a mix of fear and anticipation. "Señor Mendoza has chosen me to be at your disposal. Please allow me to serve you in any way you desire."

"While I appreciate Mendoza's gesture, I have other matters to attend to. Perhaps another time." Xavier's lips curl into a sly smile as he gazes at her with a hint of amusement.

The girls exchange terrified glances, their fear palpable. I catch the unspoken communication, realization dawning upon me. I glance at the girls and then at my companions.

"Wait, it would be rude of us to deny such a wonderful gift. Please, you may accompany us."

Both Josh and Xavier give me a look, but then understanding dawns on their faces.

"Yes, of course." Josh agrees with me, his voice filled with compassion. "Please join us. We wouldn't want any harm to befall you."

Xavier inclines his head, his amusement giving way to a sense of responsibility. "Very well, you may accompany me."

The girls, their eyes betraying both gratitude and apprehension, fall into step beside us, their presence now reluctantly accepted. We exchange a knowing glance between us, a silent acknowledgement of the unsavory realities we find ourselves entangled in. We continue walking, our footsteps steady, even as our hearts throb with a burning desire for justice.

We're led into a lavishly decorated room, a stark contrast to the brutality of Mendoza's operation. The opulence borders on obscene, the excesses of wealth and power on full display.

My gaze sweeps over the room, taking in the intricately designed furniture, the expensive artwork hanging on the walls, and the ostentatious display of wealth. It's a deceptive cover for the heinous activities that occur under Mendoza's command.

Sitting behind a mahogany desk, Carlos Mendoza commands the room. His dark eyes, as piercing as the espresso he sips, lock onto Xavier.

I swallow, my throat dry, and plaster a smile on my face, hiding the turmoil swirling within me. We have to play our parts convincingly.

As Xavier begins his dance with Mendoza, I remind myself we're here to gather information, to expose the dark underbelly of this operation, and ultimately bring Mendoza and his empire crashing down.

"Allow me to introduce Xavier St. James." I step forward to break the ice. "An entrepreneur with an appetite for the unusual and exciting."

Mendoza's gaze shifts to me, a slight inclination of his head acknowledging my introduction. "Welcome, Señor. St. James." Mendoza's voice, rich as velvet, welcomes Xavier. "I trust the heat of my country isn't too much for you?"

Xavier chuckles, a sound devoid of true amusement. "I've always had a fondness for the heat."

Mendoza appears to accept his words, a shark-like grin spreading across his face. "Good. We have a saying here, 'If you can't stand the heat, stay out of the fire.'" Amusement fills his eyes.

A waiter enters the room, bearing a tray of drinks. Mendoza gestures toward him. "Perhaps a drink to quench your thirst? Water? Or something harder? Scotch? Whiskey?"

"Whiskey for me." Xavier inclines his head. "Thank you for the warm welcome and for the gifts." He gestures toward the female slaves.

"Of course, feel free to make use of them as you please. Perhaps after dinner, you would like to enjoy additional company?" He flicks a glance to a closed door, the insinuation clear.

"I prefer not to mix business and pleasure. Your girls are stunning. Perhaps next time?" Xavier waves away the offer of company, his gesture casual, but his voice firm. He takes the offered drink, swirling the amber liquid contemplatively before raising it toward Mendoza. "You mentioned the fighting ring, but perhaps there's a misunderstanding?" Xavier's voice holds a deeper, more dangerous kind of craving.

Mendoza, leaning back in his seat, feigns surprise, although he knows exactly why Xavier is here. "If not the ring, then what interests you?"

Xavier meets his gaze squarely, a glint of excitement dancing in his eyes. "The sport of it." He states his want simply. "I'm eager to check out the boys Paul mentioned and pick a boy to represent me." He leans forward, his gaze fixed intently on Mendoza. "I find the thrill of a simple bet pales in comparison to the excitement of molding raw, untamed talent. I enjoy the sport of it."

Xavier's words hang in the air, a tantalizing offer and an unveiled challenge all in one. His focus isn't just the fights, but in the shaping of a boy into a champion. He wants Mendoza to give him access to the fighters, a dangerous demand, but one that offers a unique kind of thrill to the brutal businessman.

"Now this I can do." Mendoza echoes Xavier's desires, raising his own glass. "To new ventures among new friends."

He toasts, a subtle test of our intent wrapped in the guise of a cordial toast. We echo his sentiment, raising our own glasses, the clinking sound echoing ominously in the room.

The liquid scorches its way down my throat, but I manage to keep my smile intact. We've passed the first test, but the game is just beginning.

"Dinner will be served within the hour. Until then, feel free to explore. Take advantage of my gifts. The dinner bell will alert you when it's time, and my girls will show you where to go."

"We're not visiting your boys? I thought…" Xavier plays his role flawlessly. "I thought I would pick one out tonight?"

"In my country, it's always pleasure before business. Please, enjoy my home. Enjoy the girls. I have a few things which require my attention. I will see you at dinner, after which I can show you your potentials."

And just like that, we're dismissed.

Paul

~

Knowing not to push Mendoza, I allow the girls to lead us out of his office and command them to take us on a tour of the estate and its grounds.

His men follow us, heavy weaponry slung across their broad shoulders. We move through the main building, walking past rooms dripping with luxury. One of the girls provides a detailed account of each room's treasures. As we move through one of several courtyard gardens, I subtly release two of Mitzy's bumblebee drones.

The faint buzz blends with the distant sound of chirping crickets and rustling leaves, going unnoticed by our tour guide and his men. The girls don't question our disinterest in availing ourselves of their services. It's sad, but their relief is a palpable thing.

I don't know how Forest does it. With so many victims in the world, too many for one man to rescue, how does he handle the despair of knowing he can't save them all? With my thoughts momentarily on Forest, I worry about this latest hospitalization and whether it will delay the bone marrow transplant. My distraction, however, doesn't last long. A deep rolling gong vibrates the air.

The girls escort us to another open-aired courtyard, this one much larger than any of the others, where we're reunited with our host.

"Welcome, gentlemen." Mendoza has a silver tongue and a voice smooth as velvet. I shake his hand, feeling the weight of his power even in this simple gesture. "I'm delighted to have you here tonight and trust you enjoyed the tour of my estate?"

I respond with a gracious smile, carefully choosing my words. "The tour was absolutely captivating. Your girls did a fantastic job, showcasing the beauty you've acquired over the years. Truly a pleasure."

Mendoza's smile widens, a glimmer of pride shining in his eyes. "I'm glad to hear that. I take great pride in my estate and those who contribute to its splendor. The young lady you mentioned is indeed exceptional. I will make sure to pass on your kind words to her."

I'm sure he won't.

I take a moment to observe our surroundings, the grandeur and opulence that surrounds us. My eyes wander, taking in the lush greenery and intricate sculptures that adorn the courtyard.

The centerpiece, a grand fountain, glistens in the evening light, its cascading water adding a soothing rhythm to the atmosphere. Josh chimes in with his own praise, acknowledging the architectural beauty and natural surroundings that create a captivating atmosphere.

Mendoza's smile deepens, his satisfaction evident. The man loves praise. Eats it up. He's a peacock, needing to strut his stuff in front of others, displaying the absurdity of his wealth.

"It's my pleasure to share the beauty of this place with those refined enough to appreciate it."

"Indeed, it surpasses even my high expectations." Xavier, playing his role as a wealthy investor, adds his charismatic nod.

Mendoza's eyes gleam with delight. "Well, Señor St. James, you are in for a treat tonight. We have prepared an exquisite feast, a showcase of culinary excellence that will surely satisfy even the most discerning palate."

Josh and I exchange subtle glances, understanding the underlying darkness that lurks beneath the extravagant display. We maintain our masks, concealing our true motives as we follow Mendoza to the lavishly adorned table.

The enchanting ambiance of the courtyard, with its twinkling lights, melodic music, and alluring aromas, sets the stage for the intricate dance between deception and truth that is about to unfold.

We oblige, gracefully easing into the cushioned chairs, our eyes tracing the intricate patterns on the tablecloth as we await the culinary delights that lie before us.

The twinkling lights above bathe the courtyard in a warm, ethereal glow, casting a spell of enchantment over the surroundings as the sun fades. The soft melodies of live music weave through the air, their intoxicating rhythms harmonizing with the conversations that fill the space.

With a wave of his hand, Mendoza signals to the servers, who begin their choreographed dance and bring forth the first course. Plates adorned with artistic arrangements of vibrant colors and delicate flavors appear before us, each dish a testament to the skill and creativity of Mendoza's culinary team.

"These dishes," Mendoza declares, his voice resonating with admiration, "are the culmination of the finest ingredients sourced from around the world, masterfully crafted by my team of talented chefs. Tonight, I invite you to indulge in a symphony of flavors, a culinary journey that will awaken your senses and transport you to new realms of pleasure."

What a pompous peacock. I wish he would shut up and die.

The aroma of the dishes wafts tantalizingly, mingling with the sounds of cutlery meeting porcelain and the gentle clinking of glasses. I exchange glances with Josh and Xavier, then pretend my anticipation grows as I prepare to embark on Mendoza's gastronomic adventure.

With a flourish, he picks up his utensils, leading by example as he takes the first bite. His eyes close momentarily, savoring the explosion of flavors that dance on his palate. He opens his eyes, a glimmer of delight shining within them, and gestures for us to follow suit.

The feast begins, and we join in, allowing the flavors to envelop our taste buds and transport us to a world of culinary ecstasy. The food is phenomenal, but it sours in my stomach.

I engage Mendoza in a discussion about the intricacies of the fighting industry, skillfully probing for information while maintaining an air of casual interest. Xavier listens in, asking about how the boys are found, whether they're groomed to fight, and what he might expect with the boy he chooses.

Josh, his attention divided between the conversation and the elegant dance of the performers, interjects with astute observations and occasional bursts of laughter.

Mendoza, his charm ever-present, shares anecdotes and stories, highlighting the exquisite nature of each dish. We listen attentively, our gazes shifting between the delectable creations before us and the animated expressions on Mendoza's face.

In this realm of indulgence and pleasure, we navigate the delicate balance between savoring the culinary delights and remaining vigilant in our true mission. Behind the mask of congeniality, we keep our guard up, our senses sharp, as we gather information and seek opportunities to unravel the mysteries that lie beneath Mendoza's opulent world.

Xavier, his eyes gleaming with fascination, leans in closer to Mendoza, his voice hushed and filled with curiosity. "What other services do you offer aside from the fights?"

Mendoza's lips curl into a sly smile as he leans back in his chair, his gaze lingering on Xavier. "Ah, my dear friend," he replies, his voice dripping with intrigue. "While the fights are the heart of my operation, I pride myself on providing comprehensive offerings. I can arrange private performances, personalized encounters, and connections with those who can fulfill your deepest desires."

Their conversation dances between veiled hints and unspoken agreements, the true depths of their intentions hidden beneath polite words and delicate gestures.

After the indulgent dinner, Mendoza leads us to a secluded area of the estate where his stable of boys is kept. The training pit is a chilling spectacle of brutality, set amidst the grandeur of his estate. It lies at the heart of the estate grounds, an unholy stage built for a bloodied ballet.

"Impressive." Xavier coughs into his fist. "You hold fights here?"

"Training." Mendoza doesn't flinch, answering as if by reflex.

Dug into the ground, it forms an impressive arena that is both menacing and austere. Circular in shape, the pit spans roughly fifty feet across, ensuring that no part of the horror that unfolds within is hidden from the audience. Its walls, built from a mixture of brick and stone, rise about ten feet, the top tipped with iron spikes. These walls bear the silent testimony to countless fights, their rough surface scarred and stained from past battles.

The floor of the pit is a different story altogether. Rather than cold stone or brick, it's packed dirt, gritty and uneven. It bears the marks of furious struggles, the dirt discolored with patches of dried blood, a cruel reminder of lives won and lost.

"Aggressive training. Do you teach them to use weapons?"

"No." Mendoza's reply comes too quickly. "Let me show you the boys."

If he has an arena here, why does he use the warehouse? Is it for different clientele?

The air hangs heavy with a sense of foreboding as we step into the dimly lit corridor lined with small cells. The scent of fear hangs in the air, mingled with the mustiness of sweat and piss. It makes me wonder what happened with Alejandro. After the fight, Mendoza took Alejandro, and we haven't seen him since.

The cells are cramped, barely large enough for a single person to stand. The walls cold and grimy, echoing the despair that fills the hearts of the boys trapped within. Their faces, etched with anguish and resignation, peer through the iron bars; their eyes pleading for mercy.

Memories flood my mind, taking me back to a time when I was once one of them, standing on the wrong side of the bars.

The boys are emaciated, their bodies bearing the scars of past battles and the weight of their uncertain future. They huddle together, seeking solace in their shared misery, their spirits broken by the ruthless beatings they've endured. Each glance, each movement, betrays a deep-rooted fear, a constant reminder of the fate that awaits them.

"Choose. Any one you want." Mendoza turns to Xavier, an

unsettling anticipation glinting in his eyes. He extends his arm toward the boys as if presenting a gruesome spectacle. "You have two weeks to train him."

"Two weeks?" Xavier's brow furrows, his gaze sweeping over the boys, their frail forms huddled together in the gloom. "I need more time. At least a month," Xavier counters, his tone firm.

Mendoza smirks, a taunting retort ready on his lips. "Paul only needed two weeks." Mendoza raises an eyebrow, his gaze piercing.

"I merely conducted a proof of concept. Two weeks is not enough time for my clients to train a champion." Silence blankets us, becoming tense and palpable the longer it lasts.

"Two weeks isn't worth my time." Xavier's deep voice cuts through the silence. His gaze flicks toward me and he nods. "I require a month, and I'll take that one." His finger extends toward a figure barely visible in the back, a boy not more than eleven.

My heart stutters at the sight. I was the same age when my own ordeal began.

"Are you sure?" I gaze at the boy. Did I look that forlorn and lost when I was thrust into the ring?

"He's got something." Xavier nods, certain of his choice. "Look at his eyes. There's a fire there."

"Fire or not, he won't last a day in the ring. He needs more time. They all do." I sweep my gaze across the boys, my heart aching at the sight of their fragile forms.

"Paul's right," Josh cuts in. "That boy is malnourished and weak. Perhaps—that one." He points to another boy, his muscles rippling beneath his ragged clothes.

"I have plans for that one," Mendoza cuts in, his voice oozing with smug satisfaction.

"For what I'm paying, I was under the impression I would have my pick?" Xavier insists, his tone firm. "I want that one." He points to the boy Josh indicated.

A tense standoff follows, the air crackling with raw energy. Mendoza's lips curl into a calculated smile, and he gives in.

"As you wish." Mendoza bends slightly at the waist, conceding to Xavier's demand.

Before anyone says something else, Xavier strides toward the cell of the bigger boy. The boy—barely twelve—stands taller than the other boys, a thin layer of adolescence beginning to reveal itself on his still-childish frame. His gaze meets Xavier's, defiance sparking in his dark eyes, a silent challenge suspending the air between them.

"What's your name?" Xavier's voice is soft, a soothing contrast to the tension that's wrapped around us.

"Rico," the boy replies, his voice holding a firm edge that belies his age. He doesn't break Xavier's gaze, the same defiance burning brightly in his eyes, even under Xavier's scrutiny.

"Rico," Xavier repeats, nodding slightly toward him before turning back to Mendoza. "I want this one, and I'll take a month to train him."

"As you wish." Mendoza's lips curve into a thin smile, a glint of amusement flashing in his eyes. He nods slowly. A wicked smile plays on his lips. "You can pick the boy up tomorrow."

"I'd rather take him now." Xavier shakes head.

"Ah, but I have something special planned for tomorrow. You'll be my guest and witness the raw power of these boys, and the lengths they'll go to fight for their lives. It will help you decide how best to train your boy."

The hushed conversation sends a chill down my spine, a mix of dread and anticipation swirling within me. Rico's boldness, Xavier's unwavering decision, and Mendoza's reluctant agreement—it all points to a precarious future for us, and particularly for the young boy Xavier has chosen. Knowing we can't refuse Mendoza's invitation, I step in to conclude our transaction.

I steady my voice, forcing a thin smile onto my face. "Your invitation is appreciated, and we'd be honored to attend." The words are bitter on my tongue, but they serve their purpose— appeasing the monster before us.

"Then it's agreed." Mendoza laughs, the sound echoing hollowly off the cold walls. "The boy will be ready after the demonstration."

The tension between Xavier and Mendoza is palpable, a dangerous dance of wills.

"Tomorrow it is." Xavier's jaw tightens, a silent battle of

restraint playing out on his face. An undercurrent of frustration is clear in his tone, but Xavier knows what he's doing.

"Tomorrow it is then," Mendoza chides, smirking at Xavier's barely restrained annoyance.

The silent agreement hangs heavy in the air. I can't help but worry for Rico. We turn to leave, each step echoing with the weight of our choices. Rico's defiant gaze follows us, a potent reminder of what's at stake. A grim resolve settles within us. We have one chance to save these boys, and we cannot, will not, fail.

We have our boy, but at what cost?

As we leave the corridor, the desperate whimpers of the boys reverberate in our ears, a haunting reminder of the lives that hang in the balance.

We play a dangerous game where lives are bought and sold, and where the limits of our own morality will be tested. As we traverse the expanse of Mendoza's estate, my hand strays into my pocket, fingers brushing against another drone. When I release it, it slips from my fingers.

My heart lurches as one of Mendoza's men glances in my direction. On instinct, I stumble, letting out a grunt as I grab my ankle, masking the drone's fall. My little performance seems to work because the guard turns his attention back to our path.

The evening comes to an end, and we're escorted out of Mendoza's disgusting estate by his guards, but we'll return in the morning.

A miasma of disgust infests the air.

Tomorrow's display will be a grim reminder of the unimaginable cruelty and suffering these boys endure. It further fuels my determination to dismantle his sadistic empire, to bring justice to those who have suffered at his hands, and to put an end to the horrors these boys are subjected to.

One good thing came from today. During our day at his estate, we successfully deployed Mitzy's drones. It's a small victory. The weight of our task is heavier than ever, a constant pressure in the pit of my stomach. I catch Josh's eye, the tension mirrored in his gaze. We're in deep, and there's no turning back.

THIRTY-SIX

Paul

~

After a very disconcerting day ends, the penthouse suite falls into a hush as we grab VR-goggles delivered to our suite.

"I can't get mine to work." Josh taps his temple, trying to smack his goggles into working while I watch a three-dimensional map being built real-time in VR.

"Turn up the screen illumination," Mitzy's disembodied voice speaks from the speaker embedded in the goggles. "Not that side, the other side. And don't smack my tech. It's delicate."

I laugh, imagining the hissy fit Mitzy throws while the three of us get logged in and find our way to the VR-Suite. I have no problems with the gear because Forest loves all things VR, and when we're not fighting, fucking, or being fathers to the twins, we like to play video games in virtual reality.

I'm an old pro, but not magnanimous enough to help Josh figure shit out. It's too much fun watching him get used to being in VR. Xavier, of course, has no problems either. Like me, he sits patiently in our VR space, waiting for Josh to figure it out.

My phone buzzes in my pocket, and I quickly glance at the screen.

"Guys, Sara's calling." A surge of excitement rushes through me. "I'm going to pop out and take the call."

My hand shakes as I bring the phone to my ear. Ever since that last kiss, I'm more than eager to hear Sara's voice.

A sharp pain stabs at my chest with thoughts of Forest. By the time I get home, he needs to get his head out of his ass. I want to share Sara with him, but I can't do that until he figures out all three of us belong together.

"Hey, Sara," I greet her warmly, my voice filled with affection. "I miss you. How are you doing?"

"Miss you too." Her voice resonates through the line, comforting and familiar. "How's the mission going?"

"We're making headway, but I have to admit, I'm distracted with thoughts of Forest. How's he doing?"

"Good to hear that." Her voice carries a hint of relief. "Forest is better. Recovered from the last infection, and the doctors are optimistic about moving forward with the transplant. Should happen tomorrow."

Tomorrow? And I'm going to miss it. A growl rumbles in the back of my throat. When I get back, I'm going to beat his ass for not letting me be there for him.

"That's fantastic." A wave of relief washes over me, and I let out a sigh. "Tell him I love him and that I meant what I said when we last talked."

That should get a rise out of Forest, or at least a good ass pucker.

"He's with me right now. Wanna speak to him?"

"Of course, I do." My heart leaps at the opportunity to connect with Forest. "Does he want to speak with me?"

I seriously doubt he's in the right headspace. He knows he fucked up in dismissing me and needs time to process our talk. Truth be told, no matter what oath he swore, he always has the ability to withdraw his consent. But I know Forest. I know what he needs. It's not a man that will tuck tail and run. He needs someone who will not just fight for him but give him no choice but to stay.

There's a brief pause on the other end, and I strain to hear what they're saying, hoping to catch any indication of Forest's voice. Instead, Sara's voice is firm and unwavering.

"Forest, this has gone on long enough." Frustration edges her tone, but she's determined to get the two of us to reconnect. "You can't shut Paul out of your life forever. He cares about you, and he deserves a chance to talk to you. Stop with this nonsense."

I listen intently, my heart sinking at the resistance in Forest's voice. His words are barely audible, filled with hesitation, reluctance, anger, and hurt.

"Forest, please." Sara continues, her voice filled with compassion. "Talk to him. Give Paul a chance."

A mixture of emotions washes over me, a blend of longing and concern. My heart aches for Forest, knowing the weight he carries and the pain he endures. I understand his need for distance, yet I yearn for the connection we once had.

"I'm sorry, Paul." Sara's back on the line, sounding defeated.

"It's okay."

"Is there anything I can do to help?"

"Just keep reminding him what I said before I left."

"What did you say to him?" She's curious, but not enough to press. Especially when it has to do with the dynamic Forest and I share.

"Ask Forest." I hate keeping things from her.

Our throuple thrives because we built it on the strength of our communication, but I need Forest to talk to Sara. She's what will bridge the gap that separates us.

"I will." The rustle of fabric resonates over the line before Sara's voice, steady as a heartbeat, makes me a promise.

"Thanks." Relief washes over me, and I hold the phone a little looser in my grip.

"And Paul?" A brief pause punctuates our conversation. Her voice returns, softer than before.

"Yes?" My back straightens, alertness surging as my heart hammers a staccato rhythm in my chest.

"I love you." The words reach me like a sigh, wrapping around me like a warm blanket.

"I love you more." A chuckle bubbles up, warmth blooming within me as I tilt my head back and gaze at the ceiling.

For the first time, the words ring true. Gone is the affection and friendship. Sara and I are becoming *more*. I can honestly say I love Sara. Not because Forest loves her. Not because she's the other half of the two of us that make Forest whole. I love Sara independently of Forest.

I take a deep breath, the reality of the situation sinking in.

As I hang up the call, a mixture of sadness and determination fills my heart. I won't give up on Forest. I'll continue to be there for him, even from a distance. And with Sara's support, we'll find our way back to each other.

Meanwhile, Josh's cursing draws me back to the task at hand.

"For fucks sake." Josh feels blindly around the edge of the goggles until he finds the controls and adjusts them. "Finally." He flops back on the couch with a huff and his head roves left, right, up, and down as the VR experience sucks him in.

Mitzy's avatar pops up on the opposite side of the map. No surprise, she's as equally flamboyant in VR as she is in real life.

I still remember that day in the hospital when the band visited Forest and shaved their hair in solidarity. I would've done the same, except Forest begged me not to. He needed something in his world to stay exactly the same.

"Looks like you figured it out." Mitzy glances up from a set of controls hovering in the air in front of her.

Our VR environment is rather low frills, which is disappointing. We stand on a glossy black surface, and all around us is black nothingness. The only thing in the sim is the growing map of Mendoza's estate, Mitzy's controls, and our avatars.

"Hey, why do y'all have legs and feet and I'm just a torso?" Josh's frustration is fun to watch.

"It's in the settings menu." Mitzy doesn't look up from her controls. "If you want to play with it yourself, do it later. For now, can we focus on the madness that is Mendoza?"

"The Madness of Mendoza?" I nod approvingly. "I like that."

"That's not…" She looks up at me and shakes her virtual head.

"Whatever. Mendoza Madness it is. It's going to take the drones time to map out the entire complex. It's much larger than I imagined. I'm sending another hive of bees to you in the morning. We need more eyes."

"Did you just say a hive of bees?" Josh's rudimentary torso swivels toward Mitzy.

"What else would you call it?" She gives him a look, then returns to her controls.

In front of us, the scaffolding of Mendoza's estate takes shape. Most of the main floor is mapped out. For now, it's all connecting lines forming a basic wire diagram of the main house and two smaller structures.

Over time, I imagine Mitzy's drones, and her technical team, will continue to refine the VR sim until it's nearly lifelike.

"Your drones are fucking amazing." Josh whistles in honest appreciation.

"Thanks. They're slower than the dragonflies but are much better at getting in and out of tight spaces."

"What happens when they run out of juice?" Josh's curiosity is fun to watch.

"They return to their hive." Mitzy's avatar manages to actually snort. Seems like she's spent a bit of time in the settings customizing her avatar.

"Hive? The bees have a hive?"

"Remote charging unit. Think of them like one of those autonomous house vacuum cleaners? The ones that dock to recharge. Only, my bees are capable of inductive charging as well."

"What does that mean?" Josh asks. His avatar's characteristics start shifting. Looks like he found the avatar settings menu.

"They use electromagnetism around the electrical wires to charge themselves, in addition to the main hive base. That's being flown in by my dragonflies and will be attached to one of the trees. I like having backups."

"And backups to your backups." I can't help but chime in. "I have to admit, I'm kind of surprised how much they've mapped so far."

"They've barely mapped the first level." Mitzy makes some adjustments and the resolution suddenly doubles. In addition to a basic wire frame of the house, major pieces of furniture begin cropping up. "There are several sub-structures underneath and three levels above the main floor. That's just the main house. I've got guard shacks and staff living quarters, the pens where they hold the boys, and a lot more to map."

"We deployed a score of drones. Won't more increase the risk of exposure?" Xavier clears his throat

"The only time people pay attention to insects is when they're bothering them," Mitzy explains. "Otherwise, the insect world, the bumblebee world, goes happily about its business. I'm not worried about that. What I'm worried about is Mendoza."

"Why?" Her comment intrigues me.

For Mitzy to admit she's worried about Mendoza speaks volumes to me.

"I can't put my finger on it, but I just don't trust him. I'd tell you to proceed with extreme caution, but that's like telling a bunch of bulls to tiptoe quietly through the china shop. I just have a bad feeling about him."

"He kidnaps kids and makes them fight to the death. We all have bad feelings about him."

"I know…" She pauses for a second. "Just be careful." She looks up, stares directly at me, then gestures to the wire diagram of Mendoza's estate. "We should have eighty percent mapped by morning. Like I said, I sent more bumblebees to you, another twenty. Just make sure you get them deployed tomorrow."

"We really need that many?"

"Not to map out the structure. I want to track the guards' movements, map out his surveillance, find out any blind spots in his monitoring system. Mapping out the sub-basements is going to take time. Right now, all I know is there are three levels above ground as well as below."

"What does he keep down there?" Xavier moves closer to the three-dimensional display.

"Good question, and why I want more drones. Now, about next

steps…" She leaves me to answer that question, but Xavier speaks instead.

"I've got Ben and Chad waiting in the wings. If Mendoza wants Paul to produce more buyers, they'll step in. Otherwise, we'll use them as my security detail."

"You think he'll ask that quickly?" Her avatar arches an eyebrow. The woman's definitely spent time on her avatar, and she has features I don't have access to. That's a cool trick.

"Hard to know," I jump in. Getting one buyer in less than twenty-four hours is impressive enough, but I have a feeling Mendoza will push and test the waters. If it were up to me, I'd delay introducing other buyers as long as possible."

"It is up to you." Mitzy gives me a cold look. "This entire operation is yours."

"Then we keep Ben and Chad out for now. Xavier pushed for a month to train his boy and got it. Mendoza took Alejandro back and is likely debriefing the boy."

"In what way?" Mitzy asks.

"He's smart enough to know Josh and I have a vested interest in ensuring he wins his fights. Probably just trying to see what he can learn about us from the boy."

"Are you concerned?" She makes more adjustments to the map, filling in details in real time.

"No. Josh and I kept our covers in check, but Mendoza's going to wonder why I didn't fuck the kid."

"Why didn't you?" Her comment is rude as fuck, and this may be the first time in my life I've wanted to punch a girl.

"Because…" My eyes narrow in anger, not that Mitzy can tell. Unlike her, my avatar can't express emotion. "I don't sleep around." My fingers curl reflexively, and I physically have to cup my hand over my fist.

"I thought you and Forest were done."

"We're not done."

"You sure? Because…"

"We're not done." I modulate my voice in such a way to end that line of conversation.

My words to Forest were what they needed to be when I left. He may think he can say whatever he wants to everyone else, and pretend like we're still not tied to each other, but he heard the truth before I left.

He's mine and always will be. I'll give him a bit of grace on account of the cancer putting him in a foul mood, but he swore an oath. When I get back, I'm going to remind him what a lifelong oath means to me. As for right now, the last thing I need to be thinking about is Forest and continuing this absurd conversation with Mitzy.

The glow from the map paints her avatar's face in a blueish hue. The fine details of the simulation are crazy realistic. It's almost as if we're all in the same room rather than thousands of miles apart.

Shifting the conversation back to business, Xavier draws my attention. "We need to talk about the sublevels. Is there any possibility of gaining physical access?"

"Asking Mendoza for a private tour of his underground lair is probably not wise." While I'd love to know what's going on down there, it's not a top priority.

"You don't say?" Josh says.

"Ha, ha." I cross my arms in front of my chest. "I could try to find a reason to wander, but that's a bit too unbelievable?"

"Alejandro?" Josh moves his attention from his still floating torso, flicking his eyes between Xavier and me. "He could be a good excuse. Say you were trying to find where he was."

"Too obvious. Besides, wouldn't he be with the other boys? How about you sneak off to find one of the girls who gave us that tour?"

"That's not a bad idea." Josh figures out the directional controls and moves his avatar closer to the map, inspecting what little information we have of the basement levels. "We'll see how things shake out."

"Or maybe…" Xavier's gaze flicks between me and the three-dimensional map. "Maybe we play the ignorance card. Wander around, pretend you're lost. If you're caught, apologize profusely, feign ignorance."

"Or," Josh looks at me, "maybe we make it look exactly like it is?"

"What do you mean?" Intrigued, I glance at him.

"You're trying to scope out his operation and got nosey. Sometimes, sticking with the truth is the best option. Easier when you don't have to lie."

"So just tell him I was just poking around?"

"Poking around, but in the best interests of your clients." Josh gestures toward Xavier.

I look at him, my eyebrows rising. "That might actually work. Worst case, Mendoza will think I'm overly confident and an idiot. He'll be suspicious, but for the wrong reasons."

Mitzy clucks her tongue, rolling her eyes with a grin. "Let's focus on the mapping for now. Don't run before we can walk."

"If you've got blank spots on your map, make use of Paul's wandering and release some of those drones strategically." Josh's hands flail about as he fumbles with the controls again. "Can someone please show me how to get legs on this thing?"

Xavier chuckles, his avatar moving toward Josh's. "Let me help you with that."

A wave of tension washes off me as our focus moves toward helping Josh with his VR avatar and away from Mendoza, the fight ring, and my complicated relationship with Forest.

For a moment, we're just a group of friends navigating the VR world, the dangers of our mission momentarily forgotten. It's a fleeting moment, soon to be swept away as we plunge deeper into the heart of the enemy. But right now, it's a comfort. Something to ground me.

After Josh gets himself sorted and grows legs, Mitzy's avatar pulls up a new set of controls, and the glow of the holographic map in the VR-suite intensifies, a promise of the work still to come.

"All right, you know what these drones are capable of. They can scout out any location, even the most heavily guarded ones, but they're small and the mapping is going to take some time. By morning, I should have a fairly detailed map, but we're going to need days to get it all. A couple of weeks would be better."

"You have a month." Xavier leans into the holographic display, a calculating look in his eyes. "Can we program the drones to identify structural weaknesses? You know, stuff that isn't immediately obvious to us, but could come in handy later?"

"Absolutely." Mitzy nods. "My team will be looking for that during analysis."

"You'll monitor human patterns, as well? Track and analyze the routines of Mendoza's men?"

"We will," Mitzy confirms. "Understanding their rotation schedules and patrol routes will give us the advantage of time, know when to act."

"What about Mendoza?" Josh chimes in, "We need to understand him better. Can we use the drones to record his private meetings or track his movements?"

"Absolutely, we can get an in-depth understanding of his operations and tactics. These bumblebees are our secret weapon. They'll give us every detail we need to dismantle his empire." Mitzy grins at the suggestion.

We continue to brainstorm, trading ideas and theories, planning for the takedown of Mendoza's operation.

"Wait a second." A new idea hits me. "Can't we have the bumblebees tail Mendoza when he leaves the estate? Track his car, maybe see what he's up to outside his base?"

"Smart." Mitzy's eyes twinkle with intrigue at the thought. "We could get a broader picture of his operation, maybe even identify some allies or safe houses."

Xavier's gaze sharpens at this, his mind already running scenarios. "It'd also give us an idea about his comfort zones, his patterns outside the confines of the estate. That's valuable intel."

I nod, caught in the momentum of the conversation. "Right, and there's another thing. Remember the warehouse district where the fight was held? We need eyes on that location. Mendoza transports the boys there for the fights, has a series of cages in the back where he keeps them before their fights. If he's running these fights regularly, it would be good to know his operation there as well."

Mitzy's fingers move swiftly across the holographic controls, programming in our ideas. "Excellent. I'll send another group of the bumblebees to survey the warehouse district."

The room hums with focused energy. The drones are our eyes and ears, our unseen scouts in enemy territory. They're uncovering every hidden secret and mapping out a path to Mendoza's downfall. We wrap up for the night, each of us going to our rooms.

While I get ready for bed, my phone rings. Sara's number lights up my screen.

THIRTY-SEVEN

Paul

~

The next morning, I check in with Sara. Forest receives his transplant tomorrow. It's been such a long road, filled with equal parts hope and despair. I remember the lows, sitting up with Forest through the night, swapping out one bucket after the other while the nausea and vomiting from chemo nearly took him out. I remember the absolute joy when we identified not just any donor, but a woman who's a part of Forest's biological family.

I regret not being there while he and Lily unraveled the threads of their lives. I don't know how things stand between the two of them. Did they unravel the mystery of their parentage?

A shudder travels down my spine with a sudden flashback to the first major infection which nearly took Forest out. I'm not sure which moment was more horrifying, when he collapsed in front of the twins in shock or when he collapsed at Guardian HQ from exhaustion and we received the terrible news he had cancer.

I wish I was there for him. Instead, I call Sara, knowing she needs my support. Forest may have shut me out, but Sara and I are closer than ever.

"Hey, how are you doing?" I keep my voice steady, comforting.

We are thousands of miles apart, but I want her to feel like I'm right there with her.

"I…" She hesitates, the tension palpable even through the phone. "I'm okay."

There's a quiver in her voice, one I've grown attuned to over the past few months. I've come to understand the quiet strength that lives within her, but there's an edginess in her voice

"What's on your mind?"

There's a rustle on the other end, and then a deep sigh. "I'm scared." Her admission hangs between us, a shared fear spoken aloud. "What if… What if something goes wrong with the transplant?"

"Nothing's going to go wrong." The words seem too small for what we're facing, but they're all I have. "Forest is strong. He's got a piece of both of us in him."

Her soft laughter flutters through the line, a momentary respite from the heavy conversation. "That he does," she agrees. "Stubbornness from you, resilience from me."

"A formidable combination, indeed." I grin at that, despite the circumstances. "I miss you too."

"This would be easier if you were here." The tone of her voice shifts, turning sultry and suggestive. "I'm so angry at Forest for shutting you out. Especially when things are changing between you and me. I feel like we're just starting something and he's…" Frustration swirls in the depths of her lonely sigh.

There's an intimacy in our conversation, one that we've only just started exploring. It's both exciting and comforting. With the complexities of our unique throuple, however, it also brings questions.

And danger.

Everything we've built is been based on trust and honesty. I don't want the change in feelings between Sara and me to threaten Forest's place in our dynamic. He's our foundation. Our purpose. He's the glue—the force—that binds us together. He makes all of this work.

There's a pause on her end, but it's not one of uncertainty. It's a moment of consideration, of careful thought, and I appreciate her answer when it comes. It's spoken with such tender sincerity it's impossible to doubt her decision.

"I want to feel your touch, to experience you, and the two of us together with Forest. It feels wrong to do anything without him, but with the way he's acting? I just don't know what to do."

"I want that too. I want us to have that moment. The three of us. I think it'll be incredible."

Her answer sends a shiver of anticipation down my spine, igniting a deep longing within me. The warmth in her voice reaches out across the miles, a beacon drawing me back home.

I want to share her with Forest. The thought of the three of us in bed, bodies sweaty, arms and legs entwined. It makes me hard. Without Forest, it doesn't feel right.

"I have a confession to make," she says.

"You do?"

"Don't be mad at me."

"I won't."

"I told Forest." She rushes to explain. "I'm sorry. I know you wanted to be there so we could tell him together."

"How did he take it?"

"He said he already knew." She laughs softly on the other end of the call. "That it was about time and he was tired of waiting for us to figure it out."

"I bet he did." And if he did, I know beyond a shadow of a doubt that Forest wants me back in his life.

"He said something else."

"What?"

"That he wanted us to be together, but he thought our first time shouldn't be the three of us, but just you and me." She giggles suddenly.

"What's so funny?"

"He said since you've never been with a girl before that you were basically a virgin, and he wanted you to be experienced when the three of us finally got together. He said he probably shouldn't watch his Master fumble through his first time having sex with a chick. That it would upset the balance when the two of you were alone, and how he didn't think you'd think it was funny that he was laughing while you… Well, you know."

"He said that?" The tight band around my heart suddenly releases. Forest imagining a future with me in it means everything to me. Balancing the phone between my shoulder and ear, I trace my fingers over the well-worn surface of the coffee table.

"Are you upset I told him?"

"Never. He needed to know. The sooner the better. I'm glad you told him. Fucker needs a good kick in the ass. Now he knows I'm not going anywhere."

A lighthearted laugh rings out from the other side of the line, wrapping me in a warmth I've been missing.

"And?" Her voice is as inviting as a sunrise, a gentle tease echoing between us.

"And I can't wait to fuck you." Leaning back against the worn-out hotel room couch, I allow a smile to play on my lips.

"Oh, you are so crass. Not that I expected you to say you couldn't wait to make love to me," she replies, her voice tinted with playful scorn.

"Sorry, love. When I fuck, I fuck. I'm not a tender, sweet kind of man, but you'll know how much I love you when I make you come over and over again." My heart pounds a heavy beat against my chest.

A small gasp punctuates her response, followed by a shaky laugh. "Wow. Okay, that's… I can't wait for you to come home."

"I can't wait either." Shutting my eyes, I imagine her on the other end of the line, her cheeks flushed, her eyes bright.

"How much longer do you think you'll be?"

"At least a month. Maybe longer." Grimacing at the thought, I scratch the back of my head.

"Forest should be out of the hospital by then." Hope fills her words.

Tension seeps into my veins as I respond, "I can't wait to see him."

From the other end, Sara's voice ebbs and flows like a gentle tide, bringing with it a sense of calmness. "I can say, with great certainty, he's just as eager to see you as he is terrified." Her voice softens, a subtle mix of fondness and concern echoing in the silence of the room. "He knows he overreacted, but is too stubborn to admit it, but I'm working on him."

Raising an eyebrow, I let out a chuckle. "You are?" Shaking my head, I press the phone closer to my ear. "Dare I ask how?"

With an evident mirth in her voice, she confesses, "I keep talking about the three of us in bed."

I can't help but laugh, "Oh, I bet that got a rise out of him."

Her chuckle trickles into my ear, light and teasing. "It did. It's so much fun to tease him, and I'm learning a lot about all the positions we can try."

"Doing your research, I see?" I counter, the smile in my voice impossible to mask.

"He really wants to try two things in particular." Sara's words break the silence, the steady rhythm of her voice like a lighthouse in the storm,

"Really?" I lean closer to the phone, my heartbeat drumming in anticipation.

"Yeah." A gentle affirmation spills through the line.

"And what are those?" The suspense hangs in the air, a sweet torment. A smirk tugs at the corner of my mouth.

"He wants you to fuck him while he's fucking me."

"Definitely on the list. Anything else?"

"He wants you to fuck me together, but I'm not so sure about that."

"Why?"

"It may be something we work up to."

"That's totally fine with me." I intend on spending the rest of my life loving both Forest and Sara—and fucking them too.

"I just really want you back with us, safe and sound." Her voice, once a playful cadence, softens into a sobering lull.

The room around me suddenly feels empty, as if her presence transcended the miles to fill it, and now we're losing that connection.

"I love you." Feeling a warmth bloom in my chest, I swear to her I'll return.

"I love you too, and I miss you," she whispers back, the words carrying a weight that lands heavy in my heart.

"I miss you too." A pang of longing cuts through me, leaving an aching hollow in its wake. "When this is over, and I'm back, we'll have all the time in the world for twosomes and threesomes and all the love in the world."

"Promise me one thing?" It's not often Sara sounds so vulnerable. It's a raw side of her that never fails to pull at my heartstrings.

"Anything." I find myself promising, waiting with bated breath for her request.

"Come back to us. Come back to me." There's a tremble in her voice, a vulnerability that stings, that makes my promise carry even more weight. "I worry about you. Please be safe."

"I promise I'm coming home to you." The words resonate in the silence that follows, a solemn vow hanging between us.

We linger on the line for a while longer, our connection a lifeline. As we eventually say our goodbyes, there's an unspoken promise hanging in the air. A vow of a future, of love, of connection, waiting for us just on the other side of this mission.

Long after I end the call, her voice lingers, wrapping around me like a warm blanket. As I get ready for the day, it's with the knowledge there's love waiting for me. A love that's complex, beautiful, and all the more precious for its rarity. A love that feels as close as my next heartbeat.

Something shared between me, Forest, and Sara.

All that stands between me and our reunion is a man named Carlos Mendoza and scores of boys I need to save.

THIRTY-EIGHT

Paul

~

We're back at Mendoza's estate. Ever the charming host, he gives us a personal tour this time. Josh and I take turns releasing more of Mitzy's drones, our movements calculated and subtle. Every distraction is an opportunity to deploy more drones. The bumblebees, with their inconspicuous design, blend seamlessly into the environment, becoming just another pair of eyes in this house of horrors.

The grandeur of the place is sickening. Each piece of ornate art, each lavish room, a stark reminder of the cruelty that festers beneath the gilded surface. My heart clenches; the fate of the innocent victims of Mendoza's operation weighs heavy on my conscience.

Every corner turned, every room entered, holds the potential for disaster. There's a moment when my breath hitches in my throat, a drone skimming dangerously close to a security camera's field of view. It passes unnoticed, a small victory in this high-stakes game.

Mendoza leads us to an area of the estate that reeks of sweat and iron—the fighting ring.

We watch in horror as boys, barely teenagers, are thrown into the pit, their desperation etched onto their faces. They fight, not out of anger or hatred, but of fear, their actions fueled by desperation. The violence is sickening, their screams echoing off the walls, a testament to the brutality of Mendoza's regime.

The final match of the day is the worst. Two boys, their bodies already scarred and bruised, thrown into the pit together. Their desperation is palpable as they circle each other, neither wanting to make the first move. Their bodies shudder with the effort of standing, the remnants of their previous battles taking their toll.

Their faces contort with fear and resignation, a shared understanding passing between them before they launch themselves at each other, a final, desperate attempt to survive. The sight is unbearable, and I have to look away, a lump forming in my throat.

Once the fights are over, we're led back to the cells where the boys are kept. Rico's cell is empty. Xavier strides forward, his eyes scanning the area. A guard appears, leading Rico toward us, his body bruised, but unbroken. He meets Xavier's gaze with a flash of defiance before looking away.

"We start training tomorrow," Xavier announces, his voice firm. Rico doesn't respond, his gaze fixed on the ground. Xavier reaches out, gripping the boy's shoulder. There's a shared moment of understanding, a silent promise that things are about to change.

The drive back to our accommodations is filled with a heavy silence. We've witnessed the brutality of Mendoza's regime, the desperation of these boys, the raw violence they're forced to endure. But there's also a glimmer of hope. Hope that we can put an end to this, that we can save these boys.

Tomorrow, we start training.

Tomorrow, we start the fight for their lives.

And tomorrow comes all too fast.

"Again, Rico," I snap at the boy, my words ricocheting off the grimy walls of our ramshackle training arena. A solitary droplet of sweat weaves a winding trail down my temple, joining the moisture-soaked collar of my shirt. The relentless heat presses down, exacerbating Rico's quick, shallow gulps of air, each one reeking of raw terror.

Rico's dwarfed by the enormity of his impending fate, a mere wisp of a boy forced into a gruesome world. His knuckles blanch, a stark contrast against his dirty skin, his small fists clenched tightly. In his eyes, fear dances a macabre waltz with an unexpected partner— determination.

"Fight, Rico. If you want to survive, you must fight!" Xavier shouts at the boy, maintaining his cover as the kind of man who would use a boy in a death match. He's been an eerie specter up until now, his presence felt more than heard.

Rico gives a shaky nod, more akin to a tremble than a true affirmation, yet he manages to rally. He's just a child, scared to death, learning to fight for his life. It's too much weight for his slender shoulders.

God, he's terrified.

And we're the monsters training him to fight or die.

I hate myself.

Rico lifts his fists, a desperate kid readying to fight for his life.

But, he's just a kid.

A kid we must train.

"Up on your feet," I call Rico back to the mat. His lack of physical endurance is more likely to lead to his death than his inability to fight." I strip my tone, keep my voice bare of warmth. In this, I'm the aggressor. "Fists up. Let's go."

Again, the boy lunges forward, swinging a fist. I sidestep easily. He's quick, but his movements are unpolished, the rough edges glaring in the unforgiving light of our makeshift training arena. It's a dance we're choreographing and every beat is a damning condemnation of our role in it.

Rico stumbles, catching himself just before his small body hits the ground. His knuckles, already scraped and bruised, graze the concrete floor. Yet he's back on his feet in seconds, fists raised in a poor imitation of a boxer's stance. He doesn't have the choice to stay down. If he goes down in the ring, he dies.

"Defend yourself!" Xavier calls out. His gaze is an inferno, burning brightly with the harsh reality we're forcing onto Rico.

Rico, ever the obedient student, lifts his arms to shield his face. His chest heaves as he fights to draw in breath, each ragged inhale and exhale a testament to the fear driving him. He's not a natural fighter; he's a terrified kid pretending.

"Aim for the gut, Rico," Josh shouts, ignoring the way his voice reverberates disturbingly off the cavernous walls. He's playing his part well, but his eyes betray him; they're filled with a despair that mirrors my own.

Rico swings again, his punch landing solidly against the padded shield I hold. He winces, cradling his abused hand against his chest, but there's a spark of pride in his eyes. A spark of hope. God, I want to protect that spark, to foster it, but what we're doing might just extinguish it.

After a grueling hour, we finally call it. Rico collapses onto the hard concrete floor, his breaths coming in sharp gasps. His face is streaked with sweat and tears, a haunting image of resilience and defeat. I look away, swallowing the bile rising in the back of my throat.

Josh moves to comfort Rico, his touch a soothing balm. Rico clings to him, his tears soaking the front of Josh's shirt. The whispers exchanged between them are a secret I'm not privy to, but the result is clear. Rico stops crying, his sobs subsiding into shaky breaths.

"He's got an eight-year-old brother," Josh says. "Mendoza is using the brother as leverage." Josh's voice is barely more than a whisper.

The harsh reality of Rico's plight is a punch to my gut. It's Alejandro all over again, a cruel cycle of fear and survival.

I grit my teeth, scrubbing my face with a coarse towel. We have to make this work. For Rico, for Alejandro, for all the boys ensnared in Mendoza's vile web.

The following days dissolve into a blur of punches and desperate hopes. Every dawn spills its light onto our grueling routine, every sunset marks another day closer to Rico's judgment. We're locked in a relentless ballet of violence combatting survival.

On the third day, Rico manages to land a swift jab to my midsection. It's a small victory in the grand scheme of things, but the glimmer in his eyes says otherwise. He's beginning to believe in himself, finding a semblance of courage amidst the dread.

But that belief is a double-edged sword, it fuels him in the ring, but damns his innocence.

By the fifth day, Rico masters the basics of footwork. His movements are fluid, and he dances around with an agility that belies his initial awkwardness. Yet, every step is laced with fear, every dodge a reflection of his need to survive.

By the ninth day, Rico's punches pack more power. He strikes with a grim determination, his small fists hammering against the padded shields we hold. It's a horrifying testament to the transformative power of fear.

On the eleventh day, Rico learns to take a hit. He stumbles, but he doesn't fall. The pain in his eyes is stark, but so is his resolve. He's no longer just a scared boy; he's a fighter in the making.

But at what cost?

Throughout it all, Josh is a steadfast presence at Rico's side. His reassurances are a lifeline for the boy, a buoy amidst the stormy seas of our grim reality. Xavier, on the other hand, continues to push Rico, his fiery gaze never faltering.

Fear fuels Rico's training and Xavier is there to supply it in spades.

And then, before we know it, days turn to weeks, and finally a month passes. It arrives like a specter, a haunting echo of our shared fear. Rico's improvement is remarkable, but it's also a grim reminder of what waits for him.

As I watch Rico spar with Xavier on that final day of training, his small frame silhouetted against the bright lights, I can't help but wonder. How much of the boy we first met still remains? And how much have we shaped him into a weapon, a pawn in a game far too dangerous for a child?

Are we not the vile ones? Using him? How is what we do any different from what Mendoza does to these boys? I feel covered in filth, and there's no way to wash this stain from my soul.

Training concludes, not with a triumphant roar, but with a quiet sigh of resignation. Rico stands tall, his body marred by bruises, his spirit undeterred. He's ready for the ring, ready to fight. But at the end of it all, he's still just a boy.

A boy who should be playing, laughing, living.

Not learning to kill.

That old saying runs through my head: *The needs of the many outweigh the needs of the few.*

Or the one.

All I see is one little boy and the destruction of his innocence.

Did we do enough? Did we do too much? Only the ring will tell. But one thing's certain. We can't afford to lose.

For Rico.

For Alejandro.

For Rico's brother, Alejandro's sister, and all the innocents caught in Mendoza's sadistic games, we simply can't afford to lose.

THIRTY-NINE

Paul

~

In the hushed stillness of the final day, I reach out to Sara. My call slices through the silence of midnight, a desperate need for connection; the desire to know the things I'm doing for the greater good aren't turning me into a monster.

Though I believe in our mission—knowing that it might save countless boys—the cost it bears weighs heavily on me. Risking Alejandro's life? Rico's? No justification can cleanse that stain.

Sara's sleepy voice answers on the second ring, the roughness of disturbed slumber yet laced with an undercurrent of worry.

"Paul?" Her voice reverberates, a resonant echo reminding me of the miles stretching between us. My pulse spikes at the sound, a tangible thread of connection in the stillness of the night.

"Your voice… It's good to hear it."

"Something's wrong." Her statement, not a question, bears the keen edge of instant understanding.

Words clog my throat, tripping over each other in their rush to escape. With a deep, shuddering breath, I let them tumble out—a raw confession about Alejandro's and Rico's ordeal, the visceral terror, the relentless guilt gnawing at me.

"I need to come home," the statement slips out, barely audible, laced with longing.

"And we'll be waiting for you." Sara's voice is soft, filled with promise. "Just—stay safe. Please?"

"Is Forest there?" I steer the conversation in a new direction, my voice softening at the thought of the man at the other end.

"He is."

"Can you put him on the phone?" I ask, my tone softer now, the tenderness I feel for the man on the other end of the line seeping into my words.

"Sure, just a moment." Sara moves around before she hands over the phone. A short argument ensues between Sara and Forest while I wait.

A rustle of movement, a brief exchange, and then Forest's voice, rough and defiant, fills my ear.

"What?" His familiar defiance and challenge lingers in his tone.

"Is that how you speak to me?" My voice is laced with a hint of humor, a feeble attempt to pierce the tension.

Forest sidesteps the question. "What do you want, Paul?" His tone is bitter, laced with resentment. He spits out my name like it's venom.

Ignoring his hostility, I express my relief at the success of his transplant and his return home, a deliberate sidestep away from the undercurrent of animosity.

"I'm glad you're finally home."

After a tense silence, Forest finally responds, his voice guarded. "Is that why you called?"

"Not entirely," I confess, my tone hardening slightly. The conversation teeters on a precipice, yet I can't help but make a jab at him. "I wanted to speak to Sara, but if you're up for admitting I was right…"

"That's not happening." His laugh is sharp, grating, but it's a small victory that he didn't simply end the call.

"You sure? After all, the bone marrow drive saved your life."

"You want a fucking medal?" His retort is swift and scathing.

With an exasperated sigh, I tiptoe around the words that really matter. "You know what I want."

"That's no longer yours." The silence that follows is filled with unspoken thoughts and desires.

When it becomes clear he's not intending to speak, my irritation bubbles to the surface. "You're such an ass."

"Whatever."

"Whatever? I'm glad everything worked out. I'm happy the transplant took and that you're going to be okay. I don't regret what I did for a second. You know it was the right thing to do. And one more thing…"

"What?"

"When I get back, I'm going to make sure you understand how wrong you were to push me away. I know what you need, and we're going to stay in the basement as long as it takes for you to agree I was right all along."

He responds with a final, biting, "Go to hell," and then the line goes dead.

My fingers tighten around the phone before I throw it onto the bed; the frustration simmering within me threatening to boil over. He's not going to forgive me, at least not without a fight. I pace the room, the sound of my restless footsteps the only company in the quiet.

But isn't that the answer? The reason he and I exist? I need to remind him why he went to his knees for me. Hope flares within me because I finally see my path home to him. And when we're together, I'm going to show him all the reasons why he's such a fucking ass.

A soft tap at the door jolts me out of my thoughts. I blink, pushing off the bed. "Yeah?"

"You okay?" Josh peeks his head in, his eyes brimming with concern.

"Peachy." I sit on the edge of the bed, my hand unconsciously curling and uncurling in a fist.

"I need you on point. If something's off…" His gaze sharpens.

"I'm good." The lingering frustration from the conversation with Forest colors my words. "Just a run-in with Forest. I'll be fine."

His nod is curt, professional. "That's all I wanted to hear." With that, he disappears, leaving me alone with my thoughts.

After a day of intense training with Rico, my muscles ache for a hot shower. I strip off my gear, my mind filled with thoughts of Forest. The water cascades down, washing away the sweat and grime, but leaves the stain on my soul untouched.

I close my eyes and let the water wash away my sins. My thoughts turn to Forest, before the cancer, when he was healthy and whole. His fierce stare hinting at something wild and untamed. His desire to have that part of himself bridled and under my control. I imagine him in the dungeon, his body whipped and eager. Forest desperate to face his inner demons.

My hand travels down my body, tracing the contours of my muscles. I think of Forest, of all the ways I could dominate him, of how he responds when I touch him. I imagine him on his knees before me, eyes blazing with defiance, begging for release as I press him further than ever before. My heart races as I envision his skin slick with sweat and his lips parted with pleasure. My arousal grows, my body ready to give in to the temptation of Forest by my side.

My fingers curl around my cock, sliding up and down its length, moving faster, my breaths pulsing in and out. Heat rises inside me, the anticipation of pleasure filling me as I stroke myself. Forest yielding to my commands, submitting to my will, is a thing of rough and raw beauty. A deep longing fills me, needing to have him stand by my side once more. I picture his lips on mine, his body pressed against me, and I can almost feel the electricity pulsing between us that sets my soul on fire.

I can almost feel the rush of power that comes with knowing I hold complete dominion over him. My fantasies become more vivid and urgent with each movement of my hand. Completely lost in pleasure with thoughts of Forest, I come with an explosive release of pleasure that leaves me trembling and unsatisfied.

I stand in the shower, panting, my heart still beating wildly in my chest. An urgency fills me, the need to have Forest back in my arms, to revisit the power dynamic we so passionately share. I need to fight him to get it back, and he will resist. To reclaim what we had, I need to remind him why he needs me. Determination fuels me as I steel myself for the battle to come with the man I can never get out of my head.

All I have to do is survive this mission. I exit the shower and dry off, feeling marginally relieved after my orgasm. My hand is a distant echo of brutal sex with Forest. Crawling into bed, sleep comes slowly to me. Not because of Forest, but because of Rico.

Tomorrow, he fights. He'll either live or die. I do this for the greater good and hate myself for it. But, this is what we must do.

Mitzy and her drones better get whatever information they need to attack on Mendoza's estate and free the boys still locked inside.

FORTY

Paul

⁓

Mendoza's call splits the early morning with a shrill ring. "I'm putting Rico in the ring." His oily voice slithers through the phone's speaker and snakes its way into my consciousness. "Tonight."

"Tonight?"

"It's been one month, and I'm eager to see what he's learned and how the crowd responds. I'll send a car to pick you up."

A fight. Tonight?

It's too soon, but inescapable.

"No." I counter his offer of a chauffeur." We've got our own driver. We'll see you there."

No way in hell am I leaving our transportation at the whim of Mendoza. I don't trust the guy, and we need backup. Fortunately, I've got both bases covered.

There's a pause on the other end. Then, a low chuckle. "Very well. See you at the ring. Ten sharp. Don't be late."

"We won't. I'm looking forward to this."

His words hang heavy in the silent room long after the call ends.

It's happening. It's happening now. This match is no longer a future nightmare—it's a present-day horror.

I wake the guys, but we leave Rico asleep. He's going to need all of his energy later tonight. We slip out onto the expansive balcony of the penthouse suite and make final preparations.

Before I know it, the time has come.

A sleek, extended black SUV is our ride. Behind the wheel sits Ben, a stone-faced man with eyes that have seen too much, while Chad, quiet and watchful, takes the passenger seat. They're Xavier's men, loyal to a fault, here to provide backup if things go south.

We pull up to the warehouse—a grim testament to the monstrous deeds that are about to unfold. Stepping out of the van, the humid night air does nothing to quell the tension twisting in my gut.

Xavier leads the way, dragging Rico toward the entrance. The boy trails Xavier like a tiny shadow—a lamb to slaughter, his hands bound and a lead attached to a collar around his throat.

The fear in his eyes is a mirror to my soul, flickering with the same horrifying reality, but there's a steeliness there too. A determination to survive.

Inside, Mendoza awaits us, a predatory grin curling his lips. He's in his element, playing the gracious host to a depraved gathering. Eager bettors surround the makeshift ring, their eyes glinting with anticipation. An assault to my senses, the stench of blood, sweat, piss, and alcohol fills the air.

It's a carnival of the damned, and Mendoza stands at the heart of it, a self-satisfied smirk pulling at his lips. He's a puppet master in this grotesque theater, his eager audience hanging onto every word, every gesture.

"Ladies and gentlemen!" Mendoza's voice booms, sweeping across the crowd. "Tonight is no ordinary night." He stretches his arms wide, reveling in the spotlight that paints him as an ominous silhouette against the dim, smoky backdrop.

"Tonight, we witness a marvel of a fight to the death." His words roll off his tongue, laced with a tantalizing thrill that snags on their collective breaths and seizes their basest instincts. Their eager faces tilt toward him, each pair of eyes glinting with a perverse thirst. "A fighter," he pauses, letting the silence wring out the tension, "trained especially for this ring."

Their cheers break forth, a harsh cacophony of sound, amplifying the pounding in my skull. Mendoza lets their fervor build, a growing storm he expertly controls, his grin a chilling promise of the horror to unfold.

"A boy," he continues, his voice a venomous whisper that somehow cuts through the noise, "trained to draw blood, taught to conquer pain, built to survive!"

The crowd surges with savage anticipation. Howls and cheers rise, an untamed wave crashing against my ears. Each cheer, each clap is a grotesque tribute to Mendoza, feeding his monstrous ego, fueling his power over this depraved carnival.

He stands tall amidst the pandemonium, fanning the embers of their savage appetites.

His oily gaze swings toward Rico, his grin widening to an almost grotesque extent. "Our very own champion." He gestures grandly at the small, trembling figure by his side.

The ensuing roar of approval is deafening, a brutal slap against my conscience. With a flourish, as grand as it is sickening, he directs the boy into the blood-stained ring, presenting him to the hounds baying for a spectacle. The roar that follows drowns every other sound, a deafening applause for a perverse exhibition.

"Place your bets, my friends," Mendoza urges, his voice dripping with greed, the promise of gruesome entertainment. "For tonight, we gamble not on chance, but on skill, on bravery, on survival." His eyes scan the crowd, a silent challenge. "Who dares to risk it all?"

His words whip them into a frenzy, their screams of affirmation blending into a primal howl. They eat out of his hand, their morbid curiosity piqued, their wallets open. Their greed driving them mad.

The puppeteer has mastered his show. Mendoza's set his stage.

This is it. This is where nightmares take form.

Under the harsh glare of floodlights, Rico steps into the makeshift ring. His tiny form swallowed by the crowd's hungry anticipation. My heart hammers against my ribcage, each beat a plea for Rico's survival, a chant for the success of our mission.

"Show us what you've got, kid." Mendoza's words crack like a whip, stirring the energy in the air into a tempestuous frenzy. His dark eyes gleam with wicked anticipation.

Rico's response is a tremulous nod, his raw fear hidden beneath a brave mask. Our training, every painstaking moment, every sweat-soaked hour, now stands as his only defense in this grotesque dance of death.

Yet, as the opposing gate groans open on rusty hinges, our worst nightmare unfolds.

Alejandro steps into the ring.

My gut seizes, and my blood boils. This is Mendoza's doing.

A mirror reflection of Rico, both boys are nothing more than skin and bones. They stand gaunt and trembling with fear beneath the harsh arena light, each a specter of innocence lost.

Rico's lookalike in almost every way, Alejandro's shirt hangs loosely over his emaciated frame, a badge of his imprisonment. His skin is smudged with the filth of the fighting pit, a grim reminder of his past encounters. His hair, too, is slick with sweat, his fear-clouded eyes a mirror to Rico's own raw terror.

Both boys are barely out of their childhood, their bodies far from fully grown. Yet, they stand in the pit, pawns in a game they never asked to play. Their vulnerability a painful contrast to the ravenous bloodlust of the spectators surrounding them.

The shock hits like a punch to the gut. Our efforts to save one boy from this gruesome fate has turned into the condemnation of two. Their terrified eyes lock, two lambs led to slaughter, their lives meaningless in Mendoza's twisted game.

Guilt claws at my insides, raw and relentless, as both of their gazes flicker toward me, a mute plea for mercy in a world that offers none.

I choke on the bitter taste of betrayal. Mendoza set this stage. His knowing smirk meets my shocked stare, the silent exchange dripping with a horrifying realization. This isn't any fight.

It's a test.

An examination of intentions; a testament of our twisted double game. The corners of his mouth stretch wider, watching what I'll do. He's still unsure about me, watching me like a hawk. Looking for a crack in my veneer that will confirm his suspicions.

Poker-faced, I stare back.

Every muscle screams at me to get out of here.

It's a trap!

But I can't react. If I flinch, it'll be the end for us all.

The fight kicks off like a nightmare born of hell. Alejandro, driven by fear and desperation, lunges at Rico.

There's a flash of terror in Rico's eyes, but it's quickly replaced by grim determination. He ducks and weaves, using the skills we drilled into him, honed through countless grueling hours of training, letting Alejandro's first punch slice through empty air.

The crowd's roar echoes off the warehouse walls, a cacophonous approval of the spectacle they're witnessing.

But Alejandro's raw energy isn't easily deterred. With the ferocity of a tempest, he swings again. His fists are brutal, aiming to maim, to destroy. Each swing of his arm carries the weight of a wrecking ball. Alejandro's raw strength hits like a freight train, his punches brutal and wild.

Rico is lighter on his feet, his body honed for speed and evasion. He slips past Alejandro's wild punches, dances away from his desperate lunges. He strikes with precision, a stark contrast to Alejandro's wild rage. His punches are quick, targeted. He's playing the long game, tiring Alejandro out.

But Alejandro is unrelenting. Like a frenzied beast, he takes a hit, gives two back. His punches crash against Rico's defenses.

One punch lands square on Rico's jaw, sending him sprawling. The crowd's hunger spikes, a grotesque symphony of cheers. Rico scrambles to his feet, his teeth bared in a primal snarl.

The training kicks in. Left jab, right hook, dodge. But Alejandro isn't far behind. He fights back, an animal backed into a corner. He lands a solid punch to Rico's gut. Rico gasps, pain flashing across his face.

Their battle ebbs and flows, an appalling waltz of desperation and survival. The crowd feeds off their fear, their struggle. It's a gut-wrenching sight, two boys barely out of childhood, reduced to such raw brutality.

With each sickening thud of fist against flesh, my heart pounds in sync with each brutal exchange, each crunch of bone, each stifled cry.

From the corner of my eye, I notice a shift within the crowd. Mendoza's men. They're on the move. Subtle. Quiet. They slink through the crowd, weaving around drunken gamblers and blood-thirsty spectators. Stalking their prey, ready to pounce.

Closing in.

On me.

"They're boxing us in." I keep my voice low.

Xavier, ever vigilant, nods his understanding. His dark eyes, typically full of stoic resolve, flicker with an edge of concern. His hand slips inside his jacket, subtly checking the gun tucked there.

"We need backup." He reaches for a small communication device clipped to his belt. A short, terse command into the device follows, and Ben and Chad move toward us through the crowd, their faces hard, eyes alert.

Beside me, Josh watches the unfolding scene. He's silent, his hand resting on the knife strapped to his thigh. We trade a swift glance, an unspoken understanding passing between us.

Over the crowd's blood-thirsty roars, the sound of desperate struggle cuts through.

Rico.

Alejandro.

A symphony of grunts, groans, and the sickening crack of bone on bone. They're just boys, but here, in this ring, they're gladiators in a battle for survival.

The pervasive scent of sweat and fear. The deafening cacophony of the crowd. It all builds and builds until the tension in the air is suffocating, heavier than the heat and the stench of blood.

The crowd is too engrossed in the fight to notice Mendoza's men closing in on me. I exchange a glance with Josh and Xavier. We're ready for whatever comes next.

But for now, all we can do is watch. If we make a move, it confirms Mendoza's suspicions. We basically have to wait for the attack and watch as the fight descends into madness.

And madness it is as the two boys *we trained* turn into monsters for a crowd baying for blood.

An explosion of cheers and jeers shatters the tension like a punch through glass. It's a guttural, primal chorus, a soundtrack to the heartbreaking scene in the ring. Rico and Alejandro, no longer boys, but desperate fighters, deliver blow after punishing blow.

Rico's knuckles, bloodied and bruised, find their mark on Alejandro's jaw with a sickening crunch. Alejandro stumbles, his lip bleeding, his face a twisted mask of pain and defiance.

But he retaliates.

His leg whips out, catching Rico by surprise. The kick sends Rico sprawling onto the blood-soaked ground, a loud gasp ripping through the crowd.

But that's the last I see of the fight.

In the blink of an eye, chaos becomes my world. Men, faces twisted in savage glee, spring from the shadows. It's an ambush, a deadly dance orchestrated by Mendoza.

The first man lunges at me, his gnarled fist swinging in a brutal arc. Muscle memory kicks in, and I duck, weaving under the punch. My knuckles find the soft spot under his ribs, drawing a grunt from him. His face contorts in pain, buying me precious seconds.

But he's on me again.

As are the others.

From my right, a heavy hand swings, aiming for my temple. I sidestep, driving an elbow into his gut. The surprise in his eyes is a small victory, but it's short-lived. A swift uppercut, a gift from his comrade, sends me sprawling backward.

Around me, the battle unfolds in a violent blur. I catch glimpses of Xavier, Josh, Ben, and Chad, their bodies moving with lethal precision as they fend off their attackers. They fight like men possessed, each punch, each kick carrying a desperate ferocity.

Yet, the crowd around us is oblivious, lost in the horrifying spectacle of the boys' fight. Their roars of excitement and bloodlust fill the air, a vile symphony to our struggle.

The metallic tang of blood fills my mouth. Pain flares through me, hot and urgent, as a boot slams into my ribs. They're trying to separate me, drag me away, and fuck if that isn't exactly what they're doing.

Two men get a hold of my arms, their grip unyielding as they drag me away from Josh and into the bowels of the crowd.

Gritting my teeth, I buck against their hold, landing a solid punch on the closest face. But there are too many. My movements are hampered, my efforts blunted by the press of bodies around me.

Through the blur of pain and panic, I see Alejandro.

A scrawny, terrified boy turned into a killer, standing victorious over Rico's lifeless body.

His eyes, wide with horror, disbelief, and despair turn to me. Our eyes lock. It's a haunting image seared into my mind as I'm pulled deeper into the crowd.

The last thing I see is Xavier, his face a mask of grim determination. He fights back to back with Josh, a sight that would have been reassuring in any other situation, but they are forced to retreat, leaving me in the hands of Mendoza's men.

The others disappear from sight, their desperate fight retreating under the roar of the crowd. I catch the briefest glimpse of Josh's face, etched with a grim determination.

He mouths something, a silent promise amidst the chaos, before he and the others retreat, melting into the shadows of the parking lot.

A painful understanding passes between us.

They have to leave.

As I'm dragged away into the unforgiving darkness, the clamor of victory and defeat rings loud in the warehouse, echoing in my ears. The haunting image of Alejandro standing over Rico, the cruel delight in Mendoza's eyes, and the sight of my allies, compelled to fall back—those images sear themselves into my memory.

As the chaos of the warehouse fades, I can't shake the bone-chilling reality. My fate is now tethered to a lunatic, held captive in his malevolent hands. My mission, which began with a sliver of hope, lies in shambles.

Complete mission failure.

Worse than any of that, another pain stings sharper, deeper.

Regret.

Regret over a conversation unfinished. The words I need to

share with Forest remain locked away in the silence between us. A gaping wound that haunts me more than my own death. My thoughts remain with Forest and our fractured relationship that may never mend.

This is the price I pay for dancing with the devil.

FORTY-ONE

Paul

~

Mendoza's men move swiftly, dragging me through the crowd. Their fingers clamp down like iron manacles around my arms, but I don't give them the satisfaction of resisting. I'm supposed to be a business associate of Mendoza's. Until I figure out what the hell is going on, I'll continue to play that card until I can't.

As for my *what-the-fuck-is-this* madness, I'm in the *wait-and-see* camp.

Which means, for now, my only response to this brutal treatment will be that of irritation and discomfort.

My world narrows down to the ruthless grip on my arms. They drag me through the warehouse toward the loading dock where Mendoza waits for me.

His lips curl into a cruel smile—the kind that tells me he thinks he has won. I know better. I'm the bait, not the prey, and this is my moment to strike.

"Cocky move, Mendoza. Shouldn't you know better?" I meet his cold stare with a defiant one of my own. "Assaulting your business associate in the middle of a crowd? You've either grown incredibly brave or incredibly stupid."

Mendoza laughs, a chilling sound that echoes through the desolate warehouse. "Ah, Señor Montenegro, always quick with a response. However, bravery or stupidity isn't the question. It's about ambition. You're not my partner. You're an obstacle."

"An obstacle?" I raise an eyebrow, managing to look unimpressed. "That's a new one. And how do you plan on removing me?" I scoff, the corner of my mouth twitching upwards.

His smile widens into a predatory grin, sending a chill down my spine. "By taking your client list. I plan to cut out the middleman."

"Ambitious and premature. Your greed will be the death of you." I can't help but chuckle at his audacity, letting the sound fill the tense air. "And you think my clients will accept that? They're loyal to me, not some upstart with delusions of grandeur."

He steps closer, invading my personal space. It's a classic show of dominance that does nothing for me. His dark eyes gleam with a twisted joy. "I wouldn't be here if I thought otherwise. I'm taking over. You've outlived your usefulness. It's time for you to step aside." His dark eyes narrow, a flicker of doubt clouding his arrogant demeanor. "I can offer them a better deal."

"You think it's that simple?" I match his intensity and love the way he shifts back a step. "You're cluelessly stepping into a minefield. My clients are volatile. They trust me because I've earned it. Are you ready for the consequences?"

His gaze hardens, but I can see uncertainty seeping into his expression. Good, he needs to know he's not playing a simple game.

"You're sure of that, are you?" He tries to regain control of the situation.

"I am." I raise a brow in irritation. "And what exactly do you plan on doing to me?"

"You already know the answer to that." His lips thin into a cruel smirk as he leans back against a stack of crates. "You're coming with me where you will give me that list."

"A vacation at the Mendoza estate?" I allow a hint of sarcasm to lcak into my tone. "How charming. And what if I refuse?"

"Refuse?" His laughter rings hollow in the cavernous warehouse. "You're in no position to refuse. I don't think you understand. This isn't a request."

"Right. So you plan on forcing me to hand over my list?" I shake my head, clicking my tongue in mock disappointment. "That's a great way to lose a potential ally."

"You could hand over the list right now." His smirk falters for a moment before it hardens again. "Save us the unpleasantness of torturing you to get it."

"I think you're overestimating your influence here." I stand my ground. "I don't respond well to threats. If you want my cooperation, this is exactly the opposite way to go about it. Release me now, and I promise I won't put a bullet between your eyes."

"I think you're the one who doesn't understand. Thinking you could come into my town and worm your way into my business. Silly American." He hikes his thumb over his shoulder toward a waiting van. "Take him."

"You're making a mistake," I warn Mendoza, not bothering to hide the determination in my voice. "You won't get what you want from me."

"Is that so?" His wicked smile widens. "We'll see about that."

Mendoza's men tighten their grip on my arms and throw me into the back of the van. I hit the cold metal floor, but there's no pain. There's only hardened resolve.

I'll play Mendoza's game. I'll endure, I'll survive.

The engine rumbles to life and the van lurches forward, I prepare myself. The stage is set. The players are in position. Now, the real show begins. I hope Mitzy's tech team is on top of things.

The journey to Mendoza's estate is a quiet one. The only sounds are the rumbling engine and the occasional murmur from the men up front.

It's after midnight when they haul me from the vehicle, a harsh welcome of humid air and even hotter glares greet me. The expansive house, backlit by the moon, is a chilling silhouette against the darkened sky.

Two burly guards escort me. They guide me down winding staircases into the underbelly of the manor. The transition is surreal, from the pristine exterior to this damp, poorly lit dungeon.

We stop before a heavy metal door. One of the guards pulls out a key; the metallic echo in the silence spikes my adrenaline. The room is barren, save for a hard cot and a bucket in the corner.

"You might be here for a while, Señor." One of the guards has the audacity to smirk at me, his eyes glinting ominously in the dim light. "Señor Mendoza suggests you strongly consider his offer."

"Don't remember him making an offer, but I do remember him wanting to steal my client list."

"Señor Mendoza is not a man you say no to. Enjoy your stay." The guard's warning hangs in the air as they slam the door shut, the echo reverberating in the cold stone chamber.

Alone, I slump against the cold floor, exhaustion seeping into my bones. My body throbs with pain, a testament to the brutal confrontation, but a glimmer of hope finds its way in. Buzzing quietly in the corner is one of Mitzy's bumblebee drones.

"Hey." I wave to the drone, knowing it transmits back to Mitzy and her team. "Bit of a wrinkle in our plan." I gesture to the cell. "Looks like I've got new digs. Mendoza wants my *client list*." I use air quotes for emphasis, then laugh. "And he's going to torture me to get it. Would be nice if my friends show up sooner, rather than later."

I almost make a mistake and comment about how there is no client list, but I remember at the last minute to assume this cell is bugged. I also remind myself not to talk directly to the drone. When Mendoza looks at this footage, all he needs to see is me rambling to myself.

I settle in, get as comfortable as I can, and wait.

The first day, or what I assume to be a day, drifts by in a haze. Mendoza's men do not come. There's no trace of the man himself. The isolation gnaws at me, the silence echoing louder in my mind than any interrogation. I'm left with my thoughts, a far more insidious torture, and decide Mendoza definitely knows what he's doing. The man is softening me up, using isolation to do it.

Smart.

I spend hours tracing the cracks on the walls, committing to memory every damp line of this claustrophobic cage. I try to sleep, but it's elusive, my rest disturbed by the discordant notes of the mansion—the far-off clang of a door, the hum of a generator, the muted voices of men whose faces I can't see.

I'm kept company by the drone and the gentle buzzing of its wings. Every now and then, it disappears, lost in the shadows, only to reappear moments later. It's a small bit of reassurance. I don't feel quite alone.

As the darkness creeps in, so does the cold. Time is meaningless in my little cell, but it does pass. After days of nothing, Mendoza finally makes his entrance. His expression, when he steps under the single bulb hanging from the ceiling, is one of curious fascination. A predator sizing up his prey.

"Señor Montenegro," a tinge of amicable mockery colors his voice, "I trust you are comfortable?"

"Not so much, but if you thought your hospitality was going to change my mind…" I glare up at him, refusing to move from my spot in the middle of the room. "The answer is still no."

His footsteps echo ominously as he circles me. I keep my expression impassive, refusing him the satisfaction of seeing me squirm.

"I must say, you've piqued my curiosity." He stops, facing me, a cruel smile curling his lips. "Training my boys. Turning them into champions? It's all very—interesting."

I bite back the one question plaguing me all this time. Did Rico survive? Last I saw, Alejandro stood over Rico's motionless body. I'm really going to enjoy killing Mendoza. Fucker doesn't deserve to breathe the same air as those boys.

His words are a layered trap, a minefield of implications and accusations. I say nothing. Any attempt to explain could inadvertently reveal more than I intend.

"Perhaps, you need a bit of incentive." His smile fades into a thin line of irritation, but he doesn't lose his composure. Instead, he takes a step back, motioning for his men to come forward.

"Incentive? Maybe you didn't understand. I'm not handing over my client list. It's useless in your hands without me. I demand an apology and reparations for my *discomfort*." I gesture to the cold cell.

"It seems we're experiencing a difficulty in communicating.

Perhaps my men can change your mind." Mendoza pivots on his heel and leaves without another word.

What follows is an unnecessary orchestra of pain. His men, efficient in their brutality, weave a symphony of agony that has my vision blurring at the edges. But through the haze of suffering, I cling to my resolve. Every blow, every brutal technique, only fans the flame of my defiance.

When they finally deposit me back in my cell, my body screams in relief. The wounds on my body throb with a dull, insistent pain, a steady reminder of my predicament. Pain, I can endure.

Pain is a familiar, old ally.

And I'm fortunate in one thing. Mendoza doesn't want me dead. At least, not yet. He's keen on getting his hands on this fictional client list I hold. When it becomes clear I won't be handing it over, that's the day my usefulness to him ends.

Hours stretch into days, or is it days stretching into weeks?

Time becomes a blur, punctuated only by sporadic meals and relentless interrogations. Mendoza's men continue their brutal assaults, their zealous enthusiasm undeterred by my stoic silence. Each blow lands, each bone grinds, each muscle tears, but I refuse to give them what they want.

The drone hums in the corner, Mitzy's eyes and ears. It's the lifeline that tethers me to hope. It's the whispered reassurance that my team is out there, plotting my rescue and the rescue of scores of young boys.

What it can't do is tell me what they plan.

Mendoza has already lost. He just doesn't know it yet.

My team is out there, formulating a plan, inching closer with every passing minute. Rescue is a game of patience, and time, as they say, is on my side. Until then, I close my eyes, breathing in the dank air of my cell, and picture Forest's face, his eyes soft with forgiveness.

It's good to dream.

FORTY-TWO

Paul

~

DAYS BLEED INTO EACH OTHER IN A DISORIENTING BLUR OF ISOLATION and pain. The only indication of passing time is the ebb and flow of my bodily functions, sleep, and the sporadic delivery of tasteless meals. Still, there's no sign of Mendoza himself. The anticipation of his arrival is a form of torture, an insidious dread that twists my gut every time the door to my cell grinds open. Today, instead of food, my captor makes an appearance.

"Señor Montenegro, I trust you are comfortable?" It's a mockery of a greeting. When he finally steps into my cell, his gaze is one of fascination, evaluating my resilience and strength.

"Not so much, but if you thought your hospitality was going to change my mind..." I retort, meeting his gaze with a steadfast determination. "The answer is still no."

His following smile is thin and cold, a wolf bearing its teeth. Mendoza circles me, a hunter assessing his quarry.

"Perhaps you still need an incentive to give me what I want?" His voice is calm, a startling contrast to the fury that flashes in his eyes. He steps back, signaling his men to come forward.

As I steel myself for another bout of torture, there's no way to truly brace for the onslaught of raw brutality. It's a harsh dance I know all too well. Every punishing blow lands with a stark reminder of my past, each one a penance for the choices I've made, the hurt I've caused Rico and Alejandro.

The pain I caused Forest…

I deserve punishment for that, but amid the relentless onslaught, defiance wells up inside me. Stripped of everything else, it's the one weapon I possess—and it's powerful. It drives me to endure, to resist, to survive.

I'm going to kill Mendoza the first chance I get.

After what seems like an eternity, his men deposit me back in my cell. Each breath I draw is laced with pain, but it's a sensation I embrace. It's a reminder of my purpose.

Once they leave, my isolation resumes; the only company I have being the drone and the harsh echoes of my own thoughts. I find comfort in the faint hum of its wings, a lullaby in this otherwise silent nightmare. The drone is my anchor, and a beacon of hope in this dismal situation.

I will say one thing. Mendoza, and his men, have no talent for true torture. I should know, considering I was once the best at interrogation, dispensing pain, and breaking the strongest men with my particular brand of torture.

Mendoza does so many things wrong; it's embarrassing. I feel sorry for the guy, not that I'm going to give him pointers. And it's not like I'm not immune to his efforts.

Every now and then, I find myself teetering on the brink of despair. It's in those moments I imagine Forest's face. His eyes, always so full of understanding and compassion, they offer me a silent strength. He's the reason I'm here, seeking validation that I'm worth his forgiveness.

Is that how he survived the brutality I inflicted upon him at Snowden's fortress? Did he focus on Sara and draw strength from her?

I bet he did. Love is a powerful force and a great motivator to fight for freedom.

I find myself whispering words into the void, messages meant for him. I know they won't reach him, but the act of speaking them out loud, of sending them out into the universe, provides me a semblance of connection to the man I can't get out of my mind. It's a small comfort, but in these circumstances, even a whisper can roar.

Mendoza—what a twat—thinks he's broken me, that he's won, but he couldn't be more wrong. His sadistic game of control is a testament to his delusion.

I won't let him take over my client base—not because it doesn't exist—but out of spite. The fucker pissed me off, and I'm just wasting time. He can brutalize my body, but my spirit, my resolve, remains untamed. The man thinks to break me, all without realizing he's only honing the very weapon that will be his downfall.

Mendoza underestimates me.

All I need is patience. An opportunity. A moment of weakness on his part. I'll seize it and bring him down.

My thoughts often drift to my team, to Josh, Xavier, Mitzy, and the Guardians. They're out there, working tirelessly, piecing together the puzzle of my capture. I trust them implicitly.

They will find me.

One day, the monotonous rhythm of my confinement is broken by Mendoza's entrance. The predatory smile on his face sends a shiver down my spine, an instinctive warning of danger.

"Señor Montenegro," he drawls, delight evident in his voice. "I believe you and I need to have a—discussion."

His words are punctuated by the harsh metallic click of handcuffs around my wrists. The cold touch of steel is a chilling reminder of my situation.

My response to him is a hard glare and a clenching of my jaw.

Mendoza's goons haul me to my feet and steer me out of my cell. My heart pounds, but I keep my expression neutral, my mind calculating.

They lead me through a labyrinth of dimly lit corridors and up a set of stairs. Our boots echo ominously on the cold stone steps. The pristine facade of Mendoza's mansion comes into view, a stark contrast to the darkness I've been subjected to.

They usher me into an opulent room, its luxurious decor a cruel mockery of my condition. Mendoza wastes no time. He pours a glass of whiskey, then plops down into a plush leather chair. The amber liquid in his glass sloshes, but doesn't spill. He gestures toward a chair opposite him with a nonchalant flick of his hand as if it's a fucking invitation rather than a command. I take offense he doesn't offer me a drink.

As I take a seat, he regards me with an inscrutable expression. "I thought it might be time for a change of scenery." His voice is laced with thinly veiled amusement. "And perhaps—a different approach?"

My mind races, anticipating his next move, but his words hit like a bucket of cold water, leaving me stunned.

"I propose a fight." A perverse grin spreads across his face.

"A fight? You're fucking kidding me."

"A fair fight. You win, you walk free. You lose…" He shrugs, leaving the implication hanging in the air. "You lose, and you have a choice. You hand over your list of clients, or you choose death. Then, we can be done with all this unpleasantness between us."

"My list is nothing to you. Once my clients hear what you're doing to me…"

"But that's the thing. You will work for me."

My mind reels at his proposition. It's a dangerous gamble, one that could cost me my life, but it's also an opportunity.

I lean back in the chair, meeting his gaze. "Work for you?"

He nods and takes a sip of whiskey.

"Let's say I agree…" I'm careful to keep my voice steady. "What's the catch?"

"No catch. You win, you walk free. We cut ties. I never see you again. But if you lose, you say nothing to your clients about any of this. You work for me, no middleman, your life is mine. If you try to stab me in the back, your life is forfeit." Mendoza's laughter echoes around the room, a chilling soundtrack to our deadly negotiation. His eyes gleam with anticipation, a predator reveling in the thrill of the hunt.

I swallow the lump in my throat, forcing a smile. "Then I hope you're ready to lose." I embrace the challenge.

I don't know what Mendoza has in store for me—he's got something up his sleeve—but I know one thing for sure. My desire to kill Mendoza is greater than it's ever been.

FORTY-THREE

Paul

~

MENDOZA'S WICKED LAUGHTER FOLLOWS ME AS HIS MEN STEER ME back toward my cell. His proposal, as twisted as it is, offers a glimmer of hope.

A fight?

Against his best man?

It's a dangerous gamble. Desperate on his part.

The best part is it gives me a window of opportunity I can exploit.

For the next few days, Mendoza's men throw me scraps, enough to keep me alive, but not enough to keep my strength up. My body screams in protest; the brutal beatings and meager meals are taking their toll.

In the quiet, cold loneliness of my cell, I prepare for the fight. All the while, Mitzy's drone buzzes faithfully in the corner. It's a small comfort, a silent companion that reminds me I'm not alone in this.

When the night of the fight arrives, I'm led from my cell to the training arena within the mansion's grounds. A single, reinforced metallic gate provides the only entrance to the pit. An ominous one-way passage for those fated to enter. Mendoza's men shove me inside of it, then lock the gate, sealing me in.

Overhead, harsh floodlights cast an unforgiving glow onto the ground. It casts grotesque shadows that dance and shift. Around the pit, people pack the stone-tiered risers.

Makes me feel like I'm in a gladiator's pit instead of a training arena. Whipped into a frenzy, the baying crowd's thunderous shouts echo around me, eager for the spectacle Mendoza promised. A twisted sense of anticipation hangs in the air, a palpable excitement that turns my stomach.

I can't help it, but I'm curious how the initial betting is shaping up. Call it an ego boost. Although, I have a feeling any man stupid enough to bid against Mendoza's champion won't be around for long.

With the smell of fresh-turned dirt filling my senses, I block out the crowd and pay attention to the things that matter most. The exits and my opponent.

Mendoza's champion steps into the ring. He's a behemoth of a man, muscles rippling under a sheen of sweat, his eyes glinting with brutal confidence. His hands, the size of sledgehammers, clench and unclench in eager anticipation of the fight to come.

But I've fought bigger, stronger opponents before.

And I've won.

I fight Forest all the time. He's bigger, stronger, and a worthy opponent. It's my reach and reflexes that give me the advantage. And, as far as fighting a man such as this? I've overpowered Forest time and time again. Not because he lets me but because that's what it takes to master him.

This is going to be a piece of cake.

Mendoza's signal launches the fight. His champion wastes no time, lunging at me with a roar that shakes the very ground beneath us. His first punch swings toward my head, but I duck under it, feeling the rush of air as his fist passes inches from my skull.

I strike back, delivering a quick jab to his ribs. He grunts, more in surprise than pain, but recovers quickly. His counterattack is swift, a roundhouse kick that I narrowly block. Our fists and feet move in a rapid dance, each of us seeking an opening, a moment of weakness to exploit.

He's stronger, there's no doubt about it, but his size makes him slower. I use that to my advantage, dancing around him, quick jabs to his side keeping him off balance. But he's not to be underestimated. He adjusts his strategy, using his reach to keep me at bay, his powerful blows forcing me back.

The crowd is a deafening roar of distraction, their shouts and cheers blending into an overwhelming cacophony. They're on their feet, gasping with each near miss, cheering with each landed blow. It's a grotesque symphony, a soundtrack to my fight for survival.

Despite the odds, I gain the upper hand. I duck under a wild swing, my opponent's fist whistles past my ear, and retaliate with a swift uppercut to his jaw. He staggers back, stunned, surprise clear in his eyes. I don't waste the opportunity, rushing forward to deliver a knee to his stomach.

His breath whooshes out, his hands dropping instinctively to protect his midsection. I seize the chance, landing a solid hook to his jaw. He reels back, his eyes rolling in his skull. Before he can recover, I deliver a final punch, a right cross that connects with a satisfying thud.

He crumples, hitting the packed earth with a thud that resonates through the silent arena. The crowd is stunned into silence, the sudden quiet a sharp contrast to the deafening roars of mere moments ago.

I stand over him, chest heaving, sweat stinging my eyes. The crowd erupts into cheers, but their cries are distant, drowned out by the pounding in my head.

This is not the outcome Mendoza expected. He thought he was dealing with a soft, American businessman.

Mendoza's face is a mask of shock, of disbelief. He stands abruptly, the veneer of civility gone. This isn't over—his eyes make that promise—but for now, I've upset his game, and that's a victory I'm willing to savor.

I beat his champion—won the match—according to his rules, I earned my freedom.

But let's be honest.

He was never planning on letting me go. The man is a snake and can't afford for others to see any weakness in him.

"Enough." His eyes burn with rage. "This isn't over, Montenegro."

I upset his plans, toppled his game, and embarrassed him. In doing so, I created a powerful enemy. Not that I care. I'm tired of this whole thing, and I'm past ready to bring him down for good.

I don't know what Josh and the others have planned. There's only my faith they are planning something. There's no way Josh would ever leave me behind. The only reason they haven't shown up yet, is because they need more time.

Well, I can give them that.

I survived, proved to Mendoza I'm not his to control. Hopefully, I've given my team more time to prepare.

If Mendoza thinks he's got me cornered, he's in for a rude awakening. I'm ready for whatever he throws my way, and with every passing second, I'm one step closer to my team and freedom.

A shrieking alarm suddenly pierces the air, a blaring siren drowns out the deafening clamor of the blood-thirsty crowd. The atmosphere pivots from crude celebration to sheer chaos.

Looks like the calvary is here.

FORTY-FOUR

Paul

TERRIFIED BY THE ALARMS, THE CROWD SCRAMBLES, THEIR PREVIOUS cheers replaced by fear-stricken cries. The ground beneath rumbles ominously, adding to the confusion. As I stand, fists clenched, a twisted sense of satisfaction rushes through me. The wailing alarm is music to my ears. It's the beginning of the end for Mendoza. His world is about to come crashing down.

"You!" His bellow reverberates over the alarms, his accusatory finger pointing at me. "You did this." His voice is a garbled mixture of incredulity and fury. His face contorts, a grotesque blend of rage and terror warping his features. I rock back on my heels, folding my arms across my chest.

The message is clear.

His empire is coming down, ripped apart at the seams by the righteous fury that is the Guardians.

"You're right." I meet his gaze, the grim satisfaction clear on my features. Damn straight, I did this.

As if on cue, the reality outside the pit intrudes with a deafening roar. The imposing stone walls tremble, straining under an unseen force. Then, with a sound like the earth itself tearing apart, they give way as armored vehicles bulldoze their way through the wrecked walls. The echoing crunch of stone under heavy wheels, the billowing clouds of dust, and the sudden appearance of figures clad in black tactical gear is an unequivocal declaration.

The Guardians have arrived.

The crowd scatters in all directions; their delight turned into terrified screams. Gunfire erupts as Mendoza's men attempt to defend. The Guardians strike back. Lethal rounds drop Mendoza's men like flies.

Above the chaos, I catch Josh rappelling down from a helicopter, his rifle spitting out bullets at the frantic guards below. When he touches the ground, he sprints toward me. The others with him head toward Mendoza and his closest allies.

"Paul," Josh yells, panting as he skids to a halt beside me. His gaze scans me briefly, taking in the bloody evidence of my torture. He thrusts a weapon and several magazines into my hands. "You okay?"

"Better now." I take the weapon and secure the breech.

The earth shudders beneath our feet, a violent aftershock as another section of the once-imposing wall crumbles under the relentless onslaught.

A second wave of armored soldiers floods into the breach. At their helm is a figure unmistakable even under the bulk of tactical gear, his commanding presence undeterred by the chaos around him. Xavier and ten of his men storm the grounds, a living tide of righteous fury.

The very air crackles in their wake, a palpable current of tension and raw power. They brandish their weapons and cut a swath of destruction through their enemies. Their movements choreographed to execute precise strikes that leave Mendoza's men reeling.

Two additional Guardian teams descend upon the estate. They veer left, toward the building holding the cages of a score of boys locked inside.

"This way." Josh points toward the Guardians and we move toward them, joining the fray.

The out-building that Mendoza uses as a prison for the boys is a haunting, desolate place, an unwelcome contrast to the opulence of the main mansion. Its squat structure is stark and devoid of warmth, the rough concrete walls scarred by the passage of time and the untold suffering of its young prisoners. The air is heavy with the stale scent of fear and deprivation, making each breath a bitter reminder of Mendoza's cruelty.

The interior is dimly lit, the feeble glow of a few bare bulbs casting long, menacing shadows that dance across the damp walls. Row upon row of crude, metal cages fill the vast space, each one barely large enough to contain a mattress.

One by one, we unlock the cages. As each cage door swings open, the reactions of the boys varies wildly. Some boys rush out, desperate for freedom. Others remain huddled at the back, their bodies shivering with terror, eyes wide and uncomprehending. I help wherever I can, my heart pounding with a mixture of relief and desperation, but I'm also searching the sea of tortured faces.

The boys require a gentle hand, a soothing voice, and a promise of safety before they trust us. As I kneel down, coaxing out one boy after another, my heart aches for them. This is why we are here, why we fight. And this, right here, is only the beginning.

Finally, from the corner of my eye, I see him—Alejandro. The boy looks up at me, his face streaked with tears and dirt. Recognition sparks in his eyes, and he rushes toward me, throwing his thin arms around my waist in a tight hug. Relief washes over me; at least he's safe.

"Rico?" I ask, my voice barely audible over the chaos outside. Alejandro's face crumples at the mention of his friend's name. That's when I feel it, Rico's death.

Despair flows through me, but then Alejandro points a shaky finger toward the back of the room. My heart stops.

Together, Josh and I approach the indicated cell. Inside, we find a shell of the boy Rico once was. He's battered, bruised, his breaths coming out in ragged gasps. I can't believe he's alive. Whatever happened in the chaos following the boy's fight, Alejandro didn't have to kill his friend.

"I've got him." Josh scoops Rico into his arms, his face tight with determination and worry. "I'll get him to the medics. He's going to be okay."

I nod, my gaze lingering on the limp form of Rico before turning back to the chaotic scene outside. There's one last task for me.

"I'm going after Mendoza." His reign ends tonight. I owe it to these boys. I owe it to Rico and Alejandro.

"Copy that." With a nod, Josh carries Rico out of the building. Alejandro follows on his heels. Each of the dozen Guardians escorts two to three boys to safety.

Mendoza's desperate flight leads me on a twisted path through his mansion, a morbid testament to the spoils of his empire. Lavish and priceless artifacts flash by in a blur as I barrel through opulent halls and winding corridors. But just as I round a corner, the man himself vanishes from sight.

I skid to a halt, my breath ragged, pulse thundering in my ears.

Then, out of nowhere, they appear. An army of tiny, whirring drones, their insect-like wings buzzing with an intensity that cuts through the chaos around me. Their sleek, metallic bodies catch the light, flickering and flashing as they buzz around me. My heart surges with hope—this is Mitzy's tech in action.

The swarm breaks off into a coordinated dance, swirling and swooping in a dazzling display of aerial acrobatics. My eyes are riveted on their mesmerizing patterns, but I quickly understand their purpose. They are not here to entertain; they are here to guide.

Following their lead, I resume the chase. The drones flutter ahead of me, illuminating the path like tiny, ethereal guides through the labyrinthine mansion. Their advanced tech and precision programming make short work of Mendoza's attempts to shake me off.

Finally, they lead me to a grand set of double doors. The drones cluster at the threshold, their collective hum growing louder. I take a deep breath, drawing on every ounce of my resolve before kicking open the door.

There, cornered and wide-eyed with fear, stands Mendoza. The drones buzz around him, a living cage of whirring, pulsating tech. I can't help but savor the poetic justice. The hunter now the hunted.

In his final moments, Mendoza locks eyes with me, desperation raw in his gaze. His bravado has evaporated, leaving behind a man cornered and defeated.

"Do you think you've won?" he rasps, the bitterness in his voice fighting against the evident fear. Sweat rolls down his ashen face, making stark lines in the grime. "Do you think killing me changes anything? The world's a cruel place. You can't change that. There will always be more like me."

His words hang in the air like a toxic cloud, a last-ditch attempt to poison my victory. But I know better. This isn't about eradicating every trace of evil—it's about refusing to stand by and let this bit of it triumph. It's about facing the darkness, one Mendoza at a time.

His words dwindle to an incoherent mumble as I lift the barrel of my weapon. The cold metal feels reassuring against my skin, a solid promise of the justice I'm about to serve.

The moment hangs in the balance, a tantalizing sliver of time suspended between breaths. The world seems too quiet, the noises of my surroundings dwindling to a hushed whisper. In the solitary space of my focus, all the chaos and clamor of reality fall away.

My finger rests lightly on the trigger, familiar with the grooves and the pressure it will require. I brace against the stock of the rifle, feeling the reassuring steadiness of its weight against my shoulder. Everything extraneous falls away until there's only Mendoza and me.

My breaths align with the silent pulse of my heartbeat. As the last whisper of breath leaves my lungs, tension bleeds out from my body.

Time dilates.

In this stretch of silence, my resolve solidifies into crystalline clarity.

With slow, measured pressure, I squeeze the trigger. It's not a sudden jerk, but a gradual increase in tension. With a soft snick, a wave of recoil passes through the rifle, the jarring vibration absorbed by my shoulder. The sharp report is the physical affirmation of my action.

A cloud of expelled smoke billows from the barrel, a fleeting ghost of the violence just unleashed. The scent—metallic and acrid gunpowder—fills the air, a sensory imprint of the act just committed.

Mendoza is dead.

With a host of bumblebees swarming around me, I exit the mansion and take in the aftermath of the Guardian's raid.

Only, there are more than Guardians involved in this raid. In addition to Xavier and his men, soldiers of the Mexican military are present. No wonder it took the Guardians so long to put this together.

The Mexican military seizes control of the mansion. Mendoza's once formidable reign splinters, a crumbling empire dissolving into dust.

Guardians guide young boys into waiting transportation. Their young faces flicker between stark terror and the dawning realization of freedom. Coming from the opposite direction, Guardians escort a group of terrified women to the waiting vans. I recognize the faces of the women forced to serve us during our visit with Xavier. They too, are now free.

When the last echoes of gunfire and shouts finally wane, an eerie calm descends over the estate. The once bustling fortress, an unholy cathedral of sadistic games, stands in silence. Its imposing walls, stripped of their terror, serve as a hollow testament to Mendoza's fall from power.

A swell of pride surges within me.

We toppled a monster from his throne and freed his innocent victims. The underground death match circuit, a vile underbelly of society, was dealt a crippling blow. We won a significant battle tonight.

And a new story is being written. A story of boys who survived against all odds, and the Guardians who stood for them.

As the boys are being escorted to safety, I spot two familiar figures making their way through the ruins of the estate. Xavier and Josh, their clothes caked in dust and sweat, make a beeline for me.

As they approach, a chuckle escapes me. "Took you long enough."

Josh snorts with laughter, a smirk playing at his lips. "We had to wait for the drones to finish mapping. Plus, you looked quite comfortable in your cell. We figured a big guy like you could handle a bit of discomfort."

Xavier just shakes his head.

I roll my eyes but can't help the smile tugging at my lips. Looking around, I take in the sight of Mendoza's ruined empire. The adrenaline of the fight is ebbing, replaced with a profound sense of accomplishment. We've won. We've freed the boys and brought down a monster.

"I can't wait to tell Forest all about this." My voice is tinged with anticipation and regret.

The rift with Forest still gapes wide, the wounds of our disagreement still raw, open, and sore. It's my hope this mission might mend things between us.

Josh claps a hand on my shoulder, giving it a reassuring squeeze. "Can't thank you enough for helping with this. We did good today."

And that's the honest truth.

The hollow echo of departing engines fills the night, their rumble mingling with the hushed exchanges between the Guardians. Wind whispers across the ruined grounds, carrying away the residual stench of fear and cruelty. Mendoza's mansion, once a fortress of oppression, stands eerily quiet, its silence echoing like a solemn epitaph to a reign of terror that has come to its end.

I draw a deep breath, tasting the sweet air of liberation, my gaze lost to the far-off horizon.

Somewhere in that vast expanse, a future is unfolding, a little brighter, a little safer for the boys we saved tonight. The possibility of a world less tainted by monsters like Mendoza is a reality.

As for me, I hope for a world where old wounds can mend and shattered trust can be rebuilt. It's not much, but for now, it's the hope I hang on to.

Despite this victory, the ghost of unease lingers. Forest Summers, the man whose trust I betrayed, deserves something more than an apology. He deserves something greater.

Then there's the woman I've come to love more than life itself. Sara's caught in the middle of the mess I made with Forest. She's the glue holding us together, and I desperately pray Forest and I don't rip her apart with our issues.

I'm resolved to walk whatever path required, no matter how hard, because I'm committed to living the rest of my life with Forest and Sara by my side.

With thoughts of Forest heavy in my heart, I turn to join Josh and Xavier, their camaraderie a comforting constant in the wake of the storm. As we fall in with the departing Guardians, I'm not just leaving a battlefield. I'm stepping into a new chapter, a daunting journey toward making amends and coming home.

FORTY-FIVE

Paul

~

My heart thunders in my chest as I stand before the home I left behind. The home I once shared with Sara, Forest, and our twins. The home I plan on returning to after spending far too long away from the people I love.

I've never felt more alive, yet my body bears the scars of brutal captivity. My resolve, however, is unshaken, perhaps even stronger. I promised myself I would reclaim my place.

My rightful place is here; as Forest's Master, his lover, his best friend, and as Sara's lover.

Not just a throuple, but a true triad.

I can no longer deny my feelings for Sara. Emotions so unlike those I share with Forest.

As I push open the gate and tread the familiar path toward the front door, my mind floods with memories. Laughter, love, heated arguments, tender moments, shared responsibilities of parenting—all a part of the tapestry that makes up our life together.

I pause at the entrance, taking a deep breath before I open the door. The sight that greets me when I finally enter is as normal as it is heart-warming. Sara is in the living room, playing with the twins.

Their innocent laughter fills the room, infusing the space with a sense of joy and normalcy. Ever the stoic figure, Forest is in the kitchen, his back turned to me, but he feels me on a cellular level. His entire body tenses.

Two little bodies suddenly bolt from the living room, their delighted squeals echoing throughout the house. They rush to meet me.

"Papa!" Delia and Sebastian squeal in perfect unison. Their tiny feet thunder across the wooden floor as they jump at me, their little faces lighting up with unabashed joy.

I drop to their level, my arms extending as their small bodies crash into mine. I gather them up, their warm, soft little forms fitting perfectly against my own. Their tiny arms wrap around my neck, small fingers tangling in my hair as they shower me with their enthusiastic, sloppy toddler kisses.

I press my face into their hair, breathing in their familiar, comforting scent—a blend of baby shampoo, crayons, and the natural sweetness of youth. As I hold them, I promise myself, in the silent depths of my heart, that I will never willingly leave them again.

Eventually, I release the twins, ruffling their hair as they pull away. Their infectious laughter rings through the room as I rise to my feet, turning to face Sara. The sight of her watching us, a soft smile playing on her lips, tugs at something deep inside me. Something I'm only just beginning to understand.

I close the distance between us, wrapping an arm around her waist, and yank her against me. Her body molds to mine as if we were two pieces of the same puzzle, fitting perfectly together. Her eyes widen slightly in surprise, but she doesn't resist. Instead, she leans into me, her body relaxing against mine.

Without a word, I lean down, capturing her lips in a fiery kiss that radiates passion and intensity. It's a raw and hungry kiss filled with a yearning I've been too afraid to express before.

But now, there's no holding back.

It's a promise, a tangible symbol of the love that's been quietly building between us.

I've always considered myself gay, but this kiss… It's an

awakening, a testament to the deep-seated love that extends beyond labels and sexual preferences. Her breath comes in shallow gasps, her eyes still closed as if to hold on to the moment. When they flutter open, there's a new understanding in them, a shared promise of what's to come. I give her one last lingering look before I release her, my focus shifting back to Forest.

As I pull away, I whisper in her ear. "We'll all be together tomorrow, but I need time with Forest now."

She nods, her cheeks flushed and eyes shining with anticipation. Her fingers linger on my arm before she turns to the twins. "All right, my loves..." She gives me a knowing look, silently communicating her understanding. "Time for a walk. Let's leave Papa and Daddy and give them some time to talk, okay?"

She lures the twins away from me, coaxing them with the promise of a treat. The look on their faces is a mix of confusion and disappointment, but they soon brighten up at the prospect of an adventure with their mother.

Once they're gone, the door clicks shut behind them, and I stand, slowly turning toward the kitchen. Forest's body tenses, and he keeps his back to me. His mighty hands grip the edge of the counter, turning his knuckles white. His shoulders rise and fall with deep, measured breaths.

"Turn around and face me."

"No." His entire body shudders. "Go away."

"You can either turn around, or I can make you. Your choice."

He pauses for a moment, then ever so slowly spins around to face me.

Our eyes lock, a silent challenge passing between us, a battle of wills where every inch gained or lost is a symbol of my dominance and mastery over him. The room comes alive with the sound of his harsh breathing.

"What are you doing? You don't live here anymore."

"We're going to talk about that."

I approach, my boots echoing on the hardwood floor. He turns to face me, the look on his face a complex mix of emotions—fear, defiance, longing, anger, and beneath it all, the undeniable flicker of submission. I swallow down the lump in my throat, reminding myself this is necessary for both of us.

My mind's eye replays all the times we've come together, the visceral memories of our bodies clashing together as our wills warred with one another for supremacy. I ache to experience that again. I hunger to feel the rippling terrace of his abs tensed beneath my fingers. His biceps bulging as he struggles against his bonds. Each muscle is a testament to his body and mind's raw strength. I recall how his powerful legs shake as he struggles to fight. The way he resists my control is intoxicating. The slap of flesh against flesh fuels my desire. The low, primal grunts as I fuck him rush through my mind turning me on and guiding me forward.

I may be his Master, but Forest is a formidable opponent. He's a man imbued with testosterone, power, and a body that craves pain.

"Forest." My voice is as firm as it is gentle. "You look surprisingly well. Not as pasty white as before."

I remind myself of the promise I made to myself, a vow I made before leaving for my mission. A vow to reclaim my place, reestablish my authority, and restore our dynamic.

A moment stretches between us, silent and heavy with implications. His face is pale, his lips pressed into a thin line, but he doesn't break eye contact. He knows why I'm here; why I've come home.

More importantly, he knows why I sent Sara and the twins away.

He knows what it means for us, and for him.

As I stare into his eyes, the ghost of the man who once knelt before me is still there, Although hesitant, there's an eagerness as well.

I'm resolute in my intent, filled with resolve to reclaim the man I love and restore the power dynamic between us.

"Go away." He attempts to dismiss me, but all that does is ratchet up the tension. The energy in the room suddenly spikes.

"Downstairs," I issue the order, commanding him, absolutely assured he will obey.

Understanding dawns in his eyes, but there's a spark of resistance there too. It's that spark I need to fan into a flame, the willful defiance that always makes our power dynamic so electrifying. His entire body trembles with rebellion, and his pale blue eyes darken with the gathering of storm clouds.

"We're not doing this," he protests, standing firm. "I said no."

"You know this is exactly what we're doing, and why." I hold his gaze, challenging him. "You need this, but I need it more."

His eyes widen at that comment. It's unusual for me to assert my needs. A war wages within him, a battle between anger and the undeniable truth of my words. It's a struggle I'm familiar with and a battle I'm determined to help him win.

"Remember the oath you swore?" I urge, softening my tone and adding a layer of plea beneath the command. "You knelt for me. You gave yourself to me—forever."

A tremor runs through him, a clear indication that my words hit home. "That was before…"

"Before I broke your trust, I know," I cut him off, acknowledging the elephant in the room. "And I will spend every day earning that trust back. But you swore an oath to me—a lifelong oath. I warned you not to make it. I'm calling you out on the vow you made. Before you stepped into that circle, I warned you it was forever. Something you could never take back. You stepped over that line of your own free will, knowing you could never rescind your consent. You're mine. And I am yours. That hasn't changed. You can't deny what we are."

He remains silent, caught between the past and the present. The uncertainty and raw emotion in his eyes wreck my heart. I created that doubt within him, and I need to fix what I broke.

For both of us.

"We face our darkness together, Forest. Emerge stronger together. Today, I'm going to remind you what we are… together. I'll take you. Break you. Remake you. And I'll put you back together, as only I can."

"No." He shakes his head, but his voice hitches. "We're done."

"You don't get to walk away from this, and you'd never forgive me for allowing you to do so."

Anger flares in his eyes. "Don't I?"

"You would go back on your oath?" I step closer. "You're all butt-hurt that I saved your life. Pissed because you know I was right to intervene. You would've lost all of this." I make a sweeping gesture of our home. "You would've missed Delia and Sebastian growing up. Walking Delia down the aisle at her wedding. Showing Sebastian how to be a man. Are you really going to stand in front of me and tell me you'd rather be dead right now?"

"Watch me." His breath catches, and I see the barest glimmer of vulnerability before his walls come up again.

"I am watching you. I'm watching everything you're not saying. That hitch in your breath? The pain in your eyes. The desire swirling behind that. And let's not forget your dick. You're hard for me. Eager for the pain and oblivion only I can give you."

"Leave my dick out of it." He covers his groin and the evidence of his growing arousal.

His words ignite something within me. The dominance that has always been a part of me, the part of me he needs. It roars to life with fire and passion. Forest needs to be reminded of the power dynamic we agreed upon.

What makes everything work between us is not just removing his lack of choice. It's in obliterating it entirely.

That's what he needs.

He needs to remember the release, the solace, and the strength that comes from the loss of control and shift in power.

"No," I tell him firmly. "You don't get to walk away. Not from me. Not from us. Not from what your dick wants. But most of all, you're not walking away from what the three of us can be together. It's not just about you, and you fucking know it."

He can't consent and say yes.

Forest is incapable of bridging that gap, but bringing Sara into the conversation flips a switch in his head.

"Don't bring her into this." He makes a gesture indicating the two of us. "This is between you and me."

"I most definitely will bring her into this, but that's for later. As for now, you're right. This is about us."

"I. Don't. Trust. You." He growls out each word.

The tension between us is a physical force electrifying the air.

"I. Don't. Fucking. Care. You need this…" We trade feral stares, and an eternity passes, but it all comes crashing down in an instant when I launch myself at Forest.

I take him by surprise, but he's quick to react—a testament to his own training. This is no ordinary fight. It's a clash of titans where our very souls are at stake. A primal fight I refuse to lose.

He grunts as he pushes back against me, but I'm relentless. This fight is a battle of wills. Proof of the power surging between us. A reestablishment of our positions and our roles. It's a reset for us both.

We're a tornado of fists and fury, our bodies clashing in a chaotic dance of dominance and strength. The kitchen quickly becomes our battlefield, the sharp cracks and smashes echoing the tumult inside us. The small table is the first casualty, shattering under the force of our bodies. Splintered wood scatters around us, but we're both too engrossed in our fight to notice.

His fist flies, colliding with my jaw, a jarring force that rattles my teeth. Pain erupts, bright and sharp, but it's swallowed by the adrenaline pumping through my veins. With a low growl, I swing back, my fist connecting with his gut. He doubles over, the air forced out of him in a whoosh.

The fight rages on, with both of us locked in a dance of dominance. I pin him against the kitchen counter, the impact dislodging a cascade of pots and pans that clatter onto the tile floor. The metallic echoes of our battle reverberate through the room, a clanging symphony of discordant noise.

Forest struggles, muscles straining, rippling under my hands. His elbow smashes into my ribs, an unexpected assault that knocks the wind out of me. Stunned, I loosen my grip, and he seizes the opportunity to push me away.

He darts across the room, putting space between us, but I'm right on his heels. I close the gap, lunging for him. My fingers catch the back of his shirt, pulling him toward me. The move upsets his balance, and we both crash to the floor in a tangle of limbs.

We wrestle on the cold tiles, the harsh texture biting into our skin, but neither of us seems to notice. I land on top, pinning him to the ground.

"Submit!" It's a triumphant roar that echoes deep in my chest.

"Never." Forest's body twists and turns beneath mine, his heated skin slick with sweat. His hands claw at my arms, desperate to break my hold, but I hold firm.

My grip on him remains unyielding, a physical embodiment of the flow of power between us. Forest is always like this, a physical challenge to be conquered and claimed each time we're together.

With a last surge of effort, I pin him down. My body heavy atop his. His chest heaves under mine, each breath a testament to our struggle. Our eyes meet, locking in a violent battle of wills.

Then, sensing his resistance waning, I make my move. With a quick shift of my weight, I pin his arms above his head. His body tenses beneath me, a harsh intake of breath filling the quiet room. This is it, the turning point in our struggle.

But the fight isn't over. Forest bucks beneath me, trying to throw me off. I hold him down, my gaze never leaving his as I overpower him. The fury in his eyes gradually gives way to something else—an unspoken plea, a glimmer of the surrender I seek.

My hands, possessive and hungry, ache to travel the expanse of his body, reclaiming what is rightfully mine. I know the language of his body, the subtle clues that speak of surrender, desire, and need. I also know the fine line between pleasure and pain. How to keep him balanced on the precipice, never knowing in which direction I might take him.

"Enough," I growl, my voice a rough command echoing off the kitchen tiles. His body stills beneath mine, but his muscles continue to tremble in defiance. His eyes never once leave my face.

I don't release him. Not yet. This fight is about more than physical domination. It's not a physical contest with a victor and a loser. It's the embodiment of our relationship. The very foundation of what we mean to the other.

Forest is my equal in every way. My partner. My best friend. My lover. His submission is never about weakness. It's an acknowledgment that he willingly yields to my greater power.

And here is where everything shifts and rights itself. The underlying tension in his body, his need to be overpowered and possessed, thrums between us. It's an electrical spark that grows into a current of desire that builds and builds.

I keep my grip on his wrists, pressing them into the cold floor above his head. My other hand, free now, trails down his side, feeling the trembling that courses through his body. It's a shudder of fear and anticipation.

Submission.

His desire to submit mirrors my need to dominate and control.

I reach between us, seeking his cock, and find him hard and stiff for me. He groans as my fingers trail over his hard length, but I'm not here to pleasure him.

I'm here to fill his universe with pain.

Moving inextricably down, I find his nuts and give them a harsh squeeze until he huffs in pain.

"This is what you need." I crush his balls, my grip fierce and unyielding.

Slowly, I move my body off him, but I continue to hold his nuts in a vice. Dragging him up by his balls and shirt, he struggles weakly, but the fight in him ends. I pull him to his feet, our bodies close, his breath hitching in his chest.

"No more running, Forest," I murmur, my voice a low growl. "No more pushing me away."

I push him back until he's pressed against the wall. His eyes are wide, his chest heaving with exertion. There's a flicker of defiance in his gaze, mingling with the pain, but it's short-lived.

"Paul…" His voice is barely a whisper, an acknowledgment, a plea. "Please…"

"Quiet," I command. With a swift, calculated move, my hand slides up from his chest to his throat. I don't squeeze, but the pressure is there, a reminder of my dominance, of his submission. The fight, it seems, is over, but the look in his eyes tells me our battle is just beginning. The stakes are higher than ever.

It will take me all night to break him. Forest doesn't give in easily.

"I take what I want when I want it, and I want you.."

Before he can react, I grab his nape without mercy. Forcing his head where I want, I crush my lips onto his. It's there where I take what belongs to me.

The sudden acceleration of my heartbeat sends blood rushing to my groin. My body responds, preparing itself to take Forest as only I can. Plunder his body and consume every inch of him. Violent sex with him arouses me deeply: restraining, forcing, whipping, beating, taking, claiming. I want it all.

And when I say all, that's exactly what I mean. Physical intimacy combined with the bond of best friends, the love of two men, the family I want to create between him, me, and Sara, who gives us this space to reconnect and mend what I broke.

As for the kiss, it's not a gentle kiss, or a kiss born out of love or tenderness. It's raw, brutal, and unforgiving. A kiss between two men engaged in a power struggle, a fight for control, for dominance, for surrender. I maul his mouth, cutting with my teeth, bruising his lips.

Forest's initial shock gives way to a low growl, the sound vibrating against my lips, but then he opens for me with a guttural groan filled with desire. His fight diminishes, and his body slumps against the wall, against me. His lips part, and I seize the opportunity to deepen the kiss, my tongue sweeping inside, staking my claim. I kiss him aggressively.

Slowly, I release his throat, trailing my hand down to grip his wrist. I pull away from the kiss, our ragged breaths filling the silent room.

"Fuck…" Forest gasps, his voice a ragged whisper filling the supercharged air crackling with electricity between us.

His eyes close, and he tips his head back, baring his throat to me. His greedy fingers reach out and slip beneath my shirt. They dip down to the waistband of my jeans. His fingers curl beneath the fabric and yank my hips hard against his groin. "How the hell do you do that to me?" He tips his head forward until our gazes collide and connect.

"Because you belong to me." My voice is rough with barely restrained desire and something else—something harder to define. Something like hope.

His hunger rises, and I catch him with another hard kiss. This one isn't to claim; rather, it's filled with possession. A sense of urgency reveals itself in the way he moves and the frantic way he pulls me until our chests collide. Our mouths deepen the kiss, both of us equally invested in the outcome. Between clashing teeth and tangling tongues, this battle for dominance has been decided.

Forest wraps his arms around me, pulling me in. Every part of his body engaged in the kiss. Muscles straining. Hips thrusting. Breath surging.

The world fades away, leaving only the two of us lost in the moment, forging a connection that's unlike anything I've ever known. This is us, but it's also more.

I break off the feverish kiss, cradling Forest's face in my hands. His pupils are blown wide with arousal, lips kiss-swollen, but uncertainty still flickers in his eyes.

"You know what comes next," I warn him about what he must endure. "What must come next."

Forest trembles but doesn't pull away. Slowly, he turns his head and brushes his lips over my palm. An act of deference. His gaze meets mine, and with a fractional inclination of his head, he indicates the door leading down to the basement.

"Break me." He meets my gaze, his desire laid bare.

"I will always feed the darkness in you."

"I know." Forest bows his head, his body already trembling in anticipation of a night of intense agony and unbearable pleasure.

Joy surges within me, mixed with a surge of protectiveness. Gripping his hand firmly, I lead him toward the basement door.

He follows willingly, tension fading from his frame with each step. I make a silent promise to care for him and nurture his healing. The precious gift of his trust will never be abused by me again.

At the threshold, Forest pauses, pressing close to me. I wrap my arms around him, savoring his warmth, his presence. No matter what happens downstairs, things have changed between us.

We stand together now, wounds exposed but no longer bleeding, the first delicate strands of a profound bond taking root.

"Mine," I breathe in his ear.

He shivers.

"Yours," he agrees simply. "And Sara?"

"Also mine."

"When?"

"When you heal from what I do to you down there." I point down the long flight of stairs. "It's going to be a long night."

"I wouldn't have it any other way."

We cross the threshold together, and I lead him down to the basement he built for us.

Our sanctuary.

Our haven.

Our battleground.

He's bruised and beaten but remains unbroken. The sight fills me with a rush of pride. This is the man I claim as my own. The man who kneels for me. Stands with me. The man who will rise with me, again and again.

Together, we embrace the darkness within each of us, ready to face whatever comes next.

As one.

FORTY-SIX

Paul

~

The weeks after I reclaim my role as Forest's Master are a time of healing and reconnection.

At first, things are tentative between Forest and me—soft touches replacing rough grabs and gentle praise instead of harsh commands. I curb my dominant instincts and let Forest set the pace.

But slowly, steadily, trust is rebuilt. Forest relaxes in my presence once more, leaning into my touch rather than flinching away. Our sessions in the basement intensify, pain turning to pleasure as I feed the darkness within him and curb his darker instincts.

Daily life settles back to normal outside the basement as the three of us navigate parenting our rambunctious twins.

It's the way it should be.

As for Sara, she and I find time to steal sensual touches and fervent kisses that turn more feverish as the days pass.

I lavish affection on her, nurturing our own unique connection. We take things slow, never breaching the final threshold. That moment is reserved for when the three of us can be together.

And through it all, communication flows freely between us. No more secrets, no more misunderstandings divide us. I will never violate Forest's trust again. We talk of needs, desires, and fears. The bonds between us growing stronger after having been tested.

This is our new beginning.

After a restful sleep with Sara sandwiched between me and Forest, I wake to find Sara already up. I wander into the kitchen in boxers and nothing else, following the rich aroma of freshly brewed coffee. Sara sits at the table, damp hair pulled back, slender hands curled around a steaming mug. She smiles softly as I enter.

"Morning," I rasp, kissing her lips quickly before making my way to the coffee pot. She hums against my mouth, the familiar taste of her calming my nerves.

"Ah, that smells amazing." I inhale the rich aroma of the coffee and pour myself a generous cup, savoring the first sip, letting the caffeine work its magic.

Ah...bliss.

However, our moment of peace is short-lived, interrupted by the twins' excited shrieks and thuds echoing down the hall—the controlled chaos of morning has arrived.

Right on cue, Sebastian comes toddling into the kitchen, clutching a pile of blocks in his chubby hands. He plops himself down on the floor and begins stacking them with intense concentration, tongue poking out, his little brow furrowed.

A loud crash followed by delighted giggles signals Delia's chaotic arrival, her hair a streak of white as she zooms through the kitchen at full speed.

"No running!" I call out half-heartedly.

As usual, my plea goes unheeded, her gleeful giggles drowning out my gentle admonishment. Shaking my head in amusement, I settle into the chair beside Sara. Our eyes meet in a shared smile, bracing ourselves for the whirlwind of energy that accompanies breakfast time with the twins.

The twins are up to their usual antics. Sebastian's block tower looks dangerously unstable, wobbling with each added block. Delia zooms by again, nearly careening into my legs in pursuit of her doll.

Under the table, Sara rests her hand on my thigh, her thumb idly stroking my skin. I suck in a sharp breath when her suggestive touch moves to my crotch, sending a flare of desire coursing through me.

Ever since Sara and I started exploring intimacy, stolen touches like this have become more common. We're on the brink of taking things further, but I want to wait until Forest can join us.

"Behave," I whisper to her, catching her hand in mine before it can wander any higher.

"What if I don't want to?" She bats her lashes at me, challenging me.

After years of friendship, our relationship transformed after Forest began his battle against cancer. We've been savoring each new step, taking it slow. Though now that we've crossed a threshold, it's getting harder to keep my hands off her.

I'm a Dom and a sadist. Two things Sara isn't ready for, but she keeps teasing me with comments like that. I lean back and give her a look.

"Maybe you'll find out what it's like when I bend you over my knee and redden that ass?"

She's not into kink, but I'm testing the waters. I don't know if I can put my dominant tendencies aside and have vanilla sex with a woman, but I'm still eager to enjoy sex with her. Everything about this is new to me. Perhaps that's why I want to wait until Forest can join us.

I don't trust myself to be alone with her.

However, the way her pulse jumps in her neck tells me everything I need to know.

"You wouldn't." Her pupils dilate, and her eyes widen.

"Depends on you and how much you want to squirm. Fair warning, giving a good spanking makes me hard."

"Paul…" She looks down and away, embarrassment showing on the sudden flush in her cheeks.

"I suggest you behave, then." I'll push enough to discover her boundaries, but no further.

My entire life, I've not only identified as gay, but I've only ever experienced brutal sex. I don't know how to be soft and gentle, and there's a bit of concern on my part about how things might go when Sara and I have sex for the first time. I'm afraid of hurting her.

"I'll behave, but it's too easy to tease you. You realize you make that hard?"

"The only thing getting hard is my dick, and the more you stroke it with your thumb, teasing me, the harder it's going to get, and the redder your ass is going to become. For what it's worth, if you get me hard, I expect you to finish the job."

"As you wish." Her eyes glint mischievously, but she relents, giving my cock a playful squeeze before withdrawing her touch.

I suppress a groan and shift in my seat. We'll have to save those games for later when we have more privacy. For now, I've got a boner that needs relief.

As if on cue, Forest's heavy footsteps sound from down the hall. He appears moments later, and my cock gives a bit of a kick.

My heart swells at the sight of him awake and moving about. His recovery from lymphoma is progressing remarkably well. He's slowly regaining muscle mass. The stoop to his shoulders is nearly gone. The strength in his eyes is back with a vengeance.

Officially cancer-free, his white-blond hair is slowly growing in, long enough now to be sleep-mussed. Feet bare, he wears a loose-fitting shirt and a pair of gray sweatpants that leave little to the imagination, only accentuating his generous cock.

Like me, he woke with a woody and is standing at half-mast.

I lick my lips in anticipation.

"Morning," he rasps, quickly kissing mine and Sara's cheeks before shuffling over to pour himself some coffee.

An undercurrent of energy buzzes through him. The subtle straightening of his shoulders and the way his sharp eyes scan the twins thoughtfully as he sips his drink are all signs there must be a mission brewing.

After downing his first cup, he turns to Sara and me with an apologetic smile. "Just got a call. Wheels up in a few hours."

Called it.

My stomach sinks with disappointment. I hoped Forest would be home for a few more days, and we might finally find time for my first time with Sara.

But duty calls, as always.

"We can wait." Sara senses my frustration, squeezing my hand under the table. She turns to meet Forest's eyes. "You just focus on the mission and come home safe. Where we'll be waiting."

Forest's gaze flicks down to our joined hands, not missing the intimate gesture. A knowing grin spreads across his face.

"I'd say don't get up to too much fun while I'm gone, but that's up to Paul." His eyes land on me, tone growing more suggestive. "He may not be willing to wait and pop his cherry."

Aroused by his teasing reference to me being intimate with Sara, blood engorges my cock. Sara just laughs, well used to Forest's cheeky sense of humor.

"Oh, I'm sure we'll find ways to keep ourselves entertained." Her eyes glint mischievously, oblivious to my current state of arousal.

The playful banter and simmering sexual tension that often flows between the three of us is something I missed fiercely during Forest's illness and my banishment. Having him here and being able to engage in our usual dynamic feels like coming home.

Forest chuckles, clearly enjoying this game. He leans in close to me, dropping his voice to a gravelly murmur. "Seriously, no need to wait on my account. I know you're eager to bury your bone in more than just my backyard..."

"Forest!" Sara admonishes him. "The twins?"

"Sorry." His crassness never fails to surprise me, even after all these years. It's part of his charm.

"As for bones..." She glances over to where the twins play and lowers her voice. "The two of you fuck like animals. It's quite a sight, but maybe too much for me." Sara pushes Forest playfully. "But leave Paul alone. We'll get to it when we get to it, and don't you need to get ready for your mission?"

All this talk of boning and fucking leave me with a raging hard-on.

"Fuck that. His mission can wait." I push back my chair and stand. One hand grips my engorged cock while the other points back to the bedroom. "Bedroom. Now."

The command in my voice isn't one Forest can refuse. His pale blue eyes dilate, and his sweatpants give a little stir as his cock responds to my voice.

"Can I watch?" Sara rises from her chair, eager and willing.

"It's just a blowjob. I don't have time to fuck him properly. Besides, who's going to watch the twins?"

"The twins…" She lowers her voice to a whisper. "Are occupied and happy. We'll keep the door cracked. If they need anything, I'll deal with it, but in the meantime, I'd like to learn from Forest how you like your blowjobs. Since we're not having sex until he gets back, I should probably get checked off on that."

"Checked off?" If at all possible, my cock is harder than it's ever been before.

"I guess you could masturbate away your frustrations. Or, I could give it a go?"

"Sounds fun." Forest heads to the bedroom. "Instead of watching, you should join. Paul's going to get off with you and me on our knees serving him."

"I'm going to come in my pants if the two of you keep talking about it. Bedroom now." I give Sara's ass a light swat and love the tiny squeak in her voice as she joins Forest.

The bedroom is dark, the curtains drawn, and the lights are off for privacy. I follow them inside, then stop dead in my tracks.

"He likes it when I kneel." Forest immediately assumes the position he knows all too well. "Total power rush, and Paul loves power."

Sara follows him to her knees, her eyes wide and blown black with arousal.

Holy fuck!

My heart races as I stand between them, feeling my cock swell with anticipation. I grip the base of my cock with one hand, then place a finger under Sara's chin. "Forest is my submissive, but you are not. You don't have to kneel."

"I want to learn what you like and how you like it."

"Fuuuck…" Forest groans. "You realize you're hitting all his dominant buttons. Talking to him like that? He's going to blow his load before we begin, and you're getting me hard even thinking about…well, you know."

"He definitely likes us both on our knees." Sara grins at me. "So, how do we…How is this going to work? Do we take turns…?" She looks up at me with eyes full of lust and desire, but it's Forest who answers.

"Just do as I do. Follow my lead and obey his commands." Forest leans forward to kiss the tip of my cock.

I swallow a low moan and close my eyes while my toes curl in the carpet. That kiss on my cock is more than it seems. It's Forest reaffirming our roles.

Sara follows Forest's lead, leaning forward to kiss the tip of my cock. This is a first for her and for me.

I've never had a woman give me a blowjob before. She begins by licking my shaft from base to tip, savoring every inch of my erection. As she swirls her tongue around the head, I can't help but moan in pleasure.

"Fuck, you're good at that."

"I've taught her well." Forest takes his turn next, running his hands all over my body before taking me into his mouth. He knows exactly what I need

The warmth of Forest's lips and the rasp of his tongue is a welcome comfort. We've been together long enough, he knows exactly what I like, but then I gasp as Sara joins him, taking turns licking, sucking, and caressing me.

My breathing becomes labored as I savor every sensation, feeling my orgasm building.

She wraps her lips around me tightly and begins to bob back and forth while using her hand to stroke my shaft at an ever-increasing pace. My hips thrust involuntarily as I feel myself start to come undone, the sensations overwhelming in their intensity.

I reach down to guide her hands up and down my shaft. She strokes and squeezes me until I'm ready to explode.

Forest leans in, and she pulls off my cock. The two of them work together, their tongues swirling around my shaft, sending wave after wave of pleasure radiating through my body.

I groan as they eagerly take turns tasting and exploring every inch of me, but it's not enough.

"Put your hands on me."

Sara's tiny hand grips the base of my cock, so different from Forest's rough callouses.

"Tighter. Twist as you move." I instruct Sara as Forest takes me deep into his mouth. They work beautifully together to bring me closer and closer to the brink.

"Ahhhh…" I moan, feeling myself ready to break apart. But I hold off, wanting to savor this moment as long as possible.

Forest pulls off my dick, and the sudden chill of the air hits the tip, but it's gone in a moment, replaced by Sara's mouth on me.

"He likes his balls massaged." Forest instructs Sara on what I like. "Kind of how I like, but not as hard."

Expecting Forest's hands, I give a little jump when Sara's petite hands grab my scrotum. She squeezes, but it's not enough. Fortunately, Forest is right there to help her. With his hand over hers, he shows her how hard to squeeze.

Again, I rock back, eyes closed, immersed in the sensations of Forest and Sara pleasuring me. They switch on and off, lips and tongues exploring my body, taking turns to excite me.

Their movements cause me to huff as I push off my release.

"That's it," I say, praising them for their efforts. "I'm going to come soon; just keep working together like that."

The feeling is almost too much as pleasure builds within me. I let out a low moan and close my eyes, savoring the sensation of two mouths working together on me.

I arch my back and look up towards the ceiling, trying to contain the pleasure that threatens to overtake me. As I reach down to guide their hands, they seem to understand what I'm asking for. With a surge of anticipation, they both take hold of me in perfect synchrony, caressing and squeezing me harder with each flick of their wrists.

Though every fiber of my being aches for the release, I'm determined to make this last.

I gasp as their lips and tongues intertwine, sending waves of pleasure coursing through my body.

"More," I moan out in between breaths, guiding their hands to caress me in unison.

The sensations become almost unbearable as they work together to bring me towards the edge.

"I'm so close," I pant, feeling my orgasm building.

"He wants you to swallow every drop." Forest coaches Sara. "Are you okay with that?"

I glance down and can't believe how beautiful Sara looks with my cock shoved deep into her mouth. She gives a little nod, saying it's okay, then uses her tongue to stimulate me some more.

The sensations become too powerful. With each stroke of their tongues and every brush of their lips against my cock, I lose myself a little more. One final thrust and I come undone in a powerful wave of ecstasy that leaves me trembling with satisfaction, shuddering from the intensity of it all.

Sara swallows every last drop, and I collapse against Forest, feeling completely satisfied. Sara milks my release, not stopping until the last ripple of pleasure has left my body.

My body is overcome with pleasure, and my head swims with the intensity of their touch. Finally, after what feels like an eternity, I come back down from the high and open my eyes to admire them both, smiling in appreciation for this beautiful moment we shared. It's a prelude to the main event, which I can't wait to get here.

If not for Forest's mission with Charlie team, it would be tonight. Unfortunately, Sara and I have to wait.

"That was incredible," I say, my voice still a little shaky.

"It was amazing, and you're really hot when you get bossy." Sara gives a small smile.

"That was nothing," Forest says, "Just wait, and he'll blow your mind." He looks at me with a smirk, then glances down at his erection, tenting the gray fabric of his sweatpants.

"Go ahead." I turn to Forest. "Fuck Sara while I recover." I lean over and give Sara a kiss on the cheek. "How do you want him to fuck you?" I already know the answer, but ask her anyway.

FORTY-SEVEN

Paul

~

"I WANT HIM TO DO IT FROM BEHIND." SHE GLANCES OVER AT Forest. "Hard. Like how Paul will fuck me." With a smile, it's as if she reads my mind.

Forest wastes no time getting behind Sara. He grabs her hips and thrusts deep.

Sara moans with pleasure as he enters her, and I can't help but let out a little groan myself as I watch them together.

"Oh my God," Sara whispers. "It feels so good."

"Yeah?" Forest lets out a low growl, his eyes falling shut from the intensity of it all.

"You like that?" I ask him. "Fucking our woman?"

"Mmmhmm...I love fucking our woman, especially when you watch." He groans as he thrusts into Sara. "I can't wait for us to fuck her together."

"What about you?" I turn to Sara and whisper in her ear. "How does it feel?"

"I love it." She arches her back and meets Forest thrust for thrust.

"Good." I pull her in for a kiss and then meet Forest's eyes. "Harder Forest. Fuck her like I would. No mercy."

Forest pumps into Sara harder and faster. His hands grip her hips so tightly that I'm certain he'll leave bruises on her skin, but she doesn't seem to mind.

Soon, that will be me. Fucking Sara. Or maybe, I'll fuck Forest while he fucks her? If not for the amazing blowjob that left me spent, I'd do it now.

"Oh my God, Harder, Forest. Harder." Sara moans out as she arches her back.

Forest watches her for a moment, then obliges, fucking her even harder than before. He grabs her head, forcing her to twist her neck as he places his mouth on hers. When he releases her mouth, she's breathless, and that's when I move in to kiss Forest.

He moans into my mouth as I hold him tight. The energy between us is electric. We break away from each other, and I love the way Forest looks at me at that moment. His eyes are filled with pure passion and lust as he stares into mine, and I can tell he's just as affected by our kiss as I am.

I lean forward and press my forehead against his, kissing him once more before turning back to Sara. "I love the way you fuck her."

She watches us with a look of desire on her face, her body trembling with pleasure beneath Forest's thrusts.

He moves away from me just enough so that he can reach down with one hand between our bodies for Sara. She's dripping wet, moaning uncontrollably as Forest strokes her clitoris with expert precision while still thrusting inside her from behind.

He continues to pump into her hard, eliciting more cries of pleasure from her lips. His hands roam all over her body as he moves inside her, almost like he can't get enough of her.

I reach out and brush a lock of hair away from Sara's face before tracing my fingertips down the side of her neck. Her skin is slick with sweat, and she moans softly when I kiss her. We break away and then come back together, our tongues exploring each other as Sara moans with pleasure.

She looks at me, about to have the best orgasm of her life, as Forest's thrusts become more powerful.

"I'm coming!" she screams as she falls forward, letting out a loud moan.

Forest continues fucking her as she comes, his cock buried deep inside her.

"I'm going to come." Forest groans. He grabs Sara's hips and holds her tight, his cock pulsing inside of her.

"Don't remember you asking permission." I grind out the words, leaving no room for confusion, fiercely asserting my role with Forest.

It catches him by surprise, and he loses his rhythm for a moment. His brows tug together, but then there's a sense of rightness in his expression. A moment of comprehension and acceptance.

He stops thrusting, letting himself cool down. There's punishment for disobeying me, and unlike with Sara, it won't be a slight reddening of his ass.

What I'll do to him is much worse.

"Please let me come." He pauses, breathing heavily.

Sara stays in that position for a moment, then slowly arches her neck to find me.

"Paul, let him." She looks at me for a moment, then back to Forest.

I take a seat at the foot of the bed. The whole time, I can't help but smile as I watch them work together to make each other feel good. They have an almost psychic connection—moving in perfect harmony—each knowing exactly what the other is going to do next.

I won't make Sara beg, but Forest must ask permission. When it's just him and me, I control his releases, making him earn the pleasure. We've not discussed the interactions between the three of us when we're together, but Forest agreed to extend my area of influence over his life.

Extend my mastery over him.

This is a good time to set expectations.

"Please," he asks.

"If I refuse, you'll pull out? You'll do as I command? Here, between the three of us?"

Forest hesitates but then inclines his head a fraction of an inch. "I will." His voice is low and raspy from his exertion. "Always."

"That's all I need to know." With a wave of my hand, I allow him to proceed.

He starts thrusting again, this time with more control. He still pushes himself to the edge but not over it. His movements become more precise as he focuses on chasing his release.

Finally, after a few more powerful thrusts, Forest lets out a loud moan as he comes. His body relaxes, and he collapses against Sara. They stay like that for a moment before Forest pulls away and lays down beside her on the floor.

Sara looks up at me from where I sit at the foot of our bed. A satisfied smile fills her face, and her skin glows. "I'm definitely enjoying your dominant vibe. Now, it's your turn." Her smile is that of a tempting seductress. "No need to wait until Forest returns. We can pop that cherry now."

"Sorry, I'm spent." I lay back on the bed, trying to catch my breath.

"You're such a tease," Sara says with a laugh.

"I'm not teasing. I'm serious. I came so hard I barely feel my legs. You, my love, give phenomenal head."

"I do?"

"Almost as good as Forest."

Forest huffs a laugh when Sara scoffs at my comment.

"That's not fair. He has way more practice. That was my first time."

"Then it's definitely something we should work on." I prop myself up on my elbows, staring down at Forest and Sara lounging on the thick carpet of our bedroom. "It'll give us something to do while Forest's away on his mission."

"And gives me a reason to hurry back home." Forest shifts around to sit crosslegged facing me. "I'm going to be fantasizing about this every day."

"You're not the only one." Sara laughs again. "I don't believe he wants to wait. The twins are quiet and behaving. It's not like we can't…"

"I'm not joking." I roll over onto my side. "I think I'm going to pass out."

"You're not serious," Forest says, looking down at me. "You'd rather sleep than fuck?"

Sara looks at me as if I've grown a third head.

"I'm just messing with you." I laugh, and to prove it, I point to my groin, where my cock is ready for round two. Or rather, my first time with Sara.

"You bastard," Forest says with a growl.

"I knew you were just messing with us." Sara squirms on the floor.

"Yeah, right," Forest says, looking at me. "You're just keeping us on edge."

"Oh shit!" I leap off the bed. "The twins…"

"What about them?" Forest asks.

"They're too quiet."

"Oh shit!" Sara's up and on her feet as well, tugging on her clothes. Forest is a step behind, pulling on his pants as he races out behind us.

We burst into the kitchen, panicked at the prolonged silence from the twins. When we enter the kitchen, the scene that greets us is one of absolute chaos.

Somehow, Delia and Sebastian managed to drag a chair into the pantry. Boxes and packages are strewn everywhere—rice, pasta, cereal, crackers, a bag of flour—evidence of their attempts to scale the makeshift ladder.

The lower cabinets hang open, pots and pans pulled out and scattered across the floor. They ripped apart the bag of flour. It coats the floor and covers the twins in a fine white powder. Several brands of cereal, pasta, rice, and crackers are mixed in it.

"What a mess." I pull to a stop, unsure what to do.

Delia and Sebastian sit in the middle of it all, covered head to toe in the evidence of their antics, looking as pleased as two peas in a pod.

At the sight of us, they erupt into gleeful laughter and resume their play, clearly unfazed and eager to show off what they've done.

Sara stands in the doorway, mouth agape as she takes in the scene. I run a hand down my face, torn between shock and laughter.

Meanwhile, Forest shakes his head in amusement. "Well, at least they kept themselves entertained while we were fucking."

"Forest!" Sara cries out. "Words?"

"Sorry." His wry humor breaks the stunned silence.

Sara and I dissolve into laughter at the audacity of our determined toddlers. Delia takes our laughter as encouragement, grabbing a handful of flour and tossing it into the air.

Sebastian giggles as a cloud of white floats down to cover his head. When Delia reaches for another handful, I swoop in.

"Oh no, you don't!" I whisk her up, making her laugh. "I think you two have done enough helping in the kitchen for today!"

Sara grabs a bubbly Sebastian, who is oblivious to the mess surrounding him. She meets my gaze, and I can't help but laugh.

Our kitchen is officially a disaster zone.

"Next time we sneak off, let's at least put up a baby gate," she suggests wryly. "Or lock them in their room."

I chuckle, my heart swelling with love for our unconventional family. Meanwhile, Forest sets to work tidying up with a good-natured sigh.

Later, after the twins are cleaned and put down for a nap, the three of us work together to set the kitchen right. Amidst the shared grunt work, our eyes meet occasionally, alight with mirth and affection.

Parenthood is messy, but I wouldn't trade these crazy moments together for anything.

My mind wanders back to the first time I ever laid eyes on Sara, and I can't believe how lucky I am to have found not one person but two to love. Forest and Sara own the entirety of my heart. Everything except for the special space carved out for Delia and Sebastian.

Hours later, Sara and I collapse on the sofa while Forest packs his bag for the mission. Sara lies with her back against my chest. My arms wrap around her. The twins are down for a nap, quiet for a good reason instead of the wholesale destruction of our kitchen.

Forest wanders in with his gear, a satisfied smile on his face. He moves in for a tender kiss with Sara, then places his forehead against mine.

"You've taken me to the darkest places, but you brought me back to the light today. Thank you."

I wrap my hand around his nape and pull him in for a kiss. "Hurry back before I go crazy waiting to fuck your wife."

Sara suddenly twists in my arms. "If I'm Forest's wife, and you're his Master, what does that make us?"

"I'm not sure." I lean back, thinking about that. "My side-chick?"

"Side-chick? Hell no. I'm not going to be on the side of anything. Do better."

At some point, we're going to have to explain all of this to the twins, but that day is far down the road.

"I vote for Dom and sub. My Master, your Dom, both of us his subs. Sounds wonderful to me." With an exaggerated wink, Forest leaves me shaking my head. Even now, he knows exactly how to get a rise out of me. In more ways than one, apparently.

"We'll figure it out over time." I shoot him a look. "Just hurry on up and sort things out with Charlie team. Your wife and your Master eagerly await your return, both in bed and downstairs."

"As you command." Forest makes a grand flourish, but our playful repartee is interrupted by a wail from Sebastian waking from his nap.

Sara's up in an instant, sweeping down the hall to soothe our crying toddler, but Sebastian's cries are enough to wake his sister.

Forest heads back to our bedroom to grab something he forgot, then rushes out the door, running late. I head with him out to the driveway. No matter how often he leaves on missions, it never gets easier to say goodbye.

"Take care of our girl, yeah?"

"I will." I wave goodbye as he leaves, then head back inside to help Sara with the twins.

It takes us ten minutes of cajoling before the twins are settled. Then, we share an exhausted but satisfied smile.

The rest of the day passes in the usual blur—snacks, diapers, keeping tiny tornados contained and content.

When a rare moment of quiet settles in the late afternoon, I steal Sara into my arms, reveling in the feel of her slender curves melting against me. We trade languid kisses that gradually deepen, hands beginning to wander...

But all too soon, the peace is shattered by cries from the next room. With regret, we break apart, sharing a rueful smile. There will be time to explore each other further soon.

Despite the nonstop chaos, I wouldn't trade our unconventional little family for anything.

I miss Forest's solid presence. I retrieve my phone to send him a quick check-in text, needing that connection.

"Let him focus on the mission," Sara chides, gently plucking the phone from my hands. She sets it aside before I can hit send. Tracing a finger down my chest teasingly, she gazes up at me through lowered lashes. "I'm sure we can find ways to distract ourselves until he's back..."

I groan as she straddles my lap. My body stirs to life despite my fatigue. Still, a pang of hesitation hits me. Crossing that final threshold without Forest is wrong.

As if sensing my hesitation, Sara stills. With a soft smile, she cups my face in her hands tenderly. "We'll wait for Forest. No need to rush things."

"I just need him to be here."

"I know."

I pull her into a fierce embrace. Sara understands me. She loves me in ways I'll never fully comprehend.

And soon, very soon, the three of us will come together at last.

For now, I'm content to just hold her, trading lazy kisses, allowing our hands to roam each other's bodies, but I stop short of true intimacy.

We'll get there.

With Forest.

FORTY-EIGHT

Paul

~

SEVERAL DAYS LATER, FOREST RETURNS FROM HIS LATEST MISSION. The moment he steps through the door, the look on his face terrifies me.

"Downstairs. Now." I issue the command without hesitation.

Sara comes into the room, excited to see Forest, but I give her a look and motion for her to back up. Something happened during the mission with Charlie team, something that triggered Forest.

His mind's spiraling, heading into the darkest corners of his mind where no light shines. When he gets like this, there's only one recourse. I take him downstairs and give him exactly what he needs to reset his equilibrium.

It's a long night.

For us both.

Forest wanders into the kitchen the next morning, looking disheveled and sore. His movements are slow and purposeful. He eases gingerly into a chair with a grimace and a huff of pain. The intensity of our scene last night is clearly still affecting him. His shirt shifts, revealing lurid bruises along his ribs.

We exchange a loaded glance—arousal, shame, vulnerability, and bone-deep trust. After everything, he still trusts me with his body, his heart, his very soul.

"Morning," he rasps, grimacing slightly as he shifts in his seat.

I did a number on his ass.

Sara's gaze sweeps both of us over him clinically before meeting mine. We share a knowing look. She understands the catharsis these scenes provide him...and me. She accepts this part of us without judgment.

Our little girl wanders in, rubbing her eyes free of sleep. With wide, innocent eyes, she goes to Forest and tugs on his sleeve.

"Is Daddy having ouchies?" Delia asks, pausing her rampage to stare at Forest in concern.

He chuckles. "I'm okay, sweetpea. Daddy's fine."

She seems to accept this, resuming her high-speed adventures. Forest's lips quirk as he watches her antics. He takes a bracing sip of coffee before turning to me.

"So, last night..." His Adam's apple bobs. He gulps and shifts his feet. "We haven't gone that dark in a while. I didn't realize how much I needed it." His husky tone makes my pulse spike.

"Felt like you needed it. When you're ready to talk, I'm here." Taking his hand, I brush my thumb over his knuckles.

When Forest gets triggered, it's bad. Whatever Charlie team is up to, it's not sitting well with Forest.

The corners of his mouth turn up in a smirk. Last night was more than intense. I took us places we haven't traveled since our time at Snowden's when our bond first formed.

After a moment, Forest clears his throat, "I've got more bad news."

"More?"

Sara looks on fondly, understanding passing between the three of us.

"There's another mission. We depart in eight hours." Forest withdraws his hand from mine, though his gaze remains tender. "Seems like we can't catch a break. Every time I think we might have time to..." He glances toward the bedroom. "Something happens."

I'm not thrilled about him being called away so soon. He just returned last night, but Guardian HRS demands his attention. If not for the look on his face when he came home, I would've taken him and Sara to bed. Unfortunately, Forest needed something else last night.

Sara smiles, patting his arm. "We'll hold down the fort. Paul and I can find ways to *entertain* ourselves while you're gone." Her wink makes Forest bark out a laugh.

There's an impish gleam in her eyes, and Forest barks out a laugh. "Oh, I have no doubt about that. That's what I'm afraid of. Are the two of you gonna bone while I'm gone? Certainly, there's no need to wait for me since I'm obviously not going to be around much."

His yearning is clear. Having me and Sara together is his deepest fantasy brought to life. My pulse kicks just imagining it. He wets his lips, and his pupils dilate with thoughts of Sara and I together.

"I'm thinking about perfecting her oral skills while you're gone."

"Maybe the Guardians don't need me." Forest looks hopeful.

The truth is, Guardian HRS doesn't need Forest, but if Charlie team is spinning up to go up against a new player in the world of human trafficking, Forest needs to be there.

On impulse, I draw Sara onto my lap, claiming her lips hungrily, reveling in her softness. My hands roam possessively over the curves I'm learning to love. She responds eagerly, fingers tangling in my hair.

I'm excited and eager to be intimate with Sara for the first time. I can't wait to learn what makes her gasp and moan. The very thought leaves me dizzy with want.

We break apart breathlessly. Forest watches us, pupils blown wide. I trail my fingers up Sara's thigh, eyes holding Forest's pointedly. A promise of what's to come.

"You're a fucking asshole." Forest growls, but his smile is full of heat.

"Forest!" Sara chides. "The twins?"

"Sorry." Forest tucks his chin to his chest. He reaches down to adjust his growing erection. "Now I'm hard."

"And you're going to stay hard until you get back. No sneaking in a hand job while you're out saving lives."

"Seriously? I can't masturbate?"

"We can go downstairs and discuss it further if you want." He won't get any relief, but I'm always up for a quick fuck.

He glances at the door leading to the basement and sighs. "Still teasing me, I see. You know I have to leave." He huffs and blows out a breath. "Just call me blue balls." His eyes blaze before he shakes his head ruefully. "You two are going to be the death of me." But his smile is full of love and eager anticipation.

"I can't wait for you to get back." Sara reaches for his hand, twining their fingers together.

Forest exhales, relief and anticipation mingling. His lips curve. "Then I have something very special to look forward to when I get home."

Sara laughs, light and melodic. The sound washes over me like a caress.

Our charged moment ends abruptly with a crash. Sebastian's tower topples, sending him into wailing tears. Sara is off my lap in an instant, comforting our son.

As Sebastian's sniffles fade, warmth swells in my chest. This right here, our family, means everything to me. Forest and Sara are the best parts of me.

I catch Sara's eye and see my own emotions reflected there. Our dynamic is shifting.

Expanding.

Soon enough we're gathered back at the table, the twins occupied with toys and pancakes. The easy domesticity makes me smile.

Too soon, Forest sighs and pushes back his chair. "I really should get packed."

I draw him in for a deep, searching kiss, thumb grazing his bearded jaw. "Hurry back to us."

"I will," he murmurs against my lips.

Sara steps into our embrace, nestling against Forest's broad chest. He holds us both tightly for a long moment before pulling away reluctantly.

Sara slips her hand into mine, meeting my eyes with a soft smile. Together, we've built something beautiful. Something lasting.

Something unbreakable.

FORTY-NINE

Paul

~

For the next four days, Sara and I sink into day-to-day life. We take care of the kids, bring them to the beach to explore the tide pools, and sit side-by-side, on the couch after the twins go to bed in blissful silence.

Sara's thoughts turn toward introspection, while mine focus on the three of us. I want to give Forest the best experience the first time we're together.

Deep down, I admit to a bit of irritation. Not the bad kind. It's having to wait for Forest to return and not knowing when that will be.

Sara notices me daydreaming and takes my hand, brushing her lips along my wrist.

"You're thinking about him again," she says knowingly, her touch igniting warmth within me.

"Always," I admit with a smile.

As if my thoughts summon him, Forest opens the front door and walks in. He pulls to a stop when he sees Sara and me tangled together on the couch.

She's the first up, leaping to her feet and charging toward Forest.

He lifts her into the air, laughing as his mouth comes down to ravish her mouth.

I quickly check his mental state, praying he doesn't need another session in the basement. To my relief, the mission must have been a success. He's steady and untriggered.

I stand and join the two of them. Sara continues to cling to Forest, craving the reconnection. After so much time apart, they deserve a tender reunion before I join them.

Allowing them a moment, I stand to the side before stepping in. I clear my throat. "I arranged for Piper to take the twins tonight. We have the house all to ourselves."

Forest's eyes light up. "Tonight? Are we really…"

"Yes." I shake my head. "Take our woman to bed and warm her up for me. I'll be back shortly."

Forest grins and takes Sara's hand. Flashing her a smoldering look, he leads her to the bedroom.

I gather the sleepy twins, one in each arm, and walk the short distance to *Insanity* where my sister waits.

"Ready for an adventure?" I ask them, ushering the sleepy pair out into the night.

I arrive at Piper's door with the twins in tow, already dreading the teasing I know is coming. She gives me an exaggerated gasp of delight.

"Ooh, a special sleepover for my favorite niece and nephew. We'll have so much fun!" Then she turns to me with a wink. "And what exciting plans do you have tonight? Excited for your night of debauchery?"

I roll my eyes at her exaggerated enthusiasm. I roll my eyes, shifting the twins' bags on my shoulder. "Just catching up on chores without tiny tornadoes underfoot."

"Mmhmm, chores." She drawls skeptically. "The horizontal kind?"

I stare pointedly at the ground. "We're just looking forward to some adult time."

"Ah, Sara told me about the last time the three of you tried to sneak off." Piper props a hand on her hip. "How long did it take to clean up all that flour and the rest of the mess?"

"Which is why I owe you one."

"Definitely." She furrows her brow. "Hmm, as for adulting, is this the first time you've been with a lady?"

I choke, nearly dropping the bags. "Piper!"

"Adult time, eh?" She wiggles her eyebrows suggestively. "Will you be, uh, adulting together, or taking turns?"

I flush at her implication. "Piper!"

The twins are starting to fuss, eager to get inside. But Piper's not done teasing me yet.

"What? I just want to make sure you know how all the girly equipment works." She can't help but laugh. "So, will you be double teaming or tag teaming tonight? I can give you a quick how-to guide if you need it. Lesson one: find slot A, insert tab B. But in your case there are two tabs. Tab B and C."

"Stop."

"I just want to help. There's the obvious, of course. Tab B in slit A, with one of you left out. Or, Tab B in slit A, and Tab C in… Well, there's only one slit, but at least two more holes. Four if you count mouths. If you want to double team it, there's really only Tabs B and C in Slot A. But you need some lube and patience to get both tabs…"

"Oh my god, stop!" I shove the bags at her, face burning. She takes them, laughing gleefully at my extreme discomfort. "I swear if you don't…"

"Maybe a little of both? Double penetration and then kind of a chain gang after that." She grins cheekily. "Oh!" She claps her hands excitedly. "I forgot all about the basement. Is that something she's into?"

I snort, shaking my head ruefully. "You're incorrigible."

"But you love me." She kisses the twins goodnight. "Now go enjoy your throuple. All night long." She wiggles her eyebrows again.

"You're the worst."

"Kidding, kidding. You know I'm happy for all three of you." Her expression softens. "Really, you deserve this special time together. However, you choose to 'adult.'"

"Yeah, it'll be good for us to reconnect." With quick kisses to the twins, I take my leave, excitement building to get back home.

Laughing despite myself, I head out with a final wave, anticipation building as I walk home. Piper's raunchy sense of humor aside, she's right about one thing—we've earned this night together.

"I'm leaving now, goodbye," I mutter, quickly handing off the twins.

Laughing, Piper takes their bags. "You're too easy! Now go enjoy your throuple time. You've earned it."

With the twins safely delivered, I make a hasty exit and hurry back home. Her teasing echoes in my mind as I rush home, eager to put her suggestions into practice.

She's right—we absolutely deserve this night together. After waiting so long, tonight we explore every dynamic.

Once home, I pause outside our bedroom to take in the sight before me. Sara lays nude atop the sheets, legs tangled with Forest's, his larger frame engulfing her slender one.

Their kiss is slow and sensual as they move together unhurriedly. The tenderness between them makes my heart swell with joy.

I watch a moment longer, arousal stirring. But I won't interrupt yet. When Forest looks over his shoulder, another rush of excitement courses through me.

"You gonna stand there, or join us?" His low gravelly voice makes the air rumble. I don't normally take orders from him, but I'm eager to jump in.

I shed my clothes and stand at the foot of the bed, entirely transfixed.

Ready to join my lovers at last.

ABSOLUTELY ITCHING TO READ PAUL'S FIRST TIME WITH SARA AND Forest? I've got you covered with a no-holds-bar Bonus Epiloguc. Experience Paul's first time and Read the Bonus Epilogue HERE.

.   .   .

Forest and the Guardian Hostage Rescue Specialists don't end here. Want to read about that mission Charlie Team was on?

You can Read the thrilling beginning of Charlie Team: Rescuing Rebel HERE.

I hope you enjoyed reading about Paul, Forest, and Sara. Their story has really taken hold of me. If you missed Forest's Fall, where Paul and Forest first meet, you can read it here: elliemasters.com/ForestsFall.

ELLZ BELLZ

ELLIE'S FACEBOOK READER GROUP

If you are interested in joining the ELLZ BELLZ, Ellie's Facebook reader group, we'd love to have you.

Join Ellie's ELLZ BELLZ.
The ELLZ BELLZ Facebook Reader Group

Sign up for Ellie's Newsletter.
Elliemasters.com/newslettersignup

Cara's Protector
Rescuing Barbi
The Dark of You

Military Romance
Guardian Personal Protection Specialists
Sybil's Protector
Lyra's Protector

The One I Want Series
(Small Town, Military Heroes)
By Jet & Ellie Masters

EACH BOOK IN THIS SERIES CAN BE READ AS A STANDALONE AND IS ABOUT A DIFFERENT COUPLE WITH AN HEA.

Saving Abby
Saving Ariel
Saving Brie
Saving Cate
Saving Dani
Saving Jen

Rockstar Romance
The Angel Fire Rock Romance Series

EACH BOOK IN THIS SERIES CAN BE READ AS A STANDALONE AND IS ABOUT A DIFFERENT COUPLE WITH AN HEA. IT IS RECOMMENDED THEY ARE READ IN ORDER.

Ashes to New (prequel)
Heart's Insanity (book 1)
Heart's Desire (book 2)
Heart's Collide (book 3)
Hearts Divided (book 4)
Hearts Entwined (book5)

Forest's FALL (book 6)

Hearts The Last Beat (book7)

Contemporary Romance

Firestorm

(Kristy Bromberg's Everyday Heroes World)

Billionaire Romance
Billionaire Boys Club

Hawke

Richard

Brody

Romantic Suspense
Changing Roles Series:

THIS SERIES MUST BE READ IN ORDER.

WITH JET MASTERS

Book 1: Command Me

Book 2: Control Me

Book 3: Collar Me

Book 4: Embracing FATE

Book 5: Seizing FATE

Book 6: Accepting FATE

Romantic Suspense

EACH BOOK IS A STANDALONE NOVEL.

The Starling

~AND~

Science Fiction

Ellie Masters writing as L.A. Warren

Vendel Rising: a Science Fiction Serialized Novel

Books by Jet Masters

If you enjoyed this book by Ellie Masters, the LIGHTER SIDE of the Jet & Ellie writing duo, and aren't afraid of edgier writing, you might enjoy reading BDSM themed books written by Jet, the DARKER SIDE of the Masters' Writing Team.

The DARKER SIDE
Jet Masters is the darker side of the Jet & Ellie writing duo!

Romantic Suspense
Changing Roles Series:
THIS SERIES MUST BE READ IN ORDER.
Book 1: Command Me
Book 2: Control Me
Book 3: Collar Me
Book 4: Embracing FATE
Book 5: Seizing FATE
Book 6: Accepting FATE

HOT READS
A STANDALONE NOVEL.
Down the Rabbit Hole

Light BDSM Romance
The Ties that Bind

EACH BOOK IN THIS SERIES CAN BE READ AS A STANDALONE AND IS ABOUT A DIFFERENT COUPLE WITH AN HEA.

Alexa
Penny
Michelle
Ivy

HOT READS
Becoming His Series

THIS SERIES MUST BE READ IN ORDER.
Book 1: The Ballet
Book 2: Learning to Breathe
Book 3: Becoming His

Dark Captive Romance

A STANDALONE NOVEL.
She's MINE

About the Author

USA Today Bestselling author, Amazon All Star, and Amazon Top 15 Bestselling Author, Ellie Masters writes Angsty, Steamy, Heart-Stopping, Pulse-Pounding, Can't-Stop-Reading Romantic Suspense filled with Passionate, Protective, and Swoon-worthy Alpha men. Her writing will tug at your heartstrings and leave your heart racing. Ellie is a wife, military mom, doctor, retired Air Force Colonel, and former rocket scientist who writes about strong, accomplished, professional women finding love.

Born in the South, and raised under the Hawaiian sun, Ellie has traveled the globe while in service to her country. Her amazing husband, the love of her life, is her number-one fan and biggest supporter. And yes! He's read every word she's written.

Don't forget to sign up for her newsletter. Never miss another release, sale, or exclusive. https://elliemasters.com/NewsletterSignup

facebook.com/elliemastersromance

x.com/Ellie__Masters

instagram.com/ellie_masters

bookbub.com/authors/ellie-masters

goodreads.com/Ellie_Masters

Connect with Ellie Masters

Website:
elliemasters.com
Amazon Author Page:
elliemasters.com/amazon
Facebook:
elliemasters.com/Facebook
Goodreads:
elliemasters.com/Goodreads
Instagram:
elliemasters.com/Instagram

Final Thoughts

I hope you enjoyed this book as much as I enjoyed writing it. If you enjoyed reading this story, please consider leaving a review on Amazon and Goodreads, and please let other people know. A sentence is all it takes. Friend recommendations are the strongest catalyst for readers' purchase decisions! And I'd love to be able to continue bringing the characters and stories from My-Mind-to-the-Page.

Second, call or e-mail a friend and tell them about this book. If you really want them to read it, gift it to them. If you prefer digital friends, please use the "Recommend" feature of Goodreads to spread the word.

Or visit my blog https://elliemasters.com, where you can find out more about my writing process and personal life.

Come visit The EDGE: Dark Discussions where we'll have a chance to talk about my works, their creation, and maybe what the future has in store for my writing.

Facebook Reader Group: Ellz Bellz

Thank you so much for your support!

Love,

Ellie

Dedication

This book is dedicated to you, my reader. Thank you for spending a few hours of your time with me. I wouldn't be able to write without you to cheer me on. Your wonderful words, your support, and your willingness to join me on this journey is a gift beyond measure.

Whether this is the first book of mine you've read, or if you've been with me since the very beginning, thank you for believing in me as I bring these characters 'from my mind to the page and into your hearts.'

Love,
Ellie

THE END

www.ingramcontent.com/pod-product-compliance
Lightning Source LLC
Chambersburg PA
CBHW021229190726
48289CB00005B/1235